# A Parting of the Ways

Rachel Crowther

First published in 2011 as *The Partridge and the Pelican*.
Re-published in 2023 by Bloodhound Books.

www.bloodhoundbooks.com

Print ISBN: 978-1-916978-09-6

*For Richard*

# Chapter One

In the summer of 1983, Olivia Conafray and her friend Eve found a baby in a telephone box beside a country road in Suffolk.

It was the last week of August; an empty afternoon. The clouds had finally retreated after a week of storms, and the countryside lay quiet and listless in the tepid sunshine. Olivia and Eve had been driving around for hours in the tangle of roads between the sea and the A12, between villages with angular, unpromising names: Theberton, Knodishall, Friston. It went against the grain to admit that they were lost, but when Olivia spotted the phone box, like a red flag above the dull gold of the wheatfields, she swerved over onto the verge.

'I'm going to phone James,' she said. She glanced at Eve, but Eve didn't answer.

Olivia could taste the sharpness of salt in the air as soon as she opened the car door. Her eyes lifted to the spirit-level horizon, to the pale grey sky above. Just a couple more days, she thought, as she crossed the verge to the phone box. A couple more days and they'd be away from this strange, flat place and away from each other. Six weeks together was quite long enough.

She saw the telephone receiver first, hanging loose from the cradle, and then the bundle on the floor below, wrapped in an old blue shawl. At first she thought it was a doll, but she knelt down to look at it all the same. The way it was swaddled drew her curiosity: a tight, close binding like a shroud. She reached a finger to the tiny face, and the eyelids flickered open for a second. There was a glimpse of slate-grey iris and whites the colour of marble: the slightest hint of life.

Olivia felt a shriek rising inside her, but already she was thinking of the baby, of protecting it from noise and alarm.

'Eve!' Her voice came out somewhere between a whisper and a cry. She twisted round: Eve was still in the car, her blonde hair a blur against the windscreen. 'Eve, there's a baby in the phone box!'

It couldn't have taken more than a few seconds for Eve to join her, but it felt to Olivia as though time had stalled; as though there would never be anything but that single moment, the bundle of blue wool the same colour as the washed-out sky and the dizzy flood of disbelief. And then the moment passed, the world moved again, and there was Eve. Tall, familiar Eve, her face still shadowed by the rage that had driven them out of Shearwater House earlier in the day.

Eve squatted down beside her and Olivia swallowed, steadying her voice. 'Is it all right?' she asked. Every detail of the scene was acutely vivid now, as though impressing itself on her memory: the floor littered with cigarette butts and sweet wrappers; the metallic smell of urine.

Eve didn't touch the little parcel on the floor. She shook her head. 'I don't know anything about babies.'

'But you're a medical student. You must be able to tell if it's OK.'

Eve's eyes settled briefly on the baby, and then she rocked back on her heels, pushed herself to her feet again. 'We haven't done paediatrics yet,' she said.

Her voice sounded strange; as though she was cultivating a kind of clinical detachment, Olivia thought. Panic swelled inside her, and before she could think better of it she leaned forward and scooped up the baby. It felt warm and soft and very light: an armful of wool.

'It's definitely alive. I've seen it move.' Olivia pulled the edge of the shawl down to look at the baby's face. Its skin was pale and slightly waxy, the lips bluish. 'It must be brand new. Should we ring for an ambulance?'

Without speaking, Eve stepped past her. She grabbed the receiver, still dangling on its cord, and clicked the button on the cradle.

But the phone was dead.

Later, Olivia could hardly bear to think about the baby's mother, but at that moment she sensed the despair she must have felt. How far had she walked to find the phone box? Had she hoped to leave her child with help on the way?

'Bloody hell,' Eve said. 'What now?'

Olivia got carefully to her feet, settling the baby in the crook of her arm. She could feel its chest rising and falling, the minute movement of air that kept it alive.

'We can't leave it here,' she said. 'We'll have to find help.'

Eve didn't reply. She stood on the verge, staring down the empty road. Part of Olivia, a small, shameful part, was relieved that they couldn't summon an ambulance. She wanted to go on holding the baby, making plans for it. But Eve's mood worried her – her irritation with the broken phone and the way the baby had complicated things. And with herself, no doubt, for arguing with James. Olivia felt a flutter of doubt, but the weight of the baby in her arms spurred her on.

'We'd better take it to a hospital,' she said.

'A hospital where, exactly?' Eve demanded.

'Where's the nearest big town? Ipswich?'

Eve shrugged.

'How far's Ipswich?'

'Maybe an hour, if we knew the way.'

An hour seemed a long time to Olivia. A long time for the baby. 'Surely there'll be signposts for Ipswich?' she said.

'There aren't any bloody signposts,' Eve said. 'Haven't you noticed we're lost?'

Olivia had taken the map out of the car at lunchtime, back at the house. They'd been planning an outing, but when Eve lost her temper they'd left without James and without the map, too – just driven off without a plan. They probably weren't far from Aldeburgh, but these country lanes crossed back and forth over each other like a spider's web.

'We can't leave the baby here,' she said again.

'I'm not suggesting we leave it.' Eve sighed. 'We'd better get back in the car. Let's just get in the car and drive.'

The baby lay in Olivia's lap, its eyes shut. Olivia had unwrapped the layers of wool far enough to find dried blood caked on the inside, then covered it up again. She had no idea how much blood was normal, and only the haziest understanding of umbilical cords; she didn't dare investigate further. She gazed down at its face as if constant vigilance might keep it safe, her voice low as she negotiated with Eve.

'We could stop and ask if there's a hospital any closer than Ipswich.'

'If we stop at every house we'll never get anywhere.'

'All we need is one person to lend us a phone,' Olivia reasoned. 'We might even find a doctor or a midwife, someone who could help.'

Eve looked pale. She was tired, Olivia knew that; she hadn't been well. She felt another flutter of panic: she wasn't used to managing things, because it was Eve who always knew what to do. Eve who'd made the decisions all summer. Had she been complicit in that, admiring Eve's confidence?

'We don't know which way to go, Eve,' she said. 'We don't know whether we're going the right way.'

'For God's sake, Olivia: we haven't passed a single damn house anyway. There's the sun ahead of us, so we must be going west. The A12 is west, right? We didn't cross it earlier, so it must be in this direction.'

'OK.' Olivia nodded, trying to sound convinced. Basing their hopes on the position of the sun made the whole thing feel like a dangerous game. But the arguing was worse; she couldn't think straight while she and Eve were arguing.

When they'd arrived in Aldeburgh a few days earlier, Olivia had felt a sense of triumph. They'd spent July and August, the summer after their first year of university, driving around the coast of Britain, and this was the last leg of the tour, this week in Suffolk in a borrowed house on the sea front.

'We've made it,' she'd said, that first night at Shearwater House, and Eve had smiled. 'All this way, just the two of us.'

A mistake; she saw that now. They hadn't reached the end of the journey at all.

When they hit the A12 and the sign for Ipswich, Eve was triumphant.

'Nineteen miles,' she said. 'Closer than I thought.'

Olivia nodded. The baby was very still: too still, perhaps. She had no idea.

'When I was little,' she said, 'we had a cat who brought half-dead creatures into the house at night. Baby birds and mice; once a little rabbit.' The words sounded childish and unnatural, but she had the feeling that her voice was comforting to the baby, that she ought to talk to it. 'I'd find him crouched in the middle of the landing, yowling at them. I used to rescue them. I'd make a bed in a shoe box and feed them milk from a dropper.'

Her voice trailed away. By the morning the cat's victims were always dead. She remembered the fragile corpses, curled in postures of defeat. Even when she'd known that's what would happen, she couldn't stop herself trying.

Eve must have guessed how the story ended, or perhaps Olivia had told it before. She made a noise that might have been a grudging laugh.

'This isn't a chewed-up baby rabbit,' she said.

'You think it'll be all right, then?'

Eve glanced across at her. 'Babies are tougher than you think,' she said.

Her voice sounded tough too, but Olivia tried to feel encouraged by the words. She stroked the baby's cheek, watching the occasional, almost imperceptible flicker of the waxen eyelids. She was afraid all the noise had frightened it, the anxious rattle of the Fiat as it struggled to keep up a steady sixty-five. She watched the lorries hurling their way along the dual carriageway, the families glued behind car windows, and she thought of primitive birthing rites: even in the most precarious societies the newborn and its mother were assured seclusion and peace, fed on milk and honey for a month. The heft and shift of modern life felt all wrong. She and Eve driving a baby they knew nothing about across a strange county at dusk felt like the worst kind of foolishness.

She shut her eyes and imagined the hospital, the mirage of lights and glass somewhere in the distance. Her hand rested on the baby's chest, feeling for the thready heartbeat that was just discernible through the thick layers of swaddling.

# Chapter Two

## Oxford, September 2008

Wednesday was Olivia's morning at the day centre. At twenty-five past ten she turned her bicycle into the forecourt of the red brick building that had held various names during its hundred and fifty year history: the parish institute, the church hall, and now the community centre. The Red Cross ambulance was parked by the kerb, its glossy paintwork speckled by fitful autumn sunshine. Rex, the driver, was nowhere to be seen, though the smell of his roll-up lingered on the air. He'd be inside, Olivia guessed, drinking tea with Shirley, who ran the Wednesday Club, and casting a genial eye over the morning's proceedings.

Olivia came to play the piano. Sing-a-long Time, it was called, on the sheet that detailed the entertainment on offer. Sing-a-long Time, bingo, table games. Occasionally a special treat: a play performed by the primary school, or a talk on the churches of Oxford. Olivia's job was easy. If they joined in, it was a hit; if not, she tried something else. 'Danny Boy', 'Ilkley Moor', 'Roll out the Barrel'. The Wednesday Club regulars remembered the words to everything, deep down somewhere.

Olivia locked her bike to the iron racks. It wasn't new any more, but she still thought of it that way: a green Raleigh that Robert had bought for her fortieth birthday. At the time, she'd seen it as consolation for the final redundancy of the baby seat that had been bolted onto her old bike for almost a decade. A symbol of progress, perhaps, not that this shiny new machine had carried her much further than the community centre.

The front door was framed by bas-relief pillars and flourishes of sandstone foliage. Olivia was fond of this place. Despite its generous proportions, it looked to her like a miniature version of something else: a grandiose municipal edifice on a parochial scale, built on the enthusiasm of some liberal-minded alderman. It suggested, she thought, greater possibilities than it could rise to itself.

At the other end of the building, the playgroup children were whooping and chattering. Their mothers would be arriving to collect them by the time Olivia left at the end of the morning, calling their names as they ran ahead clutching paintings and junk models. It amused Olivia that demographic cycles had brought fashion full-circle, so that some of these twenty-first century children bore the same names as Shirley's old folk: Molly and Jack, Grace and Stanley. Different names from Olivia's children's contemporaries. It still surprised her that there was a whole new generation of pre-schoolers now, and the days of baby names and playgroups were behind her for good. Her focus had shifted, at least in this building, from the young to the old.

'Morning, Olivia.' Shirley looked up from the table where she was laying biscuits out on a plate. 'OK?'

'Fine, thanks. And you?'

The same words every week. The same plastic chairs and pale green institutional walls, and the familiar smell of old wool and Polo mints. Olivia felt a little bolus of pleasure form in her head and travel down into her chest, settling as a feeling of lightness somewhere near her heart.

She'd first come here, four years ago now, to fill in for someone else, but they'd never returned and Olivia had stayed on until it had eventually been understood that she was a permanent fixture. You couldn't call what she did here performing, but it gave her some of the same satisfaction. From time to time she caught an expression on a face, surprise or pleasure or an intensity of concentration, and knew she'd touched something that would be hard to reach any other way. There was a thrill in that, and there was the comfort of doing good. She liked the way they thought of her here.

'Good summer?' asked Shirley, crumpling the biscuit packet in one hand. 'Been away?'

'France.' Olivia laid her music case down on the piano stool and slipped off her coat. 'What about you?'

'Dave and I had a week in Ibiza.' Shirley winked, wriggling her comfortable hips in a brief parody of night club gyrations. She favoured jeans of the latest cut, and tight jumpers in bright colours that often clashed with her hair. Purple this week, Olivia noted. 'Piano's been tuned, by the way.'

Olivia tried a note or two. The piano needed a new soundboard really, but she'd played on worse. Her fingers skipped up to the top of the keyboard, eliciting a familiar plaintive tinkle. She rarely used those notes, anyway, except for an occasional music hall flourish. High frequency hearing went first; that was one of the few things she remembered from the acoustics course at university. Gabriel Fauré could only hear the middle of the piano by the time he composed his late nocturnes. Not many of the Wednesday Club regulars would be able to hear that plink on the top F.

An elderly man appeared at the door, a tiny frown on his face as he searched out his usual seat.

'Morning, Kenneth,' Olivia said. 'How are you?'

'Reasonable,' said Kenneth. 'Thank you for asking. Beautiful sunshine this morning.'

'A lovely day,' Olivia agreed.

Kenneth never sang, but Olivia often noticed that frown puckering his forehead when she got a note wrong or changed a harmony. Was he a musician? she'd asked Shirley once, but Shirley had said no, a retired doctor. Widowed early; such a shame. But he'd never missed a Wednesday morning, Kenneth. Not in five years.

Olivia scanned the room for the other regulars. There were about two dozen here, usually, although the high-ceilinged hall would have held more. There was Elsie, still full of throaty laughter at eighty-five, whom Olivia could imagine at eighteen, the centre of attention in any room. And there was William, gallant and earnest, spitting image of the Colonel in *Fawlty Towers*; and Emily, in her canary yellow cardigan. No Georgie, though.

Georgie was one of the oldest of the Wednesday Club regulars – they'd celebrated her ninetieth birthday last year, a fuss she'd endured patiently. A dying breed, Olivia thought. The generation born into the First World War, who'd lost their youth to the Second and knew what it was to put up with things.

'No Georgie this week?' she asked.

Shirley shook her head with a little warning lift of the eyebrows. 'Under the weather,' she mouthed.

It was a fine balance between capability and disability that brought them all here, Olivia knew. People who couldn't quite manage on their own, needed a bit of respite and entertainment and company, but were fit enough to be driven to and fro by Rex, and with-it enough to remember the basics of social interaction. A study in the slow, protracted business of growing old. How long might you linger at the day centre stage?

'Until they have a stroke,' Shirley had said once. 'Or a fall; sometimes a fall. Or they move into residential accommodation.'

Olivia loved Shirley's use of language. Leisure entertainment, she called Olivia's contributions to Wednesday mornings. Olivia loved Shirley full stop, her good-heartedness and patience and indestructible cheeriness. I hope there'll be a Shirley around when I'm this age, she thought. One of those little cherubs from the playgroup, perhaps.

'All right, everyone.' Shirley clapped her hands as though to staunch a boisterous flow of laughter and chatter, though in reality there was only the same desiccated rustle of conversation as usual. 'Sing-a-long time. Olivia's ready to play for us now.'


'I'm sorry Georgie's not well,' Olivia said afterwards, lingering in the kitchen doorway with her coffee cup. 'Will she be back?'

'I'm not sure.' Shirley was distracted, worrying that lunch was behind schedule, the trays of food not yet at the right temperature. 'Health and safety,' she muttered, poking a thermometer into a dish topped with what looked like pale custard. 'As if this lot haven't ever eaten anything dodgy in their lives. Hardly going to be finished off by a plate of lasagne, are they?'

'Do you know what's the matter with her?'

'Oh, the usual, I expect.' Shirley slammed the oven door shut and turned the knob decisively to its highest setting. 'Give it a burst,' she said.

'The usual?' Olivia persisted. Georgie intrigued her. Georgiana was her full name, hinting at patrician origins, but her careful dignity seemed to Olivia hard-won, not inbred. The way she held her face in reserve suggested that she'd worked her way up from somewhere and was still watching her step.

Shirley straightened up. 'She's had her ups and downs, Georgie. A hard life, poor love.'

Olivia waited, but Shirley had turned her attention to the bowl of fruit salad in the fridge. 'At least that doesn't need heating up. Come October, it'll be hot puddings again.'

'Does she have any family?' Olivia asked.

'Georgie?' Shirley checked her watch again. Outside, Olivia could hear the shrill chatter of children, and voices raised to warn them to take care, stay away from the road. 'No, no family,' Shirley said. 'She lost a baby, years ago. Never had any more.'

'I'm sorry.'

Shirley turned back to the oven. 'Must be done by now. Can't wait any longer, or we'll play havoc with Rex's timetable.'

'What're you playing havoc with now?' Rex appeared

behind Shirley, propping himself jauntily against the door jamb. He winked at Olivia.

'Get off it, Rex.' Shirley flapped her oven gloves at him. 'See you next week, Olivia. Same time, same place.'

Olivia cycled home slowly, taking the route along the towpath. She loved the canal, the lazy streak of waterway that ran through the middle of the city. For a manmade environment it had a convincingly feral air, she thought: a rural idyll overhung by a vague sense of threat, with its ducks and dock leaves and sporadic piles of rubbish, the teal-green water fleeced with scum.

The towpath wasn't busy, but Olivia passed another cyclist and a pair of runners, a young mother pushing a buggy. A narrow boat went by, smoke puffing languidly from its chimney. As she pushed her bike over the bridge that led back to the road, Olivia glanced down again at the boat, at the shimmer of sun across the water and the back gardens ranged along the opposite bank. She wasn't looking where she was going, and when she felt a sharp blow to her arm her first thought was that she'd bumped into a lamp post or a street sign, some inanimate object she'd failed to notice. But only for a split second. When she swung round, the moving shape of her assailant was clear in her field of view. As her bike clattered to the ground in slow motion and the shock of the impact shuddered through her, the man ran on without breaking stride. By the time she'd collected herself enough to say anything, he was disappearing below the bridge.

'Hey,' she called, but the sound hardly came out: more an exhalation than a protest.

Olivia leaned back against the railings and shut her

eyes, her mind a brief blur of colour. Her bag was lying on the pavement, thrown out of the bike basket when it fell. So it wasn't a mugging – but surely not an accident, either, or he'd have stopped. Had he meant to hurt her, then? To jolt her out of her complacent reverie? Perhaps she'd provoked him, dallying over the bridge without looking where she was going. But the road was empty; there was plenty of space for them both. Surely she couldn't have made him angry enough for such a powerful blow?

When she opened her eyes again, the figure retreating along the towpath already seemed remote, her memory of the encounter far-fetched. She'd only had a fleeting glimpse of him, registered short ginger hair and eyes that looked too large in a narrow face. Not a heavyweight thug: a lad not much older than her Tom, wearing combat trousers and a dark hoodie. If it wasn't for the pain in her arm, the racing of her heart and the buzz in her head, she wouldn't have believed what had just happened.

Then another figure was approaching: another man, mounting the bridge in the direction Olivia had come from only a minute or two earlier.

'Are you all right?' He was close to her age, this man, wearing blue and yellow jogging Lycra. 'Did he hit you?'

Olivia nodded. To her embarrassment, her eyes were filling with tears.

'I thought so. Did he take anything?'

Olivia shook her head. 'No.'

The man frowned, looking down at the towpath. 'I could catch him up.'

'Please don't. I'm sure it was an accident.'

He shook his head, puzzled. 'I saw him: it was a

boxer's punch. Do you want me to have a look? I'm a doctor.'

'There's no need.' Olivia felt foolish now. The attention of this stranger, his solicitude, was more than was needed. She just wanted to get home. 'Really, it was nothing. Just a bit of a shock.'

'Can I walk you home, then? Make sure you're all right?' He was looking at her with concern, and something else. Curiosity, perhaps. Did she look so ruffled? She attempted a smile.

'It's no distance. Please don't worry, I'm fine.' With an effort at composure she lifted her bike upright again. 'Thank you,' she said, as she climbed back on. 'Enjoy your run.'

When she glanced back a moment later, the man had disappeared. It wasn't until she was nearly home that she realised why he'd been studying her face so closely. She knew his, too, although she hadn't seen it for a long time. James, she thought. She was sure it was James.

# Chapter Three

## 1983

The fine weather that had followed Olivia and Eve for most of their journey had broken just as they reached Aldeburgh. The late summer storms revealed the East Anglian coast at its bleakest: the horizon was pinched thin beneath a heavy sky and the rain turned the stony shore a darker, harder shade of grey. But they were relieved to have arrived; grateful to have somewhere to hole up. After six weeks on the road, an entire house to themselves felt like a luxury.

Shearwater House was an imposing sight that August afternoon, with thunderclouds grumbling overhead and the sea marled and mottled with spume. It was a tall Victorian townhouse with Dutch gables, painted a dull pink some years before so that it now had the look of a scuffed seashell. Its name was carved into a slab of stone beside the front door in sharply angled letters, and the sky swam in the old glass of the windows.

The key had been left for them under a stone. Eve slid it into the lock and the door, warped by years of damp, yielded with a reluctant creak. Inside, the walls were painted white and hung with fading watercolours of sea scenes; blue and white china bowls sat squat and dusty on the tops of chests of drawers.

'Bit musty,' said Eve, dropping her bags in the hall.

Olivia could smell salt and mildew, a faint hint of woodsmoke. The shabbiness was misleading, she thought. It felt like a place so well known, so well loved, that everything about it was taken for granted.

'It's wonderful,' she said.

A narrow staircase rose straight ahead and a corridor ran past it to the back of the house, with doors leading off to the right: closed doors, shuttering the interior in a tranquil half-light. Olivia was conscious of the house's expectations, the familiar faces and routines it was used to, but the feeling wasn't uncomfortable. There was something about Shearwater House that made her want to belong.


They'd been best friends at school, Olivia and Eve, inseparable for almost a decade. Olivia's parents lived abroad. Her father was an engineer whose work took them from country to country: Venezuela, Iran, Nigeria, Dubai. Eve's parents lived near Chichester, barely fifteen miles from the school, but she boarded too; everyone did in her family, she said. And certainly boarding school had suited Eve better than Olivia. At eleven, Eve was already confident and popular. She could take her pick of friends, and the fact that she chose Olivia was unexpected. People found it hard to see what diffident Olivia Conafray had to offer Eve de Perreville; and so, some of the time, did Olivia.

They were at different universities now – Eve at

medical school in London, Olivia reading music at Edinburgh – but they'd promised each other they'd spend this summer travelling together. There had been talk of Italy or even South America, but in the end they'd settled for a tour of Britain in Olivia's battered Fiat 126. A quaint idea, their parents had said, secretly glad that they weren't trekking down the Amazon. Unusual, these days, to get to know your own country first.

From Chichester they'd made their way along the south coast to Devon and Cornwall, up through Wales to the Lake District and Scotland, then gradually south again until they hit the bulge of East Anglia. Eve had been cock-a-hoop when her friend James offered them Shearwater House. It was always empty in the last week of August, he'd said; the family went earlier in the summer. Where better to end their tour than on the seafront at Aldeburgh?

There had been a moment, somewhere in the long trek through Lincolnshire, when Olivia had regretted accepting the invitation. It had felt like too much of a detour to make so late in their journey, and the flat hinterland of the fens was disorientating after weeks of mountains and lakes. But now they were here she was glad they'd come. She was ready, as she and Eve climbed one staircase and then another, finding beds clothed in faded counterpanes, bathrooms with bare wooden floorboards and fireplaces filled with rushes, to succumb to the spirit of the place.

For two or three days they were alone in the house, scarcely believing in their right to be there. Like servants left behind while the family was away, Olivia thought, or evacuees placed in an empty house. The stuff of children's books.

'Do you know the family?' she asked on the first day, as they sat over cups of tea in the morning chill of the kitchen.

'Only James.' Eve poured the last of the milk they'd brought with them into her mug and glanced up at the window. The rain was coming down steadily. 'We need to go shopping.'

'We can explore when the rain stops,' Olivia said.

But the rain kept falling, and the girls ventured out only for brief walks on the storm-racked beach. They spent the days browsing through the crowded bookshelves, reading novels with battered crimson covers by authors they'd never heard of, and in the evenings they cooked frugal meals in the kitchen. They were careful not to alter anything, though: to replace books and plates and even dishcloths exactly where they'd found them. In the visitors book, which stretched back to just after the war, the same names appeared again and again, childish signatures evolving to adulthood then spawning children of their own to populate the next generation of guests. Olivia liked the idea that the house had looked exactly the same all that time.

'You know what?' Eve said one afternoon, looking up from the sofa where she was lying flat on her stomach. 'You can see from the seams how much these curtains have faded. They can't have been changed in forty years.' She shifted her weight onto her side with a grimace. 'Nor the sofas.'

'Nor the mattresses,' said Olivia. The sagging beds had become an in-joke: barely two springs to rub together, Eve had said.

The contents of the kitchen cupboards seemed to have been there for decades, too. The two girls lived on the family's supplies, heating up out-of-date baked beans in an old aluminium pan.

'Seaside food,' Olivia said. 'This must be what everyone eats here.'

'This is what we've been eating all summer,' said Eve.

But Olivia knew Eve didn't care what she ate, especially not just now. Since they'd arrived in Aldeburgh, Eve had given herself up to torpor. She seemed content to lie for hours on the lumpy sofa while Olivia absorbed herself in trying to light the fire, filling the sitting room with the smell of charred paper and damp ash.

James arrived at the weekend, during the first lull in the rain. Olivia and Eve had gone for a walk that afternoon, following the beach southwards until they reached the Martello Tower and the estuary. When they got back, they found a fire in the sitting room grate and jazz playing on the ancient turntable.

'Well,' Eve said. 'You know what they say: it takes a man to make a house into a home.' She smiled, her cheeks flushed with fresh air. She'd been saving her vivacity for him these last few days, Olivia thought. The idea raised a quiver of regret, but also of relief.

'This is Olivia,' Eve said. 'My loyal companion.'

'Pleased to meet you.' James made a little bow. 'I've put the kettle on. My mother sent a cake.'

They ate fruit cake off delicate china plates from a cupboard Olivia and Eve hadn't broached, and drank tea from a huge flowered pot that would have catered for eight. James was a medic too, a couple of years ahead of Eve at Barts. He seemed older than he was, Olivia thought, with pale, delicate skin and dark hair, a manner that was amused without being supercilious.

'So, have you been enjoying yourselves?' he asked, getting up to refill the teapot. 'Have you been won over by Aldeburgh?'

'By Shearwater House,' Olivia said, and at the same time Eve said, 'It's been too wet to go out.'

James looked at the window, where splatters of rain were making a teasing pattern again.

'Well,' he said. 'The rain'll stop now I'm here.'

After tea, James went shopping.

'What have you been eating?' he asked, surveying the empty fridge. 'Haven't you found the fish shop?'

He came back with two newspaper parcels, one containing three small sea bass which he gutted under the kitchen tap, the other a bundle of fleshy green stalks.

'Samphire,' he said, as he unwrapped it. 'Taste of the sea.'

'Is it seaweed?' Olivia asked.

'No, it grows in the marshes.'

'Wonderful name,' said Eve. 'Sand and bonfire, like a beach picnic.'

'It comes from "Saint Pierre", in fact. Patron saint of fishermen.'

James was full of this kind of knowledge. He had a mystique, Olivia decided, that was inextricably linked to Shearwater House. She could see him returning year after year, teaching his children to gut sea bass.

Over supper Eve's high spirits subsided, and

conversation was more desultory than Olivia expected. Eve played with her fish while James asked Olivia polite questions about her family, her university course, her music, and Olivia watched Eve watching her, her mind as much on Eve as on the answers she gave James. She could see why Eve liked him, why she'd been pleased when he'd offered them his aunt's house, but the two of them were strangely formal with each other, as though they didn't know each other as well as Olivia had imagined.

'Where do your family live, James?' she asked.

'Some in London, the rest scattered to the winds.' James laughed, and Olivia caught Eve's glance, a blankness in her face that might have been deliberate. She was conscious, now, of something else James had brought into the house: the possibility of competition.

Afterwards, they sat by the fire, listening to scratchy recordings of Glenn Miller and recounting the summer's adventures. Eve was more animated again, telling James about the country fair in Wales where she'd found herself inadvertently bidding for a prize bullock, the cockroaches in the sleazy Carlisle guest-house, the shooting stars in Scotland. Olivia was glad: the silent Eve was disconcerting.

'We're quite the seasoned travellers, aren't we, Olivia?' Eve said.

'But nowhere else was a patch on Aldeburgh?' James suggested.

Eve raised her eyebrows in mock-challenge. 'The sun shone all week in Cornwall.'

James laughed. 'You can't judge a place on the sunshine. That's like judging a person on their good moods.'

Eve frowned. She opened her mouth to say something, but James spoke first.

'We should have some Britten,' he said. 'Do you like Britten, Olivia?' He squatted down beside the shelf of records. 'You know he lived just round the corner? *Peter Grimes*: that's a proper Aldeburgh piece.'

There was silence for a moment, then the expectant rustle of the needle settling into the groove. Olivia felt a shiver of recognition as the overture began. She could hear the barren coastline and the turbulence of the sea. She'd missed music this summer, playing it and listening to it. Funny how you didn't notice until you heard something again.

'Have we got any of that whisky left?' Eve stretched her toes towards the fire, flexing them like a cat's.

'There's whisky here,' said James. 'Plenty of it.'

'No, we should drink ours.' Olivia got to her feet. 'We bought it in Scotland, just down the road from the distillery.'

Three glasses had been set on the low table beside the sofa when she returned.

'Cheers,' Olivia said. 'Thank you for having us.'

'You are lucky, James,' said Eve. 'Have your aunt and uncle got any handsome sons we could marry?'

'Not any more.' James emptied his glass in a gulp. 'How about a midnight swim? Either of you game?'

'Swim?' Eve laughed. 'You're not serious. The sea's freezing.'

'It feels warmer at night, when the air's colder. And the whisky'll put some fire in your veins.' He clapped his hands, suddenly energetic. 'Come on: it's a Shearwater tradition.'

. . .

The stony beach looked like a wasteland, lit by a moon as bright as a searchlight. Eve and Olivia hung back, their giggles silenced by the sight of the waves thumping relentlessly onto the shingle.

'You can't mean it,' Eve said.

James didn't answer. He ran the last few feet to the edge of the sea and plunged in.

'Come on!' he shouted.

Their shrieks of glee and horror drifted down the beach like the cries of seagulls, small and thin against the expanse of water and air. Olivia was soaked by the first breaker to hit her as she hesitated in the shallows, Eve close behind her.

It was too rough to swim properly, but they leapt over and through the swell of the surf, letting themselves be lifted and thrust back towards the shore, their energy focused on regaining their footing as each wave receded. The stones underfoot, agitated by the undertow, crashed against their ankles and bruised their feet. But it was exhilarating, life-affirming to ride the breakers as the night sky shimmered and trembled overhead. The constant movement of the waves and the effort it took to resist the tug of the current were enough, after the first shock, to block out the cold. The three of them whooped and splashed like children, the only figures to be seen along the whole length of the beach.

'We should do this every night!' Eve shouted, her voice a wisp of sound over the noise of the sea. 'Catch me, James!'

Dragged apart from the others by the roll of a wave, Olivia watched Eve teasing and splashing, and saw the elation on her face as James pulled her over in the icy water. A second later he hauled her up again, spluttering and laughing; shaking out her long hair, she reached her arms to grab his shoulders.

Olivia twisted away and plunged into the next wave. She couldn't hear their voices now; in a lull between breakers she floated, watching the moon grow fat and bright as an invisible cloud drifted out of its path. The sea seemed to be calmed by its gaze, the rush of the tide slowed briefly. For a few moments, the water lapped placatingly around her head and her spreadeagled limbs, softening the sting of whatever it was she felt: jealousy or loss or disappointment. The currents swirled inside her like pigments dropped into water, a churn of emotion she hadn't anticipated. But the effect wasn't entirely unpleasant; the ache of experience was almost welcome. This is something real, she thought. A moment to remember. She wished she could spin out forever the miraculous sensation of floating in the moonlight with the motion of the water briefly stilled and the pitch of Eve's voice subdued by the wind.

After a while she heard a shout, and she swivelled to see James waving and pointing. The others were wading back towards the beach, their laborious progress like a film reel played at half speed. She was very cold, Olivia realised. Her limbs had succumbed to a seductive numbness. For a moment she wondered whether she'd be able to fight her way out of the water, but just then a wave broke over her like a gesture of farewell, sweeping her towards the shore.

'There.' James smiled as he wrapped a towel around his pale torso. 'You've been properly initiated now.'

Eve slipped her arm through Olivia's with slight ostentation, and they ran back to the house with teeth chattering and laughter spilling out into the darkness, their feet oblivious to the pebbles. The coast road gleamed, empty and pristine, as though it had been washed clean while they were gone.

'Hot baths,' said James, when they reached the front door. 'There should be plenty of water. I put the immersion on.'

For a moment Olivia thought Eve might try to follow him, but after a second's hesitation she smiled at Olivia. 'We could both fit in the big one,' she said.

James turned at the corner landing to salute them. 'See you in the morning,' he said.

'Good swim,' Olivia called after him. 'Good idea.'

Eve found half a bottle of cheap purple bubble bath in a cupboard and emptied the whole lot under the running tap. There was more hot water than they expected, and the bath was the deep old-fashioned kind with clawed feet that you could almost float in if you filled it to the top. They climbed in carefully, one at each end. Steam filled the room like hot breath, and the smooth sides of the bath, the brush of skin against skin, had a muffled feeling after the sharpness of stones and salt.

'This is like a sauna in reverse,' said Olivia.

'Mmm.' Eve shut her eyes. 'I'm glad we got the cold part over with first, though.'

'We could do it the other way round tomorrow night.'

Eve groaned. 'I didn't mean it,' she said. 'D'you think he'll make us?'

Olivia ducked her head under the water, drowning the smell of the sea, then shifted her knee so Eve could do the same. Eve's hair spread among the bubbles like a picturebook mermaid. It sometimes surprised Olivia, seeing her close up, that Eve wasn't more beautiful. She had all the ingredients of beauty, a classic English beauty of fair skin and rosy cheeks, but the end result wasn't quite what you expected, like a portrait that somehow fails to capture the essence of the sitter. But there was, nonetheless, something complete about Eve, a sense that she had grown into who she was going to be, that Olivia was conscious of lacking. Her own features – more angular, more surprising – seemed not to have found their final form yet. Olivia looked at her face in the mirror sometimes and wondered where it was going.

'What do you think James meant,' Eve asked, sitting up and reaching for the shampoo, 'by "not any more", when we asked whether his uncle and aunt had marriageable sons?'

'Is that what he said?'

'Mmm.'

'I suppose they're married already. Are their names in the visitors book?'

'The family don't write in it. The immediate family.'

'You could ask James.'

Olivia shifted her leg so Eve could dip underwater again to rinse her hair. A heaviness was seeping into her body through the warm water, filling the space left behind by the bracing cold. She looked down at Eve's face just below the surface, its expression made unfamiliar by the water's refraction, and in that moment of silence she wondered what she was going to say when Eve came up again. It felt as though her words, even her thoughts, were outside her control; as though weariness and whisky and seawater had turned her life into a book she was reading, turning the pages to see what would happen next.

'You like him, don't you?' said Olivia's voice.

Eve smoothed down her wet hair. 'Do you disapprove?'

'No.'

'Do you like him too?'

'Not if you do.'

Eve laughed suddenly. 'God, Olivia; that's so like you.' She laughed again, her face as alive as it had been earlier that afternoon when she'd first seen James. And then, manoeuvring herself upright, she stepped out of the bath and reached for a towel from the rail.


Olivia woke late the next morning. Eve was already in the kitchen when she came downstairs, curled in the rocking chair by the window.

'You're up early,' Olivia said.

'I don't feel very well.'

Olivia narrowed her eyes, gauging Eve's complexion in the morning light. 'You do look a bit pale.'

'I feel sick,' Eve said, 'and dizzy.' Her voice sounded plaintive, little-girlish. Olivia remembered Eve being ill at school, the way people rallied round.

'Probably the swimming,' Olivia said. 'We must have swallowed a lot of sea water.' She unplugged the kettle and filled it under the tap. 'Why don't you go back to bed? There's nothing to get up for.'

Eve shook her head. Something in her face provoked a flash of doubt, not unfamiliar, in Olivia's mind. Had she said the wrong thing last night? Surely Eve had laughed at her, not the other way round. Did she ever laugh at Eve?

'Maybe you'll feel better once you've eaten something,' she said.

But Eve ignored the bowl of cereal Olivia placed in front of her. Instead, she sat across the table from James, when he came down, and watched him spread marmalade on brown toast. James ate in silence, and outside the windows the rain fell gently but steadily.

There was something in the air this morning, Olivia thought; a kind of agitation, as though they were being circled by a poltergeist.

'Was it always your aunt and uncle's, this place?' Eve asked. 'I mean, did they buy it, or inherit it?'

'They're not actually my aunt and uncle,' James said. 'It belonged to my great-aunt and uncle originally, then their daughter took it over.'

'So she's a cousin once removed, not an aunt.'

'Something like that.'

There was silence again.

'Who'll get it next?' Eve asked eventually. 'The house, I mean?'

'Sally's only fifty-five,' said James. 'I don't think she's planning on giving it up for a while.' He pushed his chair back and started gathering the breakfast things off the table, even though he'd only just finished his toast and Eve's bowl was still full. 'Have you got plans for today, you two? Have you been to Snape yet?'

'We haven't been anywhere,' Eve said. 'We've been waiting for you to show us round.'

That wasn't quite true, Olivia thought. They'd managed to get three-quarters of the way around the country without James's assistance.

'What about your parents?' Eve asked next. 'Do they come here?'

James dropped a handful of cutlery into the sink with a clatter.

'From time to time.'

For a moment Olivia imagined she'd heard something

uncharacteristic in his voice, almost a threat, but when he turned round again he was smiling.

'I know what we could do,' he said. 'We could go to Leiston. There's a museum there I loved when I was little. Steam engines and things. And there's an exhibition about Elizabeth Garrett Anderson. The first female doctor, you know?'

But Eve shook her head. 'Not today,' she said. 'I'm feeling pretty awful, actually. Is there a chemist nearby?'

So then the others were solicitous, the awkward conversation and the plan to go out both forgotten. Olivia felt a wave of relief: she'd been afraid Eve would make herself ridiculous with her insistent feverish questions. Eve was exasperating, but Olivia's loyalty went back a long way.

'There's a first aid box in the bathroom cupboard,' said James, and at the same time Olivia said, 'I'll go to the chemist for you.'

Eve shook her head again. 'A bit of fresh air might clear my head,' she said.

The rain had slowed to a drizzle by the time Eve left, wearing a plastic waterproof over her T-shirt. It was hard to credit the violence of the waves they'd swum in the previous evening, Olivia thought. The stretch of sea they could see from the front door looked quiet and tractable beneath the glimmer of rain: a docile blue, lapping peaceably over the pebbles.

# Chapter Four

## 2008

The house was quiet when Olivia got home. The boys were all at school, Robert not yet halfway through his long day in London. She was conscious of the stillness, the empty rooms like a stage-set without actors. Dropping her keys on the shelf by the front door, she went through to the kitchen to make coffee. This was a matter of habit – the cup she felt obliged to accept from Shirley stirred her sensory cravings rather than satisfying them – but today she really needed the caffeine.

Her arm was throbbing, and a similar pain was starting up in her head now. She felt fragile, precarious; certainly not as composed as she'd seemed back there on the bridge. While she washed up the percolator, her mind darted restlessly between the violence of the assault and the coincidence of that encounter afterwards, throwing out questions like sparks.

Had she met her assailant before, perhaps snubbed him unwittingly?

Did James live in Oxford now, if it really had been James?

Might the boy in the hoodie do the same to someone else, now he'd got away with hitting her?

She was surprised at herself, at her nervous excitement and the tremor in her hands. It occurred to her that she ought to be capable, a woman in her forties, of taking that momentary flare of aggression in her stride, and shame and self-pity surged through her, like hot and cold taps turned on simultaneously. She could ring Robert, she thought. She could ring the police, even. But she felt too foolish, too confused by things, to do either.

She set the coffee pot to brew on the stove, then reached up for a mug and winced at the stab of pain in her arm. There was arnica in the first aid drawer, a tub of ibuprofen in the bathroom, but instead she opened the drinks cupboard. Brandy, she thought; that was what you took to soothe the aftershocks. To buck yourself up. She wasn't quite without resources. She half-filled a glass, and before she could think better of it she emptied it down her throat. Then she leaned back against the counter, letting the warmth filter through her body and her gaze roam around the room.

What might she tell James, she wondered, about who she'd become? What would he glean from this pleasant kitchen with the breakfast things still stacked on the side, the pot plants along the windowsill? For a moment she saw it all through the eyes of her nineteen-year-old self, and she registered surprise. Curiosity. What had she imagined for herself, all those years ago? She could barely remember.

She was tempted to pour herself another brandy, but instead she went upstairs, to the bedroom she'd once decorated with such care but had hardly noticed for years, and took off all her clothes. Standing in front of the mirror, she surveyed the stretch marks of four pregnancies, the scars of minor operations, the unmistakable depredations of time. And there, on her arm, the bruise forming: a perfect fist-imprint with four separate darkening circles for the knuckles. Like a souvenir plate with a baby's handprint on, she thought, and tears welled up in her eyes.

She might have stood there for a long time, challenging herself to whatever sort of reckoning this was, but just then the smell of burnt coffee started to creep insidiously up the stairs; the unmistakable taint of blistering plastic. And then it was the irony of life that struck her: the way it offered bathos as an antidote to pathos. Humour, even: Olivia fleeing down the stairs in her dressing gown to rescue the coffee pot (which was in fact beyond rescue, its handle melted off and its insides scorched black), opening windows to let the smoke out, running cold water into the sink to drown the worst of the damage. Olivia laughing almost hysterically about the pollution of her house and her state of undress, about the absurdity of being hit by a stranger in the middle of the day, in the middle of Oxford, in front of a man she hadn't seen for twenty-five years. Who could deny life its witticisms?

She could really do with a cup of coffee now, but the smell of charred beans was still overpowering and she couldn't be bothered to dig out the old cafetière. She couldn't, for the moment, think what she'd normally do at this time of day, either. It was as though she'd been set back into an unfamiliar place after the canal incident. After seeing James. Here she was in this empty kitchen, all grown up: what now?

. . .

The house, in what had been a plain Victorian terrace, had been extended several times over the years. The properties in this well-placed side street weren't quite big enough for the people who wanted to live here now: loft conversions and rear extensions were de rigeur, back gardens gradually encroached upon by the designs of ingenious architects. Their own kitchen had been tackled by the previous owners, with plenty of glass to let in the light and exploit the view of the garden, the apple trees and ragged flowerbeds and the lawn reduced to wasteland by four boys and their ball games.

It was a decent garden, though, for a town house. And a gracious house, too: high ceilings; a sense of space. In an arch above the kitchen lintel a semicircle of stained glass, blue and amber and watery purple, offered a hint of Oxford's Victorian Gothic past. A privileged life, Olivia acknowledged that, with nothing worse to face for the rest of the day than her afternoon piano pupils. There was much to be grateful for.

She got up from the table and looked out on a collage of green and auburn, caught on the cusp between summer and autumn. And then a flash of white: the cat, stalking sparrows or squirrels. Olivia unlocked the back door and called him. He had more names, this cat, than anyone could remember. Somehow he'd managed to persuade each of the family that they were special, acknowledging their particular pet-name with a tilt of his expressive chin. He contemplated Olivia now with a haughty pretence at coincidence, and then he picked his way neatly, unhurried, towards her.

Olivia scooped him up and buried her face in his fur, and her head filled with his thrum of contentment. She envied the simplicity of his pleasure, the unrestrained hedonism that somehow didn't diminish his dignity. 'Sensualist,' she crooned. 'How can you pretend to be a hunter?' He'd been a consolation prize, the cat; acquired, like the new bike, when Benjy went to school. She was lucky, Olivia thought, that he was minded to keep her company during the long days when the house was empty.

But in a few hours her boys would be home, populating the place with their noise and their clutter. Making sense of it, Olivia always thought – and making sense of their mother, too. Every afternoon she drew the bustle about her, feeling its reassuring weight on her shoulders like a cloak embroidered with the emblems of her life as wife and mother. She was conscious, suddenly, that this was what people saw of her, this robe of office: the outward and visible signs of her growing children. Growing so quickly, too; faster and faster as they got the hang of it. Boys becoming men already. She held the cat tighter, aware of his limbs tensing, ready to wriggle free. She carried him across to the cupboard where his food was kept and felt him relax again, heavy in her arms like the after-effects of the brandy. 'Precious boy,' she whispered, half-aloud. 'Indulge me a little longer.'

Tom, her eldest, was almost the age she'd been when she last saw James. More years had passed since that summer than any of them had lived before it. Time and its curious juxtapositions spun in her head like a whirligig. If she shut her eyes she could be back in her nineteen-year-old self, not knowing what was to come: marriage, children. Tom, Alistair, Angus, Benjy.

She released the cat, and he shook out his coat and paced over to the bowl of food Olivia had filled for him. For a moment she watched him eat, then her gaze drifted back to the garden. Through the window she could see squirrels scuttling along the fence and hear the faint sounds of children next door. The first scattering of leaves lay below the horse chestnut, patterning the scrubby grass with their splayed fingers.

So this was her life, Olivia thought: the life she'd ended up with. A quiet kitchen in the middle of the day; the nagging sense that she hadn't done as much as she might, settling for teaching the piano and bringing up her children. Did that meet the requirements of whatever inquisitor she had invoked? Did it answer the questions the morning's drama had posed?

Out in the garden something stirred: a fall of light through the trees; the weight of the sun at the end of a shortening day.

# Chapter Five

## 1983

'You did the best you could,' the nurse said. She looked weary and disheartened, as though she wasn't quite inured to death; especially not to the death of a baby.

Olivia and Eve had been put in a waiting room with no windows and a sign on the door that said 'Relatives Room'. Despite the comfortable sofas and the fresh flowers on the table it had a surreal, anaesthetic quality. Olivia could only think in clichés: I feel numb; I can't believe this is happening. She tried to imagine being told that someone properly connected to her had died. Eve, perhaps.

'She must have been lying there for a long time when you found her,' the nurse went on. 'She was cold, and she'd lost a lot of blood because the umbilical cord hadn't been properly clipped off. And she hadn't been fed, so her blood sugar level was very low.'

Olivia nodded stupidly. She could tell the language was being simplified for her, but that didn't make it any easier to understand.

'She'd had a bump on the head, too. Perhaps she'd been dropped on the floor where you found her.' The nurse paused for a moment, as though waiting for corroboration.

'It was concrete, the floor of the phone box,' Eve said. It was the first time she'd spoken since they'd arrived at the hospital.

The nurse put her arms around Olivia then, knowing she was going to cry. 'If you hadn't found her she might have died without ever being cuddled,' she said.

They let Olivia look at the tiny body once more, dressed in a white gown and laid out in a little cot not much bigger than a shoebox. It looked different already, a carved effigy rather than the baby she'd carried out of the phone box. Its features were hardly there any more, mere suggestions of human characteristics. Behind her, Eve and the nurse were talking quietly, the nurse offering technical details, professional to professional. Olivia couldn't concentrate on what they were saying, but the words floated through her head all the same: she could already imagine Eve repeating them to James later. Hypothermia. Hypoglycaemia. Hypovolaemia. Infusion, intubation, infarct. Too many words, she thought. But any words would be too many for her, just now.

Eve's voice was flat when she spoke to Olivia again.

'We've got to talk to them.'

'Who?'

'The Consultant, to start with. Maybe the police.'

Olivia stared at her.

'It's all right.' The nurse smiled, moving back to Olivia's side. 'There's nothing to worry about. They just have to be satisfied it's not your baby. They need as many details as possible so they can try to trace the mother.'

'Of course.' Eve nodded, the confident witness. The reliable witness, with her medical knowledge. 'We quite understand.'

Eve had phoned James from the hospital, and when she and Olivia got back to Shearwater House at last he had supper ready for them, a bottle of wine open. They had driven all the way from Ipswich in silence. Olivia couldn't tell what Eve was thinking, whether she was still angry or regretting her bad temper; later, she realised she'd just been working out what to say to James.

'I say,' was what Eve began with when they walked in, her voice a squeaky imitation of insouciance. 'It's the Galloping Gourmet in person. How sweet of you to go to so much trouble.' She touched his arm lightly, a gesture none of them missed, then moved over to the stove and lifted the lid of the casserole. A rich scent of herbs and garlic filled the kitchen.

'No trouble,' James said. 'It sounds as though you've had a rough afternoon.'

He looked at Olivia, and she tried to smile. Although she could see him there, could feel grateful for his kindness, the world he was part of didn't seem quite real any more. She felt the ground softening, a seasick shifting beneath her feet.

'Have a seat.' James pulled out a chair. 'A glass of wine might do you good.'

Eve picked up the bottle. 'Chianti. Delicious. Shall I lay the table?'

Things went on in the same way through supper. James dished up spaghetti bolognese, and while they ate it Eve told him the story of how they'd got lost in the country lanes as though it was funny; as though the row that had sent the two of them out of the door ten hours before had never happened. She moved on to the discovery of the baby with barely a break in tone. Olivia could hear her casting herself as the dispassionate medic again, seeking James's approval as she fleshed out the story she'd told him on the phone.

'We thought they were going to keep us at the hospital forever,' Eve said. 'Didn't we, Olivia? All those questions! We might have to come back for the inquest, if the Coroner wants us there. But they have to try and find the mother first.'

Olivia tried to speak, once or twice, but the effort was too great. She could only see the world through a veil; as if she was swathed in amniotic membranes, perhaps, still tethered to the ghost of that dangling cord. Everything seemed indistinct, illusory. Had there really been a baby? Had she really believed she could keep it alive?

When she'd finished eating she pushed back her chair, walked to the downstairs lavatory and vomited up everything in her stomach. Neither James nor Eve said anything when she came back.

'I'm going to bed,' she said. 'Sorry. I feel shattered.'

'Poor Olivia,' said Eve. When the door had shut behind her, Olivia heard Eve speaking again. 'She held the baby all the way up the A12. It must have died in her arms.'

Olivia was woken by a tap on the bedroom door.

'Eve?' she whispered.

The door clicked open.

'It's James. Eve's gone to bed. I came to make sure you were OK.'

'Oh.' Olivia pushed herself up on one elbow.

'Feeling any better?'

'A bit.'

'Feeling like something to eat?'

'What time is it?'

'Late. Don't move, I'll bring something up. You'll be better off with some food inside you.'

Olivia's head hurt; the darkness was suddenly disorientating.

'No, I'll come down,' she said.

She sat at the kitchen table while James made her a ham sandwich. The curtains were all open and the sky looked very black outside. Like an eclipse, she thought, although it was just the night.

'What happened to Eve?'

'A lot of Chianti. A few tears.'

'Over the baby?'

James shook his head. He sat down opposite Olivia and pushed a plate across the table.

'Good?' he asked, after a moment.

'Yes. Thank you. It's very nice of you.'

He smiled. 'Glass of wine? There's a bottle open.'

They must have started a second bottle, Olivia realised. Or perhaps a third. She took a sip from the glass James gave her and felt it run down inside her, warm and blood-red.

'Thank you,' she said again. It felt good to be looked after, to have someone around who passed for a higher authority. An adult. Eve would scoff at that; or perhaps she wouldn't. Eve had been hard to read, these last few days.

'A nasty experience for you,' said James. 'The baby and everything.'

Olivia nodded. She could feel her eyes filling with tears again. 'We should have left her where she was,' she said. 'Perhaps someone had gone to call an ambulance.'

James shook his head. 'You did the right thing. If someone else had found her first, they'd have taken her with them.'

There was silence for a moment. Fragments of memory swirled in Olivia's head, forming and reforming like a kaleidoscope: the sea, the baby, the wine; bubble bath and empty lanes and the noise of the car's engine. She thought back to the beginning of the summer and couldn't imagine herself there again.

'I wanted to tell you something,' James said. Olivia looked up. 'Something about when I was little. Four.'

He poured himself some more wine and took a long swig.

'We used to come here every summer, my parents and my sister and I, with Sally and Jack and their boys. My second cousins, Peter and David. They were twins, a year older than me. They were wilder and braver than me; I idolised them.' He hesitated, looking at Olivia. 'One day, when it was too rough for swimming, we were playing at the edge of the sea. Peter and David were running in and out, getting soaked by the spray, while I stood at the edge and watched. Then a breaker knocked them over and the current caught them and they both disappeared, just like that. I was still standing on the beach when the adults found me, staring out to sea.'

For a moment or two Olivia couldn't think what to say.

'So you had to tell them?'

'Yes. It took a while for them to grasp what had happened.' James cupped a hand around his wine glass, cradling it lightly between his fingers. 'I wanted you to know,' he said. 'It wasn't my fault, there was nothing I could have done, but it changed things, my being there when it happened.'

'Poor you.'

'It was a long time ago. I was a little boy.'

'But you've never forgotten. You'll never forget.'

'No, I suppose not.'

Olivia let her gaze rest on him, taking in the shadow of stubble along his jaw, the translucent skin above his cheekbones. Tender, she thought. There was a tenderness about him that was more noticeable at this time of night. 'Did they have other children?' she asked.

James lifted his glass and took another mouthful of wine, swilling it thoughtfully before swallowing. 'They had another baby a couple of years later,' he said. 'Amelia. She's fifteen now.'

'It must be a burden for her.'

'What?'

'Replacing her brothers. A responsibility.'

James looked at her; a straight look, considering. 'She's not aware of that,' he said, after a moment. 'She has Down's syndrome.'

Olivia didn't know what to say. 'I'm so sorry, James.'

James shrugged. 'She's a sweetheart, Amelia. It's a blessing that she doesn't understand the gap she was expected to fill. She could never have done that, but she's filled their lives. They love her.'

In the silence Olivia heard the click and hum of the fridge, the wheeze of the windows in the breeze that comes off the sea at night.

'It changes your view of misfortune, a tragedy like that,' James said. 'What's an extra chromosome, a kink in the genetic code, if it's part of a live child? If it means you can go on being parents?'

Olivia thought of the baby – her baby – lying so still and uncomplaining in her arms. I couldn't have kept her, she told herself, even if she'd lived. I had no claim on her.

'But still,' she said. She glanced at the dresser, with its cheerful muddle of crockery and photographs. Perhaps Peter and David were among the fading snapshots of children on the beach. 'Didn't they want to sell the house after what happened?' she asked.

James leaned across the table and touched her face with his finger. A tentative touch, like a child's.

'We all love it here,' he said.

Olivia shut her eyes for a moment. She could feel the house around them, the magic of it, and the touch of James's finger lingering on her cheek. She was conscious of a new feeling threading through her body now, a twist of feelings tangled sickeningly together. Besides grief and compassion there was desire, but desire complicated by shame. She could glimpse the possibility of consolation, but she knew that accepting the invitation in James's eyes would only make things worse.

'I'd better go back to bed,' she said. 'We're leaving in the morning. We've got a long drive.'

'There's no hurry,' James said. 'We might as well finish the bottle.'

Now, when he looked at her, she was sure he could read her mind; that every turn of reason, every shade of feeling was laid bare. He smiled, and Olivia felt a wash of emotion so powerful that the world swayed again like a boat caught in a storm. She needed to keep hold, she thought. She needed something to anchor herself to; she just wasn't sure what it was.

James kept his eyes on her as he poured the last dregs of wine into her glass.


The floorboards sighed as Olivia crossed the landing, echoing the faint sound of the sea, the tide turning towards a new day. Outside the bedroom door she hesitated, and the house fell silent, waiting.

The door opened without a sound. In the dark, Olivia could just make out Eve's shape under the covers. For a minute, maybe longer, she stood and watched the gentle movement of Eve's breathing, and then slowly, carefully, she shut the door behind her. Eve murmured as Olivia lifted the edge of the sheet and slipped in beside her, curling herself around the crescent of Eve's back.

She could tell, now, that Eve was awake. She must have heard the comings and goings, the footsteps on the stairs; she must know that Olivia had been with James. Olivia could feel nothing now about the temptation he had offered or the way she had responded, but she knew she and Eve would never talk about it. After all that had happened, speech was too dangerous, too absolute.

Eve was warm, her body a simple comfort in the dark. Olivia could hear her breath, and feel the swell and fall of her ribcage against her own. She could smell Eve's familiar scent, taste the salt in her hair, perhaps even a hint of petrol to squeeze her heart tight with the memory of that afternoon. Just now, though, just for the moment, guilt and betrayal and complicity melted away as she and Eve lay pressed together, like twins placed in the same cot to remind them of the womb. They could console each other in a way they would never be able to again, without words and without any assurance for the future.

As the first glimmer of dawn seeped into the sky, Olivia was conscious of a paradox circling her tired brain. She felt closer to Eve, in the depths of this strange night, than she had ever felt before, but she knew this was the end for them.

# Chapter Six

## 2008

S arah Brewster looked out at the string of slow-moving cars ahead with a flicker of irritation. She had planned to leave work early that Friday afternoon to miss the worst of the rush hour. She'd blocked out her last two appointments. But it was always the same, she thought, as she edged along the ring road beside cars full of families heading off for the weekend: something always came up when you were in a hurry. She sighed; and then, although there was no one to observe either gesture, smiled slightly in compensation. Half an hour either way wouldn't matter to her father, but she liked to imagine herself in his eyes as a swan, not in beauty but serene competence, her arrival an effortless glissade.

Her father had just been discharged from hospital after a knee operation. He was used to fending for himself, but Sarah had insisted that convalescence required a daughter's attention. There was the wedding to talk about, in any case. She'd come prepared to ask her father's opinion about certain details, and to accept his contribution to the cost of the festivities.

Guy felt the awkwardness of this more than she did.

'We can pay for the wedding ourselves,' he'd said the week before. 'We're hardly impoverished teenagers.'

'Of course we could,' Sarah had replied, 'but he'd like to help us. He's always expected to.'

Guy had looked at her with that quizzical expression he had, poised between admiration and bewilderment, and then he'd smiled. 'The father-of-the-bride.'

'That's how he sees it.' Sarah had smiled too, relieved that further explanation hadn't been needed; that they didn't have to probe the things that weren't quite as he expected. 'I am his only daughter.'

And Guy had two parents still, she might have added, both in perfect health and requiring as little from their son now as they must have done when they sent him off to boarding school at eight. There had been few upheavals in the Dorlands' lives, and their form of ageing seemed to her to involve only a gradual desiccation, like the quinces her mother used to lay out on dishes before Christmas. Sarah frowned. Funny how things came back to you. The quince tree had gone long ago, felled by the 1987 storms, but she could still remember the smell of the fruit, sickly-sweet and pungent, turning slowly to rot.

The traffic filtered onto the motorway at last, and Sarah flicked on the radio. Guy had left it tuned to Classic FM, and she recognised the overture to *Dido and Aeneas*. They'd done it at school, years ago. As she followed the M40 towards London, the sun low enough now to flood the car with light, she listened to the first scene unfolding.

*'Shake the cloud from off your brow, Fate your wishes doth allow...'*

Olivia Conafray had been Dido, the big surprise of

the production. Everyone had assumed Eve or Julia would get the part, but the director had been right. Who'd have guessed that shy Olivia was capable of such passion?

*'Ah! Belinda, I am press'd with torment not to be confess'd...'*

Sarah had envied Olivia that triumph, but she'd been pleased enough to be in the chorus herself. She'd always been a glass-half-full person, she thought; always tried to make the best of things. She liked people to know this about her: to understand that she had a capacity for happiness. That she wasn't someone to be pitied. She was as content at this moment, for example, as any bride-to-be, even if most of her friends had been married ten – or even twenty – years earlier. She had a sense that her life was balanced between two worlds, and there was pleasure to be had, a tantalising sort of extended suspense, from the no man's land between the two. Journeying time, she thought. She'd always liked travelling, and enjoyed the way long journeys were an adventure in themselves, sometimes trumping the attractions of the final destination.

It was still twilight when she turned in through the narrow gateway. She felt a familiar lurch, and in its wake a murmur of reassurance, almost instinctive by now. She'd never have imagined that her mother's absence could be more complicated than her presence; certainly not for so long.

She glanced in the mirror before she opened the car door, pushing her hair back off her face for a moment. Her haircut hadn't altered since she left school: there was the fringe, the same slightly wayward bob, in every photograph. But something had changed recently, at least in the way she saw herself. Perhaps there was a bridal glow to her complexion, the kind of transformation you didn't think would actually happen. She frowned, then wrinkled her nose in self-parody. Perhaps she'd just spent more time looking in mirrors, these last few months.

Her father opened the front door before she reached it.

'Hello, Dad.' Sarah hugged him. 'Up and about, I see.'

Her father lifted a feathery eyebrow, indicating the walking stick in his right hand. 'Under orders from one of your tribe.'

He'd always assumed physiotherapists the world over were in league. It was rather sweet, Sarah thought – though he knew perfectly well she'd retrained as an osteopath several years ago.

'Not my tribe any more,' she said.

He looked at her quizzically, and she wished she'd suppressed the urge to set him right. He looked fragile, and pleased to see her: what did it matter?

'Leave all that,' she said, as he started towards the car. 'You're not supposed to lift.'

'Nice car,' he said, patting the flank of the vintage MG. 'How long have you had this one?'

Her father had resisted any suggestion of moving house in the years after her mother's death. Sarah could see the attraction of familiar surroundings, familiar neighbours, and she understood that his reasons were pragmatic. He didn't like change; he'd lived in the same village for forty years, and he couldn't see the point of starting again somewhere new. It had reached the point where it felt disloyal to raise the matter again, so Sarah had stopped.

'I only use the rooms I need,' he'd say, when he caught

her opening doors, peering into the shrouded darkness. 'Dust off the rest when people visit.'

The house had accommodated itself to this arrangement: it had a sleepy air, these days. Like a castle in a fairytale, her brother Andrew had said on the phone last time they spoke, hibernating around him. It was all very well for Andrew, three thousand miles away in Canada: when had he last seen the guttering?

Sarah glanced down the side of the house as she lifted her bag out of the boot. Her mother's garden had been progressively simplified over the last decade, and she noticed that another border had been replaced with lawn since her last visit. The familiar yew hedges were still there, though, and the soaring hornbeam where the swing had once hung. Across the front of the house the clematis was in full bloom, its blue flowers almost fluorescent in the dusk. Sarah plucked a couple of dead heads as she passed and rolled them between her fingers.

Her father preceded her down the hall, his ponderous convalescent gait and the tap of his stick on the flagstones giving the impression of a ceremonial progress.

'I'd have liked some of those plants from the bottom bed,' Sarah said. 'The ceanothus, or the lacecap hydrangea. I remember that being planted.'

Her father didn't turn round. 'I thought you shared the garden?' he said. 'Don't they do it for you, the developers or what have you?'

Sarah knew he couldn't understand why she'd wanted a brand-new flat. A new flat and an old car: the wrong way round, in his view.

'I could have put in a couple of shrubs,' she said. 'There's lots of space.'

'Well, maybe we can find something else for you to take back.'

'No need,' Sarah said. Another mistake. 'Don't get too dependent on the stick, by the way. Two weeks, tops.'

Her father waved it at her as she started up the stairs. 'Don't fret. I'm under an excellent woman, almost as competent as you.'

And he was almost as stubborn as her, Sarah reflected, hoisting her bag onto her shoulder to negotiate the bend in the staircase. The thought eased the jolt she'd felt when she saw him in the doorway, the recognition of his frailty.

'I'll be down in a minute,' she said. 'I've brought veg from the allotment.'

'Cup of tea?'

'Gin, if you've got it. I'm dying for a drink.'


Sarah's recollection of her childhood had shifted since her mother's death. Inevitably, she thought; but there had been some deliberate effort involved too. As she climbed to her old room at the top of the house, past a row of black-and-white photographs of the Sussex countryside, she remembered the walks on the Downs and chilly outings to the seaside when her father had explained the shapes of hills and clouds and rivers, the way the landscape had been moulded over more years than she could comprehend. Her father had taught geography at the boys' boarding school in the next town, the counterpart to the girls' school where Sarah had been a day pupil. He'd worked long hours, leaving her mother to manage the children's lives during term-time, but Sarah could still picture herself at eight or ten, listening to his bedtime stories about volcanoes and earthquakes and glaciers, falling asleep with her globe beside her bed.

It wasn't that she'd admired her father particularly, or wanted to be close to him: it was her mother she'd always yearned for. But it occurred to her now that she'd understood her father better than her mother, back then. She'd known what mattered to him; that his life was shaped by his interest in the world around him. She'd recognised the wisdom of not relying on other people for happiness. Not entirely, anyway. Sarah might have followed in his footsteps and studied geography, but her mother had sided with her headmistress in favouring what they called 'hard science'. Together they plotted a career in medicine, and Sarah had accepted their lead. But her A levels weren't good enough for medical school.

'Too much sport,' her mother had said, more than once, although she'd been pleased enough to come and watch her gawky daughter performing on the games pitch. Sarah had opted for physiotherapy instead. 'A good choice for a girl who wants a family,' the headmistress had told Sarah's parents briskly, when she shook their hands on Speech Day. Sarah had liked the idea of physio – she'd always had a leaning towards the practical – but she knew she'd disappointed her mother.

After supper her father made camomile tea.

'Will you have some?' he asked. 'It's wonderful stuff. Helps you sleep.'

The packet had come from Fortnum's, Sarah noticed. He must get it sent from London. She started to explain that it was available in supermarkets, probably even his local Londis, but this time she stopped herself. Let him have his pride in his exotic discovery, his need to be competent: if she questioned that, where might it end?

'Let's take it through,' she said. 'I've brought some bits and pieces to show you. Wedding stuff.'

Sarah caught the whiff of dead air as she opened the door to the sitting room. The furnishings hadn't changed for decades, and the garish seventies pattern on the sofas and curtains seemed out of keeping, now, with her father's quiet existence. Sarah plumped cushions and turned on lamps, dispelling the shadows. At least there wasn't too much dust, she noticed.

'Does Mrs Henderson still come?' she asked.

'Stopped in the summer. I've got another girl, though.' Her father settled in an armchair by the empty fireplace with an exhalation of relief.

'Girl?'

'The Morrisons' au pair. Nice girl. She does a few hours for me on the side.'

And would be moving on before long, presumably. But Sarah could imagine her father making conversation with a chirpy au pair; an improvement on stolid Mrs Henderson, perhaps.

'Keeps me amused,' said her father, as though he'd read her mind.

Sarah laughed, the characteristic chirrup that had always seemed too frivolous for her, then she took a sheaf of paper out of a folder.

'I'm making the dress, you know,' she said. 'And the cake.'

Her father's eyebrow lifted as he looked half at her, half at the piece of paper she handed him. 'Have you got anyone to help you?' he asked. 'Apart from, I mean...'

He made a little fuss over tapping the paper flat.

What had he been going to say, Sarah wondered? Apart from Guy, whom he assumed to have a limited interest in wedding preparations? Or had he been thinking of her mother? Her mother hadn't been mentioned between them since Sarah had announced her engagement. There would have to be a conversation – but not this time, she thought. Not yet. If growing up had been more complicated than it looked in their family, the same was true of grieving. It had turned out to be hard to share either the grief or the complications.

'Have I left anyone out?' she asked, glancing at the guest list in his hand. 'I wondered about the Phillipses – are you still in touch?'

'We needn't ask them,' her father said. 'They won't expect it.'

'I've known the Phillipses since I was tiny,' she said. 'I'd like to ask them.'

Her father smiled, unflustered. 'As you wish. I'm sure they'd be delighted. Cyril's a little doddery these days, but he is eighty-five.'

'Is he really?'

Sarah remembered helping Cyril Phillips change a tyre on his Deux Chevaux in the middle of a summer lunch party. She still thought of them as in their forties, her parents' friends, frozen at a particular stage, but of course it was her friends who were that age now. Coming home threw out her perspective. Her eyes flicked across to the photographs on the piano: her mother as a young woman, radiant in '60s chic, and the snapshots of her brother's children, sent from Canada. Her father followed her gaze, his eyes dwelling for a few moments on the photographs and then returning to his daughter.

'You deserve to be happy,' he said.

Sarah smiled: a smile that concealed, just for a second, a flash of terror.

'And Guy is a treasure,' he went on, and this time Sarah felt a surge of tears. The awkwardness with which her father said such things made them more touching. The effort that went into selecting the words.

'Thank you,' she said. 'He's rather like you, I think.'

She hadn't known this was what she was going to say, but as she heard the words it struck her that they were true. Her father had only met Guy twice, not because she'd kept them apart but because it had been, to coin a term, a whirlwind romance: she'd only known Guy for six months herself. But she was sure they'd get on, her father and her fiancé, and the thought pleased her more than she expected.

Sarah always slept in her old room when she came home. It ought to smell fusty, shut up for months on end, but instead it had preserved a dry, sweet scent that evoked in her mind hot milk and Enid Blyton and the sticky nylon sheets her mother had favoured when she was little. When she was tucked up in this bed, with its pronounced dip and the metal rails at each end, the world shrank to the size of childhood.

As she folded her clothes and laid them on the pine chest that held the last of her old toys, Sarah could hear her father moving about down below, the creak of the floorboard on the landing that had always alerted the household when anyone was up in the night. Would her children sleep up here one day, she wondered? She didn't often let herself think about the possibility of children, but here, now, alone, the hope and the doubt caught her off guard. She knew what the prospects were: how many women conceived spontaneously at forty-three, and which fertility clinics offered IVF to someone her age. She'd even made preliminary enquiries about adoption. She hadn't talked to anyone about it, though, neither the probabilities nor what she felt about them. Not her father; not even Guy, just yet. It would take a while, she thought, settling into the familiar mattress and edging her weight away from the broken spring on the left, to throw off the habit of keeping her own counsel.

And meanwhile, the wedding was enough to occupy her mind. She'd never imagined that getting married could involve so much activity, so many decisions. True to her philosophy, she was savouring the experience to the full, applying herself enthusiastically to the cake and the dress and the marriage service. And to tracking down guests. She'd been good at keeping in touch with people over the years, and it was amazing how easy it was to find lost friends on the internet. As she lay in the dark, soothed by the silence that was never quite silent in this house, a procession of names accompanied her mind towards sleep. Olivia Conafray. Grace Darwin. Eve de Perreville.

# Chapter Seven

W hen the letter announcing Sarah Brewster's engagement arrived, Olivia's first, involuntary thought was that it was bound to end badly. She stared at the letter for a moment, surprised by herself. An unaccountable reaction, she thought reprovingly, when she knew almost nothing of the circumstances or the bridegroom-to-be. Something to do with that curlicued schoolgirl handwriting, perhaps, or the recollection of Sarah's eager, guileless face.

*We met at the clinic where I'm working now,* Sarah had written. *He was a patient, and funnily enough it wasn't me who noticed him at first.* She sounded happy. But as Olivia skimmed through the lines again, the account of the brief courtship, she couldn't stop her mind running forwards through gradual disenchantment to a terrible moment of truth, and then (an unforgivably selfish thought, this) a need for Sarah's old friends to rally round and pick up the pieces. She imagined them all – their faces hazy, at this distance – wishing Sarah well at the wedding, all those people she hadn't seen for so long, and her heart sank.

Olivia frowned at the sheet of notepaper as if it might be responsible for her malice. But it wasn't the first time, lately, that she'd been caught out by a vicious note in herself. Like the Wednesday Club piano, she thought, unpredictable in tone outside the safe middle of its range.

She put the letter back in its envelope and started running hot water into the sink for the porridge pan. Did this release of spite date from the attack on the bridge, she wondered? She baulked at that idea: too much of a psychological cliché. But it was true that there had been, since that day, surges of strangely pleasurable anger; an occasional alluring feeling that violence of a specific, limited kind might be liberating. She'd allowed her trolley to catch a man's legs in the supermarket last week when he'd failed to notice her wanting to pass; she'd made a jibe, barely covered by humour, about Robert's growing paunch. Perhaps it wasn't her assailant who'd acquired a taste for hurting people from that incident, but her.

She turned back to the table to gather up the plates abandoned by her departing sons, and her eyes scanned the scattering of bills and flyers and unsolicited catalogues, the forgotten homework left on the side. This surveillance of her surroundings had become a reflex too; a deliberate act of anchoring herself, as if the detritus of family life had a talismanic power to keep the world under control. But looking at the mess and clutter now, evidence of so many lives dependent on her, she wondered how anyone could choose to take all this on so late in life, when they'd been used to the tidy existence of a single woman. But did she pity Sarah, coming so late to marriage, or resent her claiming her share of domestic bliss after all those years of freedom? Olivia didn't know what she thought, these days. Where her feelings came from.

As she loaded the dishwasher, she turned her mind towards safer ground. She'd heard from Sarah from time to time over the years: news of flats bought and sold, of walking holidays and new jobs. She knew she'd moved close to Oxford, a year or two ago. Sarah was a person you ought to like, Olivia thought – all that enthusiasm, that wide-eyed certainty. But she'd always thought of her as a character who'd found herself in the wrong kind of film, cheerfully playing it straight in the black comedy of life. And now having a go, it seemed, at the romantic lead.

The cat appeared, as he usually did when the house fell quiet after the morning rumpus. Winding himself around Olivia's legs, he made small noises of consolation and entreaty, and she bent to pick him up. 'Sweet boy,' she murmured into the thick fur at his neck. And then she carried him across to the drawer that held odds and ends of stationery. An engagement demanded formal communication, she thought: a letter, an envelope, a stamp. It was an old-fashioned business, getting married. With the cat on her knee, Olivia sat at the kitchen table and filled a card with enthusiastic congratulations.

And when Sarah rang up, a few days later, Olivia invited her to supper with her fiancé.


'Couldn't you put them off?' asked Alastair, as Olivia searched her cupboards in vain for tinned tomatoes.

Olivia turned to smile at him: Alastair the thoughtful one, the sensible second child. Alastair who might have been her favourite, if she'd been allowed to have one. 'I would if I knew her better.'

'What do you mean?'

Olivia sighed, abandoning the hunt. 'I'm afraid she'd guess I wasn't all that keen on the idea in the first place.'

She could almost believe that Fate had conspired to repay her ungenerous instincts over Sarah's engagement by making this occasion as difficult as possible. The timing had proved comically terrible: Robert was away; Tom was about to leave for a university taster course; Benjy had been off school all week with an ear infection. She'd spent the last few days carrying hot drinks up the stairs, finding lost forms and fielding fretful calls from the States. The house was even more of a tip than usual, and it seemed the larder was almost entirely empty.

'What about a takeaway?' Alastair suggested.

Before Olivia could reply the front door slammed. Angus, back from after-school football training, stomped down the hall and threw his sports bag across the kitchen. His brothers looked up as it thudded into the table leg, knocking over a glass of orange juice.

'Oh dear.' Olivia took in his furious face. How many times, she wondered, had he come home like this? She reached for a cloth to mop up the spilt juice, her eyes flicking cautiously to Benjy, curled in a chair at the far end of the kitchen with his Nintendo.

'That's the last time I'm going to football,' Angus announced, his voice dangerously calm. 'He's a complete arse.'

'Who is, darling?'

Olivia moved towards him, but Angus shied away, as if dodging a rugby tackle. He hadn't grown as fast as his brothers: he was short, for thirteen, but stocky. Strong as a pack pony, Robert's mother said admiringly, recognising her own sons in him, the Scottish farmers' genes.

'Mister So-called Sweetman. I'm the best striker in the squad, but does he care? He's totally got it in for me.'

'Just like all the other teachers?' said Benjy, without taking his eyes off his game.

'You can shut up, Mummy's boy. Wait until next year when you're out of baby school. You won't last a minute.'

'Leave him out of it,' said Alastair; but to Olivia's relief Angus was heading out of the kitchen again, towards the larder in the hallway.

'At least I've got friends,' Benjy called after him.

They had a long history, her youngest sons. Benjy's birth had been complicated – a placental abruption and an emergency Caesarian – and he'd been a delicate baby. He still aroused Olivia's protective instincts, and Angus had been swamped by jealousy from the moment Benjy was born. Not that he'd ever admit it, of course. Not that he was ever anything but the tough guy, these days.

The phone rang while Angus was out of the room. Sarah; of course it was Sarah.

'We are still on for this evening?' she asked, picking up the note of hesitation in Olivia's greeting. 'You are expecting us?'

While Olivia explained the one-way system, the intricacies of the residents' parking scheme, violence erupted in the kitchen. She didn't see how it started, but within seconds, Benjy and Angus were pelting each other with potatoes. Peeled potatoes, grabbed from the convenient supply of missiles she'd left in a bowl on the side.

'Sounds lively there,' said Sarah, as a Jersey Royal caught Olivia just below the shoulder. 'By the way, I did tell you I don't eat meat? But don't worry: I'm very happy with just the veg.'

Not when they're already in a casserole with several pounds of braising steak, Olivia thought, juggling conflicting urges to laugh and to scream. Not when the potatoes are under the table now among the crumbs and the pencil sharpenings, no longer the wherewithal for a meal but a mess to clear up.

'No trouble,' she said. 'Look forward to seeing you.'


The doorbell rang ten minutes early. Olivia opened the door onto rain in the street, her guests bedraggled in plastic macs. The happy couple, she thought. She blushed momentarily, remembering her reaction to Sarah's letter. They looked too ordinary, too well-meaning to let themselves in for doubt and recrimination.

'Welcome!' she said. 'I'm afraid Robert's not here: he's been held up in Boston. A business trip.'

'Oh dear.' Sarah hung back for a moment. 'You should have put us off. We could have come another time.'

'No, no. I've been looking forward to it.' Olivia extended her hand to the tall man at Sarah's side, holding himself a little awkwardly in the doorway. They didn't look quite at ease with each other yet, but they made a handsome couple. Each had the kind of physiognomy that ages well in their sex: Guy lean and tanned, with close-cropped curly hair that was greying attractively, and Sarah still plump, strawberry-blonde, girlish. Guy had been a mountaineer, Sarah had told her, until the accident a year ago that left him with a limp and a lot of metal in his legs.

'I really am sorry Robert's not here,' she said. 'He was excited about meeting you.'

'Oh, well–' began Guy.

'My celebrity fiancé.' Sarah beamed. 'You look well, Olivia. How have you stayed so slim, after all those children?'

Olivia smiled, then turned, gesturing down the corridor to the kitchen. 'I have a confession,' she said. 'I had a bit of a mishap earlier, so we're having takeaway curry. I hope you don't mind.' She lifted her hands in a helpless gesture. 'I can only do quantity these days, not quality. The boys simply don't notice what they're eating.'

She flushed as she reached the end of this speech, aware of sounding unnatural. Of sounding just like Sarah, in fact. A bad habit, she thought: did people notice?

'How many boys?' asked Guy.

'Four.' Sarah got the answer in before Olivia. 'Tom, Alastair, Angus, Bertie?'

'Benjy,' said Olivia. 'I'm impressed.'

'I adore curry,' Sarah said. 'And we've come to see you, anyway. What can I do?'

'Nothing. Sit. Have a drink. Here, look: help yourselves.' Olivia put bottles, glasses, corkscrew on the table. For a moment she felt flustered again; she'd hoped Alastair might reappear so she could ask him to pour the drinks, but now she was ashamed of the idea that she couldn't manage on her own.

'What will you drink, Olivia?' asked Guy.

'Perhaps a glass of wine in a minute. Sorry about the noise, by the way.'

An insistent beat could be heard through the ceiling, and the surge of canned laughter from the next room. The boys had ordered pizzas earlier, and seemed to have understood that their mother was best left to herself this evening. Not that it ever took much encouragement to scatter them to their separate entertainments.

'I'd get the boys to come and say hello,' Olivia went on, 'but – you know; a moment of peace.'

They didn't know, of course. They smiled at her, wine glasses in their hands, and Olivia smiled back, struck by the brief silence, the tableau frozen for a moment. Well, here they were, she thought: Sarah and her fiancé, large as life, and no one else to marvel at it. And was Sarah just the same as ever? Olivia wasn't sure she could tell. Less certain, perhaps? Less exuberant, but you'd expect that. It was like watching the Sarah she'd known play an older version of herself, an imaginary adult.

'So, what excitement!' she said. 'A wedding to plan. A winter wedding!'

The smell of spices filled the kitchen as she prised the lids off plastic containers.

'Epiphany's a traditional time for a wedding,' Sarah said. 'And people don't go away much in January.'

'Sarah wants a big party,' said Guy. 'She's busy ferreting people out.'

'You'll never guess who I saw last week.' Sarah raised her eyebrows, catching Olivia's eye. 'Eve.'

Olivia's hands halted for a moment.

'Eve de Perreville?'

Eve had hovered at the periphery of her thoughts since the day she'd seen James, but it was a long time since she'd spoken her name out loud. And Sarah had seen her? Eve hadn't even liked Sarah, in the old days.

'She's living in Maidenhead,' Sarah said. 'Working as a GP.'

Olivia kept her voice light. 'I thought she went abroad? Married an Australian doctor?'

'She's divorced. Second time, actually. I was surprised you weren't in touch.'

'No. I haven't seen her for years.'

Olivia had written to Eve once, during the month she'd spent in Dubai with her parents at the end of that fateful summer – a careful letter that Eve had never replied to. The following year Olivia had heard that Eve had gone to Australia with a visiting doctor she'd fallen in love with, and then she'd heard no more. There was still a small vacuum deep inside, in the space that Eve had once occupied, curiously empty of feelings now.

'I saw James,' she began – but the phrase was cut off by a crash from overhead, and in that second she thought better of it. Sarah had never known James; Olivia wasn't going to explain. She still wasn't even sure it had been him she'd seen that morning. She'd gone over it in her mind again and again, reminding herself that she'd been suggestible after the assault.

'How old are your sons?' Guy asked, glancing in the direction of the noise.

'Between ten and eighteen. All addicted to screens of one kind or another. Sorry–' Olivia strode over to the playroom door, flung it open and shouted, 'down, please, just a bit.'

'Goodness.' Sarah was at her shoulder, peering into the boys' lair. In the darkness, two bodies were sprawled half on, half off the sofa; the floor was scattered with pizza boxes, sweet wrappers, split-open files. Your perspective could shift in an instant, Olivia thought: one minute it was cheerful clutter, the next chaos and dissolution.

'This is my friend Sarah,' she said.

'From school,' said Sarah, and Tom and Angus glanced away from the television for a moment to mutter a greeting, then turned back to a scene of bloody massacre.

'That looks like fun,' said Sarah; and Olivia could tell she meant it, at some level, but also that she couldn't begin to connect these hulking creatures with any child she might ever have herself.

'Tom's about to leave school,' she said, shutting the door again. 'Amazing thought, isn't it? The same age you and I were when we were last together, Scabs.'

'The same age I was when I was last called Scabs,' said Sarah. But she looked pleased. Grinning, Olivia thought, in the same over-effusive way she used to when there was a place for her at their table in the school dining room. Poor old Scabs. Nicknames had been important, a sign of belonging, but somehow Sarah's had always had a different implication, even though its origin was innocuous enough. Sarah Catherine Brewster: Scabs. Eve's invention, of course. Olivia had another unaccountable thought: that they were partly responsible, she and Eve and the rest, for the years it had taken Sarah to find a husband.

'So Robert's heard of Guy, has he?' asked Sarah, when they sat down at last.

Olivia smiled at Guy. 'I bought your book for him to read on the plane.'

'It's very dull, I'm afraid,' said Guy. 'Have you done any climbing?'

Olivia shook her head. 'Too scared.'

'Fear's important,' Guy said. 'Climbing is most dangerous when you have no fear.'

'Did you stop because you weren't afraid any more?'

Guy laughed, and Sarah answered for him. 'It was the accident, really, but he was ready for a change, weren't you, darling?'

The endearment, an unexpected quaintness in Sarah's tone, caught Olivia off-guard. Another image entered her head: seabass and samphire, twenty-five years ago. Wondering how well two people knew each other. Then, like one wave following another, a wash of emotion: envy and regret and longing. And guilt, of course. There was always guilt, when she looked back.

'He was forever busy planning the next expedition,' Sarah was saying, somewhere in the background. 'But the accident made him realise what he was missing.' She reached out a hand to squeeze Guy's. 'He decided to settle down, and he settled on me.'

Olivia could think of nothing to say that wouldn't sound insincere – or worse, satirical. The music thudding through the ceiling was giving her a headache, even though she was entirely used to it. She felt suddenly exhausted, weighed down by things too numerous, too nebulous to name. What must it be like, she wondered, to be at the beginning of something, to have the energy to start afresh?

'So how is Eve?' she asked eventually.

'Older,' said Sarah. 'Like all of us.' She laughed, prodding her rice with her fork. 'She's thinking of adopting.'

'A baby?' Olivia was astonished – too astonished to conceal it – but Sarah was undaunted.

'From China. Apparently you can, on your own.'

'Good Lord.'

'She's only been back in the country six months,' said Sarah. 'Her parents are both dead. Between the first and second divorce, she said. She's had enough of Australia.'

'Strange, her ending up there,' said Olivia. 'Anywhere abroad.' She paused, trying to conjure Eve: a shadowy nineteen-year-old, stretching backwards in time, but not forwards. 'I never imagined her with children,' she said. 'Or wanting them.'


'It's been wonderful to see you,' Sarah said on the doorstep.

'You too. Perhaps we'll meet again before the wedding.'

Sarah looked aghast. 'The wedding's months off,' she said, with her squeaky laugh. 'Of course we'll see you. We haven't even met Robert yet.'

Guy shook her hand. 'Sarah talks a lot about you,' he said. 'I'm glad to have met you at last.'

And there it was, Olivia thought, as the door shut behind them and she stood, just for a moment, in the silence of the hall: the reunion effected. The beginning of the rewriting of history.

# Chapter Eight

The Wednesday Club had been unusually hectic for the last couple of weeks. One day there had been a problem with the lavatories, and Olivia had held the fort while Shirley placated the Council plumber, and the following week Rex had been ill. The stand-in driver had failed to collect a couple of clients and had upset a couple of others, throwing the whole morning – usually so peaceful, so predictable – into pandemonium.

But the morning after Sarah and Guy's visit things were back to normal. There was a chill in the air, an early hint of winter, but inside the centre the atmosphere was warm and serene. The first thing Olivia saw when she walked in was a giant crossword inscribed on a whiteboard, evidence of a couple of hours calmly occupied.

'Morning, Olivia,' called Shirley, wiping her hands on a dishcloth. 'OK?'

'Fine, thanks.' Olivia looked around the room. 'Still no Georgie?'

'Out of hospital,' Shirley said, 'so that's a step forward. Maybe next week.'

'What's been the matter?'

'Just a touch of pneumonia.'

Olivia remembered what Shirley had said that first week: *the usual*. Was pneumonia the usual? Had Georgie been one of those sickly children who stayed fragile into adulthood? Olivia didn't think so, somehow; you had to be tough to live to ninety. But she let the subject drop. Better to let Shirley choose her moment. Shirley liked having a story to tell; she'd want to make the most of it.

'How about a Scottish theme today?' she asked. 'Speed Bonny Boat? Loch Lomond?'

'I love Loch Lomond,' said Shirley. 'We went on holiday there once. Beautiful place.'

'Everyone seems in good spirits,' Olivia said later, as she and Shirley stood in the kitchen drinking their undrinkable coffee. 'Some new faces this week.'

'Marjorie,' said Shirley. 'Have to mind our Ps and Qs around Marjorie. She was a lady don.'

'Really?'

Marjorie had early dementia, and had enjoyed the singing with a colourful lack of inhibition. 'Bravo!' she'd called, after each song. 'Encore!'

'A lady don at St Hilda's,' Shirley said. 'Proper bluestocking. Seems a shame to me, all that learning and no family, but you pays your money and you takes your choice.'

'Didn't Elsie work at St Hilda's too?' asked Olivia. 'One of the women's colleges, I'm sure.'

'Elsie?'

'Not as an academic. Domestic staff, I think.'

Shirley raised her eyebrows. 'Who'd've thought it,' she said. 'Lady dons rubbing shoulders with cleaners. Well, we get all sorts at the Wednesday Club.'

'Funny the lives they've all had. The stories they could tell.' Olivia smiled, and let the phrase hang; felt it picked up by a current of air and wafted forwards.

Shirley reached for the biscuit tin and offered Olivia a custard cream.

'I was going to tell you about Georgie, wasn't I?'

Olivia shook her head at the proffered tin, then thought better of it. You never saw custard creams now, she thought, except in places like this. They reminded her of dismal tea parties when she was a child.

'Might as well, before they all go,' said Shirley approvingly. She settled her ample bottom on the edge of the worktop. 'Georgie's social worker told me the story when she first came here. She never mentions it herself.' She paused, peered round the door. Rex had gone outside for a smoke and there was a peaceful hum of conversation in the big room. 'She was one of those girls locked up in an asylum because they got pregnant.'

'Locked up?' Olivia was startled: whatever she'd expected, it wasn't this.

Shirley nodded. 'She was a student at Oxford, but her family disowned her. They thought it was madness, didn't they? Nymphomania or whatever. Awful.'

'Good God. How long was she in the asylum?'

'Nearly fifty years, the social worker said. Didn't get out until she was in her sixties. Too late to make anything of your life by then. You'd be institutionalised, wouldn't you? She's been in sheltered accommodation ever since, poor old Georgie.'

73

Olivia said nothing. The custard cream cloyed on her tongue; she longed for a party napkin to spit it into. Shirley sipped her coffee, savouring the effect she'd produced.

'I've heard about that happening,' Olivia said eventually, 'but you don't think about it – well, so close to home.'

'Terrible thing, in a civilised society,' Shirley agreed.

'So that's how she lost her baby? They took it away?'

Shirley nodded. 'Anyone would go mad after a while, shut up in a place like that.' She shook her head, eloquently mournful. 'Hard not to, wouldn't it?'

'Georgie's never seemed mad to me.' Far from it, Olivia thought, although it was hard to think about Georgie now without this extraordinary revelation; hard to make an assessment. 'Introverted, perhaps, but not mad.'

'Well,' said Shirley. 'Let's hope we've cheered up the last few years of her life a bit, eh? Better have a look at this shepherd's pie. And apple crumble, this week. I told you we'd be on to hot puddings before we knew it.'


Since the day of the attack on the bridge, Olivia had made a point of cycling home along the towpath every Wednesday. She imagined herself as some kind of suburban vigilante, but in truth it was more a test of her nerve. She hadn't seen the lad in the hoodie again, nor James, or the man she'd taken for James. Every week a little more space opened up between her and that morning, but the memory could still make her heart skip a beat – partly, she knew, because she hadn't told anyone else what had happened, not even Robert. The possibility of meeting the men again – either of them – gave the path, the canal, an exaggerated significance. It was as if she could hear the soundtrack to the film of her life playing in her head, overlaying the scene with suspense.

But today there was a different theme tune, another kind of emotion. It was hard to imagine, now, the scandal Georgie's pregnancy must have caused seventy years ago. Schoolboy fathers had a kind of celebrity these days; women in their thirties were blasé about the next grandchild. No one talked about sanctions, just about breaking the cycle of disadvantage. But two or three generations ago, it was enough to ruin a whole life. Enough to justify locking someone away, out of sight, until they were well past any risk of pregnancy.

Had Georgie been a wild teenager, Olivia wondered, as she ducked beneath an overhanging branch, or naïve and unworldly? Had she been seduced by a tutor at Oxford, or broken bounds to conduct an affair with a fellow student? And what had she done with her time all those years, confined in an institution? It was unimaginable. Impossible to understand how life could go on, after so much of it had been wiped out: how someone young and hopeful, taking for granted the years ahead of them, could lose so much in a single slip.

Olivia turned her bike onto the steep slope leading up to the bridge, the flicker of apprehension it induced less sharp today, and sailed down the other side towards home with a guilty sense of freedom.

*AT NIGHT THE* memory of birth returns. They held you down so you wouldn't see the baby, and you held your tongue so they wouldn't see your distress. No cries, through that forcing and splitting, that slipping away from the light. The only evidence they had of your suffering was your blood, pouring onto the floor as if it wanted to drain you dry, and the fever that racked you afterwards, conjured by your body to cauterise the pain.

The baby torments your dreams: the baby that was gone so soon that you never knew if it breathed. Its screams are silent, its head deformed by the passage it was forced through against your will; by your desperate desire never to let it go. It lies discarded on a white slab, or suspended from a wooden cross, a remnant of the faith you have no right to any more.

But some nights the seed of it is there, deep inside, the sweet secret promise they couldn't take away. The flower blooming slowly within your swelling body; the tiny fish skittering and dancing among the coral. On those mornings you wake with the pillow wet, as though your waters have broken again, and you know it is gone. You could never have held on to it: you were not fit. But when you feel it inside you again, the hidden life you were not allowed, its possibility sustains you.

You never tell them, but they know what it means, your serenity. When you don't bleed they lock you in the dark. They will not let you win.

# Chapter Nine

## Galloway, July 1983

O livia and Eve reached Scotland at the end of July. The days were long and the light thin and clear: later, Olivia would remember the sky as pure white. The colours of the landscape were simple, too. Green, grey, brown; splashes of purple heather on the hills and patriotic thistles by the roadside.

They were going to the Highlands, that was the plan, but someone they'd met in Wales had told Eve there were wonderful prehistoric sites in Dumfriesshire, and it didn't look far on the map. Along the A75, following the Scottish coastline west towards Stranraer. 'The Solway Firth,' Eve said knowledgeably. She had a way of giving romance to place names. 'We must see the Solway Firth. There are poems about it.'

'Really?' asked Olivia.

'Young Lochinvar,' said Eve. '*Love swells like the Solway, but ebbs like its tide.*'

'Uh-huh.' Olivia was tired; she'd driven all day. Somehow they'd forgotten to swap over after lunch. But she caught Eve's glance and asked, 'Who was Young Lochinvar, then?'

'*So faithful in love, and so dauntless in war, there never was knight like the young Lochinvar,*' Eve recited. 'We learnt it at primary school. Sort of a Romeo and Juliet scenario, with a happy ending. He turns up at the wedding of his true love and spirits her away on his horse.'

'Across the Solway Firth.'

'I'm not sure the route is specified.' Eve sighed. 'God, it's further than I thought.'

They were heading for Torhousekie Stone Circle. You must see it at sunset, the Welshman had said. Something about the solstice, although it was well past that now. The road veered close to the coast at times and they had a view of a wide stretch of water and the irregular outline of land beyond. The slant of the sun added a metallic glaze to the sea and the sky, disguising blue and green as silver and grey. Olivia had read somewhere that it was seven miles to the horizon, across the sea: an impossible distance to judge, unless you knew.

As the road swept up towards Newton Stewart they turned left down the side of the Esk estuary to Wigtown.

'Nearly there,' said Eve, looking down at the map. 'Just a few more miles.'

'Shall we stop?' suggested Olivia. 'Buy some food?'

It was a camping night tonight. Last night they'd stayed in a bed and breakfast, so tonight it was the tent.

'Later,' said Eve.

Olivia knew what was on Eve's mind. If the shops were shut, they'd have to go to a pub. But her budget was smaller than Eve's; she flicked the indicator and turned off the main road into the town. Eve said nothing.

Even at four o'clock there was little sign of life in

Wigtown. Olivia parked on the broad expanse of the main street outside a shop with small dirty windows and a dilapidated sign.

'What shall I get?'

'I'll come with you,' Eve said.

They were experts, after a month on the road, on shops like this. There must be whole stretches of Britain, Eve said, where people lived on the same five things. They bought sliced bread, a tin of sardines, a packet of biscuits. Then, at the till, Eve spotted a bottle of whisky on the shelf behind the boy who served them.

'I'll pay,' she said, before Olivia could object. 'Keep out the chill tonight.' She smiled, and for a moment Olivia could taste woodsmoke and sea air, the tang of friendship.

The B road to Torhousekie was lined by fields of cattle, most of them black and thick-coated, some with a distinctive white band around their middles as though they'd been assembled from unmatched pieces by a child. Here and there outcrops of grey stone could be seen, and shapely trees, scattered across the pasture land.

'Here we are,' said Eve, and Olivia pulled over onto a wide section of verge.

There was something, Olivia thought, both remarkable and disappointing about sites like this. After all just a collection of stones in a field, placed on uneven ground, with sheep's wool snagged in the barbed wire that ran around the top of the dry stone walls. But unmistakably a circle, nineteen hefty boulders dragged here and positioned with some mysterious ancient intent, and still here four thousand years later.

It was always Eve who had a sense of occasion. Without speaking she set off slowly, clockwise, around the outside of the circle, and after a moment Olivia followed.

Hocum, she thought, but perhaps no different from the urge to look upwards in a church, or to be awed by the sight of fire. There must be a reason for the potency of circles.

There were three stones in the centre of this one, two of them bigger than the rest. When she'd finished processing around the perimeter, Eve made for the largest and scrambled up onto it.

'Come up,' she called. 'There's a view.'

There wasn't, much, but Olivia obeyed, and they settled back to back on the flat summit and gazed out at the unbroken sweep of green.

'It's called the Machars, this peninsula,' said Eve. 'The bit that hangs down towards England.'

'Into the Solway Firth,' said Olivia, and Eve tried to jab her with her elbow, then lost her balance and slithered clumsily to the ground.

'Right,' she said, as she picked herself up, 'watch out.'

She grabbed Olivia's legs and pulled hard. Olivia screamed, feeling herself slipping, the stone cold and smooth against her back as her T-shirt rode up. A moment later they were both rolling in the grass, shrieking, the taste of turf in their mouths. A group of cows in the adjacent field turned their heads to watch, with the startled expressions of old men disturbed from their newspapers.

'Race you,' said Olivia, scrambling to her feet.

'Catch you,' Eve countered, and they chased each other around the outside of the circle, gathering speed until they were running full tilt, Olivia's heart pounding as though she was being pursued by a monster. The cows began to jostle each other, and soon they were lumbering along the fence beside them, a great mass of black with a slippery purple sheen in the sun, heaving and rolling like a landslide. They were too cumbersome to stampede, Olivia thought: they looked impossibly comic. By the time she and Eve circled round to meet the cows again, they were both laughing too hard to run. They collapsed on the ground as dozens of hooves thundered past, and the stones stood still and silent, unmoved by this display as they had been by all they'd witnessed in their long lives.

'Oh,' said Olivia, as she recovered her breath. 'I've got such a stitch.'

Eve rolled over and pushed Olivia's knees up towards her chest. 'Better?'

Olivia groaned.

'Good place, eh?' Eve said. 'Worth a detour?'

'Mmm.'

Eve propped herself on one elbow. 'Let's camp here tonight.'

'In the circle?'

'Wouldn't that be great? We could watch the sun set and then rise again. We could lie on that stone and watch the stars.'

'Like sacrificial virgins,' said Olivia.

But Eve was already heading for the car.

'The cows might come and trample us,' Olivia shouted after her, but then she got to her feet and followed. It was a long time until sunset, but she was hungry, and there was already a slight dampness to the ground.

'Are you sure this is OK?' she asked, as Eve held out her hand for the car keys.

'What's to stop us? It's a public place. Better than a field belonging to some farmer.' Eve heaved the tent out of the boot and slammed the lid. 'Come on. Time to open that whisky.'

The whisky, it turned out, came from just up the road. Bladnoch, on the outskirts of Wigtown, billed on the label as the most southerly distillery in Scotland. It seemed to Olivia an odd thing to boast about when the point about Scotland was its northerliness, but the whisky tasted good. All they had to drink out of were the cups from the top of Olivia's thermos, so the first tumbler-full had an edge of stale coffee to it. They drank it down – whisky was whisky, too expensive to throw away – then poured more, and swigged it with their sardine sandwiches, feeling its heat filtering through them as the warmth drained out of the day.

Afterwards, they climbed back onto the big stone and sat back to back again, taking it in turns to tell ghost stories as the sun went down towards Ireland and the cows snorted and huffled in the field behind them. Eve was a good storyteller: she had the right inflection, the proper conviction to twist cliché into fear.

'Nearer and nearer came the footsteps,' she intoned, 'and with them the sound of ragged breathing, and every minute she expected to see a face, looming out of the darkness...'

Olivia could feel Eve's spine pressed against her, the ticklish ends of Eve's hair brushing her shoulders. It seemed to her, at that moment, as though they'd come a long way; as though home was far behind them, across that silvered sea.

'To friendship,' Eve said, when the sun had set at last, and the whisky bottle had been set aside too.

'To friendship,' Olivia echoed. Eve's moods could shift as swiftly as a cloud blowing in from the sea, but the sentiment was sincere, Olivia knew that. And they were past the stage of minding each other's moods: almost like an old married couple by now.

They fell asleep early, their little tent nestled in the lee of the central stone like a sailing boat in harbour. Eve usually wriggled and grumbled for a long time in her sleeping bag, but tonight she was snoring almost as soon as they lay down, her hair furled in the hollow of her neck. Olivia lay for a while watching stars appear one by one in the strip of sky she could see through the door of the tent, then she too fell asleep.


She wasn't sure what it was that woke her: a noise, or a movement; perhaps some premonition. She couldn't tell whether she or Eve had woken first, but suddenly there they both were, alert in the darkness. Whispering in the almost-silent way you can in a two-man tent; in the way you do when you wake in the middle of the night, in the middle of nowhere.

They were frightened but giggly at first, suppressing a bubbling urge to laugh or scream. The ghost stories lingered, heightening their apprehension but undermining it at the same time.

'Maybe it's the Druids,' whispered Eve.

'Or the police.'

'Can you hear anything?'

'I'm sure I did.'

They pulled themselves upright with their sleeping bags still around them, as if they might offer protection rather than hampering their escape, and peered out through the door panel. They could see nothing except the outline of the stones, midnight purple against the dark sky, and a vague dimness over the sea in the distance.

'Shall we look outside?'

Olivia nodded. 'Perhaps it's the cows,' she whispered. 'Perhaps they've got through the fence.'

They wriggled out of their sleeping bags and crawled out onto the wet grass. Still nothing: not until they took a few steps away from the tent and turned round. Then they saw the man, sitting on the other side of the stone. Right behind where they had been sleeping, a man sitting propped against the stone. *A face, looming out of the darkness.*

Eve's scream was shocking, cutting through the night like a floodlight. Olivia grabbed her arm, wanting to calm her, shut her up, and as she did so the man leapt to his feet and ran. They caught no more than a glimpse of his face before he disappeared through the gate, a bulky figure clad in a dark jacket with fluorescent white stripes across the shoulders.

'He was probably completely harmless,' Olivia said the next morning, as they sat shivering in the car.

They'd drunk a lot more of the whisky after the man had run off; after they'd scrambled across the field to the Fiat and locked themselves in. Then they'd dozed a little through the dawn, side by side in the front seats, waking to throbbing hangovers and cricked necks, edgy with each other.

'He might not even have noticed our tent,' Olivia went on. 'We were round the far side of the big stone. It was very dark.'

'If he was innocent, why run off like that?'

That was what had frightened Olivia most too: not the man's presence, but the speed with which he'd made for the gate, the road, the distance. The sudden explosion of movement.

'We might have scared him,' she said. 'He might have been – you know, vulnerable. In need of help.'

Eve snorted. 'He didn't look it to me. I reckon we should go to the police.'

'Better not,' said Olivia. 'There might be a byelaw about camping in the stone circle. I don't suppose they'd like it, a couple of southerners showing no respect for history.'

Eve twisted sulkily at the fringe on her cardigan. 'We weren't doing any harm.'

'Nor was he. He had plenty of opportunity. Who knows how long he was there?'

'Don't,' said Eve. She was surprisingly squeamish, Olivia had noticed, about what might have been.

There was no water left and no food. No way, either, that they were capable of driving yet, even along these deserted roads. Olivia could feel the whisky sluggish in her veins still; she could smell it on Eve's breath. There was nothing to do but wait a few more hours here, but the magic had gone out of the stone circle now, the detour into prehistory a sour taste in their mouths. She could see the cows huddled together by the gate, looking expectantly towards the car. Waiting for breakfast, perhaps; or perhaps for a reprise of last night's entertainment, the chasing and squealing and laughter.

'Let's pack up the tent,' she said. The sun was up now; there was nothing to be frightened of. They could walk across those fields, down towards the Solway Firth.

# Chapter Ten

## 2008

The first Monday in October was cold and clear. Port Meadow had a sculpted look, its hollows and undulations sharply outlined before the coming of the floods that transformed the water meadows every autumn. There was hardly anyone about, and as Olivia left the path to walk across the tussocky grass she was conscious of a sense of space, and of the clarity of the landscape under the broad sky.

Not all her days had a pattern to them, but this Monday walk had become a tradition. During the years she'd accompanied Benjy to school, she'd got into the habit of walking across the meadow on Monday mornings after leaving him in the playground. Whatever the weather, she would cross the sweep of pasture to Medley Bridge, pass Fiddler's Island and Bossom's boatyard and head up the far side of the river towards Wolvercote, with the cattle and the horses and, in season, the flocks of migrating geese for company.

Benjy walked to and from school with his friends now, swapping cards or brandishing sticks and banter.

Olivia had regretted the loss of those half hours with her youngest son, as she'd regretted every rite of passage. It had spelled the end of a decade at the school gate, the daily camaraderie of motherhood. But she hadn't given up her Monday walks. It was a good way to begin the week, treading familiar ground and watching the seasons turn. A good time to think.

This morning, she was mulling over a phone call from the night before. The mother of one of her best pupils – a girl of seventeen, due to sit Grade 8 in the spring – had rung to explain that Gabriella was finding music practice too much on top of her A levels and wanted to drop her piano lessons for a while. Olivia understood what that temporising meant. It spared everyone's feelings, but pupils never came back, once they'd stopped.

When she'd first started teaching, she'd imagined nurturing children who'd follow in her footsteps, pursuing the path she'd abandoned towards the concert platform. She'd only take on students with real promise, she'd thought. She'd been sparing her own feelings back then, persuading herself all wasn't lost. But pretty soon she'd settled for more limited ambitions, for offering her pupils a little musical understanding and the pleasure of modest accomplishment. With children of her own she'd had more sympathy with those who didn't practise. But increasingly she understood that piano lessons were just a phase, a fad to be dallied with then dropped, along with Pokémon cards and skateboards. There was nothing special about music for most of her pupils, nothing distinctive about the experience except the effort involved and the slow pace of progress.

Olivia sighed. Another blow; another bit of life deftly undermined. So few of her pupils ever got as far as

Gabriella. The occasional glimmer of musical promise was necessary, a leavening that made the venture bearable, but those with some talent could be even more discouraging than the rest. It occurred to Olivia, as she walked, that she might not be able to bear teaching the piano for much longer. It was more of a career than playing folk songs at the Wednesday Club, and it had been convenient while the boys were little, but there was nothing to stop her doing something else now. Nothing, that is, except the fact that she wasn't qualified to do anything else. That she was twenty years older than most people were when they wondered what they might do with their lives.

She'd reached a broad stretch of ground where the grass had disappeared. The bare earth, cracked and swollen by the annual cycle of flooding and sunshine, had crazed into little quadrants like hopscotch squares. Olivia stopped. It looked dry enough to walk on; there hadn't been much rain recently. She took a couple of tentative steps, then a couple more. By the time she felt a tell-tale give beneath her feet she was too far in to jump back, and her panicky movements, twisting and turning in search of a firm footing, only made her sink deeper into the shallow bog. A couple of horses, grazing nearby, watched with interest as she thrashed around, before scrambling awkwardly to safety. Although there was no one to see her, Olivia smiled as she brushed off the worst of the mud, telling herself it was funny, an exploit she could recount later. And then she turned and continued on her way, skirting the mud flat this time.

As she approached Medley Bridge, she spotted a couple of boys leaning on their bikes. Truants, probably, Olivia thought, but her disappointment about Gabriella had resulted in an oddly indulgent view of adolescents in general: a sense of resignation, perhaps. Who was she to judge? But as she got closer she heard a raised voice, a chorus of laughter. She didn't catch what they said, but as she walked over the bridge she sensed their eyes on her, their whispers and giggles. Was it her muddy feet they were laughing at, or something else? The same thing that had been obvious to that lad on the canal bridge, perhaps – invisible to her, but marking her out clearly as a person to be mocked, or attacked?

In a moment she'd reached the boatyard, where launches and dinghies wintered down under their tarpaulins, and the boys were behind her. She felt a flash of relief, and then of chagrin. They were only children, no more than fourteen: they could be friends of her sons. Surely she wasn't intimidated by them, or upset by a bit of mud? She must be over-sensitive, still, to an aura of menace. But what was that about? What was happening to her – to her resilience, her self-reliance?

After the boatyard, she stopped to draw breath; to draw a line beneath the bog and the cat-calls on the bridge. Beyond the rugged pasture and the ancient willows, Oxford was a distant strip along the horizon, the whole city reduced to a narrow boundary between land and sky and its hectic activity silenced by distance. This view never failed to offer solace. Olivia gazed for a long moment at the familiar outline of roofs and steeples, and then her eyes drifted to the foreground where a group of cows grazed, the power of their jaws matched by the benign mass of their bellies and their heavy udders. She was almost close enough to feel the heat of their breath, with its sweet, fermenting smell of pulped grass.

For several minutes she stood and watched the cows,

and the silent swans on the water beyond. When she walked on she had the feeling that she was the only person in this wide landscape; perhaps the last person left on earth. Monday morning, and the world had emptied: there was nothing but the whisper of the river, the occasional call of a lonely bird.

A few hours later, Olivia sat in the little music room at the side of her house, a pair of pupils (two home-schooled siblings, as diligent as she could wish) sitting expectantly at her side as the afternoon sun sidled in through the little window.

The grand piano her parents had given her as a wedding present had always dominated this room. For years she and her pupils had edged around it, glimpsing their reflections in its dark sheen. But it seemed to Olivia today that there was something monstrous about the arrangement. There wasn't enough air in here to absorb the vibration of the strings, or to allow any of them to breathe freely.

She stared out of the window, remembering the panic that had gripped her briefly in the bog, and on Medley Bridge. The ground was treacherous today, she thought, the familiar landscape untrustworthy – and that idea filled her, suddenly, with a dangerous sort of excitement. She had the feeling that she might do something rash: something to upturn her life and set herself on a new course. But the things that turned life upside down – the things you couldn't undo – happened when you least expected, she told herself, not because you willed them. She ought to have learned that much. And then the panic distilled itself into a cold, sharp lance of fear, and she knew it for what it was. A thing she had busied herself with burying for so many years that she had almost forgotten what it had cost her. A thing which the edifice of her life would never be equal to concealing.

'Good,' she said, dragging her attention back to the child on the piano stool. He was playing a Mozart minuet, a familiar little piece rendered with flawless banality. 'It needs some dynamics now, Thomas. Can you see that this line is the same as the one you've just played? It needs to sound like an echo. Softer than the first time.'

Thomas frowned, and his sister, watching him keenly, leaned forwards as far as the piano would allow, her pigtails brushing the polished wood.

She'd been wrong this morning, Olivia thought: punctilious practisers like these two were more depressing than those who squandered their talent. But after another rendition she nodded.

'Better,' she lied, and both children grinned with relief.


Olivia stood on the doorstep at the end of the lesson and smiled in a way she didn't imagine anyone could be taken in by. But she'd regained her sangfroid. There was nothing like listening to a child murdering Mozart, she thought, to restore one's sense of proportion.

'Have we got the Grade 2 pieces yet?' she asked. 'Thomas could aim for that next term. And Elizabeth Grade 1, perhaps.'

Their mother's face sagged a little. 'I'm not sure about more exams,' she said. 'I'd like it to be – a more organic thing, if you know what I mean. All this measuring and grading. You know?'

'Of course.' Why did she feel that flash of annoyance, Olivia wondered? Didn't she complain about the parents who were only interested in the certificates, the marks achieved? She thought of Gabriella, wondering if a more organic approach would have helped her. Too much weedkiller, she thought, feeling an incongruous impulse to laugh. Too much fertiliser, week after week.

'I'll have a think about some more interesting music,' she said. 'Some duets, perhaps. Something they could play together. Would you like that?'

The children, secure now in their mother's grasp, nodded shyly. Olivia could hardly hold their mediocrity against them – or indeed against their mother, so earnestly principled. She had failed, after all, to transmit her love of music to her own sons, despite the patient hours she'd spent when they were little, singing songs and shaking maracas, hoping to instil the basics of rhythm and pitch. She hadn't tried to teach any of them the piano herself: instead, she'd sent them to a young man down the road whose enthusiasm had seemed to her irresistible. But one after another they'd rebelled, refused, charmed their way out of the process. Alastair still played the electric guitar and Angus had a drum kit; that was the sum of it. Not one with an interest in what they called her kind of music.

It was nearly half past four when she heard the click and slam of the front door.

'Hi, Mum!' Benjy's voice, and then the thud of his satchel on the hall floor.

'Good day?' Olivia called. She held her breath, wondering whether he would come through to the kitchen or head straight for his room, as he'd taken to doing lately. 'How was the maths thing?'

Benjy appeared in the doorway, pulling a face.

'It was so unfair,' he began. 'Even Mr Fletcher agreed it was. We were right in the corner. Jake, who's a total maths genius, got three things wrong because we couldn't hear properly.'

'Oh dear.'

'Anything to eat?' Benjy moved towards the larder, his attention shifting already from the day's injustice to his stomach.

Olivia found a packet of sweet French buns, the last of a bulk box they'd bought during their week in Brittany. Benjy took two, reaching for a third before he'd swallowed the first mouthful. Olivia reached a hand to touch his head – already above her shoulder, beyond the point where she could gather him in for a little-boy hug. These days, when she was allowed near, it was her head that rested on her sons' shoulders, as though they were strangers consoling her for some unnamed loss.

'Leave some for the others,' she said mildly, and Benjy nodded and grabbed another bun, then sauntered across the kitchen to find a glass.

When they were younger, this had been her favourite time: the still point between day and evening, with an empty stretch ahead before the bedtime routine began. It had been a time to savour, with her brood gathered in, the doors shut against the world. She felt the same pleasure at their return now, although arguments and silence were more common these days than cheerful chatter. But she could still feed them: they were as voracious as carrion birds, picking the biscuit tin clean, scouring the cupboards when her back was turned. And it wasn't just food they demolished. Without malice – without noticing – they kicked cupboard doors, bounced balls off lamp brackets, subjected the furniture to stresses and strains it certainly hadn't been designed for.

The door slammed again and here were the older three.

'All right, Mum?' asked Alastair, as the kitchen filled with long legs that were never still unless they were in front of a screen; with man-sized hands constantly seeking something to pick up and toss in the air. A swarm of overgrown insects, Olivia thought, all limbs and buzzing noise. At least none ready to sting today.

'What's for supper?' asked Tom.

'Macaroni cheese.' Olivia took a block of cheddar out of his hand to grate it. 'It's Monday, so it must be macaroni cheese.'

As her children's noise dispersed through the house in thuds and shouts and the throb of music, Olivia tipped pasta into boiling water. She'd been an adventurous cook once, but her repertoire had narrowed and narrowed. It wasn't all her doing: men, her friends affirmed, were intrinsically conservative, and Olivia was surrounded by men. She'd always found the predictability of her life consoling, though, hadn't she? The rhythm of it; the certainty. But here was another thing that had changed lately. The things that gave her pleasure induced a kind of pain, almost simultaneously, and the more fervently she pursued the pleasure, the sharper the pain that came with it. The pain of knowing that things wouldn't stay the same forever. The pain of knowing how lucky she was. The pain of wondering what else might have been.

# Chapter Eleven

T he clinic where Sarah worked was on the outskirts
of Oxford, just beyond the ring road where
Summertown turns into Kidlington. A few minutes walk
away was Cutteslowe Park, a model of old-fashioned civic
felicity with its aviary and its miniature railway, its
children's playpark and duckpond and bowling green.
The parade of shops which housed the Wellbeing Clinic,
between a vet's surgery and a dry cleaner, had a 1950s
feel to it too, not just because of its austerity architecture
but because of the absence of chain stores, the gentle pace
at which mothers pushed buggies and older people
wheeled trollies along the pavement.

It gave Sarah particular pleasure, this place, for
reasons she found hard to pin down. There was
something reassuringly solid about it; a sense that
everything had its place. Inside as well as out, the clinic
was unhurried and decorous. She parked her car in the
little yard behind the building and pushed the buttons on
the key pad by the back door. She was in a good mood:
she'd had the wedding caterer's quotation through the

post this morning, and had savoured it over breakfast. Canapés and petits fours were arrayed pleasingly in her imagination.

'Morning, Jane,' she said as she passed the reception desk. A vase of half-opened roses, suprisingly ugly, sat on the counter like a declaration of good faith.

'Sarah.' Jane glanced up briefly from her computer screen. She worked hard, Sarah thought, at appearing busy: she used the same verbal shorthand on patients as on her employers, as though wasting words looked slack. 'Practice meeting's in five minutes.'

Sarah halted halfway up the stairs.

'Is this new?' she called over the banister. 'This painting here?'

'Grateful patient.'

It was unmistakably France, fields of sunflowers and stone houses on the side of a hillside. Rather striking, Sarah thought, bold colours and gauzy washes giving an impression of heat. The kind of landscape she'd spent several summers walking through. She smiled to herself as she went on up the stairs. She'd met Martin and Philippa on one of those French holidays. They were a few years older than her; both osteopaths, they'd told her, running their own private clinic.

'Physiotherapy's a good background for osteopathy,' Martin had said one evening, over a glass of cognac. 'If you ever fancied a change.'

Sarah had always been protective about physiotherapy. You're not just a technician, she'd say to the students when they arrived in her department. And she was highly respected: the orthopaedic surgeons sent their private patients to her at the BUPA hospital on a Wednesday evening. But even so, she'd thought, watching the cognac swirl in her glass as the sun set over the Provençal hills. Even so. She admired Martin and Philippa, and she was flattered by their attention. And there was no denying that her life had reached a plateau.

'Where's the best training course?' she'd asked.

Once she'd got the idea into her head she was off, making enquiries and plans. Martin and Philippa offered her a place in their clinic when she qualified, and Sarah accepted. And she'd never regretted any of it, neither the change of direction nor joining the Wellbeing Clinic. Martin and Philippa were her sort of people. From the beginning, Sarah realised, they'd taken her under their wing deliberately.

The practice meeting overran by a few minutes. Sarah walked briskly down the stairs afterwards, an apology ready, but the waiting room was empty. Behind her desk, Jane was typing rapidly.

'Is Mrs Matthews not here?' Sarah asked.

'Not yet.'

'It's unlike her to be late.' Sarah frowned: Phyllis Matthews had been coming every week for five years, and she made much of her promptness, a matter of pride to her and vague irritation to Sarah. 'She hasn't rung to cancel? Left a message on the machine?'

'No.'

Sarah looked at her watch. It was almost ten past; Mrs Matthews was unlikely to arrive now. The caterer's petit fours danced alluringly in her mind's eye.

'I'm going to pop out for a coffee,' she said. 'I've got my mobile – would you give me a shout if she turns up?'

Jane nodded.

'Want anything?'

'No thanks.'

Sarah pushed open the back door again and stepped out into the mild October day. There was a little coffee shop on the corner – not a chain, but a much-loved local business. The coffee wasn't very good but the cakes made up for it. Perhaps a *tarte aux fraises*, Sarah thought. Just one. And then she saw a familiar figure coming towards her.

'Olivia!'

Olivia stopped. 'Hello,' she said. 'What are you doing here?'

'I work here.' Sarah gestured at the Wellbeing Clinic's large green sign, then smiled. 'I didn't expect to see you again so soon.'

'I've brought the cat to the vet,' Olivia said. 'His ear needs stitching up.'

'Oh dear. Fighting?'

'Hardly. I had a fighting cat when I was little, but this one's an old softie. No, I think he must have snagged himself on a bit of wire.'

'My patient hasn't turned up,' Sarah said, 'so I've escaped. Have you got time for a coffee?'

There was no one else in the coffee shop, and they sat at the table by the window. To Sarah's pleasure, Olivia ordered a chocolate éclair. She'd been afraid that Olivia was one of those women who stayed thin through rigorous self-denial. She'd been afraid, too, that it might not be easy to meet up with Olivia again: the serendipity of this encounter was delightful.

'We did enjoy seeing you,' she said, taking a bite of her tart. 'What did you think of Guy?'

If Olivia was taken aback by the directness of the

question she didn't show it. 'He seems charming,' she said.

Sarah nodded. 'He was a patient. Did I tell you that? He was referred to my boss at first. Martin's an expert on sports injuries.'

Guy wasn't exactly famous, but he was a client Martin had wanted to do his best for, so Martin had suggested he saw Sarah as well for some physiotherapy.

'It's nice to meet you,' Guy had said that first time, shaking her hand and looking at her as though he needed to memorise her face. He'd looked sallow, his tan faded by months in hospital, but his eyes were bright. Blue eyes the same shade as Wedgwood china, a surprisingly delicate colour for an outdoorsman.

Sarah grinned, remembering her brisk response.

'I didn't think he was my type,' she said to Olivia. 'Not just physically: he didn't talk much, and when he did it was hard to know whether he was shy or just brusque. I kept imagining him out on a mountain, his energy focused on some tiny outcrop of rock.'

The questions he'd asked her hardly counted as small talk. Questions about herself, admittedly, but they'd felt more like a job interview, or some form of market research.

'How long did you work as a physio before retraining?' he'd asked. 'Do you live in Oxford? Did you grow up here? Do you like it?'

Sarah had kept her replies short, because she'd thought that Guy Dorland wasn't the kind of man who'd stop you if you were making a fool of yourself. Instead she'd drummed up questions to ask him in return.

'So what do you do now that you're not–' She'd halted, wondering whether it was insensitive to imply that his career as a mountaineer was over.

'I'm an accountant,' he'd said, lifting an eyebrow. 'Climbing mountains costs money rather than making it.'

Of course she should have realised that, Sarah had thought. She'd made herself look foolish after all. But Guy hadn't seemed to mind.

'I do have a lot of time to fill, though, these days,' he'd said, with a rare smile. Sarah remembered that smile, the first one she'd noticed properly. She grinned now, and Olivia cocked her head.

'But he grew on you?' she asked.

'Not really. I discharged him after a couple of months, told him to come back if he felt the muscles tightening up again, and he said something like "I'll have to think of another excuse, otherwise." I thought he was being – not exactly sarcastic. I thought it was his idea of politeness. But he rang the next week: the receptionist told me he wanted an evening appointment. I still do physio sessions at the private hospital once a week.'

'But that wasn't what he was after.'

'No.' Sarah blushed.

Guy had answered immediately when she called his mobile number.

'I think I've got one slot left this Wednesday,' she'd told him. 'Do you know where the BUPA hospital is?'

'I do, but I wasn't thinking of seeing you there,' he'd said. 'I had dinner in mind. Or the theatre, if you'd prefer.'

Sarah sighed, putting the last bite of strawberry in her mouth. 'So that was that,' she said, smiling at Olivia. 'After all these years.'

Olivia smiled back, and Sarah thought she saw, beneath that reserve Olivia had now, that slight watchfulness, a flicker of nostalgia.

# Chapter Twelve

Faith Sargent was surprised when thoughts of marriage began to creep into her mind. They appeared at unexpected moments: a hopeful thrill when she was setting up for a function, or a wistful pang at the end of an evening, when the idea of someone to go home to hovered like a mirage above the array of wasted food and the piles of dirty plates.

She was canny enough to know that you couldn't tell, this early on, whether it was love or just infatuation – and in any case she was, as she reminded herself, an independent woman who wasn't supposed to believe in all that romantic fluff. But it was hard to resist the daydreams, even so. Even if she was young enough to see marriage as a possibility there for the plucking.

In the prime of her twenties, Faith was as loving and giving as Friday's child should be. 'Born at the end of the week,' her mum always said, 'when other people have done all the hard work. Easy enough to be loving and giving then, eh?' Her mum reckoned Faith had a charmed existence, and perhaps she was right. Things had a habit of falling into Faith's lap. The way she'd met James was a case in point: someone she used to work for, who'd run a catering business in Oxford for years, got pregnant and was badly hit by morning sickness. She'd had to pull out of a couple of bookings, and rather than cancel she passed them on to Faith, who was trying to get going on her own. One event was a reception organised by a drug company, an evening do up at the hospital – for a bunch of gynaecologists, it turned out, which seemed to Faith a neat twist when it was a gynaecological problem that had sent the booking her way. Perhaps that was what gave her the first inkling that something was up, an intriguing suspicion that Fate was taking a hand in her life.

James Young was running the meeting. He was new to the department here, he told Faith. He'd moved out from London six months before. The drug reps were a bit above themselves, treating Faith more like a glorified waitress than a professional caterer, but James made a point of coming over to tell her how good everything was.

'Those spinach rolls,' he said. 'Delicious.'

'Spanakopita,' Faith told him. 'They're Greek. Veggie finger foods are often foreign, if you think about it: samosas, spring rolls, vol au vents. British cuisine doesn't run to them. It's all sausages rolls and – well, cocktail sausages.'

She felt herself blushing. The way James raised his eyebrows, it was clear he'd taken the emphasis on sausages to be suggestive.

'I've never thought of that,' he said.

The hall where the reception was taking place was in one of those modern buildings that start to look dilapidated almost as soon as they're finished, a tall, square block of glass and concrete. The kind of building

102

Faith had gone to school in, and later to college. She hadn't had much time to look around her during the evening, but while James was talking she noticed the incredible colour of the sky, framing him through the huge windows. The days were getting shorter every week now, but at seven o'clock the dusk still lingered, lilac and pink, giving even the hospital grounds a touch of fairytale mystery.

'The pastry,' James said. 'Filo, is it? Do you make it yourself, or do you buy it in?'

By then Faith knew he was taking more than a polite interest. It was either the food or her, she reckoned, and it was a shrewd guess that he didn't spend that much time in the kitchen, a busy man like him. She looked at him for a second or two as though she was thinking, though in reality the thinking all came later.

'If you're interested in Greek food,' she heard herself saying, 'there's a new Greek restaurant on the Abingdon Road that's supposed to be really good. Really authentic.'

'That sounds like an invitation I can't refuse,' James said, and Faith blushed again. It really wasn't like her to be so brazen.

She needn't have worried, though, because her straightforwardness was one of the things James liked about her, as she found out soon enough.

'Promise you'll never go coy on me,' he said, a few evenings later, taking her hand across the table as the Greek coffee steamed between them. 'Nothing more irritating than womanly wiles.'

The food at The Olive Tree had turned out to be disappointingly run of the mill, but Faith definitely couldn't say the same for the evening. She smiled at James, and squeezed his hand back. She thought she

103

understood what he meant. In his line of work women were an open book, so to speak. He had no patience with feminine mystique: much better to be up front, up for a good time. He found Faith refreshing, he said. And he certainly turned out to be in need of refreshment.

That first fortnight they saw a lot of each other. Despite the bookings she'd taken on from her pregnant friend, Faith had a run of free evenings, and James seemed keen to fill them. After the Greek restaurant they went to an Italian in Botley, then a pub out towards Witney. Faith liked the way James was keen to try places further afield than she usually went. He was broadening her horizons already.

But she insisted on cooking for him after that. They hadn't eaten Chinese together yet, and Faith liked cooking Chinese food. All that fuss and fiddle; all those subtle flavours. It made her feel exotic and sophisticated. She spent most of the afternoon chopping and blending, rolling and simmering, in her garden flat off the Iffley Road.

In the days when the house had been occupied by one family, the basement had been taken up by a big open-plan kitchen-cum-family room, and it hadn't been altered much when the property was split into flats. People had been put off by the layout of Faith's flat – a kitchen big enough for a Victorian-sized family, and only a tiny bedroom, and tinier bathroom, carved out of the sitting area – but it suited Faith down to the ground. A flat that was mostly kitchen was the perfect place to run a catering business from.

It was raining outside, but the kitchen was full of

light. While she sliced cloves of garlic wafer-thin, she listened to Fox FM and wove a fantasy about James ringing in with a request for her. Amy Winehouse, perhaps: he knew she liked Amy Winehouse. Of course she knew doctors didn't have time to ring in to radio stations, but even so she managed a quiver of anticipation each time the announcer's voice returned. She imagined her parents tuning in and hearing it, wondering whether it could possibly be their Faith.

Faith hadn't mentioned James to her parents yet. She was biding her time, waiting for the right moment. She was an only child, and her parents had always been protective; she knew they'd be worried about the age difference. Her dad was older than her mum, but they'd see it differently in her case – and true, James was ten years older than her, not five. Thirty-five next birthday, he'd said with a shudder. Peeling root ginger, Faith grinned to herself. James would charm them, she thought. After Grant, surely they'd see what an improvement he was?

In theory Faith had still been seeing Grant when she met James. She'd been with him on and off for years; since school, in fact. Back then he'd been the boy everyone wanted to go out with, and as far as Grant was concerned he still was. One thing you could say for Grant: he didn't have a problem with self-esteem. They'd always had flexible boundaries – his phrase, not hers – so there was no reason Faith couldn't see James too, but after her second date with James she'd told Grant it was time to call it a day. He took it well, as she knew he would.

'You've met someone special,' he said, in his infuriating I-worked-it-out-for-myself way. 'I'm glad. Just hope he's special enough.'

Like hell you do, thought Faith. 'Oh, I think so,' she replied, and left it at that. She wasn't going to gratify his curiosity any further.

James was late, as he often was, but his apologies made fifteen minutes of suspense worthwhile.

'I took a taxi, so I wouldn't have to drive home,' he said. He bent to kiss her, then produced a bottle of white wine, wrapped in tissue paper, from his briefcase. 'The guy in Oddbins said this was perfect with Chinese. It all smells fantastic.'

'Let's hope.'

Faith felt bashful, suddenly, about letting him into her flat. She had a vision of his house: all Persian rugs and deep armchairs, she imagined. Oil paintings on the wall and expensive light fittings. Hers was furnished from IKEA. It was the first place she'd ever had to herself and she loved it, but she could see it wasn't the right habitat for James.

He was charming about it, though. 'What a gem,' he said.

'Me or the flat?'

'Both, of course.'

He poured them each a glass of wine, then slipped his spare hand around Faith's waist and pulled her towards him in that assertive way she liked so much.

'I wish we'd met twenty years ago,' he said, and Faith giggled.

'But I was four then, and what would people have said to that?'

She'd already discovered that James had a secretive side, but the mystery, the hint of tragedy, only added to his attraction in her eyes. It showed his sensitivity, that there were things he found hard to talk about. But he certainly wasn't evasive. If she'd had any worries on that score, they were settled that evening.

'It's only fair you should be in the picture,' he said, following her into the kitchen, picking things up from the side and putting them down again. 'Know that I'm used goods. A bit battered around the edges.' And he smiled his crinkle-eyed smile and cocked his head slightly, as if to check that Faith was real, that she looked the same from a different angle. She had the pleasant feeling, a lot of the time, that he couldn't quite believe his luck.

'I'd be more worried if you'd stayed single all this time,' Faith said. She lifted a tray of spring rolls out of the oven and smiled at the look on his face.

James didn't have children: that was one of the tragedies of his life, Faith reckoned. And it wasn't just one marriage that had failed to produce babies.

'I should never have married Susan, to be honest,' he said when they were sitting down, their plates loaded with dumplings and prawn parcels and sticks of satay. 'It wasn't her fault. I assumed it was what I needed, the best way to cope with grief. Like getting back on a bicycle when you fall off, before it starts to hurt too much.'

He'd taken off his jacket – he wore beautiful suits, properly tailored, and shirts made of expensively thick cotton – and thrown it over the arm of the sofa. Faith could see his pager clipped to the inside pocket, the reminder that he was never completely off duty.

'I was utterly devoted to Helena,' James went on, chewing contemplatively on a won ton. 'We were madly in love. We'd been married five years but we were still like newly-weds, completely silly about each other.'

He glanced up at Faith. Go on, she wanted to say. Unburden yourself: it'll do you good. Do us both good.

'I wish now that we'd started a family sooner. We didn't think there was any rush. We were married at twenty-seven; no need to fret about fertility. And—' he stopped, winced slightly '—I'm sure this will sound awful to you, Faith. It certainly does to me now. But I saw pregnant women every day, dealt with all the complications and difficulties. It didn't hold much glamour for me, the whole idea. The thought of my wife going through it.' He shook his head, leaned back in his chair. They were nearly at the end of the bottle of Sauvignon Blanc by then, but Faith didn't want to get up just now to open another. 'Well, of course that was more foolish than I could have imagined. Helena would have been happy to have a child straight away, and then I wouldn't have been left completely alone.'

Faith didn't know what to say. Poor James; she could see what it had cost him to admit to all that. He looked older, all of a sudden; the lines around his eyes looked careworn rather than humorous. She sat quietly for a moment, then she got up and fetched another bottle of wine.

'What happened to Helena?' she asked, when she was sitting down opposite him again.

'She drowned,' James said. 'A sailing accident. Freak wind. She was an expert sailor, thoroughly competent, but it was – I don't know, some kind of mini tornado, the coastguard said. The rest of the sea was flat calm, so they didn't expect anyone to get into trouble that day, and by the time they realised her boat had gone down it was too late. It took weeks for her body to be washed ashore.'

His eyes had filled with tears, Faith noticed, with a sort of thrill that she immediately felt guilty about.

'I was on duty that weekend, or I'd have been with her,' he said. 'And I spent most of the next year wishing I had been.'

He sighed, shook his head. He'd ruffled his hair while he was speaking and he looked like a little boy, sweet and uninhibited.

'I married Susan eighteen months after Helena died. It took me about two weeks to work out that I'd made a hideous mistake, and almost two years to extricate myself with as little damage as possible on both sides. I guess you could say I've felt a bit – wary, since then. Battle-scarred.' He grinned, managing to look both rueful and full of lust at the same time. 'Until now, of course,' he said, and Faith smiled and laid her finger on his lips.

# Chapter Thirteen

'Georgie's back,' said Shirley, when Olivia walked into the community centre the following week. And sure enough, there she was, in her preferred seat in the corner. Olivia felt a jolt, a sort of shyness. Georgie had been so much in her mind, these last few weeks, that Olivia had almost forgotten what she looked like in person: the long nose, its sharpness exaggerated by age, and the steel-grey hair cut aggressively short, lacking the pampered, fluffy look favoured by many of the Wednesday Club regulars.

'Is she better?' Olivia asked.

'Tough as old boots.' Shirley beamed, as though Georgie's indestructibility was something for them all to be proud of. 'All the same,' she said, lowering her voice and leaning forwards in a way that could hardly be missed if you happened to be watching the conversation, 'not quite her old self, if you get my drift.'

Olivia surveyed the room, her gaze passing over Georgie and on to the others. Kenneth, absorbed by a puzzle whose pieces looked too numerous for a morning's entertainment. Elsie, holding forth to a small group gathered around her. William, Marjorie, Grace, Dorothy.

Georgie was sitting a little apart from the rest, staring straight in front of her, dressed as plainly as always, in a white blouse and dark skirt. They reminded Olivia of photographs she'd seen of schoolgirls in India, streaming into the dusty streets in their spotless outfits.

'It's not a uniform, is it?' she asked. 'Her clothes? I mean – did she have to wear a uniform in the asylum?'

'I don't know.' Shirley frowned. 'She wouldn't've kept it up after she was let out, though, would she? After she could choose what to wear?'

Olivia wasn't sure. Something about Georgie's clothes suggested a desire to blend in, although the irony was that she didn't. The other women wore flowered dresses made from some synthetic material with give in it, or the kind of trousers Olivia's grandmother used to call slacks. But wasn't the point that Georgie had never chosen anything in her life? That she'd never had the chance either to fit in, or to stand out?

'What happened to her baby?' Olivia asked, as she took her music out of its case. 'Was it a boy or a girl, do you know?'

'A little girl.' Shirley sighed. 'She was adopted: no choice about that, I'm sure. She was dead by the time Georgie came out of the asylum. Tragic, isn't it? A car accident, in her twenties.'

'No...' Olivia froze, a book of folksongs in midair. She hadn't thought the story could get any worse. 'How did she find out? Did she try to trace her daughter?'

Shirley shook her head. 'There was a note in her file, according to the social worker. Crying shame, but there it is. All in the past now.'

Georgie looked up for a moment and Olivia caught her eye, but Georgie gave no sign of recognition. There was a fretful look beneath her usual composure, a twitch and tremor of her facial muscles.

Shirley followed Olivia's gaze.

'Not quite her old self,' she said again. 'A tad confused, poor old Georgie. But I said I was happy to have her, even so. She won't be any trouble, not Georgie.'

The singing seemed lacklustre to Olivia today. Even the old favourites failed to arouse any enthusiasm: 'She'll be coming round the mountain'; 'It's a long way to Tipperary'. Had Georgie's malaise, whatever it was, infected them all? Or was Olivia boring them, ploughing through the same old repertoire? After three or four numbers she stopped and leafed through a book of Irish songs she didn't often use. 'The Rose of Tralee' perhaps? She hadn't played that for them before.

She didn't expect them to know the words. She sang the first line herself, softly, enjoying the bittersweet lilt of the melody, the major key that sounded more like minor.

'The pale moon was rising above the green mountain...'

Then suddenly she wasn't singing alone: out of nowhere came a tenor voice, a little cracked but still resonant.

'The sun was declining beneath the blue sea...'

She looked up: Kenneth, his face intent, hands gripping the arms of his chair. He might be a retired doctor, Olivia thought, but his voice had been trained, once upon a time. Shooting a glance at Shirley, standing listening in the kitchen doorway, she let her own voice fall

112

away, and Kenneth carried the ballad with a gusto she had never seen or heard in him before.

*'When I strayed with my love to the pure crystal fountain*
*That stands in the beautiful vale of Tralee.*
*She was lovely and fair as the rose of the summer,*
*Yet 'twas not her beauty alone that won me;*
*Oh no,'twas the truth in her eye ever dawning,*
*That made me love Mary, the Rose of Tralee.'*

There was silence when they got to the end, complete silence of the kind that conveys some shared feeling. An extraordinary voice, thought Olivia, even if it was four decades past its prime. An extraordinary thing to hear an old man singing a love song with such fervour, shaping the words and scaling the leaps of the melody as though it was newly minted. Small wonder that he didn't wheeze along with the rest, most weeks.

Kenneth was looking at her expectantly. Olivia had forgotten there was a second stanza, but she smiled and nodded and started again.

*'The cool shades of evening their mantle were spreading*
*And Mary all smiling sat listening to me;*
*The moon through the valley her pale rays were shining*
*When I won the heart of the Rose of Tralee.*
*She was lovely and fair as the rose of the summer,*
*Yet 'twas not her beauty alone that won me;*
*Oh no, 'twas the truth in her eyes ever dawning,*
*That made me love Mary, the Rose of Tralee.'*

Olivia sat very still on the piano stool. Kenneth's voice had begun to give way towards the end of the second verse, but he sustained his tone with a sureness that revealed the strength of his technical training. It was rare, very rare for her to feel so moved by music these days. It had become bread and butter to her, a facility she could trade on. She turned to smile at Kenneth.

'Thank you,' she said.

He looked bewildered now, as though he was stunned by what he'd done, now it was over. As though he'd got up and run around the room, whooping and yelling like a schoolboy. Olivia looked across at Shirley, waiting for her to say something. But before either of them could speak they were both distracted by something else: a sob, and a little crooning moan, and a catching of breath.

Georgie. Over in her corner, behind all the others – who were beginning to murmur and exclaim now, to ask each other whether they'd known Kenneth had a voice like that – Georgie was weeping.

Olivia was closer than Shirley, and she moved faster. In a few seconds she was at Georgie's side, squatting down, taking Georgie's bony hand in hers.

'That was a treat, Kenneth,' she heard Shirley saying. 'You've kept that voice quiet, haven't you?'

Georgie was saying something too, muttering words Olivia couldn't understand.

'What is it, Georgie?' she asked, and Georgie gripped her hand harder, staring into her eyes, and tried again.

'I don't want to go back.'

'Back where?'

'Don't let them. You don't know what they do.'

'No one's going to hurt you,' Olivia said. Georgie's skin was very smooth, very soft: as though it had been preserved in a museum case, Olivia thought. Kept from the world.

'Horrible,' Georgie said, 'horrible,' and then the words were swallowed by muttering and grunting.

Shirley was standing beside her now.

'Remembering the asylum,' she mouthed, the hiss of the 's' like a threat. She touched Olivia's shoulder. 'It's not your fault: anything can set her off these days, poor love.'

# Chapter Fourteen

For the third night in a row, Olivia woke in the early hours to an instant alertness. She had the feeling that she'd been woken by a crying baby. Someone pushing a wakeful infant around the streets to quieten it, perhaps? She listened again, but there was nothing to hear except the wind and the rain. A storm was racketing at the windows and whipping the bare branches of the silver birch tree back and forth through the beam of the streetlight. Not a night you'd take a baby out for a walk. It must have been a dream.

And then the dream she'd woken from slipped back into her mind; a dream she hadn't had for years. That summer with Eve. The flatness of the fens, and the baby in the phone box. Olivia shut her eyes, feeling again the weight of suspense, the hope and dread of that August day. Dreams never faded, she thought; the passage of time offered no protection from their power.

She lay still for a few minutes, listening to the storm. Robert had stayed in London after a late meeting, so the bed felt cold, and her mind thrummed now with questions. Was it the mention of Eve during that evening with Sarah that had brought the phone box baby back? Or Georgie's sad story: one child abandoned by its mother, and another forcibly removed?

Georgie's plight had haunted her these last few days. Had Georgie been allowed to hold her daughter, she'd wondered, perhaps to keep her for a few days? She'd been tormented by the idea of Georgie, barely more than a girl herself, grieving for the loss of her baby, and that other childless woman overjoyed to receive her, then devastated by her early death. A double tragedy: two mothers mourning the same child.

Olivia pushed back the covers. She wouldn't go back to sleep now, she knew that. She took her dressing gown off the back of the door and crept out onto the landing.

The kitchen was full of noise: the rain ebbing and flowing; the rattle of the dustbin lid being teased up and down the passage beside the house. The moon was bright despite the storm, and Olivia didn't put the lights on. Filling the kettle, reaching in the cupboard for tea bags, she wasn't aware, at first, that there was anyone else in the room. And when she was, it was exactly that: an awareness. Not a sound, but the sense of someone else's presence.

Olivia turned towards the little sofa in the corner of the room. A girl was curled in the corner of it, neither watching Olivia nor avoiding her. It was curious, Olivia thought, her quality of detachment. Detachment and a kind of acceptance, like a baby lying where it has been put down, waiting for someone to do something with it. A shiver ran through her, not quite of fear.

'Hello,' she said. 'I didn't see you there.'

Except that she wasn't sure whether she'd said it or not, especially when the girl didn't move. She must be a friend of Tom's. Perhaps more than a friend, if she was still here in the middle of the night. Olivia's head was still swirling with fragments of dream and memory, but it was reassuring to fall into a familiar role: the practised mother, unfazed by the unexpected.

'I'm making a cup of tea,' she said, louder, to be sure. 'Would you like one? Or a glass of whisky?'

The girl uncurled slightly, raised her head to look at Olivia. Slowly, unhurried. 'Whisky would be nice,' she said.

Olivia put the tea bags back in the cupboard and reached instead for the bottle Robert had bought duty free on his way back from the States. She carried two glasses to the far end of the room and sat down in the armchair opposite the girl. She felt a pleasurable whisper of expectation now, and something else: a sort of evaporation from her mind, like the molecules coming off the surface of the whisky. A part of her floating free.

'Laphroaig,' she said. 'My husband's a Scot.'

'Thanks.' The girl glanced towards the window, and the moon lit her profile for a moment. Her features were small and delicate, her throat hidden by a thick rollneck jumper. 'It's horrible out,' she said. 'I didn't fancy walking home in this.'

Olivia watched her lift the glass to her lips. She had the feeling that she could taste the whisky too, coursing down her throat too fast, like hot tar. She still hadn't put the light on, and she wondered whether it would seem stranger to do so, now, than to leave the room in darkness. Tom should have given up his bed for her, she thought. Or did he think she'd gone?

The girl shifted slightly on the sofa, unfolding her legs from beneath her. Taking care, Olivia noticed, not to disturb the cat, who was curled beside her, a perfect powder-puff ball.

'Beautiful cat,' she said. 'What's his name?'

'It depends who you ask.'

'Oh.'

'We could never agree on a name. He answers to anything, more or less.'

'Sensible,' said the girl. She stroked the cat's head, starting between his ears, smoothing out the ruff on the back of his neck.

'You're a friend of Tom's?' Olivia picked up her glass, smelling the peat and the sea.

'I'm Lucy.'

'From school?'

Lucy shook her head, made a little laughing noise. 'No, I left a few years ago.'

Olivia made an effort to smile. An older girlfriend wasn't what Tom needed, she thought, when he should be gearing up for A levels.

'So what do you do now?' she asked. 'Are you working?'

'I'm studying photography.'

'Oh, yes? Documentary photography? Journalistic stuff?'

'After a fashion. The purity of the image, you know.' Lucy made inverted commas in the air with her fingers.

Olivia tried to imagine her in a war zone, picking her way among rubble and broken bodies. She didn't look robust enough for that. She looked tiny and fragile, her hair long but wispy, as though it had taken a long time to grow.

'Tough way to make a living,' Olivia said.

Lucy shrugged, and shook her head slightly, as if to indicate that money was tedious.

Olivia wasn't sure what to make of her: there was something unnerving about her, she thought, although she couldn't put her finger on what it was. Perhaps it was just the way the two of them had fallen into conversation as if they'd met somewhere ordinary, on a train or a bus. But it was a novelty, having someone to talk to in the middle of the night. For a moment she allowed herself the fanciful thought that Lucy had been sitting down here night after night, waiting for sleeplessness to drive Olivia from her bed.

'I've got some prints with me, if you want to see.'

It was a statement more than a question. Lucy reached into a rucksack on the floor beside her and held out a large plastic envelope.

A moment later, registering belatedly a frisson of anticipation, Olivia wondered what she'd expected from the photographs. Some clue, perhaps, to Lucy's life? Scenes from an interior, or faces? Instead they were landscapes, black and white, beautiful. A bare sweep of hillside bisected by hedges; stone walls with the sea beyond. A church spire, perfectly positioned.

'These are good,' she said.

'The purity of the image.' Lucy tipped her head in self-mockery.

'Where are they?' Olivia asked. 'A field trip?'

'Norfolk. Where my grandparents live.' Lucy took another sip of whisky. 'Near Diss, you know?'

Olivia shook her head.

'Beautiful,' Lucy said. 'Empty. There are millions of

people on this island, but there are still huge spaces with no one in them.'

The whisky was starting to have an effect, loosening something inside Olivia's head. This conversation could go anywhere, she thought, like a party game that starts with trivia and leads deeper and deeper into the bizarre or the tragic. Truth or dare. Consequences.

'I'm not often away from other people, I suppose,' she said. 'Except that I am, these days. Alone and not alone.'

'My grandfather would say if you belong in the landscape you're never alone.'

'What about in a city?' Olivia asked. 'Aren't they supposed to be the loneliest places of all?'

'Maybe.' Lucy looked at her. 'Are you lonely, then?'

Olivia laughed, a strange throaty laugh that didn't seem to belong to her. 'No,' she said. 'No, I'm not lonely.'

And then, quite suddenly, Lucy got to her feet. 'I'd better be off,' she said.

The rain had stopped, Olivia noticed. But even so ... 'We've got a spare bed,' she said.

'No, that's fine. I should be going.'

'I could drive you.'

Olivia knew as soon as she'd said it that the offer sounded ridiculous; that there was something undignified about not wanting the girl to leave. Lucy looked at her curiously for a moment, and then she smiled, an attractive, crooked sort of smile.

'It's not far,' she said. 'Thanks for the whisky.'

Olivia followed her to the front door and watched her slip out into the night with the curious feeling that she was watching a ghost disappear. Where do you live, she wanted to ask? What were you really doing in my kitchen? Though it was none of her business, of course. She'd always kept open house for the children's friends: it had always seemed a wise thing to do. Her unease wasn't Lucy's fault.

Back in the kitchen, Olivia put the whisky bottle away and stood for a moment looking out into the dark garden. The clock stood at four thirty, but she wasn't ready to go back to bed yet. Instead she drifted restlessly around the room, touching the surfaces, the cold steel of the draining board and the scrubbed pine of the long table, uncovered at last after years of plastic tablecloths. When they had finally been removed, Olivia had been amazed by the pristine surface of the wood beneath, left intact amid the hurly-burly of family life.

She sat down in the corner of the sofa where Lucy had been, and the cat stretched, relaxed, settled his weight against her leg. But his purring wasn't enough to absorb Olivia's thoughts. She'd hoped Lucy might banish the bad dream, but instead her departure had left its imprint more distinct in her mind, the memory of the phone box stark against the sparse light of the kitchen.

That baby had cast a long shadow over her life. It had tainted the rest of her time at university, propelled her too early into adulthood. Her own babies had been born sooner than they might have been, Olivia thought, because she'd picked that child up from the damp floor of the phone box and held it in her arms. Because of the way things had turned out that day. That was why she'd married Robert barely a year after they graduated; why she'd been so impatient to get pregnant, not just once but again and again and again, until her sons satisfied, or at least dulled, the need she'd uncovered that summer in Aldeburgh.

But even that hadn't been enough. For years she'd

immersed herself in breast-feeding, nappy-changing, pram-pushing; in constant servitude to the demands of motherhood. And now look what she was left with: four hulking boys with only the slimmest connection to her, unless she held tight to their resemblances and their familiarity. Young men who would circle her for a few more years, with their needs and demands, before spinning off into their own orbits.

And where am I, Olivia wondered, in this perpetual motion I have created: left at the still point of the whirlpool with my bad dreams?

# Chapter Fifteen

'St Catherine's asylum,' the social worker said. 'A Victorian monstrosity on the eastern fringes of London.'

Her name was Mary Baldwin – a short, competent woman in her late fifties with cheeks that were permanently flushed, as though in indignation. Olivia had tracked her down after that morning at the Wednesday Club, the 'Rose of Tralee' morning.

'And that's where Georgie was, all that time?' Olivia asked.

'Forty-seven years: from 1935 to 1982. Hard to credit, isn't it?'

Mary sighed, leaning back cautiously in a battered swivel chair that was wedged tight between a filing cabinet and an ugly chest of drawers that looked to Olivia like an upended coffin. The room was tiny, shelves stacked high with box-files and books and papers, no decorations of any kind.

'It would have been bad enough when it was first

built,' Mary said, 'but at least there was a park then, somewhere to walk. But for the last thirty years they had no one to look after the grounds, so it turned into a wilderness. With a great high wall round it, like a prison.'

'Were they all unmarried mothers there?' Olivia asked.

Mary laughed briefly, a sound like a whistle. 'Lord, no. Most of them had learning disabilities. The mild end of the spectrum, usually, though after years in that place... And some had mental health problems. There were separate sections, in theory, though Heaven knows what actually went on.'

Olivia tried to picture the place: the smell of urine and disinfectant, the long bare corridors, the isolation.

'Cruelty,' Mary said. 'Plain cruelty.'

'Locking them up, you mean?'

'I mean worse than that. The stories that have come out... Like a prisoner of war camp, someone described it. The staff free to do what they chose. No respect at all; treating the clients like animals.'

Clients. The contemporary term jarred in Olivia's ears: so far from the horror that was being described, she thought. She could see now what such careful terminology had been a reaction against; what people like Mary Baldwin, overworked, fighting for a hopeless cause in some cases, were trying to do.

'Why did Georgie end up in Oxford?' she asked.

'I don't know. Usually we'd try to settle people where they had a connection to the community. Georgie had been a student in Oxford, maybe that was why. Or maybe there was just a suitable placement here for her at the time.' Mary shrugged her shoulders. 'I don't know

Georgie well. I met her five years ago when she was moved into her current placement, and I was asked to reassess her needs when she was in hospital recently. Fascinating woman, though. Amazing.'

She might have been more amazing, Olivia thought, if things had been different. There was a limit to what you could make of yourself if you were locked up until you were sixty-five.

'A lot of them died, you know,' Mary said. 'TB, or some other infection. Flu or pneumonia. The medical care was rudimentary, and they didn't have much reason to keep living, most of them.'

'Broken hearts.' Olivia felt a little foolish, saying it, but Mary nodded.

'Broken lives.'

'So what's kept Georgie going, all this time?'

Mary smiled. 'Pure spirit.'

Perhaps, Olivia thought. Perhaps pure stubbornness; a refusal to surrender completely. Or perhaps there was something Georgie wanted from life, still.

'What about the daughter?' she asked. 'I understand she died.'

A frown flickered on Mary's forehead. Olivia understood: general information was one thing; personal details were another.

'Sorry,' she began.

'No, it can't do any harm,' Mary said. 'She's dead, as you say. The parents too. Georgie's parents.'

Mary lifted a thick manila file off the desk beside her: Olivia hadn't realised it was there until now. She hadn't realised how hot the room was, either. Hot and airless. No wonder Mary's cheeks were crimson.

'Her parents lived in Bury St Edmunds,' Mary said,

after a minute or two. She studied the file as if she was trying to make up her mind about something, then closed it gently. 'Birth mothers have no right in law to information,' she said, 'even when there's been a forced adoption. Terrible, but there it is. But when St Catherine's closed, the social worker who handled her discharge – she was a wonderful person, tireless – she traced the child. Found out what had happened. And she told Georgie. She thought she ought to know her daughter was dead, that it might help her settle. Close that chapter once and for all.' Mary raised her eyebrows, looking straight at Olivia. 'That's all she told her,' she said.

'But?' Olivia prompted.

Mary sighed. Behind her head a small window looked across a narrow courtyard to a row of similar offices opposite. Olivia could see people moving around inside them, answering the telephone, carrying cups of coffee. A whole building full of people in the business of managing other people's lives. Were there so many Georgies?

'Supposing I told you that it wasn't uncommon for babies to be adopted within the family, in these circumstances,' Mary said. 'By a sibling, say. Georgie's surname is unusual: there aren't many Quickshalls in Essex.'

'So it might be possible to find out where her daughter ended up?' Olivia asked.

'Tracing family trees is easy these days,' Mary said. 'There are dozens of websites dedicated to genealogy.'

'But what more is there to know, if the child died years ago?'

Mary chewed her lip. 'Adoptive mothers sometimes had other children. Birth children, after the adoption.

127

Even if they'd had trouble conceiving before. Something to do with hormones.'

'So there might be siblings? Nephews or nieces of Georgie's?' Olivia thought for a moment: born in the late 1930s, perhaps, or the 1940s. In their sixties; quite likely still alive.

Mary stood up, opened a drawer to replace the file. 'I can't tell you any more,' she said.

'Why didn't your colleague tell Georgie all this when her daughter was traced?' Olivia asked. 'If there were relatives left alive, couldn't she have put her in touch?'

Mary turned, her hand still resting on the filing cabinet, and looked at Olivia. A long, compassionate look. 'It's hard to imagine what sort of state people like Georgie were in when they first came out of those places. Especially Georgie. There'd been so much trauma already. The risk of another rejection by the family...'

'Surely by then—'

'If Georgie had wanted to find her brother or sister she could have asked us to help,' Mary said, more firmly. 'No one had the right to make that decision for her. And if the family had wanted to see her, ever, they'd have found her. Some families did, when the institutions closed. Or before.'

'And others?'

Mary shrugged. 'Guilt. Whitewashing. A secret never told to the next generation. Georgie's nieces and nephews were most likely told she'd died young, if her name was mentioned at all.'

There was silence for a moment.

'I should be going,' Olivia said. 'You've been very generous with your time, satisfying my curiosity.'

Mary looked surprised. 'Not just that, surely,' she

said. 'Georgie's been different since that last stay in hospital. She might not have long left. You're right, it might be the moment to look into it again, see whether there's anything else we can give her. Closure of some kind.'

*NOTHING IS YOURS. There is nothing left to remind you, not a trace of who you were. They took your clothes, your books, your home. Sometimes, if you try too hard to hold on to it, they even take away your name.*

*You have a bed and a cupboard with no lock; no place to keep things safe, even if there is nothing to keep. When you make, in this space, a place where you can begin to live, they move you. You are not safe with yourself, they say. The poison, the illness, is inside you, and they must stop you from finding anything there to comfort you. The outside world has been stripped to bare walls and silence and they will strip the inside too: they will not let you be at peace with yourself or your wickedness. They are certain of this, zealous in their quest to reduce you to a hollow shell.*

*You know what they are doing – that is your salvation and your downfall, that you know what they are doing, despite the pills they feed you, the wires they use to probe and cleanse your head. You don't know how long it has been but you know it will go on and on, that they will never give up.*

*Others escape, leaving their bodies shrouded by drawn curtains, but your body is too stubborn. Your body resists the tumours and fevers that claim the weak here.*

*Your body carries you out, when it is permitted, into the air that no longer smells of freedom. It forces its way through the mud and the roots and the nettles that surround the walls. It sustains itself on so little that you would marvel, if you were able to, at its resilience.*

# Chapter Sixteen

G uy's head was framed by the wings of his chair. Sarah stared at him for a moment: his pose reminded her of a painting they'd seen the week before in the Ashmolean. The man of action lately returned home, she thought, ready to be portrayed with the accoutrements of his life spread about him. The *Economist* and the world atlas tellingly at his elbow. She judged that he was only half-occupied by the newspaper he was reading, but even so she hesitated before speaking, clearing her throat to announce her intention of distracting him.

'The modern words have a sort of freshness, don't you think?' she said.

Guy looked up from the business section with an indulgently non-committal expression. 'You're leaning towards the revised service, then?'

'I think it might sound more meaningful. As though you're saying something that's not completely taken for granted.'

They were in Guy's house this evening, a tall, narrow

townhouse near the city centre. Guy had lived alone here – when he wasn't away climbing mountains – for fifteen years, and it sometimes felt to Sarah as though there was someone else in the corner of the room: not a ghost, exactly, but perhaps another version of Guy, the confirmed bachelor people might have thought he was. She could feel a sense of regret, or possibly disapproval, emanating from the rows of Folio Society volumes in the bookshelves (not a novel among them, she'd realised, when she went looking for something to read). She felt too loud here, too definite. It was as if every move she made disturbed things that had been just as they were for years.

Guy was watching her with an expression of mild consternation now, as though he wasn't sure whether anything more was expected of him. She couldn't explain it to him, Sarah thought. She'd said, once, how unfussy the décor was, but that wasn't what she meant. What she meant was that it was masculine, solitary, self-sufficient: that she didn't belong in his house, even if he planned to admit her to his life.

'Your judgement about these things is so much better than mine,' Guy said, with a smile that lingered for a moment on Sarah's face before his eyes flicked back to the newspaper. 'Did you read about this débâcle at Prime Minister's question time?'

Sarah shook her head, and returned to her perusal of orders of service. But she couldn't absorb the words any more; they floated through her head and out again the other side.

She suspected that Guy had similar reservations about her flat in the landscaped development where everything was bright and new. She could see through his eyes the too-green lawns and the recessed ceiling lights, the pale veneer doors and paper lampshades. She could see him watching his step, as though he'd found himself on a stage-set where things might topple over if he knocked into them.

Sarah sighed. Houses were only houses, she told herself, and they both knew marriage meant compromise. They could look for somewhere with enough space for both of them. A family house. Opposite her, Guy was deep in the newspaper again. She watched the small movements of his face as his eyes scanned the leader page, the infinitesimal registering of amusement and surprise and dissent, and she felt a rush of emotion so powerful, so unexpected that for a moment she couldn't tell what it contained. She shut her eyes, heat suffusing her cheeks, grateful now that Guy wasn't paying attention.

She knew what had caused it, that flood of feeling. She knew it was an aftershock, a consequence of what had happened this morning. She'd hoped the marriage service would distract her, that concentrating on the words that would join the two of them inextricably together would keep all that at bay.

She sat very still for a moment, and then she shut the books in her lap and levered herself out of the deep armchair.

Jane the receptionist had looked up when Sarah came through the door of the clinic that morning, her face revealing something that might almost be curiosity.

'Phyllis Matthews' son is here,' she'd said.

'Her son?'

'Instead of her. Martin took him up to your room.'

Sarah had felt a flash of conscience: she'd meant to

ring, after Mrs Matthews' non-appearance the previous week. Running into Olivia had distracted her. She ran up the stairs now, pausing for a second to compose herself before pushing open the door of her consulting room.

Harry Matthews' big hands rested awkwardly on his knees as though they weren't used to being idle. He stood up when Sarah came in.

'I'm sorry I'm late,' she said, although she knew she was precisely on time, and the appointment hadn't been for him, anyway.

He shook his head. 'I was early. I wasn't sure of the traffic.'

Sarah sat, not in her usual chair, but in another one at right angles to his. She was conscious of a restlessness, an edginess about him, but she was mystified as to its cause. If his mother wanted to stop coming, all she had to do was ring up. Could it be a complaint, a question about her treatment?

'Your mother,' she began.

Harry Matthews nodded. 'I'm afraid she's dead,' he said. 'I wanted to tell you myself, because I know how much you meant to her.'

Sarah stared at him. Several thoughts fired at once in her head, not quite forming into questions.

'I'm so sorry,' she said. 'That must have been a shock.'

'Yes,' he said. He hesitated. 'We had no idea how much the pain got her down. I don't think anyone knew except you.'

Sarah could make even less sense of this. On her desk she could see Mrs Matthews' thick brown folder. Martin must have got it out, perhaps left it for the son to read, if he wanted to. Sarah knew exactly what he would find in there: unexplained back pain in a patient who insisted on returning week after week; five years without progress. She'd felt guilty about Mrs Matthews as well as exasperated by her. The two were related, in fact, guilt leading to exasperation and back again. She felt another tweak of disbelief and – almost – fear.

'I'm afraid there wasn't much I could do for her,' she said. Her heart was beating fast, but she felt she had to say this; she couldn't have the son thinking better of her than she deserved.

He shook his head vigorously. He had the kind of complexion that flushed easily; a mottling of crimson spread like a cloud over his cheekbones. 'It was the only thing that helped,' he said. 'She wanted me to tell you that.' He hesitated. 'It was in her letter. Her note.'

Now Sarah's heart jumped and recoiled.

'Her note?'

The son nodded, an unexpected compassion in his face, as though he understood more than he possibly could. 'She took her own life,' he said. 'She couldn't bear the pain any more.'

Sarah shut her eyes. Not that, she thought. Not that. Her encounters with Phyllis Matthews rolled through her mind on fast-forward: her own barely-contained frustration; her suggestion that pain killers were part of the problem, not the solution; her progressive loss of interest. Shame surged through her, the heart-sink acceptance of responsibility.

'She wanted you to know she was grateful,' the son was saying. 'She asked me to give you this.'

Sarah opened her eyes again and saw a small parcel in the hand he held out to her. She unwrapped it with as much composure as she could muster. She couldn't let herself speak, but she met Harry Matthews' eyes briefly and saw in them his own distress, the difficulty all this had caused him. He must blame himself too, she thought. Of course he must blame himself.

Inside the wrapping was a tiny Bible, leather bound, with an embossed silver cover. Sarah's heart tumbled again.

'I understand you're getting married,' Harry said. 'My mother was given this for her wedding.'

'I can't take it,' Sarah said. She shook her head, as much to shake away the tears welling in her eyes as to emphasise her meaning. Phyllis Matthews hadn't been a vindictive person; she couldn't have meant to cause this tidal wave of guilt. But even so, it was more than Sarah could bear. 'Whatever she said, I did nothing to help. Whatever she thought. It was the idea of the treatment, that's all.'

Harry Matthews looked at her blankly. 'But isn't that what it means, therapy?' he said. His voice was gentle, for such a big man. 'Treating a person? Making them feel better?'

Sarah kept shaking her head. For a moment she saw her professional life, the career she took such pride in, with devastating clarity. She saw a series of encounters in the white-walled cleanliness of the clinic; the half-hour slots allocated to each patient; the notes filed in identical brown folders. She saw her attempt to bury herself in work, efficiency, achievement. Mrs Matthews' face loomed in her mind, then dissolved and reformed in the shape of her mother. Just when she'd thought she was home safe, she thought; that things might at last work out all right.

As the tears welled out of her eyes Harry Matthews reached across to take her hand.

'Please,' he said. 'Don't upset yourself.'

Sarah brushed her other hand across her face in an attempt to staunch her tears. Harry picked it up gently when she let it drop. There was something wonderfully soothing about the contact between them, the way they made a closed circle, both her hands clasped in his.

'I let her down,' Sarah said, but the words didn't sound as she expected. Instead of slowing, her tears flowed faster. She was conscious of Harry Matthews looking aghast and earnest and intent, of time spinning out and away from her as he pulled her forwards, lifted her upwards until they were both standing and he had his arms around her. And even then a part of Sarah – a wisp of conscience, or consciousness – was surprised more by the consolation she felt than by the fact that she was in the embrace of a stranger.

When they were at Sarah's house Guy cooked, and vice versa. It had been her idea: a good way to get to know someone, she'd said, to find your way around their kitchen. It was certainly a good idea tonight, anyway, to have something to occupy herself with.

Guy's kitchen was elegantly appointed, but it seemed to Sarah that its contents had been chosen with a view to appearance rather than practicality. There was a whole battery of stainless-steel saucepans, but she had no idea how he managed without a non-stick frying pan or a decent sharp knife. She was often tempted to lapse into bachelor fare here: cheese on toast; sausages cooked under the grill with much spitting and smoke.

She found the packet of pasta and the jar of pesto she'd left here the previous week, and filled the kettle under the unwieldy retro-design tap. Someone's idea of chic, she guessed, but presumably not Guy's.

While she chopped tomatoes for a salad she forced her mind back to the order of service she'd left behind in the sitting room. She wasn't really a churchgoer – not one to allow the Holy Ghost much truck, as a rule – but she'd turned out most Sundays recently, in advance of the reading of their banns. And sometimes, especially at evensong, which always evoked the school chapel, the fervency of adolescence, she'd been surprised by the feeling that it wasn't so much at odds with the rest of life to repose her trust in the Lord and affirm her faith through the creed she still knew by heart. It was a good basis for marriage, she thought. A help, when things were difficult, to feel that you weren't going it alone.

And then she stopped, resting against the kitchen worktop. Oh God. Please God, pay attention for a moment.

She hadn't expected her encounter with Harry Matthews to take root like this. It had been a chance occurrence; a congruence of circumstances. She'd never see him again, and she shouldn't want to. It must be something to do with this tipping point in her life, she told herself, this time of limbo before the wedding: she must be unusually vulnerable to emotional turmoil. To absurd romantic suggestion.

If only Guy would fold away his newspaper, she thought. If only some instinct would prompt him to come through to the kitchen right now. If he put his arms around her, held her tight and told her all was well, then surely it would be. This hitch, this glitch, would be banished like a playground jinx that could be undone with the right form of words.

But he didn't. Of course he didn't. He had no idea what was needed of him.

Sarah put one of Guy's shiny saucepans on the hob, filled it with boiling water and turned on the gas. She knew well enough that one moment could determine the future as powerfully as the accumulated actions and decisions of months and years. That the course of life could be altered in an instant. But surely she wouldn't stake her marriage, like a gambler, on the flip of a coin: heads he comes through now and everything goes on as it was; tails he doesn't. How could she judge Guy, their future, her happiness, on an action whose importance he had no inkling of?

# Chapter Seventeen

## August 1983

'We should tell James about Torhousekie,' said Eve.

It was the night of the big storm in Aldeburgh: the night the grumbling rainclouds flared into a full-blown display of thunder and lightning that drove the remaining holidaymakers inside to huddle around unseasonal fires. The curtains were drawn in the kitchen at Shearwater House, but the wind and the sea roared and shushed beyond them. Eve had got up from her sick bed for the first time that morning, looking fragile after three days of illness, and the three of them were making supper together.

'Mmm.' Olivia was chopping onions, her eyes stinging as she sliced them into half-moons and threw them into a chipped enamel pan.

'It was an amazing place, wasn't it?' Eve turned to James. 'It's one of the best preserved stone circles in the country.'

She'd bought a guide book after their visit and had fed Olivia facts as they drove north through Scotland, weaving the dramatic events of that night into a story that stretched back through centuries of myth and legend. The three stones in the centre were known locally as King Galdus's Tomb, Galdus being a Scottish king who was supposed to have fought off the Romans in AD 80. But Eve preferred the story that the Druids had built it. As a court of justice, she'd said. Just imagine being tried there: the elders in their robes, banging their staves on the ground as they passed sentence. The cows watching, Olivia had added.

'There's a tradition,' Eve said now, 'that you have to drop a pebble into a hole in this big stone nearby when you visit. An offering, so you can pass in peace. Maybe that's where we went wrong.' She raised her eyebrows, looking first at Olivia and then at James.

In theory they were all helping with the cooking, but Eve had been occupied for half an hour with a bowl of green beans that she was topping and tailing at a dilettante pace. Cooking was a decorative act for Eve, Olivia thought; it represented womanly virtue in the abstract.

'We camped in the middle of the circle,' Olivia said. 'Braved the ghosts of the Druids.'

'And we had an adventure,' said Eve. 'Perhaps we did disturb some ghosts. The spirit of the place.' She paused for effect, a long, slender bean poised in her hand. 'It was a beautiful evening, and we sat on top of one of the stones and watched the sun set.'

'Not like Stonehenge,' James said, 'where you can't get anywhere close.'

He was rolling pastry, his arms and chest dusted with flour. Olivia couldn't work out what she thought about his proficiency in the kitchen – all this pastry-making and fish-gutting, the swift movements of his hands. Like a surgeon: was that what he wanted to be?

'It's not as dramatic as Stonehenge,' she said. 'Just a ring of rather dumpy stones.'

'Still,' said Eve. 'It's four thousand years old. Not the kind of place many people have camped. Anyway, there we were, asleep in our tent, and in the middle of the night we were woken by a noise. And what do you think? When we opened our eyes we saw a man's face. Crouching there in the dark, just staring at us.'

Olivia frowned, but she was silenced by the expression on Eve's face.

'A local farmer, I should think,' said James. 'Wondering what you thought you were doing.'

Eve shook her head in a slow, deliberate way. 'No. Definitely not a farmer. He had – oh, a hideous face. Great heavy brows. And as soon as we moved, he ran away. Definitely not an innocent local, or why run like that?'

'But not someone who meant you harm, either,' pointed out James, 'or why run away from two – sorry, but – from two girls?' He lifted the pastry onto the rolling pin and held it in midair for a moment before lowering it into the flan dish.

'But if he didn't mean us any harm,' said Eve, 'why follow us around the country?' She looked at Olivia. 'He did, didn't he? We kept seeing him.'

'We thought we did,' said Olivia.

Eve glared. 'A few days after that, we were in Oban,' she told James. 'There's this huge folly on the hill above the town, a bit like the Coliseum, built by some Victorian philanthropist.'

'McCaig's Tower,' said Olivia.

'It's empty inside, just a kind of park,' Eve continued, 'but the views of the sea and the islands are wonderful, everyone told us, so we walked up there one afternoon. This was – what, three or four days later? And two hundred miles north?'

'A hundred and fifty,' said Olivia.

'We'd forgotten all about the man at Torhousekie by then. We'd stopped in Glasgow, seen lots of different things, and there we were in Oban, climbing up to the folly. The entrance is very dramatic, a great archway with rows of empty windows on each side. It's not spooky, exactly, but it's – awe-inspiring.'

Bright sun and shadows, Olivia remembered. No one in sight except seagulls.

'Like a film set,' said James, and Eve's eyes widened.

'Yes,' she said. 'Exactly. And as we came through the archway, there he was. Standing in the shadows, looking out of one of the windows at the path we'd just walked up.'

'The same man?'

'The same man. We only caught a glimpse of his face, but he was wearing the same jacket, dark grey with these thick white stripes across the shoulders.'

She turned to Olivia with an expression somewhere between command and entreaty. Olivia made a tiny gesture of equivocation.

'We were sure it was him,' she said. 'It was pretty startling.'

'And then what?' asked James. 'Did he run away again?'

'He slipped out through the archway and headed off down the hill.'

'Well, well.'

Eve frowned. Her bowl of beans was going down slowly, a small pile of green tips gathering on the table in front of her, cut off with little jerky movements of the knife James had given her.

'You might call that coincidence,' she said, 'but we saw him the next day on Mull. He was waiting when we arrived back at the port at Craignure, leaning against the railing, wearing the same jacket. We were so spooked we walked away and waited for the next ferry, even though it meant hanging around for another two hours.'

'Although if he was a tourist like us, it's hardly surprising he went across to Mull from Oban,' said Olivia.

'But then I saw him again when I went for a walk above Loch Ness that weekend,' Eve insisted. 'You only missed him that time because you stayed behind to read your book.'

Olivia said nothing; she could see that Eve was on the brink of tears or losing her temper, or perhaps both at once. She didn't want to provoke her.

In the little bed and breakfast at Drumnadrochit, on the edge of Loch Ness, they'd slept in twin beds squeezed so tightly under the eaves that it had felt more like being in the tent. The sky was heavy and dark the next morning, and she'd decided to stay in bed while Eve went out for a walk. She remembered the bliss of a day of silence, a whole day alone. Then Eve had come back, late in the afternoon, full of excitement and something like triumph. 'Guess who I saw', she'd asked, and Olivia had said, 'Nessie?'

'It was a bit of a saga,' Olivia said now, in a voice she could tell was wrong; too placatory, as though she was talking to a child. 'We wondered whether he was stalking us, didn't we? Where he was going to turn up next. But he didn't follow us south from Scotland. We threw him off the trail in the end.'

She smiled, but Eve stared down at the table, her eyes widening dangerously.

'Drink,' said James. 'How have we gone this long without a drink? It must be half past six. Red or white? Eve? Olivia?'

The man hadn't appeared again after Drumnadrochit, but Eve's flashes of bad temper had. Olivia marked off the days in her head, the towns and villages and mountains and rivers. Aberdeen, she remembered: a bustling city perched at the very edge of the land, coming as a surprise after miles and miles of open country. Eve had sneered when Olivia said the front of Marischal College reminded her of the Houses of Parliament, and insisted they stay at an expensive hotel where the sheets weren't even clean. Then St Andrew's: the castle, the botanic gardens, the fearsome row in a medieval tea shop.

Olivia felt weary, suddenly, even though they'd done nothing today. Even though Scotland was behind them and Eve was her friend and there had been all those picnics by the sea, too, and singing along to the radio with the car roof open and the glens empty of anything except air and heather.

'White,' she said, 'please,' and James poured her a glass as lightning flashed through the gap in the curtains.

# Chapter Eighteen

## 2008

Faith's catering business took off with a bang in the month after she met James. She had him to thank for it, partly. He'd given her card to a few people at the hospital, and one booking had led to another, and then another. Word of mouth was the way to do it, everyone said so – but you needed a break, and Faith was lucky to have got hers. All kinds of parties came her way: wedding anniversaries, twenty-first birthdays, engagements, retirements. She even had to take on a friend from her Cordon Bleu course to help out.

'You're a jammy sod, Faith,' Erica said, looking through her bookings diary. 'You've walked into a goldmine.'

Goldmines weren't the kind of thing you walked into, Faith thought, but she didn't want to annoy Erica by being clever-clever. She was an asset, Erica, a quick worker and good with the clients. Reliable, for all her flash comments. If things went on like this, she was going to need Erica to stick around.

'Is this all through that doctor boyfriend of yours?' Erica asked.

Faith shrugged in a nonchalant sort of way. 'He's certainly given the business a boost.'

'My last boyfriend didn't give me anything except chlamydia,' Erica said, and Faith laughed, although she knew that was just a line.

They were in Faith's kitchen, rolling out puff pastry for a batch of vol au vents. No one did vol au vents any more, but people liked them. They were becoming one of her trademarks.

'The only problem with being so busy is I don't get to spend enough time with James,' Faith said. 'What with his weekends on call and his private work, we've hardly seen each other lately.'

'My heart bleeds.'

'If I didn't know how hard he worked I'd wonder whether he'd got someone else on the side,' said Faith, and then she laughed, to make sure Erica didn't take it seriously.

But James evidently understood her frustration – felt the same way himself, maybe – because the next time they met he suggested a weekend away.

'I've got a reception on the Saturday evening,' Faith said. 'Up at Boars Hill. A party in one of those huge houses.'

She made her mournful face, and he stroked her cheek.

'Couldn't Erica handle it?' he asked. 'Wasn't that why you took her on, so you wouldn't have to do everything yourself?'

'I guess so.' Faith had her doubts about leaving Erica

to it – not because she wasn't competent, not that at all;
more because she was too competent. She didn't want
Erica stealing her clients. But the way things were going
she was never going to have a free weekend to spend with
James, and they needed it. 'You're right,' she said. 'It
would be fantastic to get away together.'

'My cousin has a house in Aldeburgh,' said James. 'It's
beautiful there. You'll love it.'

'Where's Aldeburgh?' Faith asked. She'd had Paris in
mind, but she tried not to let her disappointment show.

'On the Suffolk coast.'

'I like the beach,' said Faith, thinking as she said it that
the English coast in November wasn't exactly what she'd
call a beach. But even so it would be romantic, all
windswept and bleak. They could snuggle up together,
listening to the sea.


It rained all the way to Aldeburgh, five hours' drive
from Oxford. They could have been in Paris by now,
Faith thought, as they covered the last few miles with
the windscreen wipers working double speed to keep
the road in view. The previous night's event had
overrun – it had been two o'clock before she got cleared
up – and she was dead tired. She'd fallen asleep a
couple of times in the car. She didn't like to think what
she must have looked like, lolling forward in the
passenger seat, and she'd woken up with a stiff
neck, too.

'You're not doing any cooking this weekend,' James
had said when he picked her up, and she'd been cheered
by the thought of cosy suppers in country pubs. That was
something to look forward to, anyway. Unless she had

stuff over from functions she ate rubbish, most of the time. Certainly couldn't be bothered to cook for herself.

'OK?' said James now, seeing that she was awake again. 'Nearly there. We're just coming into Aldeburgh.'

Faith peered out of the window but she couldn't see a thing through the dark and the rain. She looked at the dashboard display: nearly ten o'clock. She was famished, she realised. She hadn't had time for lunch.

'Will the pubs still be serving?' she asked.

'I've brought food,' James said. 'I'm going to cook for you.' He grinned at the look on her face. 'Don't worry. I learned to cook at my grandmother's knee.'

'So that'll be dumplings and junket, then?'

James squeezed her leg. 'Actually, though I hesitate to say so to a pro, I'm not a half bad cook. And I've got a damn good bottle of Chablis in the cooler, so at least we can enjoy the drinking.'

It was still pouring when they pulled up opposite the house. James lent Faith his mackintosh to pull over her head for the dash to the front door. He followed with the bags and they slammed the door behind them, dripping wet just from that short sprint.

The house had the damp, mildewy smell of the seaside and all the furniture was old and battered, but at least it was warm. They left the bags in the hall and went through to the kitchen. The big old range cooker and the slate worktops looked original, Faith thought, and there was even a huge butler's sink in the corner.

'Wow,' she said. 'This is a real period piece. How long has it been in your family?'

James was unzipping the chiller bag, pulling out a bottle of wine and a series of packets and Tupperware boxes.

'For Madam's delectation,' he said, 'Chablis Valmur Grand Cru, 2006. I think Madam will agree it was an attractive year, and that the classical austerity of Chablis is nicely balanced here by the weight of the finish.'

'Gosh,' said Faith.

James laughed. He reached in a cupboard behind him for a couple of wine glasses, then pulled the cork out with a flourish. 'That's what the label says, anyway. Cheers.'

'Delicious,' Faith said, and it was. It didn't taste like wine at all, or not the kind she usually had. It was sweet and sharp at the same time; rather how she thought of James, in fact. The thought made her giggle and want to slide her hands around James's waist right away. God, if she was going to get pissed this quickly...

'This certainly beats a conference on vulval surgery,' said James, removing the film from a packet of king prawns.

'What conference?'

'Didn't I tell you? I was supposed to be at a conference in Florida this weekend, that's why my diary's clear. No private patients booked in.'

'You could have taken me to Florida,' said Faith. 'I'd have liked a bit of sun.'

He looked fondly at her and shook his head. 'Lots of boring seminars and lectures,' he said. 'This is much better: I've got you all to myself. And the sun will come out tomorrow, I promise.'


But it didn't. The rain kept up for the whole weekend, and although they made the best of it Faith was disappointed that they hardly even saw the sea.

'We could borrow some wet weather gear and go for a walk on the beach,' James said, when they woke on Sunday morning to a steady patter against the windows.

'I suppose so,' said Faith doubtfully. One day spent doing nothing had been great, but another might be a bit much. She didn't want them to get scratchy with each other from being cooped up too long.

'Or we could go for a drive,' James suggested. But they had the drive back to Oxford ahead of them, and Faith didn't want to spend any more time in the car. You couldn't see anything except clouds and rain, anyway.

In the end Faith had a long bath in an antique bathtub with clawed feet, then James brought up brunch on a tray for them to eat in bed. Bed was the right place for them, Faith thought; a safe bet for a good time. She felt like a courtesan, with James feeding her fingers of toast while the towel slipped off her shoulders. He'd turned out to be a good cook, just as he claimed, and she found that sexy too: watching him cut up vegetables in a methodical, efficient way, frowning as he checked for some herb or spice in the cupboard.

'I'll tell you what,' James said when they'd finished, 'why don't I find us a nice pub on the way home? We could head off late morning, and stop for a late lunch to break the journey.'

Faith couldn't imagine eating another thing, after bacon and eggs and fried tomatoes, but she could see the sense in ending on a good note. And much as she'd looked forward to the weekend, she didn't want to be too late home. She'd got a frantic week ahead.

'I'll google the Good Pub Guide,' James said, as though her hesitation had to do with the practicalities.

He'd brought his laptop, and while she was getting dressed he sat at the kitchen table and checked his e-mail.

Faith hadn't paid much attention to the house so far, except to approve of the old-fashioned kitchen and the old-fashioned bath and the working fireplace in the sitting room as suitable props for their romantic weekend. It needed a bit of money spending on it, she thought now, pulling her clothes on slowly and watching her reflection in the long mirror. A coat of paint and some new furniture would spruce it up no end, make the rooms look bigger. Maybe next time they came she could make some suggestions.

While they were packing, the rain stopped and the clouds lifted – sod's law, James said – and at last they could see the sea from the bay window in the bedroom. It looked cold and uninviting, even with a wintry sun in the sky, but at least it was the sea, Faith thought. It made a difference, being by the seaside: a change from landlocked Oxford.

'Was this where...' she began – and then she stopped.

'Where what?' James had finished his packing. He held up one of her dresses (what had she been thinking, bringing so many clothes for one weekend?) so she could take it from him and fold it into her case.

'Where Helena came,' Faith said, her heart beating fast suddenly.

James looked stunned, as if all that had been so far from his mind that it was a surprise to remember it, and Faith kicked herself. Idiot; why did she have to spoil things?

'She came here, yes,' he said. His voice didn't change; Faith wasn't sure whether that was a good sign or a bad one. 'But she drowned off the south coast. We had some friends with a house there.'

'I'm sorry,' Faith said, and she was. But things didn't go the way she expected after that. James dropped the dress on the bed and took her in his arms.

'God, I'm glad I've found you,' he said. 'You're my redeeming angel, do you know that?'

# Chapter Nineteen

'Are you busy on Friday?' Sarah asked, when Olivia picked up the phone. 'I'm going to look at lace for my wedding dress.'

It was the first time they'd spoken since the chance encounter in Kidlington, and Olivia was surprised by how pleased she was to hear Sarah's voice. How flattered by the invitation, too. She'd have imagined Sarah having dozens of friends more suitable for such an expedition.

'I'm not much good on lace,' she said, 'but why not? Where are you going?'

'There's a shop on the way to Cheltenham. I could pick you up.' At the other end of the phone Sarah hesitated. 'It sounds beautiful, the shop. The lace. It should be fun.'

The hesitation was touching too, Olivia thought. She squirmed, now, when she remembered how she'd reacted to Sarah's letter a few weeks ago. How uncharitable she'd been.

Friday was wet, a day of low skies. There was a lot of

traffic on the roads, as though everyone was trying to get away from the rain.

'I'm making the dress,' Sarah explained as they crawled along the A40 towards Burford. 'I know it's mad. I'd be better off with a dressmaker who knew how to flatter my figure, but I've always wanted to make my own wedding dress. Remember Mrs Darnley in Home Economics, saying if we practised enough we could do tiny, dainty buttonholes like the ones on Princess Diana's wedding dress?'

Princess Diana, thought Olivia. That dated them. 'I hated Mrs Darnley,' she said.

Sarah laughed. 'You were always off doing music. You never got any better at sewing.' They reached a section of dual carriageway and Sarah's MG put on an effortless spurt of speed to overtake the lorry they'd been trailing for the last five miles. Olivia had been surprised by the car, but she had to admit it was fun riding in something designed for pleasure rather than practicality.

'What happened to your music, anyway?' Sarah asked. 'Do you still play?'

'I teach,' Olivia said. 'I practise barely enough to keep my fingers moving these days.'

'That's a shame. You used to play so beautifully.'

Olivia thought of her irascible teacher in Edinburgh with his regime of technical exercises, and the professor of piano at the Royal College of Music who'd encouraged her to specialise in the early Romantics.

'When the boys were first born I imagined peaceful hours at the piano, lulling babies to sleep with Chopin nocturnes,' she said. 'But it didn't work out like that. They tolerated me playing nursery rhymes, but only if they could sit on my knee, and even then they screamed for the same tunes over and over again.' She used to blame Robert for their musical taste; it had become an in-joke.

'Ungrateful brutes,' said Sarah.

Olivia glanced sideways at her, remembering the sight of the boys sprawled in the TV room, and Sarah's smiling incomprehension. Did Sarah want children? Olivia imagined her with one of those new buggy-to-car contraptions, a tiny creature strapped deep inside it.

Sarah pulled in behind a sluggish Mini with a little click of annoyance.

'How's your mother?' she asked.

'Fine,' said Olivia. 'Busy.'

'That's good.'

'She's turned herself into an expert on old buildings. Not exactly the hands-on granny. Robert's mother sees more of them: she comes down from Scotland for a week at a time.'

There was silence for a moment. Olivia couldn't remember what had happened to Sarah's parents; whether she was supposed to know. After a little while she asked: 'Yours?'

'My mother's dead,' Sarah replied. 'Twelve years ago now.' She flushed, and lifted a hand from the steering wheel to push her fringe back from her forehead. 'I found her wedding dress last time I went home to see my father, tucked away in a box on the top shelf of her wardrobe. Such a beautiful dress. It wouldn't fit me in a million years.'

Olivia looked at her, the competent shoulders clad in red lambswool, and couldn't think what to say. She didn't remember Sarah and her mother being especially close; not like Eve. She didn't remember much at all about Sarah's mother, in fact – a slightly austere figure, perhaps, despite her solid Englishness? Intent but distant, on public occasions, and Sarah always anxious to please her.

'She was so elegant,' Sarah said. 'Do you remember? My brother and I were the wrong way round. He was delicate and winsome, with long lashes like some romantic poet. I was plain and plump, no good at all for dressing up.'

'Rubbish,' said Olivia, but Sarah shook her head.

'She always wanted to see me married,' she said.

Olivia waited for her to say more, but she didn't. They slowed for a roundabout, then accelerated away again. The rain had stopped but the sky was still heavy, clouds fissured with streaks of sharp blue like faultlines.

'You shouldn't feel bad about enjoying it,' Olivia said after a while. 'The wedding, I mean.'

Sarah laughed, a sudden chirp that was surprising in so small a space, followed by a string of sounds that might have been laughter or something quite different. 'I'm doing my best,' she said. There was a deep flush along her jawline now, but otherwise she looked entirely composed. 'Believe me, I'm doing my best.'


The shop was smaller than Olivia had expected, a dark room with delicate pieces of lace laid out in glass-topped cabinets. On the walls were framed engravings – tiny and intricate themselves – of lace-makers at work in cramped Victorian cottages.

Sarah rang the brass bell on the counter, and Olivia drifted towards the other side of the room. She felt a touch of unease, now, about this outing. She hardly knew Sarah; she had no idea what had happened to her in the last twenty-five years. It was all very well thinking you could pick up a friendship after so long and find nothing substantially changed, but she and Sarah hadn't really been friends to start with.

But the shop was fascinating. There was something strange and rarified about the atmosphere, as though the silence was made up of a myriad of unseen breaths, held in suspense so as not to disturb the stillness. As her eyes adjusted to the dim light, Olivia gazed in awe at the samples. Had people really made these tiny stitches and minuscule knots? They looked like a blend of cobweb and snowflake, too perfect for human handiwork. Even the names sounded magical: Honiton, Mechlin, Valenciennes. Tambours, flounces and lappets.

'I want ivory,' she heard Sarah saying, 'not cream.'

Olivia glanced across to see her handling the lace with an assurance she couldn't help admiring.

'That length of Honiton there,' said the assistant, a thin, grey-haired woman wearing a white blouse with an elaborate collar, 'we've a veil in a very similar pattern if you wanted to match it.'

She opened a door at the back of the shop. Sarah turned to Olivia with a smile, and they followed the woman through to an inner sanctum where wedding veils and christening gowns trailed from padded hangers. The assistant moved among them, looking for the one she wanted, then lifted down a length of lace and held it out to Sarah. The design looked different on a piece this size: the swirl of flowers and leaves was clearly discernible, the twists of the thread invisible. Patterns of light and shade, Olivia thought. She had a sudden urge to dress up; to drape herself in fairy cloth, like a little girl.

'Let me see it on you,' Sarah said, as though she'd read Olivia's mind.

Olivia's own wedding had been low-key, her dress off-the-peg from John Lewis and the reception demure. One branch of Robert's family was teetotal Presbyterian. Olivia hadn't minded the limitations on drinking and dancing: she'd been more concerned to get married than to have a wedding to remember. Whatever you did it was only one day, she'd thought. Here and then gone. But now, twirling in slow motion in front of the mirror, her dark hair edged with tiny flowers, she understood Sarah's excitement. The thrill of transformation; the urge to be a princess for a day.

'It's gorgeous,' she said. 'You try it.'


They had lunch, afterwards, in a tea shop in Burford, as old-fashioned in its way as the lace shop. Waitresses well over sixty, wearing white aprons, served croque monsieur and omelettes.

'It was beautiful, wasn't it?' Sarah asked. 'I hope you're glad you came.'

'Yes.' Olivia hesitated. 'It's odd to think it would be nothing without the holes,' she said. 'The lace, I mean. It's defined by what isn't there; by the gaps as much as the threads.'

'Like life,' Sarah said.

Olivia stared at her, and she blushed.

'Exactly,' Olivia said. 'The things you turn away from.'

'Presence and absence.'

Olivia nodded slowly. 'Maybe that's all life is,' she said. 'Empty spaces woven together. A flimsy thing held together by a few well-placed knots.' She took a deep breath, and let it out on a long sigh. 'Do you ever have the feeling that if you pulled one thread, the whole thing would unravel?'

Sarah took a sip from her water glass as if to prevent herself speaking too hastily. 'There can't be much room in your life for empty space,' she said. 'Your sons, your marriage, your teaching.' She looked at Olivia, her expression inscrutable. 'Or isn't that what you mean?'

Olivia stared back at her. Perhaps the gaps in one person's life, she thought, might be the threads in another. Or perhaps – perhaps we see things differently from outside. The pattern inverted, as if the lace had been pressed into soft clay, turned into something solid and substantial. She teased that thought round her head for a moment, and then she reached for a piece of the buttered bread that was stacked in a basket between them.

'I don't even know what I mean,' she said.

Sarah's eyes were still on her, as though she, too, was reaching for something she couldn't quite express. 'There is something extraordinary about lace, though,' she said after a moment. 'All those hours of work in a frill.'

'A throwaway detail,' Olivia agreed. 'A veil to cover your face when you get married. There's a symbolic gesture if ever there was one.'

Sarah frowned. She'd said the wrong thing now, Olivia thought. Or perhaps...

'Don't you think symbolic gestures matter?' Sarah asked. 'Isn't that exactly how we weave our lives out of – out of nothing, if you like? How we stop them being nothing? Maybe it doesn't matter what you do, as long as it's–'

The oldest of the waitresses banged through the door from the kitchen, carrying two plates. Two omelettes, liberally sprinkled with cress, were set down in front of them.

'Go on,' said Olivia, when the waitress had disappeared again, but Sarah shook her head. Olivia wondered suddenly whether Sarah's determination, the indomitable momentum of the wedding preparations, was designed as much as anything to carry Sarah herself along. She steeled herself, took a risk.

'Does it feel odd, getting married now?' she asked. 'When you've been used to a different kind of life?'

'It's what I've wanted,' Sarah said. 'I feel very fortunate to be given the chance.'

'But?'

But Sarah just smiled. The chink that had opened up for a moment had closed again, Olivia saw. She couldn't blame Sarah. Much better to let the elaborate framework of life be what it was: an appealing fiction, constructed knot by laborious knot.

# Chapter Twenty

Olivia had a plan for tonight. Robert was flying to Germany in the morning, and she thought she'd feed the boys early so the two of them could have supper alone when he got home – a rare event, these days. People said you had more time for each other as your children grew up, but Olivia hadn't noticed that yet. By the time the boys left home, she thought sometimes, she and Robert would have forgotten how to be alone together. And the lace shop had lodged something inside her: some need, or want, or hope.

As she chopped onions for the boys' spaghetti bolognese, she remembered the first year of their marriage: both of them twenty-three, playing house together. Robert had commuted into the City to his grown-up job while Olivia, who only had to go into the Royal College of Music twice a week, spent most of her time at home, practising the piano. Robert carried the air of the outside world into the tiny flat when he returned, the eddies of grown-up London escaping from his briefcase, shaken out of his hair, and they'd have the whole evening ahead, just the two of them. There were stand-by tickets for plays and concerts, Sunday walks in London parks and Olivia's experiments in cooking, hampered by the landlord's battered pans that they'd never thought to replace; the recipes redeemed or ruined by a last-minute ingredient.

Olivia didn't often think about those years. Was that, she wondered now as the water came to the boil, the only time when she'd been properly an adult, that time when she'd thought she was playing at being grown-up?

She remembered, then, the day Robert had come home early, his reliable figure blurred by anxiety. Black Monday: the day of the stock market crash. Rumours had spread fast, and Robert's boss had acted promptly to rationalise his team. Robert had come home in the middle of the afternoon, jobless, not knowing what to do with himself. Olivia smiled, remembering. She'd taken his clothes off, his Austin Reed suit and striped shirt, and taken him to bed. They'd opened a bottle of champagne from his Christmas bonus hamper, drawn the curtains against the autumn sunshine, hidden away from the world. He had relied on her, that day, to set things right. Never mind, she'd said; we're young, we have each other, we can do anything we want. We could go and live on an island. For an afternoon and an evening they had flown free, far away from the grime and crush of London.

But the next morning there'd been a call from the office. No hasty decisions, they'd said; too valuable to the team to lose you that easily. So Robert had put his suit back on and disappeared back to his other life, the one that had paid the mortgage ever since, fostering their progress from Leyton to Islington to Oxford and providing all those Babygros and football boots, those summer holidays and new boilers. It hadn't occurred to Olivia to feel regret, but she saw now that that was the moment when things had been settled, finally, between them. When their course had been fixed. Her own life had filled out since then, year by year, child by child, but looking back she could envy the simplicity and completeness she'd felt then: the sense of possibility. And the music, every day.

She was lost for a moment when Tom came into the kitchen, stranded in an earlier life he hadn't been part of. She smiled blandly at him, adjusting her focus back to the present.

'See you later,' he said. He'd exchanged his school clothes for uniform of a different kind: jeans narrow around the legs, T-shirts and sweatshirts layered artfully into dishevelment.

'OK.' Olivia nodded, conscious of the neutral expression she adopted these days for her oldest son – one that avoided expectation or reproach or enquiry. She jabbed at the blackening onions in the frying pan. 'Want anything to eat before you go?'

Tom shook his head. 'Might bring some friends back.'

'Fine.' Olivia thought, as she had once or twice before, of mentioning Lucy, but she resisted the temptation. It was better not to ask unnecessary questions. Tom had always valued his privacy: even as a little boy he'd had boxes of secrets under his bed, notices on the door warning people to keep out. Last year, he'd taken over the attic and created a lair from which a stream of friends now came and went at all hours. If she showed too much interest in all that, Olivia thought, he'd take more trouble to conceal it from her. The delicate equilibrium would be upset.

'Homework?' she asked.

Tom shrugged. Olivia was spared a decision about whether to press him further by the ringing of the phone.

'Ma,' she said. 'How are you? Good trip?'

As her mother replied, Olivia heard the front door closing at the other end of the corridor.

For an eighteen-year-old Tom was, Olivia knew, remarkably little trouble. He went to school without complaint; he engaged in the same old banter with his brothers, the same lion-cub scuffles. But Olivia had almost no idea what went on in his head these days. She told herself that was to be expected. Watching the boys grow up, she'd felt pleasure and regret at each new step, but also relief – like taking a cake out of the oven and finding that it's risen, just as the recipe promised. It proved her competence, refuted her nagging suspicion that she was an amateur mother getting by on a wing and a prayer. And she had three more after Tom, a long way to go before her nest was empty.

But even so it felt strange, the beginning of letting go; the sudden presence of all these almost-adults in her house, friends and strangers drifting through.

'Hi,' Olivia would say, as a waft of perfume and cold air swept up the stairs. She'd catch sight of her face, sometimes, in the hall mirror, and realise she was her mother's age now.

Her mother: that was another thing. Her mother who always seemed to ring at the wrong moment, often after weeks of silence. They had never been very tightly bound to each other, but after her father died Olivia had assumed that she and her children would be a necessary fixture in her mother's life. She'd been pleased when her mother cultivated new interests; surprised and pleased when they took shape as a career. But now her mother wasn't even in the country, half the time. She was spinning off into her own life, just like her grandson.

'D'you know, they're way behind us in Italy,' her mother said, sounding oddly distant at the other end of the phone line, even though she was at home this time, calling from her London flat. 'It's hard to credit, with such treasures to their name, but I suppose that's the point. An embarrassment of riches. Anything less than priceless gets overlooked.'

'Three months in Florence,' said Olivia. 'How lovely.' She could see her mother, stylish in her long black coat, standing in a Romanesque church, surrounded by frescoes and conversing with a handsome Italian architect. She could pass for an Italian herself, elegant at sixty-five with her strong features and her tiny frame. Haloed by shafts of sunlight through stained glass as she gave her opinion on the stonework.

'Not so lovely at this time of year,' said her mother, 'but you can't have everything.'

'Your mother,' Robert said, when Olivia related the conversation to him later – much later: there'd been a problem with the trains – 'is remarkable.'

'In what way?'

'In many ways.' Robert sat back a little in his chair and smiled at her. 'Though not as remarkable as you, of course.'

'Rubbish,' said Olivia. She looked at the array of food on the table, the lamb tagine and the dish of couscous elaborately constructed from a recipe book Robert's sister-in-law had given her last Christmas, and realised she wasn't hungry any more. Too much cooking, she thought. They could just as well have had spaghetti bolognese too, and then she could have helped Angus with his homework. 'What do you mean?'

'In the way she carries her responsibilities so lightly.'

'What responsibilities?'

Robert raised his hands, a comic gesture of surrender. 'In the way she's reinvented herself, then, if you prefer.'

'I don't prefer at all. It makes me feel weary.'

Robert looked at her for a moment; she saw in his face a well-worn path, and she regretted sending him down it. It wasn't what she'd intended for this evening: she'd had in mind those flurries of fresh air carried into their half-bare flat, the sense of space in those tiny rooms.

'You have decades ahead of you,' he said. 'Your mother didn't start on this conservation kick until she was – what, fifty-five?'

Olivia nodded. The future snaked away from her, furtive and unknowable.

'And you have plenty to show for your life already.'

Robert leaned across the table towards her. Olivia knew she should be grateful that he took the trouble to offer reassurance.

'I've made other lives,' she said. 'That's not the same as making something of my own life.'

'You'll always have your music.'

Olivia sighed. It was what he always said at such moments, and she knew he meant it sincerely. But the truth was more complicated: music is something you have to live, she wanted to explain. She'd tried to explain, many times. The fact that she'd once been able to perform

Chopin's Revolutionary Étude or Bach's Musical Offering wasn't a consolation; it was like a garment she'd put away years ago, something she would never wear again.

She stood up, gathered the plates from the table. 'It's late,' she said. 'You've got an early start. Let's get to bed.'

# Chapter Twenty-One

Sarah's wedding reception was taking place at St Saviour's College, where Guy had once been a graduate student. One November morning Olivia and Sarah went to meet the domestic bursar, a bald man with a comically oversized moustache who treated Sarah like a wayward student.

'Two hundred,' he said, his hands on his plump waistcoated hips, 'is the very maximum we can accommodate.'

'That's what I was told,' Sarah said. 'It won't be more than that.'

The bursar harrumphed, as if to say it wasn't the first time he'd heard that story. Behind him, around him, the eighteenth-century hall soared in graceful arcs. The ridiculous and the sublime, Olivia thought. She imagined the wedding reception as a scene from a costume drama, the bursar as a comic cameo.

'Will you be returning to the Combination Room after dinner?' he asked. 'Coffee can be taken in there if you prefer.'

Sarah looked at Olivia. 'People might like to move around, mightn't they?'

'We usually find guests spill out into the grounds.' The bursar frowned. 'Even in winter.'

Olivia suppressed a smile. Was he going to ask Sarah to insist her guests brought scarves and gloves? Perhaps they could line up their wellies in the panelled passage, like a primary school cloakroom. Apparently oblivious to the bursar's air of reproof, Sarah consulted her checklist of questions.

'Will there be someone in the Porters' Lodge to direct latecomers?' she asked.

Olivia felt a sudden sharp tenderness for her; for the way she ploughed on regardless.

'Naturally.' The bursar cleared his throat. He led them into the servery, where heated trolleys were lined up like engines in a shunting yard. 'Will your caterer supply her own crockery?' he asked. 'Or will you require ours?'

Since the visit to the lace shop, Olivia had been drawn gradually but irresistibly into Sarah's wedding preparations. To keep her company, she told Robert, but that wasn't the whole truth. Olivia had no daughters, no mother-of-the-bride flummery to look forward to: why not make the most of this opportunity? Why not absorb herself in the relative merits of florists and caterers? And the lace outing had sealed a bond between them. Despite her initial qualms – despite the way she and Eve used to sneer – there was something persuasive about Sarah's approach to life. Olivia hadn't felt the lack of Sarah's friendship all these years, but she valued it now more than she'd expected. It sometimes felt as though the last twenty-five years were being gradually rubbed out, and replaced by a version in which she and Sarah had always been the best of friends.

For one thing, Sarah filled a gap which Olivia hadn't ever acknowledged. It was easy to be so absorbed by children, by the momentum of family life, that you didn't notice the absence of friends. But since the night she'd met Lucy, Olivia had thought a lot about loneliness. The women she'd called friends when the boys were little had slipped out of her life, one by one. Now and then she would run into someone she'd spent hours with in that former existence, in the days of watching small children play and comparing notes on teething and tantrums. They'd recognise each other across a café or a cinema lobby, and they'd smile and exchange a word or two, and a look that conveyed quite clearly that intimacy wasn't expected any more. It was as though the years of nappies and intractable tiredness were a secret it wasn't polite to mention once you'd left them behind. As though the weaknesses that phase of life had revealed – the neglect of ambition and fashion and current affairs – might betray you unless you moved on, up, out, away. Most of those women had gone back to work and immersed themselves in other worlds, other friends, but piano teaching was a solitary occupation. No scope for office camaraderie for Olivia.

But now here was Sarah, waiting, hoping, to start out on the path Olivia had already trodden. Sarah, who seemed as oddly bereft of female companionship as Olivia. Who seemed to need her.

Sarah was tentative at first, phoning on another pretext and dropping a visit to a marquee company into the conversation as if it were an afterthought. ('You

171

wouldn't believe the catalogue. Five different chairs!') But not for long. She didn't work on Fridays; she called it her wedding planner day. After a couple of weeks, she assumed Olivia's Fridays were her own too.

'Hello!' she would chirrup, usually early on Friday morning, before the boys had left for school. 'What are you doing today?'

Olivia could have left the phone, of course; no one else rang that early. Instead she picked it up eagerly.

Later that morning, Olivia and Sarah sat on a log, watching the river idle past. Prompted, perhaps, by the bursar's reference to wedding guests straying outside, Sarah had assumed they were free to wander in the grounds after their meeting. The gardens of St Saviour's ran down to the water: gardens that were lovingly tended but not manicured, with some areas allowed to run wild. In a fringe of woodland, fallen trees had been left where they lay, creating impromptu seats with a view across the lawns in one direction and the river in the other. On the opposite bank, a dog ran ahead of its master, its tail flying like bunting.

'It must be wonderful,' Sarah said, 'to have such a well-established family.'

'What do you mean?' Olivia's mind flitted first to the cool, well-regulated life of her childhood. Her family had been too slight to count as well-established, she thought: the hard-working father, the dutiful wife, the solitary daughter. But of course that wasn't what Sarah meant.

'Four sons, almost grown up,' she said. 'You're the uber mother. The definitive matriarch.'

Olivia laughed. 'Hardly,' she said. But she was

gratified, even so. She'd imagined Sarah was quietly horrified by her domestic situation: the noise; the general chaos.

'You're very lucky,' Sarah said. 'Not that I don't appreciate what I've got – what I've had – but I envy you your fairytale ending. Happy ever after.'

'You've got a fairytale ending too.'

'Who knows.'

Olivia remembered that moment over lunch in Burford, seeing the same flutter of doubt cross Sarah's face now. But as she grasped for whatever it was that hovered between them, she found, instead, an insight into her own life: despite the excitement of the wedding, she realised, she didn't envy Sarah her chance to start afresh. Whether or not she would choose the same path again, she was happy to have travelled this far along it. It was the next bit of the road that troubled her; the bit she'd never thought about.

She picked up a conker from the path, turned it over in her hand then threw it into the river. A ring of ripples spread swiftly across the surface then died away, leaving the conker floating, barely visible, in midstream.

# Chapter Twenty-Two

S arah opened her car door onto a thin drizzle that had turned the swathe of tarmac behind the flats into a dark slick. She was late back from work tonight, and she was tired and hungry. In the short time it took to walk to the front door, the rain insinuated itself beneath the collar of her jacket in a filmy trickle.

It was Monday: Sarah had spent the weekend at Guy's house and she knew the fridge was empty. The heating had come on at six but even so the flat felt cheerless, as though it could tell it was on the point of being abandoned. And Monday was running night. Sarah had spent last Monday evening at a dinner with Guy; she really ought to go this week. As she filled the kettle, she bargained with herself. If it stops raining, I'll go running and buy fish and chips on the way home. If it doesn't, I'll go to Sainsbury's and do a big shop.

She and Guy were planning to spend their honeymoon walking. Not climbing, he'd assured her; no ropes or pitons. They were going to New Zealand, where it would be high summer, to walk the Milford Tracks.

Guy had produced several brochures about the landscape and the wildlife to whet her appetite.

Sarah wasn't worried about the walking. She'd been on dozens of walking holidays over the years, and the terrain in New Zealand didn't look so different from Europe. It was hardly the Himalayas, and Guy still wasn't fully fit after his accident. Even so, when she heard about a running club that met in the local park, she decided to join them. A little extra fitness wouldn't hurt, she told herself. But as the weather grew colder her resolve had begun to flag. It took an effort of will to drag herself out on nights like this.

While she drank her tea, Sarah sewed a couple of buttonholes on her wedding dress: tiny buttonholes, but not as dainty as Princess Diana's, despite her best efforts. It would be going too far to say that her resolve was flagging on the dressmaking as well, but it seemed to be taking forever to work her way down the back, and she still had the sleeves and the hem to finish. Thank goodness, she thought, that she'd found that wonderful veil, and the long lace train that would cover a multitude of sins.

After a while she got up again to check the weather. The rain had stopped; the moon glimmered in a gap between clouds. Sarah's heart sank, but a deal was a deal. Running it was.

The Striders were diminished this evening. Only a small straggle of people had gathered in the car park, waterproofs over their running gear, and conversation was sparse as they warmed up.

'This is devotion,' said Mandy, a plump thirty-five-year-old who always looked as though she was hating every minute.

'To what?' replied her friend Liz, and they both laughed and stretched their hamstrings and groaned.

'Is this the Striders?' asked a voice behind them. 'I spoke to someone called Kevin. Am I in the right place?'

The voice was familiar. Sarah straightened up and found herself looking straight at Harry Matthews.

'Oh!' he said. 'Dr Brewster.'

'Sarah.' She managed a smile; an unconvincing cover for the knot that had wound itself into her guts in that instant of recognition. He was taller than she remembered, his burliness less awkward in running gear than the tight suit he'd been squeezed into last time they met. She thought of the little Bible, wondered if she ought to have written to thank him.

'Are you one of the Striders?' he asked.

'Yes.' She pointed to the far side of the car park. 'Kevin's the one over there in the red jacket.'

Harry nodded, hesitated. 'Thank you.'

Sarah was glad to get going along the track. The physical effort was a relief, pushing herself to keep up with the leaders as the group spread out along the first stretch. But she wished fervently that she'd stayed at home this evening. She'd managed to put Harry Matthews out of her mind. She shouldn't have played games with Fate again, staking her decision on the fluctuations of the weather.

The park was almost empty, which was hardly a surprise. It was dark and cold and the drizzle had started up again, just the slightest shimmer, as if the air was too saturated to hold any more moisture. A solitary runner passed them in the other direction, wearing a blue Lycra jacket with a yellow streak across the chest; he raised his hand in greeting and ran on.

As they passed the cricket pavilion, settled into a steady pace by now, Sarah allowed herself to think back to that morning in the clinic, trying to get straight in her head what had actually happened. Surely the emotional power of the encounter had all been in her mind? Harry had comforted her; she had stayed in his arms longer than he might have expected, but then she'd shaken his hand and thanked him for coming and said goodbye. He couldn't have known how agitated she'd been, afterwards. He couldn't have known that she ran with the Striders, either. It was pure coincidence that he'd turned up this evening. She just needed to keep going, to keep a safe distance between them. She lengthened her stride, feeling the pleasurable ache of exertion in her muscles.

When the going was firm, the Striders extended their course by circuiting the water meadows on the far side of the park. Sarah had expected that they'd stick to the tarmacked running track tonight, but at the corner near the duck pond Kevin cut off towards the river.

'Bit of mud,' he called over his shoulder.

Sarah was tiring by now – the missed week was telling, she thought – but she wasn't going to let up her pace. If she kept pushing herself, it wouldn't be possible to think about anything except the pain in her legs and the rush of blood and air through her chest.

They were nearly at the river when she slipped. There was an uneven bit of ground, a patch of mud, and she slid a couple of feet and fell awkwardly. Almost at once, there was a small group around her: Mandy and

Liz, puffing, grateful for an excuse to stop; and Harry Matthews kneeling at her side, putting his hand on her shoulder, looking at her with an expression of anguish out of all proportion to the severity of the situation. But perhaps not out of all proportion: when Sarah tried to move, a sharp pain shot through her ankle and up her leg. Despite herself, she yelped, then groaned as a second wave of pain clamped around the twisted joint.

'Is it broken?' Mandy asked.

'Sprained, I expect,' said Liz. 'God, Sarah, you couldn't have done it much further from the car park.'

'I'm fine,' Sarah said. 'I'll be fine.'

She could feel Harry's hand, its warmth too comforting. She shut her eyes for a moment, marshalling her strength.

'I can carry her,' she heard Harry saying.

'No,' she said, more vehemently than she intended. 'You go on. It's your first run; there's no need.' She looked up at Mandy, hoping her appeal would be understood. Mandy's face was a benign moon against the dark sky.

'We'll help her back,' Mandy said. 'Won't we, Liz? We can always join in again on the next circuit.'

Sarah didn't want to look at Harry. She knew he'd be hurt, that he wouldn't understand – or worse, that he would.

'Thank you,' she said, as he stood up. 'It's nice of you to offer.'

Hobbling back across the field between Mandy and Liz was a heavy price to pay: the pain in her ankle was worse by the minute. Even if there was no fracture, she thought, it was a bad sprain.

'When's the wedding?' Liz asked. 'You'll be OK by then, won't you?'

'I'm sure I will,' Sarah said, although she wasn't sure at all. 'Six weeks still. Ow!' She squealed as the bad foot was jolted by an awkward step, and Mandy and Liz tightened their grip on her.

'What do we look like?' Mandy said. 'Limping across some field in the pouring rain like a bunch of drunks. Lucky there's no one to see us.'

But there was. The runner who had passed them earlier was approaching, slowing down; the man in the blue and yellow running gear.

'Are you hurt?' he asked.

'She slipped,' said Liz. 'Sprained her ankle.'

'Can I help? I'm a doctor.'

'We just need to get her back to the car,' said Mandy.

'Let me carry her,' offered the man. 'It's a long way.' He smiled as they hesitated. 'Compulsory NHS training: manual handling and lifting. I knew it would come in handy one day.'

Sarah was in too much pain now to object. He wasn't young, the man, but he was tall and he looked fit. He hoisted her into a fireman's lift and set off for the car park. Her foot dangled painfully, but it was better than trying to walk. To her relief, Mandy and Liz followed.

'We should call your fiancé,' Mandy said. 'You're not going to be able to drive home.'

'He's away,' Sarah said. This fact, forgotten until now, came as a tremendous, guilty relief. She didn't want to set Guy any more tests, she told herself. 'He flew to Prague this morning.'

'Men,' said Liz. 'Where are they when you need them?' She glanced at Sarah's rescuer with a grin. 'Present company excepted, of course.'

When they reached the car park, Mandy opened up

179

the boot of her Discovery and the man set Sarah down on its wide lip. Carefully, he removed her running shoe and felt the swollen joint. Sarah wondered if she ought to ask his name, mention her own professional credentials, but instead she sat still and let him examine her foot.

'It needs an X-ray,' he said. 'Is there someone who could take you up to A and E?'

There was a tiny pause. 'I could,' said Mandy. 'I could ring the babysitter and ask her to stay on, then if we dropped Liz–'

'No,' said Sarah. 'Really. I'll call my friend Olivia. Can you – her number's in my mobile, in the car. Olivia Conafray.'

She was looking in the other direction, passing Mandy her car keys, but she couldn't miss the man's reaction. Not unlike hers when Harry showed up, she thought. Curious.

'Do you know Olivia?' she asked.

He smiled, composure restored. 'I don't think so,' he said. 'Now–' he checked his watch, frowned slightly '–if you're OK here, I should really be getting back.'

'Sorry,' said Sarah. 'I've held you up.'

'Don't even think about it. Hope the ankle's better soon.' He smiled again, and then he was off, jogging across the car park to the black Mercedes parked by the gate.

'Well,' said Liz. 'He was in a hurry, suddenly.' She raised her eyebrows at Sarah. 'Do you know that other bloke?' she asked. 'The new one who was running with us?'

'Not really. His mother was a patient. I just – you know, it's awkward when people feel some kind of obligation.'

Sarah blushed; she'd never been a good liar. Then,

alarmingly, she felt tears starting behind her eyes. Her ankle hurt; she wanted to be at home in bed with a hot water bottle and a glass of whisky. She wanted a mother who'd come and look after her.

'Sorted.' Mandy was coming back towards them. 'She's coming. Should be here in fifteen minutes.'

'Thank you.' Sarah tried to smile. The pain in her ankle was getting steadily worse. The thought crossed her mind – another guilty, welcome thought – that she wouldn't be able to run again for a good few weeks.

'We'll wait with you until she gets here,' said Liz. 'Have you got a spare coat or anything, Mand? She's shivering.'

'Only a dog blanket.' Mandy reached into the car for a rug to drape around Sarah's shoulders. 'Bit hairy, but better than nothing, eh? Did he go, your knight in shining armour?'

'Took off in fright.' Liz laughed. 'Anyone want a Polo? Only three calories.'

Sarah shut her eyes, adjusting her mind to the rhythm of the blood throbbing in her ankle, and to the prospect of a long evening in A and E. Was she right to have called Olivia? Martin and Philippa would have come, or her downstairs neighbour. Perhaps she presumed too much on Olivia. It was hard to tell sometimes, she thought, what Olivia was thinking, whether she was enjoying herself or just going along with things.

And what about her? demanded an internal interrogator, seizing this unguarded moment. Was she enjoying herself, or just going along with things? What did it mean that she was relieved Guy was away when she'd hurt herself? And that Harry Matthews could upset her equilibrium so easily?

181

By the time Olivia's car turned into the car park, the other Striders were trickling back. Sarah caught a final glimpse of Harry Matthews as Mandy slammed the passenger door and Olivia slipped the car into gear, and then they were off towards the hospital.

# Chapter Twenty-Three

In the second week of November, Benjy had a bout of tonsillitis. He was too old, really, to need coddling in the way he used to, but Olivia was still quick to respond to any suggestion of fragility in her youngest son. She spent several days trudging up and down the stairs, bringing him hot lemon or cold squash, extra pillows, more painkillers. Much as she loved her proto-men with their video games and their football boots, this, she admitted, was the kind of mothering she knew best – and Benjy savoured the comfort of being looked after. While Olivia sat on his bed and read to him, the rest of the world receded into the shadows beyond the bright circle of the bedroom. It felt to Olivia like one of those vivid moments before the end of an era: the summer before war breaks out, or the *fin-de-siècle* brilliance of a doomed society. By rights this time should be past, and it soon would be, but its last vestiges were precious. For a few days and nights, nothing else mattered very much.

On the fourth night, Benjy fell asleep before the story

was finished. His fever was almost gone, the penicillin Olivia had coaxed out of the GP working at last. Olivia was exhausted, but back in her own bed she lay wide awake. There was plenty to occupy her thoughts once they were let loose at this hour: plenty of anxieties, set aside this week, to loom large in the darkness. She drew up her knees against the cold, letting the latest note from Angus's year head, the latest argument with Tom about family holidays, filter through her head. The orthodontist, the PTA meeting, the leaking dishwasher. The ordinary flotsam of her life, familiarly insistent.

But there was more than that on her mind at the moment. There were the ghostly figures in the shadows, waiting for her to attend to them.

She'd done nothing about Georgie since her meeting with Mary Baldwin. Georgie was still vague and distracted, and Olivia was squeamish about interfering in her life. Perhaps the vagueness was welcome, she thought; perhaps Georgie's past was drifting out of focus at last, and she should leave well alone. But she couldn't escape the nagging awareness that Mary expected something of her. Every week at the Wednesday Club, she felt a stab of guilt and of cowardice.

And then there was Eve. A few weeks after Sarah had first mentioned her name, Eve had rung one evening, out of the blue. Sarah must have given her Olivia's number, although Eve didn't say so. They'd both said hello, and goodness, how many years was it, and then Eve had cleared her throat.

'Perhaps we should meet for lunch,' she'd said, her voice stilted, as though Olivia was a stranger whose standing she wasn't sure of.

Olivia had responded too eagerly, the way she always had to Eve's suggestions.

'One day next week?' she'd said.

'The week after would be better.'

Eve's tone was measured, restrained, and Olivia had kicked herself. The same mistakes, always.

The whole conversation had lasted only a few minutes: there was too much to say on the phone, or too little. And now the prospect of the meeting hovered in Olivia's mind like a mirage; something hardly to be believed in, certainly not relied on. Most of the time she wished fervently that Eve was still in Australia with her flying doctor husband – but some small, incautious, fatalistic part of her was counting off the days. Almost, she thought, like waiting to meet a lover wounded in battle, unable to bear the suspense before seeing his injuries for herself.

The next thing Olivia knew it was light, and there was noise downstairs, the clatter of plates and the raising of voices as her sons ate their breakfasts. She lay still for a few more seconds, then she rolled out of bed and went down to the kitchen to dispense lunch money and arbitration.

Benjy was feeling better this morning. After his brothers had left, he settled himself in front of the television, wrapped in his duvet. Standing in the doorway, watching him absorbed in a re-run of *Friends*, Olivia felt suddenly fretful and airless. Cabin fever, she thought: she'd been cooped up for too long this week. It was the morning the cleaner came, and when she'd made Benjy a jug of honey and lemon and kissed him on the forehead (something she knew would be forbidden again by tomorrow), Olivia left him in Agata's care and slipped out through the front door.

The morning was cold and damp, but it felt good to be outside. Out of habit, she made for the canal and followed it down to Port Meadow, and then she crossed the river and turned north through the boatyard before halting to survey the view, her view, back towards the city.

As she stood there, a solitary figure came into sight on the far side of the water: a runner, moving steadily across the northern stretch of the meadow. He was too far off for Olivia to see him clearly, but she recognised the distinctive colours of his Lycra jacket, blue with a strip of yellow across the front. For a few minutes she stood and watched, aware that her position gave her the freedom to observe unseen: the willows along the bank would block her from view if he happened to look her way. In her head danced the faces of men half-recognised, and ghost stories and cold water, and the cries of seagulls, sharp as labour pains. Was it James, across the river? How could she imagine she'd recognised him at that distance when she hadn't been sure of him close up? She shook her head, chiding herself, and turned to walk on towards the lock.

She was almost home when she saw him again. As she approached the turning for her road he came into sight, running south from Wolvercote, heading directly towards her. It was definitely the same man who'd helped her the day she was attacked. And beyond doubt James. She waited in the middle of the path, wondering what they would say to each other, and in those few moments Shearwater House came vividly, stridently back to her, along with the muddle of regret and grief that had smudged its memory afterwards.

As the man came closer, Olivia was sure he'd seen her too. There was a second, no more, when it was inevitable that they would meet – and then he ducked away from her, across the road, and before she could call after him he had sprinted off towards the canal.

# Chapter Twenty-Four

Olivia had the strangest feeling: that she was not in a restaurant but a church, before a funeral, surrounded by the whisper of mourners' voices as they waited for the coffin to appear. If she shut her eyes, she could imagine the quiet organ music, the scent of the lilies.

But instead there was the rustle of lunchtime conversation, the swish of waiters, the glasses on the table in front of her. A different kind of expectation.

She'd arrived more than usually early. Despite herself, she'd been anxious not to keep Eve waiting, or to imply that she wasn't keen to see her. Eve, apparently, was not anxious about these things. The clock on the wall was moving towards ten past one, and Olivia was wondering about ordering a glass of wine. A gin and tonic, even. When did she last have a gin and tonic at lunchtime?

And then suddenly there was Eve, coming through the door – unmistakably Eve, although Olivia could hardly have said what she recognised in this woman. She looked older than Olivia had bargained for, her skin deeply lined by the Australian sun. Blonde still, but a harder shade, and wearing clothes Eve would never have worn: gold and flowing, like expensive curtains.

Olivia half-stood, began to wave, as a waiter pointed and Eve turned towards her.

'Well.' They both spoke at once, grinning sheepishly, guardedly, like schoolgirls brought to the Head's office to make up after a fight in the playground.

'You haven't changed,' Eve said, and she laughed briefly, as if to say that she knew she had.

'I was just going to order some wine,' said Olivia.

Eve lifted her hands. 'Not for me. No good at that any more, I'm afraid.'

Olivia blushed, flustered. Had she missed something in Sarah's briefing? Some medical detail?

'Not at lunchtime,' Eve said, sliding into the seat opposite. 'Or I'll misbehave.'

'Pact.' Olivia was stupidly relieved. 'Stay sober and behave.'

Eve had suggested this place, on the river near Marlow. Halfway between us, she'd said. Not too expensive. She knew the menu, and knew what she wanted to eat already. Olivia stared for a moment, then pointed at the first thing her eye lit upon. Choice, she felt, was altogether too complicated for today.

'So, reunited by the inimitable Sarah.' Eve raised her eyebrows, and Olivia felt a flicker of the old conflict between the pleasure of mockery and the proscription of her conscience.

'Sarah's leg's in plaster,' she said. 'Poor thing, she fell over on a run. Broke some bone in her foot.'

'Lord – is she going to hobble up the aisle in a cast?'

'She's hoping not. But you know Sarah, never daunted.'

'And you're miles ahead of all of us, I gather. Four sons.'

Olivia was wrong-footed, briefly, by the change of direction. 'If you call that miles ahead.'

'How old?'

'Between ten and eighteen.'

'Eighteen! A grown-up son, my goodness. You certainly don't look old enough for that. Did Sarah tell you I'm planning to adopt?'

'Yes.' Olivia met Eve's eyes, taking care over her response. 'From China, she said.'

'It's a hell of a process. Years, literally. Forms and interviews and references and more forms. And I've had to go back a stage since I came back home.'

Home, Olivia thought. After twenty-five years on the other side of the world, this was still home. She felt sorry for Eve at that moment, for the thought of her being in exile all that time.

'How much longer now?' she asked.

'It's in the lap of the gods, or at least the Chinese authorities. All the preliminaries are done. I'm waiting to hear when there's a baby available.'

Eve's face quivered, with pleasure or anxiety or perhaps a mixture of the two.

'How exciting!' Olivia said brightly, though she felt her own quiver too, a queasy foreboding at those words. *A baby available.* How time changed things. And how strange, how awful, for motherhood to be reduced to forms and foreign officials. Would she have wanted a baby that much? Even she, the uber mother?

When the waiter arrived with their food, Olivia

realised they'd ordered the same thing. Salade niçoise with a twist of parmesan on top, thin as a leaf.

'Cheers,' she said, lifting her water glass.

'You know what?' said Eve. 'I think I do need a glass of wine. I was horribly nervous about this. God knows why.' She laughed, a bright, brittle trill, and Olivia thought: that I recognise. She grinned. That I remember.


To Olivia's surprise Eve ordered pudding, a crème brulée with stem ginger sliced on top, as thin as the parmesan.

'It must be the wine,' she said. 'I don't usually eat anything at lunchtime.'

She did look thin, Olivia thought. She was strangely gratified by Eve's appetite, as if she was watching one of her boys tucking into something she'd made.

'Good?' she asked.

Eve nodded. 'Want a bite?'

Olivia shook her head. She'd never had a sweet tooth; Eve would know that.

Eve lifted her spoon to her mouth, licked it with an elegant deliberation, then laid it on the edge of the dish. 'If we're going to do this,' she said, 'this reunion business, then I think we have to talk about things, don't you?'

She looked straight at Olivia then, with the narrowed eyes of the old Eve, and Olivia felt as if something had hit her in the stomach. Something she ought to have seen coming. No: something she'd anticipated but had foolishly hoped to avoid.

'Haven't we been talking?' she said, although she knew that would irritate Eve. We've managed some treacherous ground, she meant. Haven't we acknowledged the past, between the lines?

Eve made a brief, dismissive gesture.

'I was pregnant that summer,' she said. 'I found out while we were in Aldeburgh. It was James's, naturally. James's child.'

The words came in a surge: like the way a baby's head is born, Olivia couldn't help thinking. 'Bloody hell,' she said. And you never told me. She couldn't say that, but surely Eve could hear the words. Surely she must have anticipated them.

'I'd slept with him a couple of times, earlier that summer,' Eve said. 'You probably guessed that.'

Olivia shook her head.

'I suppose I was too presumptuous. When he arrived at Shearwater I behaved as though we were together, even though we weren't.'

'I don't remember it like that.'

As she stared at Eve across the table, the events of 1983 loomed and blurred in Olivia's mind. She remembered Eve's face when James ducked her in the sea, and her mermaid hair floating in the bath. Everything was distorted, now, by the secret Eve had kept from her all these years. Her trump card, Olivia thought: her *pièce de résistance*, saved up for this occasion.

'So,' Eve said. 'That's why no babies, you see.'

Olivia waited.

'Actually,' Eve went on, in a tone that seemed to be aiming for jauntiness and falling dismayingly short, 'it probably wasn't the abortion. Probably the chlamydia. A double whammy from dear James.'

'I'm sorry.'

'It went on for years,' said Eve. 'Tests, waiting, IVF. Divorce, more IVF, another divorce.'

'Bloody hell,' said Olivia again. Although she was

thinking, this time, that they were too much, all these words. Eve had always liked words; liked taking refuge in them.

'Anyway,' said Eve. 'There'll be a baby now, I hope. One that has nothing to do with all–' She swept her hand in a grand gesture.

Did you tell James? Olivia wanted to ask. When did you tell him?

She reached a hand across the table. Imagine Eve, waiting all this time for a baby. Imagine her tiny embryo bumping along in the front seat of the Fiat that day, while Olivia held someone else's baby in her lap. Imagine another loss.

'I'm so glad it's all worked out,' she said, conscious that it wasn't enough. 'I'm glad there's a happy ending.'

'Not yet,' said Eve.

No surprise, really, that her face should be set hard.

Olivia was exhausted as she drove away up Marlow High Street. There was never any way of knowing how things would go with Eve, she thought: that had been true twenty-five years ago and it was still true now. They'd avoided what Olivia dreaded most, but in its place there had been enough shocks to dislodge her hold on the past. There was another baby to take account of, another slant on history.

But the darts of venom that had punctuated the lunch had come as a relief, in a strange sort of way. She'd been afraid of finding Eve softened, subdued, after all she'd been through. But it was clear that Eve hadn't altered so much. That essential core, sharp and selfish and clear-sighted, was still there. The part of her that expected, commanded, attention; that knew she was more highly-coloured than the great mass of humanity. Whatever else had changed, Eve still had you sitting on the edge of your seat, watching your words, hoping against hope for a smile.

As she rejoined the motorway, Olivia found her mind surveying the long years of their separation, and it was as if, when she thought of some particular event, she could feel Eve looking over her shoulder, recalling her own part in it. Visiting when Tom was born, or approving the new house, the stripping of floorboards and reinstatement of fireplaces. These flashes of false memory made Olivia's heart race with agitation as well as pleasure, and remembering that Eve hadn't been there after all, hadn't seen any of it, she felt an unaccountable sense of loss. It was as if she had lived her life without the person whose presence would have made sense of it for her. This was regret, surely. The omission of a subtle flavouring that would have made all the difference: the dash of puffer fish poison that supplied a vital piquancy Olivia couldn't do without, once she'd acquired the taste for it.

# Chapter Twenty-Five

Since the day of 'The Rose of Tralee', a gentle gloom had settled over the Wednesday Club. Kenneth had become increasingly withdrawn – fading fast, Shirley said, with her inimitable combination of compassion and gossipy curiosity.

'Funny, isn't it?' she said one morning, when the trees were almost bare and the dead leaves were layered thickly on the forecourt where Olivia parked her bike. 'He's never been the same since that day he sang with you. Like it was – you know, his last gasp.'

'His swansong,' said Olivia.

'His swansong.' Shirley nodded. 'That's a beautiful way to put it.'

He *had* been a singer, Olivia had discovered. Kenneth had told her himself, after his gala performance. He'd studied in Italy as a young man, at the conservatory in Florence, but he'd always been destined for doctoring, and after a year he'd come home to finish his medical training. After that the singing was confined to amateur

Rachel Crowther

performances. He named oratorios, a handful of operatic roles, his face animated, and Olivia wondered whose decision the return to medicine had been. A father whose parental licence had been stretched as far as it would go? A fiancée waiting for a steady doctor's salary? He might have made it as an operatic tenor, Olivia thought. Though she was a fine one to talk.

Georgie had remained subdued too, slow to recover from her stay in hospital. But this morning when Olivia smiled at her she looked back with a clear, sharp gaze.

'She's perked up,' Shirley said. 'On good form today.'

Olivia felt the same pang as on that first morning of Georgie's return, the blend of guilt and diffidence that comes from knowing someone else's secrets. She'd thought a lot about Georgie since the lunch with Eve: she'd needed the distraction; welcomed having something else to occupy her mind. But she hadn't got any closer to resolving the dilemma of what to do. Would it be better to know whether there were any relatives left alive before getting Georgie's hopes up? Or was it wrong to go poking around in someone else's life, finding their long-lost family, without their permission?

All the time she was playing the piano, Olivia pondered. Had she taken an absurd liberty, going to see Georgie's social worker? She'd been frank about her position, but Mary Baldwin might have assumed a closer connection than actually existed. True, Olivia had known Georgie for several years now, but she knew precious little about her beyond the secret history Shirley had disclosed. Not nearly enough to predict her response to what Olivia was contemplating.

Rex was helping Shirley in the kitchen when Olivia reached the end of her appointed slot. She moved casually across the room and slipped into the chair next to Georgie as if it was a spur-of-the-moment impulse. Her heart was beating fast now. Phrases turned in her head, offering themselves one after another.

'How are you today, Georgie?' she asked.

'Very well, thank you.' A schoolgirl's polite response. 'It's a beautiful day, isn't it?'

Olivia glanced up at the window, the grey-blue sky and the skeletons of trees patterned against the leaded panes. A stark sort of beauty, she thought. The voices of the playgroup children drifted over from the little yard at the back of the building; there was a sudden flurry of noise that might indicate the discovery of a beetle or a disagreement over the slide.

'My children used to go to that playgroup,' she said. 'Yesterday, it seems. Amazing how fast time passes.'

She blushed, appalled by her clumsiness. But Georgie gave a little nod of acknowledgement, and she stumbled on. There was no easy way, after all. No point looking for a connection between their lives that wouldn't seem impossibly awkward.

'Do you have family, Georgie?' she asked. 'Nieces or nephews?'

Georgie looked at her with the directness of the very old. Olivia had a sense, in that moment, that Georgie could see straight into her mind: that she was wise to all the deceptions people played on her. What was said and what was not.

'I lost touch with my family long ago,' she said.

Olivia nodded slowly. 'Perhaps you could find them again. It's easy to trace people, these days.' Georgie's face moved slightly; nothing that could really be called a smile.

'I could help you,' Olivia went on, seizing her courage. 'If you'd like to find out, I could help you.'

There was a long silence. Georgie stared straight ahead, and Olivia wondered whether her concentration had drifted, or whether she was willing Olivia to go away and stop pestering her. This is my only chance, Olivia thought: I can't bring it up again if I don't get an answer now. But perhaps Georgie's silence was enough of an answer.

Just then she caught sight of Shirley, struggling to move a table.

'Excuse me for a moment,' she said. 'Shirley needs a hand.'

She left her books on the chair beside Georgie, proof of her intention to return, smiled at Elsie and William as she passed.

'Having a chat to Georgie, were you?' Shirley asked, as they dragged chairs into place for lunch.

'I've been wondering if she has any family left,' Olivia said. 'Anyone we could trace for her.'

Shirley raised her eyebrows. 'Does she want to find them?'

'I'm not sure.'

Olivia looked back at Georgie, at the expression that seemed, at this distance, full of intelligence. There was no doubt, she thought, that Georgie was capable of understanding today, of making a judgement. That, at least, was reassuring. Her mind hadn't slipped so far into the shadows.

Even so, it was a shock when Georgie's first words, on Olivia's return, picked up their conversation exactly where it had been left.

'No,' she said. 'No, I don't think so. Let bygones be bygones.'

The look she turned on Olivia then was unmistakable. The spirit that had kept her alive for so long was clearly visible in her eyes: a defiance and a self-reliance that made Olivia shrivel. The necessary arrogance, she thought, of the survivor.

# Chapter Twenty-Six

F aith felt rather sorry for herself on the journey back from Aldeburgh. It had been a lovely weekend, she thought, but – what? Was this just the usual down-in-the-dumps feeling you got at the end of a holiday, or had there been something missing; something she'd been expecting from the trip – apart from the sunshine, of course? Something about James, perhaps. Not feeling as sure of him as she'd hoped after two days together. But that was stupid: how could she doubt anything after that last half hour?

'Thank you for taking me there,' she said.

He glanced sideways at her. 'I thought you'd like it. Everyone loves Aldeburgh. Shame we didn't get into the sea, though. Have to do that next time.'

James had found a place near Chelmsford that served food all day, according to its website, and they were both surprisingly hungry by the time they arrived. It looked promising from the outside, a pretty village pub with hanging baskets planted up for winter colour, but when they got inside there were no other customers and a sour atmosphere you couldn't mistake. The barman glowered at them as though they'd walked in on a private argument, which perhaps they had. They could hear dogs barking furiously out the back somewhere.

'Yes?' he demanded.

James and Faith exchanged glances. They ordered a drink each, downed it in a hurry and walked out again, leaving a tenner on the bar. For damages, James said, though Faith wasn't quite sure what he meant by that.

'What the hell was going on there?' he asked, as they pulled out of the car park. 'All those dogs howling?'

Faith laughed, fighting off disappointment. 'God knows.'

James raised his eyebrows. 'Perhaps they're on the menu? When he's finished cooking up his wife, that is.'

'Don't.'

As they drove through the outskirts of the village, between rows of identical grey houses strung along the main road that led to the dual carriageway, he put his hand on her knee. 'What shall we do? Try somewhere else?'

Faith wasn't exactly hungry, but she'd been looking forward to the lunch. They didn't pass anywhere else that looked open, though, and it was almost three o'clock by now, too late for even a late lunch. When they stopped for petrol on the M25, James bought some sandwiches and a couple of packets of crisps. He grinned when he saw Faith's expression.

'Oh dear,' he said. 'I've let you down. What can I do to make it up to you? Shall I take you out to dinner when we get back to Oxford?'

'Don't worry,' Faith said, although she hoped he'd insist.

'Another night, then? When are you free?'

Faith shook her head. 'I've got functions all week,' she said. 'My first free evening is next Wednesday.'

'Is that the 20th?'

Faith nodded.

'Perfect!' James grinned. 'That's my birthday. Where shall we go? Back to that Greek place?'

'Oh, no! If it's your birthday I should cook for you.'

'No need. You cook every day. Let me treat you.'

'I'd like to,' Faith insisted. 'Please. I cook for a living because I like it. And anyway, it's different cooking for you.'

James shrugged. 'If that's what you want,' he said.

'Shall I bring it to yours?' She hadn't been to his house yet. She didn't even know exactly where it was, except somewhere in the posh bit of North Oxford. She was curious to see what it was like.

'I've got builders in next week, I'm afraid. Dust sheets everywhere. I could come to you straight after work, though. Six thirty-ish?'

'Seven,' said Faith. 'Then I'll be cleared up and ready.'

She leaned her head across the gap between them, aiming for his shoulder but finding herself propped at an awkward angle against his elbow. She extracted herself with a little wriggle and they both laughed and things felt better.

'Shall we have some music on?' said James. 'Less than an hour now, I reckon.'

Faith cleared the afternoon of 20th November to cook for James. She put on the CD of Katie Melua he'd given her and put a bottle of white wine in the fridge so she could pour herself a glass when it got to six o'clock. She rarely drank anything when she was cooking for clients, but there was nothing nicer than a glass of cold Chardonnay while you did the finishing touches.

She'd spent ages thinking about what to make. It was like miniature painting, she'd thought, cooking for two. And that had given her an idea. She'd make everything extra-small, a taster menu with eight or nine bite-sized courses. All things she could prepare in advance, so she wouldn't have to keep jumping up and down while they were eating.

She'd had so many ideas that it had been almost impossible to choose, but in the end she'd got it down to a selection she was happy with. An amuse-bouche first, foie gras on little circles of fried toast with caperberries on top. Soup, served in espresso cups: chestnut and field mushroom with truffle oil. Then ceviche, made with thin slices of Dover sole and salmon, marinaded in lime juice and ginger, served with a dash of soy sauce and a hint of wasabi. As a savoury, mini cheese muffins, made in petit four cases, slipped into the oven when she got the soup out. A pink grapefruit sorbet to clear the palate, one melon-ball-sized scoop each in a shot glass, followed by miniature beef Wellingtons and baby vegetables: new potatoes the size of cherries, leeks narrow as cigarettes. Chocolate soufflé served in egg cups, white and dark swirled together and garnished with morello cherries. A cheese board filled with whole, tiny cheeses, crottins and mini mozzarella balls and a few others she'd found in the cheese shop in the Covered Market, and then doll's house sized petits fours: minute rounds of shortcake topped with slivers of crystallised orange peel and dipped in melted chocolate; blocks of fudge cut so small you almost needed tweezers to pick them up.

So much effort, she thought, for such a small volume of food. Erica would think she was mad. But Erica had gone away for a few days with her new boyfriend – Scarborough or somewhere. Not as classy as Aldeburgh, Faith told herself smugly, though maybe one bit of sea was much like another, if it was in England in the middle of winter. Anyhow, if Erica didn't understand the pleasure of putting so much care into preparing a meal for someone, she was missing something. Faith felt like a geisha, lavishing her skills on James's pleasure, and the thought made her melt inside, just like the fudge she'd allowed herself to taste earlier on.

By six o'clock she'd finished most of the preparations. Just the garnishing left to do, the presentation and decoration that would turn what she'd made into a work of art. An exhibition, she thought with satisfaction, carefully planned so not just the flavours but the colours and shapes and textures followed one another in a pleasing way. Oh, she was good at this.

She poured herself a glass of wine and lifted her best plates down from the cupboard. She'd bought tiny pink rosebuds for the table and dug out the linen cloth she'd brought back from Ireland one time. The table was the perfect size for two: with any more guests, she had to serve buffet-style, plates on knees.

At six thirty she had a shower, opening a new bottle of ginseng shower gel, then blow-dried her hair and slipped on the dress she'd bought for the occasion. You always needed little black dresses, as her mum was fond of saying, and her old faithful felt spoiled from being worn to serve up at so many functions.

By seven she was absolutely ready, Katie Melua back on the CD player, another dash of wine poured into her glass. She'd bought James a book about the British coast, since he seemed so keen on the seaside, and it lay on the dining table beside the rosebuds and the candlestick.

James was often a bit late, and she knew he couldn't always ring if he was still at the hospital, but at seven thirty she began to wish she'd gone with his suggestion of six thirty. Maybe that way he'd have got away a bit earlier. Perhaps she'd have another glass of wine now, anyway, to keep her occupied. So she didn't feel so twitchy, sitting waiting.

When eight o'clock came she felt a twinge of annoyance – not at James, of course, no one would willingly miss their own birthday celebration – but at the job that kept him tied up so late, and so unpredictably. At whatever crisis had delayed him. Wasn't there anyone else who could deal with it? Surely he wasn't on duty, not on his birthday? It must be a private patient, she thought, some demanding woman who thought she could buy his attention at any time of day or night, sod her.

It was surprising how soon she realised he wasn't coming. Near the end of the bottle of wine, a moment of clarity: he must have forgotten, because he'd certainly have rung her by now, otherwise.

And another thought: could it really be his birthday, because who would forget what they were meant to be doing on their birthday? But why would he tell her it was, though, if it wasn't? To make it feel like a special occasion? To make her feel special because he wanted to spend his birthday with her?

Faith lurched to her feet, walking awkwardly now in her heels. A small part of her wanted to tip all the food in the bin, just to show how much it didn't matter, all that effort, and how much it did. But her professional instincts ran a checklist: ceviche, beef, soufflé mix and cheese would all keep in the fridge. The sorbet was already in the freezer. She was hungry now, and she ate the amuse-bouches and the petits fours, all of them, including the spares she'd made in case James wanted seconds, standing in the middle of the kitchen. One, two, three, four, five, six, seven, eight, one by one, straight after each other.

She'd opened the red wine in advance, as James had taught her. She poured herself a glass now and drank it to wash down the petits fours, then followed it with another. What did you say, the austerity of the fruit aromas? The full-bodied finish of the flinty whatnot? She ladled the soup into espresso cups and drank it down: delicious, the flavouring perfect even without the truffle oil which she'd been going to drizzle on at the last minute. One, two, three, four espresso cups. Lucky he wasn't coming now, because the food was going fast. And the wine. She opened up the freezer and scooped out a dollop of sorbet which she ate straight from the spoon, and then she opened the fridge and took a handful of the dainty crottins and stuffed them in her mouth. What a stupid idea, she thought, food in such small bites you can barely taste it.

She hardly heard the doorbell ringing the next morning. No one ever rang her bell: why did they have to choose today? She pulled the covers up over her head and shouted at them to go away. She'd been in the middle of a dream, a weird dream where armies of tiny cupcakes and pork pies were circling her, blowing whistles.

No, that was definitely the doorbell. Bugger it, what was it? The police, to ring so bloody-mindedly, not giving up and going away?

'All right!' she shouted, her voice thick and croaky. 'All right, I'm coming.'

In the few seconds it took to cross the floor, her sluggish brain thought out options. Erica, back from Scarborough early. Her mum, about some family crisis. Oh God, the flat looked dreadful. She must have knocked into the table on her way to bed, spilt the water and scattered the flowers on the floor, the poor blameless rosebuds. And there were dirty plates all over the kitchen, as though there'd been a whole rugby team through here last night, making merry.

James. The one person she didn't expect, in his best suit and polished brogues. She put words in his mouth, in the moment she stood staring at him: I can explain, he'd say, or, you must be furious, or even, can you ever forgive me?

But he didn't say anything. He stood there, looking at her, and then he laughed, and she laughed, even though she knew she looked terrible, and he came down the last steps and shut the door behind him and took her in his arms.

'God, you look good when you're hungover,' he said eventually, when he'd kissed her and held her for a while and taken in the chaos in the kitchen. 'Did you have a good time all on your own, my poor little love?'

'No,' said Faith.

'Well, I suppose I'm glad to hear that.' He held her at arm's length then, looked at her seriously. 'I've got an hour,' he said. 'I've cancelled all my new patients this morning. Shall I come and crawl into bed with you, or shall we clear up some of this mess?'

Faith didn't remember the call she'd made to his mobile in the middle of the night, but he was glad she'd rung, James told her, even if it had been a bit tricky understanding what she was saying. He'd been so tied up he might not have realised what an ass he'd been until it was too late to make amends.

'So what was going on, to make you forget your birthday?'

'A bizarre situation.' His voice was crooning and soft, his shirt-sleeve arms wrapped around her. 'Something you don't expect these days. A young woman turned up at the hospital with a massive post-partum haemorrhage and no record of delivery.'

'A post what?'

'Heavy bleeding after giving birth. But as far as we knew she hadn't given birth. No baby. No record of her in the maternity unit.'

'Maybe she had it somewhere else.'

'Her parents insisted there was no baby. Said she'd never been pregnant. She'd gone away for a night to stay with a friend and when she came back in the morning she was poorly, and the next thing they knew there was blood everywhere.'

'So where was the baby?'

'Someone found it early this morning. Abandoned somewhere in Blackbird Leys.'

Faith curled against him as he recounted the details. She felt warm and safe; the muddle of last night didn't matter any more, now he was here. She could see the funny side of it, all that doll-sized food sitting waiting in the fridge.

'Is the baby OK?' she asked.

'I'm afraid not.'

'What about the mother?'

'She'll be fine. Needed a lot of blood, a bit of stitching, but she'll be fine.'

Faith pushed herself up on her elbow and craned her neck round to look at James. 'So will it be in the papers, then?' she asked. 'Will you be in them? Local hero?'

James smiled faintly and lifted a finger to stroke her cheek. 'She's only fourteen, the mother. It'll be covered by a confidentiality order – no publicity, to protect her. But I'll be your hero, if you like.'

# Chapter Twenty-Seven

## 1983

The weather had stayed squally throughout their week in Aldeburgh. Every morning Olivia hoped they might wake to find the clouds had been blown away, but there was never more than an hour or two of milky sunshine before the rain returned.

While Eve was ill it hadn't mattered so much. Olivia had been happy to potter around the house or to brave the short walk to the beach, and James seemed to have an inexhaustible list of errands to occupy him: a new washer for the kitchen sink, a broken shelf in the bathroom. Olivia found his industriousness oddly restful. While he came and went she tinkered with the old piano, amused by the translation of Beethoven and Schubert into honky-tonk. She imagined she could hear the rustle of waves and the wail of seagulls in the piano's rusty workings. Decades of sun-bleached Junes and stormy Januaries, she thought, since it was last tuned. She looked out on the little garden at the back of the house and daydreamed about being here in the full heat of summer, lying on a deckchair on the straggly lawn.

But a sense of restlessness had descended on the house since Eve had emerged from her bed.

'It's practically autumn,' Eve said on the morning after the big storm, the well-intentioned supper spoiled by that uncomfortable conversation about the Torhousekie stalker. She was standing in the kitchen, shivering theatrically in the threadbare dressing gown she'd found on the back of a door. 'It feels too early for the summer to be over. It hasn't even been my birthday yet.'

Eve's birthday was on August 28th, right at the end of the school holidays. Eve always used to bring a cake to school at the beginning of term, and woe betide anyone who'd forgotten to buy her a birthday present.

'We could have a party,' Olivia said. 'Go out for supper or something.'

'It's my half-birthday too, on Monday,' said James. He stopped, waiting for them to react.

'The 29th?' said Olivia. 'You must be a leap year baby, then.'

'What do you mean?' Eve frowned.

'If someone's half-birthday is the 29th of August,' Olivia explained, 'they must have been born on the 29th of February.'

Olivia had thought that Eve would be delighted to share a celebration with James, but she shrugged dismissively, as if to say that a half-birthday was a secondary consideration.

'I feel like a game,' she said. 'Is there a Monopoly set here?'

Something in Olivia's upbringing, the trace of Protestant asceticism, made Monopoly after breakfast feel rather louche. But James brought the box down from the top of a bookshelf and they set it up on the kitchen table.

'Bags I the boat,' said James.

Eve played aggressively, buying everything she landed on and building houses as soon as she could, but the luck of the dice went Olivia's way. Within half an hour she had Park Lane and Mayfair and three of the four stations.

'Lucky sod,' said Eve, as Olivia's Scottie dog landed on Piccadilly.

'Not so lucky. I've got Leicester Square already.' James waved the card as proof, grinning at Olivia. 'But we could go into partnership. What do you say, oh mistress of the board?'

'Not allowed.' Eve scowled.

'I'll leave it,' said Olivia. 'Don't want to overextend myself.'

'There's a surprise.'

Olivia was an only child, but she'd played enough Monopoly to know that every family had an Eve in it. Monopoly, she thought, was definitely not the right choice for this occasion.

After a few more minutes James yawned. 'I could do with stretching my legs,' he said.

'It's pouring still.' Eve was facing the window; the others followed her glance towards the rain-streaked glass. 'We can't go out in that.'

'How about hide-and-seek?' James gave Eve a beseeching look, disarmingly boyish. 'Just for a break. We can come back to this. It's a great house for hide-and-seek.'

'Sardines,' Eve bargained.

Olivia shrugged her shoulders. Three people wasn't enough for either, but she was happy to leave the Monopoly board for a while.

'Sardines,' said Eve again. 'You hide, James, and we'll look for you. Come on, Olivia, we'll go and count.'

The downstairs cloakroom doubled as a laundry room, with an old top-loading washing machine and a drying frame suspended from the ceiling. On the wall, racks held sou'westers, fishing rods and the other paraphernalia of seaside holidays, smelling of salt and damp winters.

The two girls hadn't been alone together for several days, except for Olivia's fleeting visits to Eve's sickbed. Olivia was conscious of an awkwardness between them. Watching Eve count aloud, Olivia felt a sudden urge to reach out and take her hand. But Eve had got to fifty already.

'You go first,' she said. 'I'll wait a bit longer. We have to keep out of each other's way or it won't be any fun.'

Olivia looked in the kitchen first. There were a couple of full-height cupboards, but James wasn't in either of them, nor wedged behind the high-backed chair in the corner. As she went through to the garden room at the back, she heard Eve heading up the stairs, and she felt an odd mixture of excitement and detachment: they were too old for this, part of her said; it was a silly thing to be doing in the middle of the morning. But something about concealment, about the chase and the quarry, stirred a primitive thrill in her belly.

The garden room was still and silent. Faded cushions slumped deep in the seats of old wicker chairs, and a heavy sideboard leaned against the wall, its doors swollen tight. After a cursory glance, Olivia doubled back through the kitchen and into the sitting room. The ash from last night's fire fluttered in the draught, spilling the scent of charcoal into the air.

When she reached the first floor, she could hear Eve searching the bedrooms. Olivia glanced into the airing cupboard outside the bathroom, piled high with folded sheets and towels, then climbed the second flight of stairs. She and Eve had explored the top floor on their first evening, but they hadn't ventured this far again. The furnishings were sparser up here: the attic bedrooms, presumably intended for children, contained nothing but bunk beds and frayed rag rugs. But on the landing stood an ornately carved blanket box, made of some dark old-fashioned wood. Olivia lifted the lid carefully and there was James, half-sitting, half-squatting in the bottom. He grinned and raised a finger to his lips, then held the lid open so Olivia could climb in.

The box was empty, but even so there was only just room for the two of them. When James let the lid down it was very dark, only a peephole of light where the key should have been.

'OK?' he whispered, so quietly that it was almost not a sound at all.

Olivia nodded. In the darkness her hearing felt heightened, like a bat's. She shifted her limbs carefully and felt laughter welling up inside her – the gurgling, childish laughter of suspense, but something else as well, something skittish and secretive that she knew she shouldn't examine too closely. Then she felt James's arms threading around her, helping to settle her into a more comfortable position. As she lay back against him to ease her arm out from behind her she heard Eve's footsteps on the stairs and she froze, curled in James's arms, so that when Eve flung open the lid that was how she found them: wedged into the blanket box like twin foetuses, looking up blankly at the sudden light.

'Oh,' said Eve, staring down. She held the lid half-open for a few seconds and Olivia thought she might let it drop again with a crash, but instead she lifted it back against the wall so they could climb out. 'My turn to hide, then.'

'Why don't we stay here to count?' said James. 'Give you more choice.'

Eve frowned. 'You'll be able to hear how far down I've gone,' she said. But she lowered the lid of the box reluctantly, sealing Olivia and James in the dark again.

Whatever that illicit pleasure had been, in the few seconds before Eve discovered them, it was magnified now. Olivia was uncomfortably aware of its effect – on her, on Eve, and even, possibly, on James. While he counted, they both stayed so still that their immobility seemed to communicate something: an awareness of their closeness and of the pressure of their bodies against each other; the implication of even the smallest movement. When James reached fifty he paused, squeezed Olivia's waist gently, then lifted her away from him and reached up for the lid.

Olivia went first, this time, scampering down the stairs like a child released from its room after a punishment: light-footed, sharply conscious of the risk of further trangression. Her head spun with freedom and danger. She paused on the landing, collecting herself. It would be better to let James find Eve first. She pushed open the door of the master bedroom, where James had been sleeping; an unlikely place for Eve to hide, she thought.

The sheets were tumbled on the double bed. For a moment Olivia thought she could make out a form under the covers and her heart throbbed at the thought of Eve burrowing into James's bed, waiting for him to come and find her there, but there was nothing but heaped up pillows. She let out a little giggle and as she did so she heard James's footsteps, heard him hesitate outside the door and then go on down the stairs, and her cheeks burned with the threat of discovery.

Then there was another noise, a tiny creak from the built-in wardrobes that covered one side of the room. Olivia stood silent, her eyes straying over the dressing table with its floral skirt, the mantelpiece littered with forgotten treasures, as she waited for another clue. She glanced through the bay windows and noticed that the rain had stopped, that the sea was lying slate-blue and tranquil beyond the beach.

Eve was in the wardrobe, she was sure about that, and she ought to walk away and leave her for James to find. But instead she tiptoed across the room, past the chair where James's suitcase lay open, until she was standing in front of the first of the wardrobe doors. Was this really what Eve wanted – to be found, brazen, in James's room? Olivia reached a hand to the wooden handle and pulled. Inside, coats and jackets gave off a smell of mothballs and old wool. She rustled her hands between the clothes and, finding nothing, closed the door gently.

Another hesitation; another chance to walk away. The next door opened onto a tall stack of shelves, some fitted with drawers. Nowhere for anyone to hide in there. Olivia shut it again quickly and before she had time to think she pulled the third door open and there was Eve, shrouded in summer dresses, staring at her in disbelief. Olivia stared back, and within a second Eve's expression evaporated.

'You took your time,' she said. 'You've been in the room for ages.'

Olivia grinned sheepishly.

'Get in, then. There's plenty of room.'

Olivia found herself in the dark again, wedged against Eve, steeped in the subtle, stifling scent of old perfume. The texture of silk against her hair and her cheeks was soft but insistent, like the wings of a butterfly folded around them both, and she could hear Eve's breathing, steady and shallow.

The wait seemed longer this time, not full of suspense or anticipation but something duller. Long childhood afternoons, Olivia thought; empty rooms stippled with dust motes. She could detect nothing in Eve now except a sort of neutrality that might signal resignation.

But when James finally opened the door Eve burst out like a jack-in-the-box.

'Boo!' she said, her face strained into an expression of surprise. 'Two skeletons in your closet!'

James gave a brief smile. 'There you are,' he said. 'Are you desperate for a go, Olivia, or shall we have lunch?'


Olivia helped James get things out of the fridge: bread and cheese, the remains of a salad they'd had the previous night.

'We need to go shopping,' he said.

Olivia looked guiltily at the empty shelves. They had let James provide for them all week, she thought. No tinned sardines or horrible jam for days.

'I could do that, after lunch,' she said. 'And we should cook, tonight. You've done loads.'

'Listen to you two,' scoffed Eve, sliding the Monopoly

board along the table intact, as though they might resume later. 'Just like an old couple. *What shall we have tonight, dear?*'

'You're welcome to contribute,' James said shortly. He sat down at the table and reached for the bread knife. 'The weather's looking up. We could walk along the coast path towards Thorpeness this afternoon.'

'Where's that?' asked Eve. 'I don't feel like walking too far.'

'There's a map somewhere,' James said.

'I'll get ours from the car,' offered Olivia.

'That's a road atlas, not a walking map,' said Eve.

'Better than nothing,' said James. 'Wait until you've finished, though, Olivia. There's no rush.'

But Olivia was suddenly desperate to be outside. She ate her sandwich as fast as she could, then she put her plate in the sink and slipped out of the front door, leaving Eve and James facing each other across the table.

The car was parked very close to the house, but she didn't go straight to it. Instead, she went down onto the beach and stood on the ridge of wet shingle, letting the sea air fill her lungs. She thought of James's hands holding her, and Eve's body pressed against her, and she stretched her arms wide into the buffeting breeze and let it support her, alone on the wide swathe of shore.

It had been a good summer, she thought, a very good summer, but she was glad it was nearly over. In a couple of days she and Eve would head south again, and then she'd fly to Dubai to spend a fortnight with her parents. That thought made her happy – the prospect of being away from Eve and James and the depressing monochrome of this coastline – but at the same time she felt a wrench of betrayal. She remembered the three doors of the wardrobe, and how she had opened each of them in turn, pressed on until Eve was exposed.

For a few more minutes she stood looking along the beach, her gaze taking in the now-familiar landmarks of the town, and then she turned slowly and made her way back to the car.

The atlas was lying on the passenger seat. It was dog-eared from a summer of use; a reminder of the fun they'd had, she and Eve, and all the places they'd visited. Olivia slammed the car door and crossed the road again to Shearwater House.

As soon as she pushed open the front door she could hear Eve shouting. Before that, perhaps: the harmonics that hover above the human voice, a primitive warning system for conflict. Bracing herself, she went on down the passage to the kitchen, letting the words fly past her.

They didn't stop when she came in. Olivia put the map book down on a chair and stood uncertainly by the door, wondering whether to intervene or to stay out of range.

'I didn't ask you to come and join us,' Eve was saying – a sob, almost.

'You'd hardly be here without me.' James had seen Olivia: was his tone gentler because of it?

Suddenly Eve burst into tears. 'Fuck you,' she shouted, the words shocking on her lips. 'I don't want to be here any more, anyway.' She swivelled round. 'Come on, Olivia, we're going.'

'Going?' Olivia didn't move. 'Packing up?'

'Just going,' said Eve. 'Away. Out. Are you coming or not?'

# Chapter Twenty-Eight

## 2008

One Monday morning at the beginning of December, when ice had spread across Port Meadow, Olivia abandoned her usual walking route and made instead for the middle of town. Along St Giles, the ancient buildings stood staunch against the vicissitudes of the weather. Olivia looked up at the familiar wonder of turrets and gargoyles dramatic against the fretful sky. Below them, the city pursued its business. The streets were filled with Christmas shoppers, the pubs and cafés doing a steady trade, and the hoarding around the Ashmolean made cheerful claims for the improvements underway inside.

Walking in the city centre felt strange, Olivia thought. Following the course of the river, the turn of the seasons, didn't require any justification, but among all these buildings and busy people she felt the lack of a purpose. She turned left into Broad Street, past Blackwells and the King's Arms, then halted in front of the beautiful façade of the Holywell Music Room. Twenty years ago she'd given a recital here, and held a masterclass in the

Sheldonian, just along the road. That was hard to believe now. Had she been too ready, she wondered, to make sacrifices for motherhood? Other people kept playing when they had children: had she been too greedy, bearing four boys in such close succession? Or too fearful of failure, as a mother if not as a pianist?

The smell of coffee bloomed invitingly from a tiny café, offering a welcome distraction. There were only three tables, but one of them was empty. Olivia ordered an espresso and took a copy of *The Independent* from the rack beside the counter. At the next table, a young couple talked in low voices that proclaimed the vital importance of whatever they were discussing; beyond them, a man her own age spoke loudly into a mobile phone. Olivia half-listened, wondering about these people's lives, and how they came to be sitting here in the middle of the morning.

'Espresso?'

The waitress smiled as she set the little white cup down, and Olivia recognised her as a contemporary of Tom's, the daughter of one of those baby-group friends who had disappeared rapidly back to her law firm. The girl was called Imogen, Olivia remembered. A phrase hovered on her lips – *Are you...?* – but she didn't speak it. Too complicated; too many years to fill in. Instead she smiled her thanks and let her gaze dip back to the newspaper.

Although she scanned the news with an appearance of attention, Olivia's thoughts drifted away – lighting, as they had done so often lately, on Eve. Several times since that lunch in Marlow she'd thought of picking up the phone, to propose another meeting or simply to hear Eve's voice again, but each time something had stopped her. A kind of shyness, you could call it; the difficulty of being such familiar strangers. But she knew that was only part of the answer.

The businessman concluded his phone call with a hearty laugh, stared at the phone for a moment as though surprised by its sudden silence, then slipped it into his top pocket and pushed his seat back.

'Excuse me,' he said, when he knocked Olivia's chair on his way out, but he didn't look down at her.

'No problem,' said Olivia. She caught the waitress's eye and they both smiled. Nice girl, Olivia thought. Nice smile. Funny how you came across people again. So many people, lately.

But without Sarah, what was the chance that she and Eve would have met again? Would Eve ever have sought her out, after she came back to England? The bonds between them were hard to fathom, Olivia thought. That conversation over lunch had seemed momentous at the time, but the things that remained unsaid, unmentioned, still loomed large; the ghosts they might never lay to rest. Perhaps they had long ago passed the point where ordinary friendship would ever be possible again.

She caught the waitress's eye and ordered another espresso, even though the caffeine was making her head spin. What possible futures, she wondered as she sipped it, might there be for her and Eve? It was entirely possible that they'd never see each other again. That lunch might turn out to be a bizarre epilogue to their friendship: something she'd scarcely believe in after a while. But if there *was* another meeting, what would it be like? Would the past be pushed aside entirely this time, or would Eve's new taste for truth-telling prevail?

Each of these possibilities filled Olivia with a

different kind of horror. The long silence between them hadn't changed anything, she realised: it had merely delayed the moment of choice. She knew instinctively that the choice would fall not to her, but to Eve – and Eve surely knew it too, whether she attributed her precedence to Olivia's lack of courage or to some complicated equation of blame and guilt.

But perhaps Eve had made her choice already. Perhaps she'd said all she wanted to. Each day that passed, Olivia decided, made it more likely that she would never hear from Eve again, and the thought made her feel both giddily relieved and utterly bereft.

When the phone rang that afternoon, Olivia picked it up without a thought. But in the instant before she heard the voice on the other end she knew it was going to be Eve's. They'd never spoken much on the telephone: it felt like a dream where you meet someone who's been dead for years.

'I've got a date,' Eve said. 'To go to China.'

'For a baby?'

'Of course for a baby. They've sent the details. Photos.'

'My goodness.'

'Can I come and see you?'

Eve sounded tremulous; Olivia's heart raced in sympathy. She'd made everything too complicated, she thought. She'd let it all fester and ferment.

'Of course. Any time. Robert's away for a couple of days: come for supper.'

'Tonight?'

Olivia made rapid calculations. She had pupils from

four until six, but she could get to the shops now before
Benjy got back. She looked around her kitchen, imagining
Eve here.

'Sure.'

'Sure?'

Olivia could hear Eve reading her mind, wondering at
the juggling and scurrying that went into a simple
arrangement.

'Yes,' she said. 'Seven-ish?'

# Chapter Twenty-Nine

'I had trouble parking,' Eve said. There she was, standing on the doorstep. Coming into the house.

Olivia held the door wide. 'I've got a vistor's permit, if you need it.'

Eve shook her head. 'I found a space round the corner.' She looked up at the ceiling. 'This is nice. It's exactly the kind of house I imagined you living in.'

'A pigsty?' Olivia's laugh sounded nervous.

'A proper house. Original features.'

'Boringly conventional.'

'Why not?' Eve looked straight at her, and Olivia quailed, recognising too late her own tactlessness. 'If you can be conventional, why not?'

Benjy was sitting at the kitchen table with his Nintendo. Olivia was absurdly grateful, at that moment, for the presence of her youngest son.

'This is Eve, Benjy,' she said. 'She was at school with me.'

Benjy looked up, briefly curious. 'Hi,' he said.

'Hi, Benjy.' Eve had that over-careful tone children

pick up instantly, like an animal recognising a scent. She stared at him for a few moments. 'Sweet child,' she said.

He did look like an angel, his blond hair wild, narrow shoulders hunched inside his school jumper, but Olivia could tell Eve was already fixed on her own image of a child. A little Chinese girl.

'So show me the pictures,' she said.

The photos were better than Olivia expected, close-up shots of the baby's face. She had beautiful eyes that looked directly, untroubled, at the camera.

'Her name's Huan,' Eve said. 'It means happiness. Let's hope that's prophetic.'

'She's a darling,' Olivia said, but part of her was bewildered by the idea of this child becoming Eve's daughter. A child she knew nothing about, who could have belonged to anyone. What an extraordinary thing to do. Especially for Eve to do.

Eve was looking at her, waiting for something more.

'How old is she?' Olivia asked.

'Six months. I'm lucky, they're often older. A year or more in an orphanage is a terrible thought.'

Eve was frowning now; looking to her as the expert, perhaps. Olivia wasn't used to that idea. 'D'you want a drink?' she asked. 'A glass of wine?'

'There's all this stuff about early interaction,' Eve said, taking the photographs back while Olivia busied herself with glasses and a corkscrew. She was wearing another of her flowing outfits, in some grey material that Olivia imagined had been more expensive than it looked. She didn't look dressed for motherhood, Olivia thought; and then she thought, what a ridiculous notion. What were mothers supposed to look like?

'The neuronal patterns get established within the first year,' Eve went on. 'Don't you think that's important?'

Olivia remembered this feeling of walking a tightrope, second-guessing Eve's train of thought.

'But there's more to childhood than the first six months,' she said. She thought of Georgie; of the way people could be damaged at any age.

Eve shook her head. 'They're hideously under-resourced. You can imagine.'

'Isn't she lucky to get you, then?' Olivia handed Eve a glass. 'Cheers,' she said, 'and hurray for Huan,' although the toast sounded wrong, once she'd said it. Too flippant and too earnest, all at once.

'Odd how things end up,' said Eve. 'Still, you've done exactly what we all imagined.'

'All?'

'At school,' Eve said. She lifted the wine glass, considered its contents. 'You were always going to get married and have hundreds of children.'

'I was going to be a concert pianist,' Olivia protested.

Eve laughed. 'Since when? You were an earth-mother in training at thirteen.'

There was no point rising, Olivia thought. Even less point now. Another memory: never being sure whether Eve's throwaway remarks were meant to be hurtful.

The oven timer sounded, breaking the silence. Olivia had wanted to cook something imaginative, but it was safer to fall back on the things you could do blindfold. She lifted a casserole dish out of the oven, releasing reassuring wafts of bolognese sauce, and set it down on the side.

'Top up?' she asked.

'Better pace myself. I'm driving.'

'You could always stay.'

It was a reflex; the kind of thing you said without thinking. But when Eve didn't answer Olivia turned her head and caught an unfamiliar expression on her face. Wanting something, Olivia thought. And perhaps not quite wanting to admit it.

'We've got a spare room,' she said, wondering even as she heard the words whether she would regret pressing the invitation. 'I'm not going anywhere tomorrow morning.'

Eve didn't smile. 'I suppose I could,' she said.

Olivia turned back to the stove, her hands suddenly clumsy. She didn't know what to think now: was Eve lonely, or frightened? Perhaps she'll never leave, she thought, as she filled a pan with water. Perhaps she'll move in here with her little girl, like the plot of some big-hearted film.

Eve was better with the boys than Olivia expected. She talked to Tom about his university applications and was charmed by Alastair, as everyone was. Angus told jokes: progressively dirtier jokes from *Family Guy*, his latest passion. Even Benjy joined in, describing *The Sims* in patient detail. Olivia's head hurt after a while, from tension and tiredness and everyone talking at once, but she felt proud of them, nonetheless. Even of Eve, coping with culture shock. Which of the options she'd considered in the coffee shop would this count as, she wondered, with a shaft of self-deprecation?

After supper the boys disappeared, ignoring Olivia's remonstrations about washing up. Olivia gestured resignation.

'At least I don't have to put them to bed any more,' she

said. 'No more scrabbling around for toothbrushes and pyjama bottoms.' She scraped back her chair and started clearing the last things off the table. They'd finished a bottle of wine already.

'Do you miss all that?' Eve asked. 'The baby bit?'

'Sometimes. It's weird to think they'll be more or less gone, the lot of them, by the time I'm fifty.'

It was a shock to hear herself saying these things to Eve. It was as though the conversations she'd run in her head over the last few weeks were being played live; as though some interminable rehearsal was over. She took another bottle of wine out of the rack on the side. She'd have a hangover tomorrow, but it was worth it. She felt a twinge of guilt about Sarah, usurped by her old adversary, but it didn't last. Eve was Eve. Back from the dead.

'Maybe you could adopt a baby too,' Eve said.

Olivia laughed. 'Robert would hit the roof. Four lots of university fees to pay already.'

'A little girl,' Eve wheedled.

Olivia shook her head. I've had my turn, she wanted to say, but that was obvious, tactless even.

'Didn't you ever want a daughter?'

Eve always did have a way of probing, Olivia thought. Pressing James about his family, not realising there were things he didn't want to talk about, that had nothing to do with her. Though perhaps this had everything to do with her. She forced the tip of the corkscrew through the foil, her back to Eve, and waited to see where the conversation was going.

'Four boys – that came as a bit of a surprise,' Eve said. 'I always thought of you with girls.'

Olivia sat down, placing the wine on the table between them.

'I always thought of you with that baby, I suppose,' Eve said. 'The phone box baby. The way you held her.'

'Her' was the word that struck Olivia. At the time, Eve had said 'it'. Olivia thought of Eve's unborn baby again, of the fact that Eve had been pregnant before her. She thought of that last night in Aldeburgh, holding Eve in the dark, and the tiny creature that had been lodged inside her. She felt her heartbeat quickening.

'Yes,' she said.

Go on, she meant. Truth or dare: I'm ready for it now. Somewhere upstairs she could hear the thump of rock music; a strange reassurance.

'The pelican mother,' Eve said. 'That's you to a tee, isn't it? Piercing your breast for your babies. For any babies you could get your hands on, back then.'

'What do you mean?'

Eve laughed. 'Of course, I forget you're not Catholic. Don't you have pelicans in your churches? The mother surrounded by chicks, wounding her breast to feed them her own blood? They thought that's what pelicans did, before they understood that they kept fish in their bills for their young. It was too good an image to waste, anyway. Self-sacrificing parental love, like the sacrifice of Christ for his flock.'

'I've never heard of that.' Olivia's heart was beating fast. It was clear from Eve's tone that they were heading for danger.

'Olivia the pelican,' Eve said again, the edge of mockery in her voice stronger this time. 'Whereas I, of course, am a partridge. A stealer of other birds' eggs.'

'Is that—'

'More medieval iconography,' Eve said. 'The

partridge steals other birds' eggs to raise as her own. Unless they die first, of course.'

Olivia tried to speak again, but Eve silenced her with an impatient flick of her hand.

'I know you thought I was vile that day,' she said. 'Heartless.'

'No,' Olivia said, although she knew there was no point in denying it.

'Perhaps knowing I was pregnant alters things a bit, but even so. You'd have been even more full of anguish if you were pregnant, wouldn't you? Even more zealous to help her.'

All of a sudden Olivia felt horribly sober. Did she really have the courage for this? She could feel herself chickening out already, before they'd even begun.

'It's a long time ago,' she said at last.

'I want you to know I'm not a monster,' Eve said. 'I want you to believe I'm going to be a decent mother, and that I deserve this chance. This baby.'

'Of course you are. Of course you do.'

'It doesn't work out for the partridge,' Eve said. 'The stolen babies fly back to their real mothers when they hear their cries.'

Olivia could feel herself trembling. Eve's vulnerability had always frightened her more than Eve's manipulations.

'You're not a partridge,' she said. 'And the phone box baby has nothing to do with yours – with Huan.'

Eve picked up her wine glass then put it down again roughly, slopping wine onto the bare surface of the table.

'All that week, I watched James looking at you.'

Again, a change of tack Olivia wasn't ready for. 'James?'

'Maybe you didn't mean to lead him on. Maybe you didn't even realise what the game was, until that last day. You must remember that: how I found you in the blanket box on the top landing, wrapped in each other's arms.'

Olivia remembered the smell of the wardrobe where she'd stood shoulder to shoulder with Eve, the lingering scent of adult lives. She remembered the rest of that day too, every detail of it. She'd lived through it time after time, grasping at the primitive belief that enough effort of will, enough regret and remorse and repentance, could change the way things had ended up.

'It was just sardines,' she said. But Eve ignored her.

'I'd known I was pregnant for a while,' she said, her voice preternaturally calm. 'I should have known, anyway; I did my best to ignore it. But then I couldn't ignore it any more, the nausea and the tiredness, being upset by the least thing.'

The man at the stone circle, Olivia remembered. The rows that had become more frequent as the summer went on.

Outside, a siren raced past on the main road.

'I bought a test after we got to Aldeburgh. I was ill, do you remember?' Eve gave a little ironic emphasis to the word 'ill'. 'I lay in bed and hoped it would go away. Things were different back then. I wasn't sure whether they'd let me back into medical school with a baby. I wasn't even sure I was going to tell James. But every time I saw him looking at you–'

Olivia shook her head slightly, almost involuntarily, and Eve looked straight at her, something close to hatred in her eyes. Olivia remembered that last night, the wine and the family secrets, and she blushed crimson.

Eve raised her eyebrows, letting the silence harden for

a moment. 'I had an image of us,' she said. 'Me and him and the baby. I wasn't sure it was what I wanted, but I didn't want it taken away from me, either.'

She stopped, took a mouthful of wine and swilled it down. Olivia noticed the lines around her neck, the definite way she'd aged. Almost as if someone had taken the Eve she knew and applied layers of stage make-up, a dash of grey to her hair. For a moment she felt it wasn't quite convincing, this disguise; that the old Eve was still underneath, waiting to peel back the mask.

'Then there was that other baby,' Eve said. 'The phone box baby. God, I don't know if I can tell you what that felt like. The reality of it, showing me what I was carrying around inside me. What I was planning to kill.'

Olivia couldn't speak. She had assumed that the tragedy of that day was all hers; that Eve had been untouched by the guilt, the repercussions.

'You can accuse me of whatever you like,' Eve said, 'but you took away the possibility of my family. Even if I could have talked James into standing by me, how could I do it when I knew he preferred you – even you – to me?'

Olivia lifted her eyes to meet Eve's and saw that she was shaking.

'He was horrible.' Eve made a noise that could have been a sob or a choke of anger. 'I told him that night, after we got back from the hospital. You went to bed, and I knew I had to do it then. I was hideously nervous, after the argument at lunchtime, but I thought he'd be nicer after the baby incident. More understanding.' Eve shook her head. 'He said all the things men say in these circumstances. All the worst things. That it was my problem, my decision; that he'd assumed I was on the pill.

He could be cruel, you know. You never saw that, but he could.'

Olivia thought about what James had told her, later that same night. The drowned cousins, and their younger sister. That didn't excuse his behaviour, but it showed that he understood life was complicated, and that he'd had his share of tragedy too. But she resisted the temptation to tell Eve. What good could it do?

'It made me want to have my baby,' Eve said. 'It made me want it desperately, but I knew I had to get rid of it before it was too late. Before it took me over.' There were tears on her cheeks now. Olivia didn't think she'd ever seen Eve cry before, not properly. 'How could I know it was the only chance I'd ever get?'

'You were only nineteen.'

This seemed to Olivia, suddenly, to be the final truth of the matter: they had been little more than children. Not a partridge and a pelican; not anything so definite or irrevocable. She felt a great compassion for Eve, back across the years, and with it a gushing sense of relief. She was on safe ground again: she could be the mother, the adult, now. 'We were both so young,' she said.

But Eve showed no sign of having heard her, and when Olivia reached her hand across the table, she withdrew hers.

'There,' she said. 'Now you know it all. And now I think I'll go home, actually.'

'Please don't,' Olivia said. 'You've drunk too much. It's too late now.'

She had no idea what time it was – but that wasn't what she meant. She meant it was too late to stop now.

'I'll take the risk,' Eve said.

'Why?' Olivia's voice sounded querulous, but she didn't care. 'There are other things to talk about still.'

'Such as?'

Olivia recognised that look: Eve's eyes set hard, unyielding. Such as the rest of the story, she thought; the parts that mattered to her.

'We haven't talked about your baby,' she said instead. 'Huan. About when you're going to China, what happens next.'

Eve shook her head slowly. 'I don't want you to have anything to do with my baby.'

Olivia gaped at her. 'But that's why you came, isn't it? To show me the pictures, to talk about it?'

Eve went on shaking her head. 'I came to set the record straight,' she said. 'I needed to get it off my chest, all that ancient history, before I went to China. I needed you to hear it. I don't care whether you understand, or whether you still blame me. I'm done with you now.'

'No,' Olivia said. 'Please don't let's leave it like this. We were friends, that's what matters. That's what mattered most about that summer for me.'

And it was, she realised. The most precious thing she had lost that summer wasn't James, nor the baby, for all the dreams and the heartache and the obsessive pregnancies that had followed. It was something simpler than either of those things, something smooth and certain like the pebbles on the beach at Aldeburgh: the pure, hard core of her friendship with Eve.

For a moment she thought Eve was wavering, but the quiver at the corner of her mouth was quelled before it was more than a shadow.

'Maybe,' she said. 'But this is something I'm going to do on my own. Something I'm going to have for myself.

You have everything you could want, Olivia: a reliable husband, four perfect sons, a beautiful house. You have your music and your life here, twenty-five years of history to look back on.'

This last speech was so fluent, delivered in such a headlong stream of words, that Olivia was sure it had been rehearsed, or at least thought about, imagined, over and over again. Perhaps the whole evening had been planned. Had the look on Eve's face earlier revealed a desire not for reconciliation but for revenge?

'You've had your career,' Olivia said; a last-ditch plea. 'You're a doctor; you're still a doctor. I gave up my career for my sons.'

'That was your choice.'

Eve got to her feet and Olivia followed, her head suddenly empty. She trailed Eve to the door and waited while she buttoned her coat.

'I'm sorry,' she said, her voice sounding calmer than she expected. 'I can see I'm to blame, and I'm sorry. I hope everything goes very well with the baby.'


When the door had shut behind Eve, Olivia let herself slide to the floor in the narrow hallway. She thought she would cry, but she didn't: her eyes were dry, her heartbeat steady. She could hear it throbbing in her ears when her fingers pressed them shut. Perhaps I have a heart of stone, she thought. Perhaps that's the truth, that all along I was the one with no feelings. It wasn't her fault that she hadn't known Eve was pregnant; it wasn't her fault James hadn't wanted Eve. But even so she'd failed Eve. Failed to understand.

Through the kitchen door she could see the plates

stacked on the sideboard and the bottle of wine, almost full, standing on the table. The cheerful domestic scene looked like something from a horror film now, full of foreboding rather than comfort. Olivia knew it was ridiculous to stay here, sitting on the floor, but it was equally ridiculous to get up and fill the kettle as though nothing had happened. Once upon a time she would have sought solace in the piano, but nothing satisfying and complex, nothing capable of diverting her mind, would flow through her fingers any more. So here she was, trapped again in a moment when time seemed to have stalled; when none of the paths she could take seemed right or possible. Not so much a crossroads as a full stop: the place on the boys' old train track where the buffer marked the end of the line.

After a long time, long after all the noise from upstairs had stopped, the throb of music and the banging of doors, Olivia got up. She usually said goodnight to the boys, but they didn't need her any more. They'd go to sleep when they were tired. Even Benjy would doze off over his Nintendo: she'd find it blinking on the pillow beside him later, when she went up to bed.

She went through to the kitchen and opened the cupboard where they kept spirits and mixers, bottles of dark rum and crème de cacao that hadn't been touched for years. There was the whisky she'd drunk with Lucy. Duty free Laphraoig. She reached up and lifted it out of the cupboard. She could have done with Lucy's company tonight, she thought. With someone to drink with, at any rate.

# Chapter Thirty

Olivia was woken the next morning by the ringing of the telephone. She was conscious of her head throbbing, then of the dismaying memory of the previous night. Oh God. Might it be Robert on the phone? Or Eve? Eve saying she was sorry – that Olivia had done her penance?

The ringing continued. The answerphone must be off, the boys all still in bed. What time was it, anyway? Light was seeping around the sides of the curtains. Should she be awake? Might it really be Eve?

She had forgotten, of course she had forgotten, that the only person who rang her this early in the morning was Sarah.

'Did I wake you?'

She sounded so blithe, Olivia thought, so unsuspecting. Irony would be a waste of energy.

'Yes.'

The heating hadn't come on yet: why was that?

'Are you free for lunch?' Sarah asked. 'Say at the Lebanese place in North Parade?'

Olivia scrabbled on the bedside table for her watch. It was ten to eight already. She shut her eyes for a few seconds, then levered herself out of bed.

'Boys!' she yelled through the door. 'Breakfast! Hurry hurry!'

A cold breakfast, it turned out. No toaster, no kettle, no microwave. The electricity was all off.

'It's supposed to tell you where the fault is,' Olivia muttered, frowning at the row of switches in the fuse box.

'Mum. Chill.' Alastair stood behind her, a bowl of cereal in one hand. 'We've got to go, anyway.'

'Have the others eaten?'

'Tom's gone. Prefect duty.'

Angus and Benjy stood in the middle of the kitchen with schoolbags over their shoulders, holding a piece of white bread each. Despite herself, Olivia laughed.

'Look at your faces. No one would guess you beg me to buy that stuff.'

'For *toast*,' Angus said. 'It's disgusting like this. It tastes like cardboard.'

'I'm glad you've noticed.'

At least they hadn't noticed the state of her, Olivia thought. At least the lack of electricity had put a damper on the usual squabbling as well as on their spirits.

'Go on,' she said. 'Don't be late. Have a good day.'

When the door slammed behind them Olivia was tempted, just for a moment, to sink down again in the hall as she'd done the night before. There had been something easeful and comforting in simply giving in to emotion, letting time slip away. But it wouldn't do. This was the point, surely: that she had a life to run, four sons to occupy her.

A life to run, an electrician to call, and a pupil coming

239

in half an hour. At least she could teach the piano without electricity.

Five hours later, Olivia looked across the table at Sarah.

'I saw Eve last night,' she heard herself saying.

'Oh?' Sarah raised her eyes from the menu with a smile. A bland smile, Olivia thought with momentary viciousness, measuring her against Eve. But she ought to be grateful for blandness, today of all days.

'She invited herself for supper,' she said. 'Brought the photos of her baby to show me.'

'Oh!' A different tone this time: expectant, but not, Olivia thought, sentimental.

Olivia hesitated. She hadn't intended to say any of this to Sarah.

'Did I ever tell you about what happened at the end of our driving tour, years ago?'

Sarah shook her head.

'We were staying in a house in Aldeburgh with a friend of Eve's,' Olivia said. 'Another medical student, called James.'

'Ladies?' The waiter was standing beside them.

'Shall we have the meze?' Sarah suggested.

'Sure.'

'Two meze,' Sarah said. 'One veggie. And another bottle of sparkling water, please.'

She shifted slightly, a spasm crossing her face as she moved her plaster cast to a different angle.

'Are you comfortable?' Olivia asked. 'Is it hurting?'

'It's fine,' Sarah said. 'Much less painful now. Go on.'

Olivia realised then, in a moment of clarity, that she was going to lie to Sarah. No: she checked herself. Not quite that. The facts were beyond doubt. But she couldn't help giving them her own slant; telling her own version of the truth.

Isn't that what Eve had done last night, though? Isn't that what everyone did?

'Eve and I were out in the car one afternoon,' she said. 'We got lost, and we stopped at a phone box so we could ring James – but the phone was out of order, and there was a newborn baby lying on the floor.'

Sarah's eyes widened. 'Alive?'

Olivia nodded. 'Her mother must have abandoned her.' She swallowed. 'We took her to the hospital in Ipswich, but by the time we got there she was dead.'

'How awful.'

Sarah looked at her for a few moments and Olivia looked back, her gaze steady.

'The thing was–' Olivia broke off. Following the direction of the sun, she remembered; travelling west as it started to sink over the fields. Eventually she said, 'We reacted differently, Eve and I. We argued. I thought we could save the baby, that we'd be the heroes of the hour, but Eve just seemed to be annoyed about it. To see it as a nuisance.' She felt tears pricking then. 'I never understood. But when we met for lunch a couple of weeks ago, Eve told me she was pregnant that summer. She'd done the test a couple of days before we found the baby.'

'Goodness,' said Sarah. 'Poor Eve.'

'We talked about that day last night,' Olivia said. 'We'd never done that before. And Eve told me – James, the boy we were staying with, was the father of her baby. And according to Eve he spent the whole week in Aldeburgh flirting with me.'

Sarah raised her eyebrows. 'Did he?'

'No,' Olivia said. 'No, he–' She shook her head slightly. 'It was a long time ago. We were very young, all of us.'

'But it still rankles? With Eve?'

'She said that was why she'd come to see me last night: to get the stuff about Aldeburgh off her chest. To accuse me of being responsible for her abortion.'

'You?'

'She said James made it clear he didn't want anything to do with the baby. Eve wanted to keep it, but she decided she couldn't when she realised he preferred me to her. That was the final straw.'

Put like that, it sounded ridiculous. A trumped-up charge. But even though they were Eve's words she was repeating, Olivia knew she wasn't being completely fair. She was guilty of misrepresentation, of partiality, just as she'd known she would be.

'So what did you say?' Sarah asked.

'I didn't really get a chance to reply. When Eve had said her piece, she walked out of the house saying she never wanted to see me again.'

Sarah frowned. 'She always was a bit unpredictable.'

For some reason her tone threw Olivia into a rage. Like a mother who dismisses her child's distress with a platitude, she thought. *What would you know?* she almost said. *What the hell did you ever know about Eve?* But what was the point? What was she doing, anyway, telling Sarah all this?

The waiter reappeared just then with a tray laden with little bowls: taramasalata, moutabel, houmous. She was hungry, Olivia realised. She hadn't had any breakfast. No wonder she was irritable. She took a deep breath, conjured a smile.

'This looks good,' she said.

'I love this place.' Sarah smiled, perhaps with relief. 'The trouble is, now I can't take any exercise the wedding diet is going into reverse.'

'You can always let the dress out.'

'I'm not that good a seamstress. Don't let me eat too much. I never did have any self-control.'

That wasn't how Olivia thought of Sarah. Her life had always seemed meticulously controlled.

'Do you remember,' she said suddenly, 'that party at Eve's house? A whole lot of us went for the weekend in the Easter holidays.'

Sarah nodded. 'We all slept on the floor.'

There had been a startling array of alcohol at the party – bottles of wine and beer and a fruit punch that grew more and more potent as the evening wore on. Eve's older brothers had invited their friends too, though only the boldest of the girls had dared to speak to them.

'Vomit on the carpet,' said Olivia. 'Milly Mason out in the garden with Eve's brother Paul.'

She remembered Sarah, bright and chirpy the next morning, helping Eve's mother clear up. And Eve's father standing at the front door when they arrived: a huge man offering bone-crushing handshakes. His bonhomie had always alarmed Olivia. The sanctioned debauchery had alarmed her too: packets of cigarettes circulating freely, and the adults conspicuously absent once the party got underway.

'What hopeless innocents we were.' Olivia dipped a strip of pitta into tzatziki, feeling a pang of nostalgia, or perhaps regret. 'Where did you think you'd end up, back then?'

'I was still hoping to do medicine.'

'Like Eve.'

'Eve was never in doubt,' Sarah said. 'Not about anything.'

No, Olivia thought, surprised by a sudden insight, that wasn't true. There *had* been doubts for Eve; more than anyone realised, perhaps. She remembered the way Eve had seemed diminished rather than augmented by being at home. She remembered, too, dropping Eve off at the end of that summer. The last time she'd seen her, before this year: Eve and her mother on the doorstep, watching her drive away. Olivia let that thought hover for a moment, then pushed it away, discomfited by the unexpected dart of pity it induced. Eve had been in the ascendant back then, she reminded herself. Think how unkind she'd been to Sarah. She smiled across the table and tore off another piece of bread.

The restaurant was almost empty now. When the waiter came to collect their plates, Olivia ordered coffee and baklava, more to spin out the time than anything else. She'd recovered, now, the reassuring feeling she'd had in Sarah's company these past few weeks – a muffling, simplifying sort of reassurance. So be it, she thought. Let Eve go, let it all lie. She felt a kind of relief she couldn't fully embrace but badly wanted to believe in: the possibility of absolving herself.

She sipped her coffee, thick and grainy and flavoured with cardamom.

'How are things on the wedding front?' she asked.

'The wedding's fine.' Sarah cut a small piece of baklava into two smaller halves which disintegrated into a heap of pastry flakes and crumbled almonds. 'The plaster should be off by Christmas. It's all fine, really.'

It hadn't occurred to Olivia that Sarah might have had a particular reason to propose lunch today. She'd monopolised the conversation, she thought, and Sarah had been too polite to claim her portion.

'But...?' she offered.

Sarah sighed; a long, slow sigh. 'Oh, it just seems – such a change. A lot to get used to.'

Olivia tried to recall what it had felt like, getting married. An adventure, she thought. But she could hardly remember, now, what life had been like before. 'I've never lived on my own,' she said. 'You've got a whole life set up. It must feel strange.'

Sarah picked up another piece of baklava, contemplated it for a moment as though she wasn't sure what to do with it, then slipped it into her mouth.

'I know it's my fault for leaving it so long.' She sighed again, more gently. 'Robert's away a lot, isn't he?'

Was he? Olivia digested this statement. 'He has been away a lot recently,' she said. 'He's working on some big deal.' But that wasn't what Sarah meant, she thought. She meant, surely, that Guy wasn't going to be travelling much any more. 'Is this,' she said, 'to do with Guy, or...'

'I don't know. There's nothing about him – oh, it's silly. I shouldn't bother you with it.'

'I bothered you with Eve,' Olivia said, and Sarah smiled gratefully.

Neither of them said anything for a moment. It was her move, Olivia thought. Sarah was waiting for her to speak.

'Have you talked to Guy?' she asked. 'Said any of this to him?'

Sarah shook her head. 'It's hard to explain,' she said. 'We get along very well, but we don't seem to have a way to say things. Some things. It's as if we've learned each other's language but we've missed out a whole chunk of vocabulary. We can't do *à la maison*. Does that make any sense?'

Olivia thought of Robert; of the dwindling of their conversations. Had they had a common language and let it slip away?

'Maybe it's something you need to practise,' she said. She was conscious of her voice sounding unnatural, unconvincing. She hadn't had much call for this sort of talk for a long time.

The waiter was hovering, out of Sarah's field of view. Keen to move them on, Olivia thought.

'You know what?' Sarah said. 'All the time I was single and everyone else was getting married, having babies, I used to think, "I'm fine like this. There are plenty of compensations." But I never completely believed it. I always thought... Now I wonder whether I fell in with Guy's proposal without thinking properly about it.'

'Because you love him,' said Olivia.

Sarah stared back, her usual assurance disconcertingly absent. 'I don't know,' she said. 'Is that what you need, to make a marriage work? Is it essential?'

'Among other things,' said Olivia helplessly. The truth was that she'd got married so young that she'd never considered what it might require of her. Twenty-two, blithely giving up an independence she'd never recognised for what it was.

The waiter sidled closer and Sarah turned abruptly towards him. 'Two more coffees,' she said.

Olivia didn't demur.

'The thing is,' Sarah said, the words coming in a rush now, 'I didn't mean to tell you this, to tell anyone, but I've had a – I think I might have fallen for someone else.'

'An affair?' Olivia was startled. She remembered her doubts, all those weeks ago when she'd read Sarah's letter, but surely this wasn't what she'd anticipated? But Sarah was hurrying to deny it.

'No, not an affair. Just a – nothing at all, really. I met someone by chance, at work, who isn't my type at all, who I hardly know anything about. A silly crush.' She flushed. 'It's so unlikely I can't help feeling I've – sort of invented it, to test myself. Or to test Guy maybe. To talk myself out of marriage. You can see why I can't say anything to Guy: *I don't know whether I should marry you because I've got the hots for a complete stranger.*'

'Are you seeing him? The other man?'

Sarah shook her head miserably. 'The last time I saw him was at the running club the night I did this.' She gestured at the plaster cast. 'He turned up out of the blue. I thought it was some cruel twist of Fate, but it turned out the cruel twist Fate had lined up was for my ankle.'

Olivia laughed, then checked herself.

'But you're still thinking about him?'

Sarah shrugged. 'About *it*,' she said. 'About what it means. Am I only marrying Guy because he seems so suitable, or has this ridiculous crush only happened because I'm committed to Guy now, and being illicit makes it more exciting?' She moved her leg again with a grimace. 'I keep wondering what would have happened if I'd met him – Harry – six months earlier.' She picked up the last crumbs of baklava with the pad of one finger, then flicked them back onto the plate with her thumbnail. 'People fall in love in arranged marriages, don't they?' she went on, her tone almost pleading now. 'And other people love each other madly but don't manage to live together for more than a few months.'

Olivia thought about her own marriage: the routine, the babies, the history. How much really depended on who you chose, she wondered, and how much on what you made of it? Then she thought about Robert, who was coming home that night, and she felt her skin tingle.

'Love is important,' she said. 'But it isn't straightforward. It's not the only thing that matters, and it's tangled up with the rest of life, the practicalities and eventualities, more and more as time goes on.' She looked out of the window, where the light was already beginning to fade. The boys would be home before long, she thought. 'But maybe – maybe it's what makes all those empty spaces into lace. Makes it feel as though there's a pattern, a meaning to life. At best, I think that's what it does.'

The coffee arrived, set down without a word.

'I don't need this,' Sarah said. But she picked up her cup and took a sip.

'You'll never know unless you try,' Olivia said. 'That's what I think. If it doesn't work out, it'll be awkward, but you can undo it. You're both grown ups. You have to take a chance, sometimes. You're good at making things work.'

But was that, she wondered, the coward's way out? The predictable advice of the long-married woman who liked things to follow their appointed path? An odd sense of responsibility niggled at her; the thought that seeing Sarah married would settle some ancient account between them.

'I just don't know if it's for me,' Sarah said. 'For a long time I didn't think it could be.'

'Because you hadn't met the right person, perhaps?'

'Because I didn't think I had the right.'

'The *right*?' Olivia was astonished. 'How could you not? Isn't it in the Declaration of Human Rights, even?'

'I didn't think I had the right to be happy, I mean. Even though I *was* quite happy, really, as I was. Oh, I'm sorry, I'm being a bore.'

'You're certainly not,' Olivia said. 'Bemusing, but not boring.'

To her relief Sarah smiled. 'We'd better go,' she said. 'I expect they want to shut.'

Sarah reached across the table and squeezed Olivia's hand, then she swivelled in her seat and caught the eye of the waiter, who was leaning against the counter as though he'd given up hope of them leaving.

'The bill, please,' she said. 'And could you call me a taxi?'

They hugged goodbye on the pavement: the occasion seemed to demand it. Olivia held the door of the taxi while Sarah slid awkwardly into the back seat.

'Marriage isn't the be all and end all,' Olivia said. 'I'm like one of those financial advisors who have to warn you that they only sell their own bank's products. I can't give you a balanced view; I have to believe what I did was the right thing.'

Sarah nodded. 'I could do with a sign,' she said. 'But life isn't like that, I know.'

The phone was ringing when Olivia opened her front door. She didn't reach it in time, and instead of interrupting the answerphone she stood and waited for the machine to stop flashing, then pressed the play button.

Robert, making her heart skip a little. *Hello darling, it's me. The plane's landed, I should be back by six. Hope all's well.* Robert who had been away a lot lately; whom she could do with having home again.

# Chapter Thirty-One

'This is a good idea,' Robert said. 'You always have good ideas.'

He lifted his glass to her and Olivia smiled. She'd been looking forward to this evening, but now they were alone at last she was no longer quite sure what she wanted from it; what she'd imagined them saying to each other. Robert looked at her across the table with that open, enquiring look of his and she felt the same nervousness as she had with Eve.

It had taken several days to manage this outing. Olivia was out of the habit of asking for attention, used to managing on subsistence rations. 'You look weary,' Robert had said on his first evening back, and she'd demurred. Not because she was many things as well as weary – not because she hardly knew where to begin – but because she knew his mind was still elsewhere. And because there were plenty of other things to occupy him, now he was home.

He'd spent the first evening investigating the fuse box and speculating about what could have blown so many circuits at once. (An unusual flow of energy, the electrician had suggested, or a rogue appliance, and Olivia had thought that either of those descriptions could apply to Eve, although it was probably one of her sons' electronic devices.) Then there had been the Physics project Alastair had saved up for his return, the problem with Angus's computer that his older brothers couldn't or wouldn't fix. And the backlog of sleep Robert always brought home from business trips. He never slept well without Olivia, he maintained. She knew she should be flattered, but she wished he didn't always come back so tired.

But here they were now, a bottle of wine between them and a candle alight beside it. Here they were, and Robert didn't seem inclined to fill the silence by telling her about his trip, or by discussing the boys' homework or his mother's plans for Christmas. Robert was good at filling silences, but he was good at leaving them alone, sometimes, too. Olivia had forgotten that.

'You've been away a lot recently,' she said.

'I suppose I have. There's been a lot going on. We're lucky to be so busy in the current climate.'

Olivia took a sip of wine, cold and delicious.

Robert watched her face. 'It should be better after Christmas,' he said. 'Less travelling. Once the takeover in Germany's sorted out.'

'Good.'

They were surrounded by couples around their age. They all looked so assured, Olivia thought. As though they had life taped. Did she and Robert look like that too?

'So,' Robert said. 'You had a visit from Eve?'

'She upset me rather,' Olivia said.

'Didn't she always?'

'Not always.' Robert had never met Eve; she wasn't going to let him get away with that. 'We were always friends, though, and now it seems we aren't. She wanted me to feel I'd done something wrong. That I'd caused her harm.'

'What kind of harm?'

Olivia took another sip of wine. 'She thought her boyfriend liked me better than her.'

Robert laughed. 'What, twenty-five years ago?'

'She was pregnant,' Olivia said. 'It spoiled everything, in her eyes.'

'Hardly your fault, though.'

'Maybe I was partly to blame.' Olivia stopped, considering the words at her disposal as though selecting flowers for a daisy chain. Essential to pick the best ones, and to link them delicately so you didn't spoil the careful work of half an hour, or half a life. 'Maybe I should have guessed she was pregnant,' she said.

'How could you have done? She was the medical student, not you.'

'We spent the whole summer together,' Olivia said.

Robert raised his eyebrows. 'You didn't have any experience of pregnancy back then. I don't suppose you'd miss the signs now.' He glanced down at the menu, hesitated. 'What do you think: fish or steak?'

Suddenly Olivia knew she didn't have the heart for this conversation tonight. There were lots of other things they could talk about. Robert was looking anxiously at her, as though worried he'd made a misstep. She smiled.

'Fish would be nice with the Sauvignon,' she said. 'They've got skate.'

·   ·   ·

Mary Baldwin rang the next afternoon when Olivia was teaching. Olivia didn't usually answer the phone in the middle of a lesson, but when she heard Mary's voice on the loudspeaker she slipped out of the room with a mumbled apology.

'Any news?' Mary said, when Olivia picked up.

'About?'

'About Georgie. Have you made any progress?'

'Oh.' Olivia leaned against the worktop behind the kitchen door. 'No. I talked to Georgie and she said she didn't want to know about her family. I took that – she was very clear about it.'

There was a long silence at the other end. Olivia could hear silence from the music room too, Bach abandoned in her absence. She cupped her hand over the receiver and called through the door: 'Bar twenty, Natasha. I'll be back in a moment. Sorry,' she added, to Mary.

'Here's the thing,' Mary said eventually. 'Of course respecting the client's wishes is paramount. Especially for Georgie, whose wishes were trampled over for years. But sometimes it's very hard not to do something you're sure is in their best interests. You had the same thought as me, that some sort of reconciliation...'

'Maybe Georgie will come round to the idea in time,' Olivia said.

'There may not be much time left. Georgie's much frailer since that bout of pneumonia.' Olivia could hear Mary pursing her lips before she spoke again. 'I'm bound by a code of conduct: you're not. You could at least find out whether she has any relatives left to be reconciled with.'

Surely Mary could research Georgie's family in her

free time, Olivia thought, if she had scruples about making it official business? But of course it was she who'd raised the matter, gone to see Mary in the first place. Of course Mary would assume she was keen to help.

'I'll think about it,' she said. 'I'm sorry, I'm teaching. I really have to go now. I'll be in touch.'

Natasha was staring out of the window, watching a squirrel digging in the bed nearest the house.

'They bury conkers all over the garden, then forget where they are,' Olivia said. The squirrel looked up, its head cocked as though it had heard her. 'Now.' She smiled. 'Let's look again at that tricky bit, shall we? Try the left hand on its own from the third line.'

Olivia dreamed that night about the man she and Eve had seen at Torhousekie. In the dream his malign intent was beyond doubt. They were running down a mountain, she and Eve, in flowing white nightgowns like something out of a Victorian melodrama, and the man was just behind them, closing in with every step. Olivia thought she recognised Loch Ness far below, dark and menacing in the moonlight. She tripped over a rock and fell to the ground, but the man didn't stop. He was after Eve, she realised, with a flood of relief and guilt. All that time, it was Eve he'd been chasing, not her.

In the dream the man was clearly recognisable, but it wasn't until her eyes opened to the darkness of her bedroom that Olivia realised who he was. That it was the face of Eve's father she had conjured.

For several minutes she lay still, her heart pounding. It was a dream, she told herself; just a dream. And there'd been nothing to it at the time: it hadn't been the same man

even the second time. She'd been sure of that, whatever
Eve said. Eve had made him into a bogey man for reasons
of her own. It was what those reasons might be, though,
that made Olivia's pulse race now.

In her mind's eye she could see Eve telling the story to
James, her eyes wide. Olivia had seen her at the time as a
little girl used to having an audience: Eve the idolised
daughter, the popular schoolgirl. But now, seeing it
through a mother's eyes, she suddenly understood that
Eve had believed in the story. Like her sons' recurring
nightmares, it had represented some truth for her, as
though she'd already learned to expect the worst from
men before James had disclaimed responsibility for her
baby. Before her two marriages had ended in divorce.

Olivia pushed back the covers and climbed out of bed.
She'd considered Eve from all angles in the last few days,
conducting in her head the conversations she couldn't
have with anyone else. Not Robert, it seemed. Not Sarah,
either. Sarah's view of Eve was coloured, still, by the past:
*she always was a bit unpredictable.* That phrase had
infuriated Olivia, but it was a generous assessment, Olivia
thought, as she fumbled in the dark for her dressing gown.

It was hard to explain what had distinguished Eve
and Sarah at school, made them chalk and cheese from
the very first day. They'd both been blonde, confident,
outgoing, but Eve had been the centre of attention, the
girl whose lead everyone followed, and Sarah the butt of
her jokes. Her nickname was a case in point – and Scabs
had stuck fast, even after nicknames had gone out of
fashion. Eve was capable of cruelty: that was beyond
doubt. But it occurred to Olivia now that the cruelty
might have come from the same place as the Torhousekie

stalker. That Eve had never been as sure of herself as everyone believed.

The loose floorboard on the landing yielded beneath her foot, and Olivia's nerve ends tingled. She'd lost enough sleep lately, she thought, for her mind to conjure its own phantasms. She hadn't seen Lucy again since the night of the whisky, although she'd looked out for her among the trickle of Tom's friends passing through the house, and she wondered now whether she might have been a mirage, the whole thing a dream. A strange girl in her kitchen in the dead of night. It wasn't hard to imagine what subconscious need might have summoned her.

The kitchen was empty tonight, and utterly quiet. Olivia stood for a moment in the doorway, and then she moved slowly around the room touching the daytime things that became totems, symbols, at night: the vase of Honesty pods, the wooden knife block, the wicker fruit bowl. The garden was silvered by the moon, an uneven oval, almost full.

'Olivia?'

She turned with a shock. Not Lucy: Robert.

'Are you all right?' he said. 'You look as though you've seen a ghost.'

His hair was tousled, his face crumpled with sleep. The sight of him like that, his night-time self, made Olivia's eyes fill with tears.

'What is it?' he asked. 'Couldn't you sleep?'

'I think I *have* seen a ghost,' Olivia said.

'Whose ghost?'

Olivia hesitated. It wasn't too late to make a joke of it. 'A girl called Lucy,' she heard herself saying. 'I found her in the kitchen one night.'

Robert frowned. 'A friend of Tom's? They seem to hang around until all hours.'

'That's what I thought at the time, but I didn't recognise her.'

Robert put an arm around her shoulders. 'Why would you be seeing ghosts?'

'I've had things on my mind.' Olivia felt the tears stinging now. 'Eve, and that baby we found. And Georgie, the old lady at the day centre I told you about. The one whose child was taken away.'

Robert said nothing.

'All those baby girls,' Olivia said. There was a tremor in her voice, a shifting of the ground beneath her. 'All dead.'

'Not your fault,' he said, and Olivia had the feeling that this was what he'd said for ever and ever. Ever since he'd first met her: *it's not your fault*. As though he'd always known she needed absolution.

'But I can't get them out of my mind,' she said. 'This girl – this ghost – I thought she might be one of them.' *Had* she thought this, or had the idea come into her mind just now? It seemed obvious, now that she'd said it aloud. Obvious and absurd. 'She's about the age the phone box baby would be now,' she said. 'About the age Georgie's daughter was when she died.'

Robert sighed very gently. Not a sigh of impatience or disbelief, but of concentration. Olivia rested her head against his chest, gratitude making her head swim.

'But they're not connected, the two of them?' he asked.

Here was another thing Olivia didn't realise she'd considered before. 'They could be, if Georgie's daughter had a child. A daughter. She could have been the right age to give birth in 1983.' It was mad, impossible, but Olivia's mind wouldn't give up the trail. 'They came from East Anglia, Georgie's family, not so far from Aldeburgh. And Lucy – she told me her grandparents lived in Norfolk.'

She could feel something throbbing inside her chest now that was surely too painful to be her heart. Something fragile and urgent, insisting on being heard. In the silence she took a deep breath, began to couch the words that would prepare its way, but Robert spoke first.

'That's something you could find out.'

'What?'

'Whether Georgie's daughter had a child.'

Olivia twisted her head to look up at him. She felt dazed, now, by what she had not said, and by the possibility that she might have said it. Giddy with the reprieve Robert had offered her. She shut her eyes, and when she opened them the world looked different, no longer the domain of ghosts and dreams.

'Georgie's social worker rang me yesterday,' she said, and her voice sounded different too. Strangely normal, like the dead flat sound when you come out of an echo chamber. 'She wants me to look up Georgie's family on one of those genealogy websites.'

'Georgie does?'

'No. But the social worker thinks it's a good idea.'

'Well, then.' Robert stroked her hair. 'Maybe you should. Maybe that would be a good plan.'

'Do you think I'm going mad?' she asked, as the tears spilled over onto her cheeks at last. 'Poor Robert: I'm sorry. What a dance I lead you sometimes.'

'Rubbish,' he said. 'Think what a boring life I'd have

had without you. I'd have married some dull Scottish farmer's daughter.'

Olivia gave a little sniffle of laughter. 'Robert Burns thought rather highly of Scottish farmer's daughters.'

'Rabbie Burns had a poet's imagination.' Robert squeezed her shoulders. 'Speaking of which, I might have a dram of whisky. Will you join me?'

So that was it, Olivia thought, as she watched him pour Scotch into two shot glasses. That was the closest she would come to telling him. A good thing, she supposed, but the relief she felt was salted with a dark tang of dismay. This particular secret had been shut away inside her for a long time, but there was a difference, all the difference in the world, between not now and not ever. Between twenty-five years and infinity.

But she had reckoned without Robert.

'There was something you were going to tell me,' he said, as he handed her a glass.

Olivia didn't move. Robert took a slug of whisky, raised an eyebrow.

'When we went out for dinner the other night, there was something you were going to tell me about Eve, wasn't there?'

# Chapter Thirty-Two

## 1983

'We're running out of petrol,' Eve said.

It was the first time either of them had spoken for a long time. They'd turned off the A12 and were following signs for the city centre and the hospital, approaching Ipswich along a road with fields on one side and big suburban houses on the other. Clutching the baby in her lap, Olivia felt like a countrywoman coming in from the wilds in search of a doctor. Would they understand, at the hospital, why she and Eve had acted as they had? Would they think they'd done the right thing?

'Did you hear?' Eve said.

'Yes.'

The noise of the car was something they'd learned to deal with over the summer: the need to shout, if they were going above thirty miles an hour. The petrol gauge was another: as a warning system it was approximate at best. They'd ground to a halt on a B road in North Wales, late one July evening, after a few puttering protests from the little engine. Nothing in sight but sheep and mountains. If it hadn't been for the lorry driver who'd picked them up, Olivia thought now, sparing them a twenty mile walk to the nearest garage, that might have been enough to kill off the whole venture.

'We'll have to stop,' Eve said. She turned to look at Olivia, her face unexpectedly drawn. 'Unless you want to risk it.'

'No.' Olivia lifted the baby gently, and the little eyes opened. 'Oh,' she said, 'look.'

But Eve had turned back to the road. 'I haven't seen a garage,' she said, 'but there must be one along here somewhere.'

'There!' Olivia pointed. On the far side of the road, in the middle distance, was the red and yellow sign of a Shell petrol station. She smiled: it seemed a good omen. They were nearly there, the baby was alive, they weren't going to run out of petrol. 'What a day,' she said. 'I can't believe we've almost made it.'

When they reached the garage, Eve veered across the road with a sudden sharp turn of the wheel.

'Hey!' shouted Olivia, as a van coming the other way swerved to avoid them with a resonant blast on its horn. 'For God's sake, Eve, are you trying to kill us all?'

Eve slammed the brakes on, narrowly missing the concrete pillar that housed the pumps.

'You can do the petrol,' Eve said. 'The smell makes me feel sick.'

'There's probably an attendant.' Olivia held the baby protectively, conscious now of additional perils: petrol fumes as well as unexpected noises and sudden jolts. 'There, there,' she murmured.

'Shut up,' said Eve. 'Just shut up with your bloody crooning.'

'Eve,' said Olivia. She didn't mean her voice to sound reproving, mother-like, but it did. 'For goodness' sake.'

'Give me the baby,' Eve said. 'Give me the baby and deal with the petrol.'

'I'll go and look for someone.' Olivia released the handle and eased the door open carefully with her foot, trying to avoid crashing it against the concrete. Eve's sudden lunge took her by surprise.

'Eve!' Olivia was shouting now, clasping the bundle of wool tight. 'What the hell are you doing?'

'Give me the baby, I said. Just give me the bloody baby.'

'I'm going to look for an attendant.' Olivia twisted her body towards the narrow gap between the door and the pump, keeping the baby close to her chest. A primitive protective instinct had taken over now: it seemed suddenly vital to get the baby out of the car. She didn't want to be alone with Eve any more, didn't want to have to rely on her. She made a final effort to escape as Eve yanked at the fringe of the blanket.

She couldn't have said, later, how it happened: couldn't have said whether it was her pulling or Eve's sudden letting go that launched the baby out of the door, sent it smack into the concrete pillar and then down, sickeningly down out of sight, onto the grimy floor.

And then, after the shouting, the tussle, there was silence. Nothing but Olivia's whimpering, and then the clunk and slam of the driver's door as Eve got out and went round the back to fill the car with petrol.

'Oh God,' Olivia whispered, as she gathered the baby into her arms again. 'Oh God, I'm sorry. I'm so sorry. But we're nearly at the hospital. You'll be all right, little one. Little baby.'

But she knew already that it wasn't. She didn't feel again for the heartbeat, just wrapped the tiny body tightly in the shawl and held it against her as though her heart might work for both of them. As though sheer will might be enough to sustain its tenuous hold on life for a little longer. She could feel herself trembling with shock and fear and anger. At least there was no one around; at least the position of the car door meant not even the cashier could have seen what happened. But with that thought came culpability. She heard her mother's voice: it takes two to make an argument. Why hadn't she handed the baby over when Eve asked? She knew Eve well enough to read the signals.

By the time Eve returned Olivia was weeping quietly.

'Stop it,' Eve said. 'For God's sake stop snivelling. The hospital's only a mile down the road, OK? Five minutes. Pull yourself together.'

'We needn't have stopped,' Olivia said. The enormity of that fact filled her mind as Eve pulled back out into the early evening traffic. The chasm between stopping and not stopping. If they'd filled the car with petrol earlier in the week; if they'd known how close the hospital was. If they'd never passed the phone box, someone else might have found the little bundle.

'I think the baby's dead,' she said.

Had Eve realised? Was that why she'd capitulated over dealing with the petrol? Was she hurrying on to the hospital because she thought there was still hope, or because she wanted to get the whole thing over with?

Olivia couldn't ask her. Neither of them could speak any more, about what to do or what to say or what had happened. They passed a golf course, crossed a roundabout, and there was the hospital on the left, a low-slung, sprawling building like an organism that has grown and spread haphazardly. The Accident and Emergency department was clearly signed just inside the entrance. You weren't supposed to park there, but Eve stopped at the edge of the ambulance bay and they both got out. Olivia felt sick with guilt and grief. She knew what it meant, their silence: it spelled complicity, the willing withholding of information. As they passed through the glass doors, the weight of the baby felt like an immense nothingness in her arms.

Eve stayed behind her, letting Olivia's agitation speak for both of them as she made for the reception desk, called out to the nurse who was busy with a pile of forms.

'We've got a baby,' Olivia said. 'We've found a baby, abandoned in a phone box.'

# Chapter Thirty-Three

## 2008

R obert said nothing for a long while when Olivia had finished speaking. No absolution this time, she thought, and she was grateful. Grateful for the silence that surrounded her like a lake around an island, the water stretching glassy calm to the distant shore.

She'd always thought she knew what the effect of disclosure would be: that despite the years of care and sacrifice, she would be revealed as an unfit mother. Her life would unspool before her eyes. But all she felt now was emptiness. Like the loss of a tumour, she thought, that had grown inside her for years and years, pressing for space, shifting everything out of alignment. Like the loss of a baby.

'You poor darling,' Robert said eventually, and although Olivia didn't want, didn't expect his sympathy, she began to weep with a violence she'd rarely known before. Twenty-five years of tears, she thought. Enough to fill the lake, to flood the island.

'I should go to the police,' she said at last.

'No.' Robert sat beside her, holding her hand.

'It was manslaughter, at least that. You're sheltering a criminal.'

'My love, it was an accident.'

'There must be some sort of penalty. There would have been, if we'd told the truth back then.'

'I don't know,' Robert said. 'You might have been charged with something, but I can't imagine it would have merited more than a reprimand, in the circumstances.'

'Even so, we escaped that. There ought to be some redress.'

'To whom?' Robert took her other hand, drawing her in closer to him. 'What on earth would it achieve, raking it all up now? Who is there to make amends to, if the mother was never identified?'

Olivia closed her eyes for a moment, trying to staunch her tears. 'The baby,' she said. 'She was a person. She had a life ahead of her, just like one of our babies.'

'The baby would probably have died anyway. Didn't they say so? Hadn't she lost a lot of blood?'

Olivia remembered the little eyes opening, those dark grey newborn eyes. 'She was alive when we arrived at the petrol station.'

'I think you've paid your penalty, Olivia.' Robert's voice was very gentle. 'Years of living with this awful secret. Don't you think you've grieved for that little baby more than the mother who left her to die?'

'These days there'd be CCTV.' Olivia had often thought about this; filling up her car with petrol, she'd looked up at the cameras, imagined the grainy images. She and Eve fighting over that helpless bundle, and then the brief lunge and drop.

'Think about Eve,' Robert said. 'If you broadcast this

now, she won't be adopting that baby. Does it make her an unfit mother, this thing that happened so long ago?'

Hearing those words, exactly the words she had expected to hear applied to herself, made Olivia shiver.

'That's what it's about with Eve, isn't it? All this time, neither of you could talk to the only other person who knew what had happened.'

Olivia nodded. But it wasn't within their power to forgive each other, she was thinking. They could only have made it worse by discussing it, agreeing to keep the secret. That would have been a greater conspiracy.

'We blamed each other,' she said. 'Eve thought I was being sentimental. Possessive. I thought she was being a selfish cow.'

'And do you still?'

'No.'

'Then write to her. Tell her. She needs your blessing, whatever she said to you. If you need to do something to make amends, do that. You have me to share it with now; you can be generous with her.'

'I don't think Eve wants my generosity,' Olivia said. 'She blames me even more because of the boys. She thinks having my own children has cleared the slate for me.'

This was the irony, she thought: neither of them believed they deserved to be mothers. All these years she'd felt guilty because she was so abundantly fertile, and she was suddenly sure that, for all her medical training, Eve believed she was infertile because of her guilt.

'Sometimes being generous means offering something that might be rejected,' Robert said. 'It's hardly generosity if you expect gratitude in return.'

He squeezed her hand, then got up to fill the kettle. Olivia stared out of the window, where dawn was edging into the sky. Was it a question of generosity, she wondered? Did she have the right to absolve Eve?

'Do you know about the pelican?' she asked. 'The myth about the pelican piercing her breast to feed her babies with her own blood? That's how Eve described me. She said I was the pelican and she was the partridge, stealing eggs from another bird's nest. She sneered at the pelican's self-sacrifice.'

Robert didn't say anything. Perhaps he was right, Olivia thought, that making a formal confession would only gratify some perverse desire for self-flagellation, while telling Eve she had nothing to fear could do some good. She understood all too well the healing power of babies: surely Eve had a right to that, at long last. Eve had suffered enough too – and not just because of those two deaths, the phone box baby and her own tiny foetus. Perhaps not just because of the agonising rounds of IVF and divorce, either. Olivia remembered her dream, and the suspicion it had awoken. Was that why Eve had run away to Australia, leaving even her mother behind?

Olivia felt fragile the next morning, but it was a peculiar, an unfamiliar kind of fragility. Like a seedling planted out at last where it could grow and flourish, she thought, conscious of being fanciful but too relieved, this morning, to care. As the metaphor took hold she could almost feel her cramped roots probing their way into the soil, extending beyond the bounds that had kept them in check for so long.

She had resolved, before she reached the Wednesday Club, to get on with tracing the Quickshall family tree. It was partly a need for atonement – a desire to sustain

269

herself with good deeds – but it was more that she understood now that the consequences of facing up to the past might be infinitely different, infinitely better than you expected. And that sometimes it took a third party to push you into it.

And if she needed a final spur, it was provided by Georgie's absence from the club that morning. Just a cold, Shirley said, but even so Mary Baldwin's words seemed prescient. Who knew (who ever knew?) how much time was left? Kenneth wasn't coming back again; he'd moved into a nursing home, his health deteriorating fast. Poor Kenneth. Whenever Olivia thought of him now she heard the words of 'The Silver Swan' in her head, and imagined him singing them in that poignant, cracking tenor that still contained the echoes of its heyday: *Farewell, all joys; O Death, come close mine eyes.*

That wasn't one for the Wednesday Club, Olivia thought. Pathos wasn't quite their style, though Shirley would no doubt have found something soothing to say about it.

As she cycled home along the canal she was conscious of the after-effects of the night before: a tight little headache was pressing between her eyes, and a bilious swirl of emotion boiled up at the least provocation. At the thought of Georgie or Kenneth, of Eve or James or Lucy. Certainly at the thought of her sons, riding their own course through the world, oblivious to its perils and pitfalls.

She was tempted to retreat to bed when she got home, but she knew that would only prevent her from sleeping later. Better to stay awake, to keep herself busy. She made a sandwich, then sat down at the computer in the little study next to her bedroom and typed 'family history' into Google.

She couldn't believe how fast the process was. Within half an hour, having supplied her credit card details to buy a month's subscription to an ancestry website, she had found Georgie's birth certificate. Georgiana Christina Quickshall, born 17th March 1917, in the Lexden district of Essex, to Thomas Quickshall, clerk, and Ann Quickshall, née Walters. The sight of the names and dates in black and white gave Olivia a thrill of satisfaction. There was a link that would allow her to order a facsimile copy of the document, but she was eager to press on. For now she clicked the button to print off the details as they appeared on the screen.

After another half hour she had found the records of Thomas and Ann's marriage, in May 1905, in St Mary's Church, Dedham, and of the births of two other children: Henry Thomas in 1908 and Eliza Frances in 1910. Both a good deal older than Georgie, Olivia thought. She had been the baby of the family.

And then – another thrill – there was the birth of Georgie's daughter, named (though presumably not by her mother?) Jane, in another part of Essex in March 1935; father unknown. Known to Georgie, Olivia thought, with a pricking qualm at the consciousness of what she was doing. This wasn't a story, but real life, the proof of Georgie's tragedy. She let the thought rest for a moment, then nudged it gently aside. She wasn't committing herself to anything beyond this, she thought. Beyond finding out for herself, for Mary.

Adoption records, Olivia discovered, could be searched in a microfiche at the General Register Office, but not online. But some of the other details could be filled in: the ones she was most interested in, that brought her closer to the answers she was looking for. She was so absorbed that she didn't hear the doorbell the first time it rang. An insistent, sustained ring roused her: her Wednesday afternoon pupils, of course.

On the doorstep, the earnest mother and her dutiful offspring were waiting. With an effort, Olivia rallied her mind to teaching. She had taken some trouble over these two lately. Since the day of the bog. She had felt they deserved better from her.

It was five o'clock before Olivia could continue her search. For once she stood impatiently while Benjy told her about his supply teacher and Angus related a hilarious incident from his Biology lesson. Today she was as eager to get back to her screen as they were to theirs: how ironic that today, of all days, her sons should choose to be so chatty after school.

'Really?' she said, half-listening, 'and what did he say to that?'

At last they drifted off to homework and television, and Olivia scuttled back upstairs. The search pages were open, stacked one in front of another on the screen just as she had left them, and a growing pile of printouts lay in the tray at the side of her desk. The cat was curled up in her chair – every member of the family wanting her attention today, she thought. Olivia lifted him carefully, and when she sat down he draped himself across her knee like a cushion. As she typed and clicked and waited for the website to respond, her mind drifted back into the story of this family who could have had no inkling that a stranger would one day uncover the details of their lives and deaths from a computer screen in Oxford.

No death certificate was listed for a Jane Quickshall

any time between 1950 and 1960, but Olivia wasn't
surprised. Her name would surely have been changed
when she was adopted. Olivia moved on through the
family tree: Thomas Quickshall had died in London in
1940, aged fifty-eight, and Ann Quickshall in Colchester
in 1950, aged sixty-six. Georgie's parents had both been
dead for more than half a century. Neither of them, she
guessed, would have lived to see the death of their ill-
fated granddaughter – assuming that Mary was right
about Georgie's baby being adopted within the family,
and that the Quickshalls had stayed in contact with their
other children after Georgie's disgrace.

Henry Quickshall, Georgie's older brother, would
have been a hundred this year if he'd survived, but he
hadn't proved as long-lived as his sister. He'd died in
1983, in Ipswich. A frisson passed through Olivia: there,
she thought, was a trace of a connection between the
Quickshalls and the phone box baby. Perhaps Henry's
family had sat, that same year, in the same relatives' room
where she and Eve had waited for the nurse to come and
talk to them about their tiny foundling. Although there
might not have been many grieving relatives for Henry,
who had not married, as far as Olivia could discover, nor
fathered any children.

Georgie's sister Eliza was the next link in the chain. It
didn't take long to find the record of her marriage: Mary
Baldwin was right, the rare surname was a godsend. Eliza
Quickshall had married a man called Edwin Charles
Shotter in October 1930. Another unusual name, thought
Olivia with satisfaction. Although there were more
Shotters than Quickshalls on record, it wasn't hard to
home in on the details of their family. Eliza and Edwin
hadn't had children of their own until 1938, when Eliza

had borne two sons in quick succession: Clive Thomas Edwin, followed by Philip Henry Andrew a year later. Was Mary right about this, too, the childless couple whose fertility had been unleashed by an adoptive child, after a long wait? Two precious sons, given three Christian names each.

The door opened silently behind Olivia and she jumped when Benjy spoke.

'Mum,' he said, 'are we having supper tonight?'

Olivia glanced at the clock on the wall behind her: it was half past seven. Not so late, she thought. Could they tell that she was absorbed by something that had nothing to do with them?

'Yes,' she said. 'Of course. What do you fancy?'

Benjy's eyes narrowed slightly, as they did when he sensed a possible advantage. As they had since he was a tiny boy. Oh, she could deny him nothing, this last child, Olivia thought. This golden-haired cherub. Did he really have to grow up so fast?

'Chinese?' Benjy ventured.

Olivia smiled. 'OK. The menu's on the board in the kitchen. Ask the others what they want.'

'Can I order it?'

'Sure. See if Tom or Al would go with you to pick it up.'

Olivia turned back to the screen. Nearly there, she thought. Just in time for a celebratory takeaway.

'What do you want?' Benjy called back, already halfway across the landing.

'Anything,' said Olivia. 'Dad likes chow mein, remember.'

She heard Benjy going from room to room, his excited treble met by his brothers' laconic baritones; a minor fracas with Angus as Benjy let his role as catering co-ordinator tip over into dictatorship. A door slammed, and there were Benjy's footsteps heading back downstairs.

Olivia's attention had returned to the Shotter clan. Two sons, she thought, three and four years younger than the adopted daughter. If there *had* been an adopted daughter in that family, as she had begun to assume. Had they called her Jane, plain Jane, or had she too been given a string of euphonic Christian names to mark her welcome into the family? A picture began to form in Olivia's mind of a little girl who could never quite throw off the taint of her birth, her association with the outcast mother who would spend nearly fifty years shut away for the sin of her conception.

Perhaps at first her aunt and uncle, childless for five years already, had been glad to have her; had done their best to see the good in her. She had Eliza's blood in her veins, after all. But when those boys were born, just before the war – a time when masculinity was important, when bearing sons was something to be especially proud of – they must surely have eclipsed little Jane in their parents' affections. And she would have been just at the age, Olivia knew from experience, when sibling jealousy was at its worst. Her animosity couldn't have been easy for the ecstatic new mother to bear, holding her very own babies in her arms at last. Small wonder if Jane's place in the family had dwindled further as the vicious circle played itself out. Small wonder if she had grown up to fulfil her adoptive parents' worst fears by turning into a rebellious adolescent. Small wonder, perhaps, that she had died young, in a car crash. Poor Jane Quickshall, doomed, after all, by her scandalous origins.

Olivia stared at the screen as if the names and dates

staring back at her could answer this question as well as the rest. The cat stirred on her knee, rearranging his warm bulk. Olivia stroked him absently, the softness of his fur a surprise after the flat keyboard. Then she shook her head gently, to dispel her doubts and dislodge the vestiges of the headache that was gathering again at the base of her skull. The facts could only carry her so far, but she hadn't finished with them yet.

She didn't expect either Eliza or Edwin to be alive still, and indeed they were both long dead. Dead long before Georgie had been liberated from St Catherine's, even: in the late sixties, within months of each other. There was another story, Olivia thought, that she couldn't tease out of names and dates alone. Another avenue for speculation. Had they been a devoted couple who couldn't live without each other, or was the explanation more prosaic?

There was no Clive Shotter in the death records, but she found a match for Philip Shotter: yes, that was him, Philip Henry Andrew, born July 1939, died December 2005. So, one surviving nephew, Olivia thought. Possibly. One surviving nephew who might be on the other side of the world, for all she knew. Here was the next challenge: to trace a living person by his name and date of birth.

Olivia heard the front door click open, and Robert's voice in the hall. Time to stop, she thought. Time to return to her own family. But the lure of all that information waiting for her, humming out there in cyberspace, was too much. She typed 'find UK address' into Google, and a moment later she was on the British Telecom address search webpage. All she needed was a surname and an area. Essex, she wondered? They hadn't moved far, this family. London? Somewhere else in the Home Counties?

Her fingers darted over the keys – quick pianist's fingers, more used to Couperin than computers but agile, nonetheless. Before Robert had reached the top of the stairs she had found him. Clive T. E. Shotter, obligingly listed with his full initials, as if he was still aware of how much he had meant to his parents. Clive T. E. Shotter, living at an address in NW1.

'Hello.' Robert sounded amused, peering over her shoulder. 'Have I driven you to the Lonely Hearts? What does Mr Shotter have that I don't, may I ask? GSOH? Well-honed biceps?'

'He's Georgie's nephew,' Olivia said. 'I've found him.'

'Just like that?'

'Just like that,' Olivia agreed. She pressed print, and closed the last window on her screen with a signing-off flourish. 'A few hours on Google, and Bob's your uncle.'

'Georgie's your aunt,' said Robert. 'Congratulations. I suppose this means the kitchen's closed tonight?'

'Benjy's gone for Chinese.' Olivia stood up, dislodging the cat at last, and stretched her arms above her head. 'Goodness, I'm stiff.'

Robert bent to kiss her forehead.

'Nice to see you smiling,' he said.

***THEY KEEP YOU*** *locked in the present. You are not supposed to remember the past and there is nothing to anticipate except the blankness of a future that is always the same. Each day is an empty space, indistinguishable from the one before and the one after. Row upon row like a hall of mirrors, they taunt you if you lift your head to look at them. Each week, each month, a chain of identical images that slip through your grasp, allowing no finger hold. Time here has no beginning and no end: you go on existing; that is all they allow you.*

*But the past is still there, washed on the tide of drugs and sorrow. There are glimpses, sometimes: a flickering image beneath the surface, the sharp glitter of something bobbing in the distance. And when you least expect it the tide goes out, leaving pictures you could call memory. A memory without words, but it is simpler that way.*

*There is a girl you know to be you, a child with plaits, buttoned into a winter coat, her hands held by a sister and a brother. Older: twice your size, they seem. She seems happy, this child, and you are glad for her, although her happiness arouses a dull rage that you cannot locate.*

*You see her again and again, always the same child, sometimes younger and sometimes older. A sickly child, often in bed. The kind brother who sits with her; the sister who runs off to play, who dresses up for parties. The father who looms and sways, leaning against the door frame. The mother with a hard life and a hard face. The coldness of the house, always.*

*She is rarely at school, this child, but she reads and*

*reads and one day, one hot summer, she finds a way out of the chilly house and the flat, bare land that runs all the way to the sea. Her family do not understand how, or why, but she goes, with her parcel of books and her clothes packed into a leather bag. She goes, but she takes with her something that none of them know about, none of them suspect. Something that will end in disgrace and despair, in the long blank corridors and white rooms where there are no books. No words. No explanations.*

*Something else penetrates your dreams. A horror like the birth: another passage you resisted with silent screams, that ended bloodied and torn. In the darkness you sense it coming and you can do nothing. None of them will save you: the kind brother, the sister who is married and gone, the silent mother. The father sways and lurches and you have always been powerless, a sickly child with pale limbs and hollow eyes. A child lost in other worlds, dreaming of escape.*

# Chapter Thirty-Four

## 1983

I t seemed to Olivia, driving south, that the seasons had
turned overnight: that summer had yielded, after the
furious stormy battle of the last week, to a peaceful
autumn. Fields bleached brown through July and August
showed a shimmer of green again; crops steeped in
sunshine all summer were swelling, ripening towards the
harvest. The chill in the air and the stillness of the sky
were welcome after the stifling heat and its tempestuous
aftermath.

The atmosphere inside the car, however, wasn't the
companionable quiet she and Eve had often shared that
summer, but a silence in which powerful emotions were
barely contained. It surrounded them, Olivia thought, like
a bubble: memory and misunderstanding swirled on its
iridescent surface, and inside it the past and the future
dissolved into the emptiness of the present.

The seed of it had been there when they fled from
Shearwater House the previous day, a tiny bubble that
sealed away the echo of the shouting and the ugly words
as she and Eve drove without purpose through the

featureless East Anglian landscape. During that afternoon – at the phone box, the petrol station, the hospital, and on the way back to Aldeburgh – it had swelled and strained to enclose all the things they couldn't talk about, couldn't dispel or ignore or acknowledge. And last night, when Olivia had left James in the kitchen and climbed the stairs and opened the door not of her bedroom but of Eve's, it had settled around them as they slept, pressed together for comfort in the dark. It was the last thing they could share, Olivia thought, this shroud of silence. Glancing at Eve now, she remembered with a fierce clutch of regret their camaraderie earlier in the summer, the nights in the tent or the incommodious double beds of guest houses when proximity had been effortless and unremarkable.

As the hours passed, two then three then four, Olivia coaxed her mind away from the events of the previous day and the past few weeks. In two days time she would be in Dubai with her parents. It felt almost as odd to be leaving the beginning of the English autumn for the subtropical heat of the Arabian Gulf as to be leaving a person who felt like a stranger after a whole summer spent in each other's company. But when she thought of the colours, the smells, the sounds of Dubai, she felt a pressing impatience. Surely the weight of loss and guilt would feel different there. The foreignness of the Middle East would be welcome, this time: the expat routine of her parents' life would be a comfort.

Before that, though, they had to get Eve home. Olivia had driven to the de Perrevilles' house before, but she didn't know the way by heart. As they drove west along the A27 she braced herself to speak, but it was Eve who broke the silence first.

'You need the next exit,' she said. 'We turn off before Chichester.'

There was something adult in her voice, a world-weary overtone, as though she'd tired of the adolescent game they'd been playing all summer. She'd used the same tone when they'd said goodbye to James that morning, the kind of flat disappointment parents betray when their children misbehave, and Olivia had felt implicated even though she had held Eve in her arms all night; even though she could have accepted the invitation to James's bed and had not.

She clicked the indicator and pulled off onto the slip road, following Eve's staccato instructions until they were in a country lane that wound its way south through the Sussex countryside.

'Strange to be back here,' she said, 'after all the places we've been.'

Eve nodded; a barely perceptible movement. She looked ill again, her face drained and pale. Like mother of pearl, Olivia thought, an unearthly sheen to her skin. It occurred to her that neither of them would ever look as wholesome and innocent again as they had at the beginning of summer.

'There's a right turn in the village,' Eve said. 'After the pub.'

'I remember.'

The de Perrevilles' house wasn't huge, but it had the approach, the setting, of a house on a grander scale. Stone gateposts flanked the entrance, and the façade was seen first across a sweep of lawn fringed by silver birch trees. It ought, Olivia thought, to represent a happy compromise between domesticity and gracious living, but it looked to her just at that moment like a doll's house forgotten in the corner of a playroom, unprepared for visitors.

They hadn't rung ahead to let Eve's parents know they were coming. Neither of them had thought of using the telephone at Shearwater House, and after yesterday a phone box was out of the question. As the car hit the gravel in front of the house Olivia felt a qualm of misgiving.

'Have you got a key?' she asked.

Eve shook her head. 'My mother will be here.' She was leaning forwards now, craning her neck, taking no trouble to conceal her impatience.

And as they drew to a halt the house sprang to life. A dog came bounding round from the back, a stiff little wire-haired dachshund barking furiously, and then the front door opened and there was Eve's mother, framed between neo-Classical pillars and wearing the kind of pale draping clothes that would have suited a Greek statue.

'Darling!' she called, 'what a lovely surprise!' There was a wobble in her voice that made Olivia feel instantly excluded; she thought of the cool welcome her own mother would offer at the airport in Dubai. While Eve ran up the steps, Olivia opened the boot of the car and lifted out Eve's bags, setting them down carefully on the gravel.

'What have you done, Mummy?' she heard Eve say, and the laughing reply: 'I slipped on the stairs, clumsy me.'

Olivia glanced over, and realised that the impression of flowing garments was partly due to the sling that supported Mrs de Perreville's right arm.

'Is it broken?' Eve asked.

'I'm sure not, just bruised. And a black eye too: such

283

drama! Would you believe it, all the way down with the tea tray in my hands?' She laughed again, and pressed her daughter against her chest with sudden ferocity. Eve nestled in like a little girl, all her resilient independence gone as she gave herself up to her mother's embrace.

Then Mrs de Perreville lifted her good hand behind Eve's back to greet her daughter's friend. 'How lovely to see you too, Olivia, safe and sound.'

Olivia smiled, mumbled greetings. The closeness of these two was familiar, the hermetic bond between mother and daughter that she'd always – what? Envied? Admired? Watching them now, she was conscious of another perception: for a moment she saw the survivors of some natural disaster, clinging together on the threshold of their ruined house. But the house stood square and solid; Eve and her mother had nothing but a sprained wrist and a lingering bug between them. If they were holding tight to each other, it was because they'd been separated for so long, because they depended on each other in a way Olivia could never completely understand.

'Will you stay for supper?' Eve's mother asked, when the bags had been carried up the steps. 'We can rustle up a homecoming feast.'

Olivia shook her head. 'I'd better not,' she said, even though she was very hungry, now she thought about it. They hadn't stopped for lunch; negotiating that would have been too difficult.

'At least a cup of tea,' Mrs de Perreville pressed.

'I should be getting on.' It was what her father said, on these occasions. An allusion to other demands on one's time.

'But where are you going, Olivia? Are your parents in the country?'

'I'm going to stay with my guardian for a couple of days.'

A schoolfriend of her mother's had looked after Olivia for half terms and exeats while she was at school, and her house had become a comfortable refuge over the years. Olivia's last postcard, sent the day after they arrived in Aldeburgh, had suggested that she might have a day or two to spare before her flight, and she knew she'd be welcomed without any more notice. If she left now she'd be in time for supper, she thought. The only fixed point in that pleasantly unstructured household: supper at seven thirty, when Frank returned from the station in Liphook after his day in London. Steak and kidney pudding, perhaps. The associations of Margaret's stolid English cooking were suddenly heavy with nostalgia.

Eve disentangled herself from her mother then and came down the steps, like a child remembering her manners at the last minute.

'Goodbye, Olivia,' she said. 'Have a nice time in Dubai.'

They hugged awkwardly, and then Olivia climbed into the driver's seat. She circled the little car around the wide oval of gravel and headed back up the drive.

As she approached the gateposts again she glanced in the mirror and was surprised to see Eve and her mother still standing at the top of the stone steps, two willowy blonde figures gazing after the retreating car. She was the last person they needed, Olivia thought, but even so she couldn't avoid the feeling that she was abandoning them.

# Chapter Thirty-Five

## 2008

I t was Robert who suggested a long weekend away –
an early birthday present, he said, but he didn't labour
the pretext. It was one of his skills, that sort of tact: the
kind that could almost pass for absent-mindedness, for
missing the point altogether.

Olivia wouldn't have chosen Suffolk, but Robert had
already booked the Swan in Southwold. A colleague had
recommended it as the perfect place for a winter break,
and it lived up to his description – a place of gentle
pleasures, of craft shops and beach huts, open grassy
spaces and fine Georgian houses. Olivia and Robert
walked along the beach, read newspapers on the
comfortable chintz sofas in the lounge. The days passed
slowly but too fast, one running into another.

On the final day, they drove down the coast to
Aldeburgh. This was Robert's idea too, and it occurred to
Olivia, as they drove out of Southwold, that it had been
part of the plan all along. She thought of asking, but since
the night of her confession there had been a strange
shyness between them; a sense, on Olivia's side, that she

shouldn't push her luck. Instead she stared out of the window, remembering a documentary she'd seen about evacuees being taken back, in old age, to the windswept village where they had spent the war years.

She hadn't been back to Suffolk since 1983, but she remembered the A12, the tangle of lanes on its seaward side. She'd got better at navigating since then: it was hard to imagine how lost she and Eve had been that day, even though she could see the spider's web laid out on the map now. This must have been where they were, somewhere in this circle. Theberton, Leiston, Knodishall, Sternfield. Olivia remembered Theberton, but none of the rest. Were they Viking names, she wondered? She spoke them under her breath, hearing the chink of armour, the rush of the wind. And Knodishall was in two different places, either side of the B1119: how was one supposed to manage that?

The weather had looked promising earlier, one of those misty winter mornings that often lead on to sunshine, but although Olivia kept glancing towards the sea as they drove, hoping to see patches of blue sky, the mist lingered until it was absorbed by swathes of cloud. Those heavy skies, Olivia thought, and the flatness of the land: she remembered that. The great stretch of it, punctuated by those extraordinary churches built in the region's wool-trading heyday. Blythburgh, with its angels. All of it ready to be swallowed in one bite if the sea level rose, as they said it soon would.

'Do you want to stop at Snape?' Robert asked. 'Explore the Maltings?'

They had never made it to Snape, in 1983.

'On the way back, perhaps.'

Nothing about the outskirts of Aldeburgh looked familiar. Had it changed so much, or had she forgotten?

She hadn't meant to look for Shearwater House, but when they turned right along the seafront, there it was. Olivia recognised it instantly, although it wasn't exactly as she remembered. There was one of those little jolts of memory, where what is recalled and what is before you are superimposed for a moment.

'That's lucky,' said Robert, swinging the car into an empty space. 'I didn't expect to be able to park so close to the sea.'

Olivia sat in the car while he researched the parking regulations. The beach was a few feet away over a concrete ledge, the steep ridge of pebbles blocking the view of the sea.

'Pay and display,' Robert said, when he opened the passenger door to attach the ticket to the windscreen.

Robert rarely spoke unnecessarily; it was petty of her to notice.

'Whereabouts did you stay, that summer?' he asked, as she got out of the car.

Olivia pointed.

Shearwater House was blue now, not pink, although the paintwork looked as weathered as ever. A faded flower, not a scuffed seashell: an end of season forget-me-not. The plaque beside the door must be the same, made out of some hard stone that would resist the salt and the wind, but it looked different too, the lettering more deeply engraved than Olivia remembered. She could see the clouds reflected in the plain, square windows, and behind them the faint edges of curtains, pulled back. It was impossible to tell whether they were the same ones whose seams Eve had examined twenty-five years before.

Then as she stood, not immediately in front of the house but quite obviously staring at it, the front door opened and a woman emerged, carrying a battered canvas shopping bag. Olivia looked past her into the hall. The ancient chest of drawers was still there, but with a vase of flowers on top instead of the bowl of seashells Olivia remembered. The woman hesitated for a moment on the doorstep, as though wondering whether to say something to someone inside the house, then she pulled the door shut behind her. In that moment she noticed Olivia and smiled, and Olivia stepped forward.

'Excuse me,' she said, 'are you–'

Then she stopped. She couldn't remember the name of James's aunt, and anyway she must be in her seventies by now, and this woman was closer to Olivia's own age. She could be anyone, Olivia thought; at best, the connection between them was trifling.

But the woman was waiting, her face open and enquiring. *I'm sorry, I've made a mistake,* said a voice in Olivia's head, but the words that came out were different, seizing on the only name she remembered.

'I wondered if Amelia was here,' she said.

The woman looked puzzled, but she smiled again.

'I'm Amelia,' she said. 'Do I know you?'


Robert didn't understand. They walked in silence along the beach, stones crunching beneath their shoes, but Olivia could hear the questions that hung unspoken in the air. Picked up by the seagulls, perhaps, as they swooped to and from the horizon. Olivia said nothing because she didn't know where to begin, how to explain her desire to speak to the woman or the mistake she'd made. She felt the same tumult of confusion and shame that she'd felt on that long ago day, slipping out of

Shearwater House to fetch the map from the car. The same feelings, and the same place, the sea and the sky and the pebbles. She let the wind lift her hair, the waves fill her head, and then she took Robert's arm as people do when they walk along the beach.

They had lunch in a pub on the sea front and talked about the boys. About Tom's university offers and Benjy's move to senior school, the fortunes of Angus's football team and Alistair's band. About extending the house, converting the loft, building a workshop or a den or a music room in the garden. This was what marriage was about, Olivia thought, having so many things to talk about that you could avoid talking about anything in particular. She reached across the table and took Robert's hand.

'Thank you,' she said. 'It's been a lovely few days.'

But as they walked back up the beach Olivia could feel the lure of Shearwater House growing stronger again. She couldn't help staring at it as they approached, letting the chalk-blue paint settle into her mind. Samphire and *Peter Grimes*, she thought. What an extraordinary way to live, as a student. Swimming in the sea at midnight where your cousins had drowned. She remembered the lumpy sofas, the lumpier beds, the ramshackle dresser in the kitchen, and felt a stab of nostalgia so strong it filled her belly with stone.

The door was shut now, but the sun had moved inland so that the sky no longer filled the windows, and she could see inside. She could see the fireplace in the sitting room to the right of the front door. She remembered those few blissful, rainy days when she and Eve were alone and things were easy and peaceful. Eve lying on the sofa while she tried to light the fire. Books no one had read for decades. Baked beans.

'So who was she, that woman?' Robert asked, when they were safely away, heading out towards Snape.

'I don't know.'

'But you knew her name.'

'She had the same name as someone else,' said Olivia. Perhaps that was it, she thought: a simple coincidence. She might not be anything to do with the family, this Amelia.

'Then why–' Robert stopped. Olivia could see him processing, speculating. She owed him more, she knew that.

'When I stayed there with James and Eve,' she began, 'James talked about his family one evening. About how his two little boy cousins had drowned, years before, and his uncle and aunt had had another child afterwards. A girl.'

'Amelia?'

'Yes. But that Amelia had Down's syndrome. So this must be another Amelia.'

'I see.'

'It threw me, that's all. The whole thing threw me, coming back and finding the house a different colour. It used to be pink.'

Robert drove in silence for a few minutes, then he said: 'As a matter of interest, did he get you into bed, this James?'

Olivia looked sideways and saw the downward curl of his lip, the crease in the middle of his forehead.

'No,' she said.

Strange; on this score she was blameless, but even so she had felt guilty, all these years. She had never proclaimed her innocence, even when Eve had seized her chance to accuse.

They halted at the junction with the A12 and turned north towards Southwold.

'Not that it's any of my business,' said Robert.

'I saw James not long ago,' Olivia said. 'The day I was attacked.'

Robert turned so sharply that the car almost swerved off the road.

'The day you what?'

She had forgotten – how had she forgotten? – that she had never told him about the assault.

'You were away,' she said; and then, because that sounded as though she blamed him, 'it was nothing. Some lad thumped me in the arm while I was wheeling my bike over the canal bridge. There was a man running along the towpath who came to make sure I was all right, and I realised after he'd gone again that it was James.'

'Were you hurt?' Robert asked. He stared straight ahead at the road – either because he wanted to avoid another near-miss, Olivia thought, or because he wanted to avoid her eyes.

'Not really. A bruise.' Her heart was beating fast again. 'I didn't realise it was James until he'd gone,' she said. 'I'm still not entirely sure it was him.' Except that she was, of course. Sure of that, but not of why she felt in jeopardy suddenly.

'Perhaps we should go back,' Robert said.

'Back where?'

'To the house. To speak to that woman.'

Olivia's scalp tingled. 'Why?'

Robert turned towards her for a moment, and she saw that his expression was troubled rather than angry. Had she expected anger? Or suspicion?

'Because otherwise you'll keep wondering,' he said.

'Won't you? This whole thing – it's not just the baby, is it? It's all of them. James and Amelia and the lot of them.'

'No,' said Olivia.

'Come on: you've had more on your mind today than the baby.'

'Because I was confused,' Olivia protested. 'Because of the coincidence over the names.'

'Is it a coincidence?'

She was riled now. 'What are you suggesting? What on earth does it matter who she is, anyway? She's nothing to me. To us.'

There was a layby just ahead, and without speaking Robert slowed and pulled into it. For a minute or two there was no sound except a periodic rush and shudder as cars sped past, heading up the coast or down it, making for home as the light drained out of the winter landscape.

'Olivia,' he said eventually. 'Forgive me if I've got this wrong. But it seems to me that this thing – what happened that summer – is too important to let it go. I need to be sure that we've sorted it out, all of it. If you still hold a candle for this James, I'd like to know. If there's still some mystery somewhere, let's look into it. I want to get back all of you when we're done with this. I don't want to be floundering among things I don't understand for the rest of my life. I want you to tell me everything there is to tell.'

'Oh, Robert.' Olivia put a hand on his knee, and he laid his own over it, calmly, conceding nothing. Her mind was a muddle, loose ends flailing. Every time she reached for one it dipped out of sight again.

'I may be wrong,' he said.

'No,' said Olivia, 'and yes. I don't know. I feel so – confused, lately. I can't work out what matters any more.'

'I matter,' said Robert. 'Just tell me something. Anything.'

Olivia shivered; the heat was beginning to seep out of the car now the engine was off. Perhaps she wasn't quite innocent as far as James was concerned, she thought. She had resisted temptation that night, but she had regretted it afterwards, for longer than she might have anticipated. Perhaps she should tell Robert that when she imagined James taking other girls to Shearwater House and cooking them sea bass and samphire, she wondered whether she should have ignored her scruples. Perhaps she should admit that part of her believed the ghost of the phone box baby would have been banished sooner if she had accepted James's offer, that the ache of loss might have been silenced before it could take hold of her. Perhaps she should confess that she had thought these things again, in the last few weeks.

'James has nothing to do with the baby,' she said at last, 'not really. Except that we were staying at Shearwater House when it happened, and we went back there afterwards, and that night, after Eve was in bed, he told me the story about his cousins, the little boys and Amelia. He told me to make me feel better, because he'd stood on the beach while his cousins drowned, but instead it made me feel worse.'

'Why?'

'Because he was blameless and I wasn't. Because I wanted him to think well of me, but I knew I didn't deserve it. Because I knew people would go on feeling sorry for me, and I wouldn't ever tell them the truth.'

'And because you liked him.'

'Yes.'

'And you went on liking him.'

294

'Yes.' She hesitated. 'He was unusual, among the people I knew back then. Cultured, witty, sure of himself. He was very kind to me. I suppose I measured myself against him and saw I wasn't worthy. I imagined how different things would have been if he'd been with us when we found the baby.'

'How different things would have been if you'd judged yourself worthy of him?'

'God, Robert, what are you saying?' She turned to face him, feeling something different suddenly: out of nowhere, a powerful erotic charge. The knowledge of being desired. 'My love, you were the one who rescued me. Who keeps rescuing me.'

And that was the truth of it: James had offered her nothing, just as he had offered nothing to Eve, whose claim was so much greater. Why should she imagine that James would ever have bothered with her? How could she imagine, even if he had, that it could possibly have been better than what she had?

'Good old Robert.'

'Wonderful Robert,' she said. 'Truly wonderful Robert. I don't care about any of them, James or Amelia or the wretched aunt and uncle. Let's for God's sake get back to the hotel now, and let them stew.'

# Chapter Thirty-Six

The taxi carried Olivia around the top of Regent's Park and past London Zoo, where the aviary rose beside the road like a giant Meccano model. It must be five years, she thought, since she last took the boys to the zoo – the time Benjy fell and grazed his knee so badly that she'd spent half an hour at the first aid point with him. She remembered him limping proudly towards the penguin pool to rejoin his brothers, his spindly leg adorned with a fat bandage.

Five years had transformed Benjy, but the image was still sharp in Olivia's mind, and the outline of the aviary as familiar as something she passed every day. The past was collapsing behind her, she thought, telescoping like some ingenious device designed to store her memories tidily. Like whole shelves of photograph albums condensed onto a single CD: a reminder that the space occupied by human lives was out of proportion to their importance. And what about Georgie, she wondered, who had no memories to speak of? What space would her life occupy in a world of gigabytes and cyber-reality?

The thought of Georgie brought Olivia back to the task in hand, and her heart skipped a beat or two as the taxi turned into the network of streets northwest of Primrose Hill. Towards Clive Thomas Edwin Shotter, a man who had borne, all his life, the names of two of Georgie's closest relatives – her father and her brother-in-law – but whom she had never met. A man whose existence Georgie was unaware of, and who was almost certainly unaware of hers.

Olivia had found Clive Shotter hard to place, on the phone. He sounded younger than seventy, a man still hanging on to the prime of life. Well-spoken, witty, with a flirtatious edge to his voice and an easy manner that made Olivia feel more than usually tongue-tied. An actor, perhaps, with those rounded vowels, that impression of vigour? A roguish Falstaff, preserved by good living?

'You don't know me,' she'd said. 'I wanted to talk to you about a family matter.'

'That sounds intriguing.'

'It's rather difficult to explain on the phone. I thought–'

'Come and see me, then,' he'd said, briskly cheerful. 'I'm laid up, so to speak. Knee replacement. Pottering around. Happy to receive visitors.'

So here she was, pulling up outside an immaculate Victorian terrace of white stucco, paying off the cab, ringing the doorbell. And here he was, Clive Shotter, opening the door, leaning on a stick as though it was an amusing accessory. Not a trace of Georgie in him, Olivia thought. He was twice her size: a big man, in every sense of the word. His presence filled the doorway, spilled down the broad steps and onto the pavement.

'Hello!' He lifted the stick in a sort of salute. A pug

peered between his feet, implacably comic. 'Olivia? Bang on time. Come in.'

The house bore the signs of recent arrival – or at least, Olivia thought, of its occupants not having moved in fully. There was almost no furniture in the sitting room they passed (a single armchair; a coffee table stranded in the middle of the polished oak floor) and Olivia spotted a couple of packing boxes stacked behind the door of what might have been a dining room. The walls had been hung with pictures, though. They seemed incongruously well populated, looking down on half-empty rooms.

'My watercolours,' Clive said, following her gaze.

'Are you a painter?' Olivia asked, although she realised almost immediately that the question was foolish. Clive didn't laugh: she warmed to him for that.

'Just a collector, but like all true passions it verges on obsession. That's why my ex-wife got the furniture.' He smiled genially, holding a door open for her. 'My den.'

This room, at the back of the house, looked like a cross between a student bedsit and a don's study from an episode of *Morse*. Clive Shotter had evidently crammed most of the furniture left to him in here: an old-fashioned desk; a sofa large enough to sleep on; a couple of high-backed chairs. A heavy sideboard in the corner housed an elaborate hi-fi system and a full-sized Italian coffee maker. The walls were almost completely lined with books; in the only empty space, above a small fireplace, hung a watercolour of London Bridge.

The pug trotted ahead of them and settled itself without demur on the hearth rug.

'Like to have all my kit around me.' Clive chuckled, surveying his territory with satisfaction. 'Coffee? It's my speciality. New toy.'

'Thanks,' said Olivia.

'Do sit: no booby traps.'

Olivia chose the chair nearest the fireplace, which had a view of the garden. A city garden: paving and gravel flanked by easy-care shrubs, and in one corner a beautiful tree (a cherry, Olivia thought) which must provide a pretty view in the spring.

'It's nice of you to see me,' she said. 'I'm sorry to have been so mysterious.'

'Woman's prerogative.' Clive was busy with the coffee, tamping down grounds and pressing buttons. The machine began to growl and splutter, filling the room with a rich smell of arabica beans. Expensive coffee, Olivia thought.

'It's about your aunt,' she said.

Clive turned. 'Lydia?'

'No.'

He frowned. 'I only have one aunt,' he said. 'Had, rather. She died last year. Game old bird, almost ninety.'

'You have another aunt, as it happens,' Olivia said. 'Georgiana Quickshall. Your mother's sister.' She hesitated. 'Your mother was Eliza Quickshall?'

'Née Quickshall, but no sister. Brother, Henry: no sister. Here, Pooch!' Clive opened a lacquered tin and took out a bone-shaped biscuit. The pug cocked his head hopefully but didn't stir, and Clive laughed. 'You'll have to do better than that. Lazy so-and-so.'

Olivia smiled; a public smile, steeling herself to go on. 'You must think I'm mad, arriving on your doorstep and claiming you have an aunt you've never heard of. A complete stranger. I'm sorry to launch it on you like that.'

'No, no; don't apologise. I like aunts. Rather short of

Rachel Crowther

relatives, in fact. Long on ex-wives, short on solid blood relations. How d'you like your coffee?'

'Just as it comes.'

'Espresso?'

Olivia nodded. Clive manoeuvred himself across the room with some awkwardness to deliver Olivia's coffee, then settled himself with a sigh on the sofa.

'Shouldn't really have more, myself. Doctor's orders: too much caffeine. Better than breaking out the Scotch at this hour, though, eh?'

Olivia had the feeling that if she let the subject drop Clive wouldn't mention it again: that he'd pretend he hadn't heard, or that it had been Olivia's little joke. She imagined he might talk pleasantly about watercolours and play games of temptation with the dog all afternoon, if she let him. But she was wrong.

'So Ma had a sister?' he asked, after a moment.

'Yes.'

'Still alive, you said?'

'She's ninety-one.'

Clive pondered. 'Separated at birth, or something?'

'Later than that.'

'Emigrated?'

Olivia shook her head. 'It might come as a bit of a shock, this,' she said.

Clive downed his espresso in one gulp, then grinned at Olivia. 'Ticker's solid,' he said. 'Gippy knee, but the rest of me's sound. Won't pass out on you.'

'Let's hope not. First aid's not my forte.' Olivia smiled back, took a sip of coffee. 'Your mother had a younger sister who was – disgraced. She got pregnant when she was eighteen and the family disowned her.'

'I say.'

'Mmm.'

'So where's she been all these years? She and this long-lost cousin of mine? She did have the baby, did she?'

'She was locked up,' Olivia said, 'in an asylum. It was what they did, in those days. 1935.'

Clive's eyes widened. 'And she's still there?'

'No, she was released in the early eighties. Rehabilitated, to an extent. She lives in sheltered accommodation in Oxford now.'

'Well, bugger me.' Clive shook his head. 'That's quite a skeleton in the old family closet. You sure about this?'

'Absolutely sure. I've checked all the facts, seen the documents. Birth and death certificates.'

'And the child?'

Olivia hesitated. 'Did you have a sister?' she asked.

Clive nodded. 'Isabella,' he said. 'She died young.'

'In her twenties? A car crash?'

'That's right. Terrible thing.'

'And she would have been – what, three years older than you? Born in 1935?'

Clive stared at Olivia. 'Are you telling me Isabella wasn't my sister?'

'I'm not sure,' Olivia admitted. 'I haven't looked up the adoption records. But I think she was probably your cousin. Your aunt Georgiana's daughter. I think your parents adopted her.'

Clive was silent for a few moments. He reached his stick to prod the pug, which stirred itself with a grunt and waddled over to its master. Clive scooped the dog onto the sofa beside him and it settled its head affectionately on his knee. It was an appealing creature, Olivia thought, despite its unprepossessing physiognomy.

'Great little dogs, pugs,' said Clive. 'Not that Pooch

here is the liveliest specimen.' He tickled the dog's rumpled neck and it wheezed with pleasure.

'Tell me about your family,' Olivia said. 'Your parents; your grandparents. What were they like?'

'Beats me why none of them ever said anything,' said Clive. 'Even after Bella died, they could have said something.'

'I may be wrong,' said Olivia, 'but it fits. If you look for her birth certificate – Isabella's – I don't think you'll find it. I think she was born Jane Quickshall, daughter of Georgiana.'

Clive levered himself to his feet and moved back towards the coffee machine. His limp seemed more pronounced than it had done when Olivia arrived, the stick a more necessary prop.

'How did you find me?' he asked, his back to her once more as he emptied out the damp grounds.

'I found your birth certificate. And your brother's.'

'My brother's dead.'

'I know; I'm sorry.' Should she tell him that anyone interested, for any reason, in the Quickshalls or the Shotters could find out all about them in a single afternoon? 'I traced the family tree.'

Clive turned to face her again. 'Why?'

Why indeed? 'Because I know your aunt. Through the day centre she attends.'

'And she wants to meet me?'

That was the rub, of course. 'She doesn't know you exist,' Olivia admitted. 'I thought – I thought it might be better to find you first. She has good reason to be wary of her family.'

Clive Shotter laughed suddenly.

'You're quite a woman,' he said. 'So you came to check me out, make sure I'd pass muster?'

'No, of course not–'

'Eminently sensible.' Clive waved his stick as if to dismiss Olivia's embarrassment. 'I feel protective of her already, this aunt. Glad you're not springing any old nephew on her. She's not gaga, is she?'

'Not yet.'

Clive nodded slowly, as though conjuring Georgie's image in his mind.

'Tell me about your family,' Olivia said again.

Clive leaned against the sideboard for a moment, then pushed himself upright with a wince.

'Tell you what: got to take my constitutional. Limber up the new joint, you know? Come with me and I'll fill you in on the whole clan.'

Olivia stood at the top of the steps while Clive made his way down, grasping the ornate black rail. The sun had come out while she'd been inside, revealing one of those perfect winter mornings that are particularly lovely in city streets. The clarity of the light gave the white stucco the glistening sheen of icing sugar.

'This is a wonderful place to live,' she said.

Clive was breathless from the effort of manoeuvring himself down to the pavement.

'Lucky,' he agreed.

They made their way slowly along the couple of blocks that separated Clive's house from the green space of Primrose Hill. Olivia didn't know this area well, but she remembered walking here once before, a long time ago, with a young Irishman she'd known at university. The 'Rose of Tralee' man, she called him now, in her head.

The original 'Rose of Tralee' man. A mad interlude before Robert came along. The awkward nostalgia the memory provoked felt lighter here, in the sunlit anonymity of this elegant enclave of London. Almost anything, Olivia thought, would feel easier to bear, gilded by the ambience of early Victorian prosperity. She imagined Sylvia Plath walking these pavements, towards the hill and its views of the London skyline. Not that it had done her any good.

'You know what?' Clive said, as he settled into a steady walking pace. 'I'm rather chuffed about all this. To tell the truth, I was expecting worse.'

'Worse?'

'After your call. Woman with a grievance, sort of thing.' He chuckled, making the allusion to sexual intrigue sound charmingly old-fashioned. 'My loose ends are all tied up, far as I know, but there's the next generation. Sins of the fathers, and all that.'

Olivia thought of her boys; of the prospect of receiving phone calls from weeping girlfriends or their irate mothers. 'You have sons?' she asked.

'Two. High fliers, both of them. Not much time for their ageing Pa. Good boys, though. Got some steady blood from their mother.'

They crossed the road into the park and started up the broad asphalt path that led to the summit of the hill. The grass was still green, the soaring trees and cast-iron lampposts silhouetted against the sky.

'There's a slogan painted on one of the paths,' said Clive. '*The view's so nice.* Comes from a song, apparently, that mentions Primrose Hill. Do you know it?'

'I'm afraid not.'

'Haven of peace,' Clive went on, puffing now from the effort of the incline. 'Not always, though. Lots of famous duels. Murders. Old Mother Shipton said – phew – said the streets of London would run with blood if the city ever grew to enclose the hill.' He halted, leaning on his stick. The pug pulled up at his heels, lifting its face towards Clive. 'Worth the climb,' he said, more to convince himself than Olivia, perhaps. They didn't speak again until they reached the top – and then there was London, laid out before them. Olivia recognised the Post Office Tower and St Paul's among the landmarks in the distant skyline. Worth the climb indeed, she thought.

'I don't know much about my maternal grandparents,' Clive said, when he'd got his breath back. 'Old man Quickshall died when I was a baby.'

'In the war?'

'During the war, not in it. 1940, I think. Or '41. He wasn't spoken of much. I had the impression Ma was frightened of him. Small wonder, if he'd packed one daughter off to a loony bin.'

'A tyrant?'

'A drunk, is my guess. Free with his fists.'

'What did he do for a living?' Olivia remembered the marriage certificate: Thomas Quickshall, clerk.

'He did well for himself.' Clive lifted his stick to demonstrate. 'Worked his way up. East Anglian building society. Started out as a scribe, ended up chief accountant.'

'And your grandmother?'

'Granny went on until I was twelve or thirteen. Not your warm, cosy grandmother: bit of a cold fish, in fact. Lived alone, ten miles from us, but rarely visited. Sunday lunch, once a month, right up to the end. Mind you, I reckon she was the one with the aspirations.'

Those flowery names, Olivia thought. Eliza Frances

and Georgiana Christina. Hauling up her family by the bootstraps, christening them into the middle classes.

'More Hardy than Dickens, my family,' said Clive. 'Even without today's revelations.'

'More than their fair share of tragedy, you mean?'

Clive turned away from the view and began to walk down the hill again. A slower pace than the ascent, Olivia noticed. Wasn't that the way with knees?

'Isabella was the tragedy. Enough tragedy for any family. She was the life and soul, Isabella. Kept us all alight. When she died, everything fell apart. Ma's heart was broken: nothing Phil or I could do to make up for it.'

'She loved Isabella?' Olivia was agog.

'Adored her. Everyone adored her. You couldn't not. She was beautiful, clever: too good to be true, really. Too good for this life, Pa said afterwards. That was the kind of thing he said; drove Ma mad.'

Olivia tried to remember the dates on the documents she'd printed off: had Edwin and Eliza both perished soon after Isabella?

'How old were you when she died?' she asked.

'Twenty-one.' Clive didn't hesitate. 'June 1959, end of national service. About to go up to university.'

'So she was–'

'Twenty-four.'

'Not married?'

Clive shook his head. 'Lots of beaux, to quote Ma. In no rush to choose between them.'

'No child?' ventured Olivia.

Clive turned sharply towards her, but all he said was, 'No child.'

So that avenue was closed, anyway. That fanciful

idea. Olivia chided herself. Ridiculous to imagine that life could deliver such a coincidence.

As they reached the street again a young mother passed with a baby in a pushchair and a toddler trailing behind, tears streaming down his cheeks. Red hands, red cheeks, red eyes, Olivia thought. The gruelling drag through the winter, cold mornings and long afternoons. That was another thing about memory: you didn't exactly forget the boredom and the tiredness, but they were stored in a different place from the technicolour images burned onto the hard disc for future viewing. Benjy looking comical with his giant bandage, solaced by sweets from the ample-bosomed first aider, not the half hour of screaming beforehand. Not the anxiety about time running out on the parking meter, the accident on the M40 that added an hour to the journey home.

'You haven't told me much about my aunt,' Clive said, as they turned into his street.

Olivia felt a spasm of anxiety: she tried to imagine Georgie, austere, withdrawn Georgie, meeting this garrulous, worldly-wise nephew.

'You have to bear in mind that forty-seven years in an institution has an indelible effect,' she said. 'She's not the woman she might have been. Sometimes I feel there's no more than a shell left, a suggestion of her.'

'But there must be something,' Clive said. 'Something about her, to make you go to all this trouble.'

Olivia smiled. 'You're right,' she said. 'There is. The shell of a remarkable person.'

Olivia had expected to take her leave soon after she and Clive returned from their walk on Primrose Hill. She'd imagined that he'd asked her to come so early because he had business to deal with later on, or perhaps because he'd need a rest at lunchtime. When they reached his front door she began to make noises about calling a cab, leaving him to get on with his day.

Clive halted with his key in the lock. The face he turned to her looked older, suddenly; sagging, like the pug's. The effect of exertion, Olivia thought, and the pain in his knee.

'We haven't had lunch yet,' he said. 'You don't really have to go already, do you?'

'Well, not immediately, but—'

'Stay for lunch,' he insisted. 'I'll take you to a little place round the corner. Italian. You like Italian?'

'You don't have to take me out,' said Olivia. 'I could make us a sandwich.'

Clive laughed cheerily. 'Not unless you go shopping first,' he said. 'Not a crust in the house.'

Clive was evidently well-known in the restaurant, an intimate little place on a side street run by three Italians who could have been brothers, and who looked at least Clive's age.

'Signora.' They beamed at Olivia, ushered her theatrically to a table in the window. She smiled, imagining herself in a long line of women brought here by Clive, fêted by the waiters, discussed afterwards. Putting her hand lightly on Clive's arm as he held her chair for her, she smiled at the four old men, feeling like a minor celebrity. She was glad she'd worn her decent coat.

There was, apparently, no menu.

'Food's wonderful here,' said Clive with satisfaction. 'Not vegetarian, are you?'

Olivia shook her head.

'Glass of Prosecco to start? Toast my aunt Georgiana?'

'Why not?'

The food was indeed wonderful. They could have been in Italy, Olivia thought, as a plate of lobster ravioli was laid before her.

'Nice place to have round the corner,' she said.

'One reason I've stuck around.' Clive reached for the wine bottle; Olivia was too slow to prevent him refilling her glass. 'Love it here: couldn't imagine moving. Hettie took off to the country after the divorce. Surrounded by cows.' He chortled.

'What did you do?' Olivia asked. 'For a living, I mean?'

'City.' Clive shrugged dismissively. 'Heyday long gone.'

'Yours?'

He laughed. 'No, the City's. Long lunches; gentlemen's agreements. Rat race, now. My older boy's a currency dealer: wouldn't want to be in his shoes.' He put his fork down for a moment. 'Tell you something, though. Not sure I'd have got where I got if it hadn't been for Bella.'

'How do you mean?'

'My parents weren't interested, after she died. Gave up on us. Could have gone two ways after that. My brother Phil went down the tubes, but I was buggered if I was going anywhere but up. Set my sights. Not as meteoric as Grandpa Quickshall, but I stuck it out.'

'What happened to Philip?' asked Olivia.

Clive shrugged. 'Not a lot. Bit of speculating. Wasn't bad at it, until he was. Spent his money, such as it was, on women and wine.' He laughed suddenly. 'Unlike his big bro. What about you? What's your line?'

'I teach the piano.'

'Ah!' Clive looked interested; more interested than people usually did. 'Play, too?'

'Not much any more,' Olivia admitted.

'I'm involved in a little charity,' said Clive. 'Music lessons for underprivileged children. Maybe you could help us out a bit.'

Olivia was taken aback. 'I'd be glad to, if you've got children in Oxford needing teaching.'

'No, no. Advice, I meant. Strategy, sort of thing. We need musicians on the board.'

It was Olivia's turn to laugh. 'I don't know anything about strategy,' she said. 'And I'm hardly a musician any more.'

Clive shook his head. 'Nonsense. You're just the kind of person we need. Bit of time on your hands, eh?'

'What makes you think I've got time on my hands?'

'Enough time to come up to London on a wild goose chase like this.'

Olivia raised her eyebrows, but she didn't reply.

They ate in silence for a while then. It struck Olivia as deeply ironic that she should be eating a slap-up lunch with Georgie's nephew while Georgie, still unaware of his existence, was at home in Oxford, sitting out another identical day of her impoverished life. How could she explain that to Georgie? How, indeed, could she explain what she'd done without her consent? Because it was clear to Olivia that Clive Shotter wouldn't give up his newly discovered aunt now without a struggle. How could she raise the subject again with Georgie after the flat dismissal she'd received last time?

'Why bother learning to cook?' said Clive happily, as he chased the last parcel of ravioli around his plate, gathering the traces of sauce. 'Perfetto, Alessandro,' he declared, as the youngest of the waiters hovered into view.

'Grazie, signore.'

'So,' said Clive, when the plates had been cleared. 'Question: are you going to break it to my aunt that you've sniffed me out, or am I going to pretend I've got a yen for family history all of a sudden?'

'What do you mean?'

He shrugged. 'If you could find me, I could find her. Odd name like Quickshall: not that many around, I imagine.'

Olivia felt a rush of relief. 'Why would you do that?'

'Plenty of people look into their forebears. Perfectly natural thing to do.'

'No, I mean why would you present it like that? Pretend it was your doing?'

Clive twinkled. 'Don't much fancy a rebuff before I've clapped eyes on the old bird,' he said. 'Good reason to be wary of her family, you said. As translated: had no idea you were coming to find me. Am I right?'

Olivia blushed. 'You might still be rebuffed,' she said. 'She's a person of strong will. You'd have to be, to survive that long in the kind of place they put her in.'

'I'll polish up the old charm,' said Clive. 'Take the pooch along. Never met an aunt yet who didn't fall for the pug.' He grinned. 'Now: better get you on a train before your husband sends a search party.'

# Chapter Thirty-Seven

Faith's business went through a quiet patch in December. Not that she minded: she'd been flat out since September, and she reckoned it was about time she had a rest. She needed to look for new premises, too. Some of the contracts she'd been getting lately were beyond the scope of her kitchen, and the business was steadily taking over her whole flat. Her paperwork was stashed in a drawer under the telly, and her second fridge-freezer jostled for position in the living area with the wardrobe that wouldn't fit in the minuscule bedroom. Maybe she was doing well enough, these days, that she could afford to live in one place and work in another. Keep herself above board with the planning regulations, too.

She certainly needed a bit of time to take stock, but it was a fine line, how much of a lull she wanted. She'd got plenty on over Christmas, but not a lot yet after the holiday season. No good planning for expansion if she'd come to the end of a run of good times. No telling how soon the credit crunch would bite, either, though everyone said Oxford was a good place for a catering business right now.

So when an enquiry came through about a wedding, a last-minute contract for a big do in one of the colleges in the first week in January, she was relieved – even if it was going to be a tall order managing something on that scale.

'I'll be quite frank,' the bride said on the phone. 'I've lost confidence in the people I'd booked. It's disappointing; I took a lot of trouble over choosing them. But I found out yesterday that the person I've been dealing with all this time wasn't even going to be there on the day. I don't know how they think they can get away with it. A wedding's a wedding, after all.'

'Absolutely,' said Faith. 'Your big day: you want it to be perfect.'

'Exactly.' The woman paused. 'I take it you don't have any other bookings that day?'

'I never have more than one function the same day,' Faith assured her. 'Unless it's, like, a small cocktail party after a private lunch, something like that. I'd never double up on a wedding, no way. The advantage of a small operation like mine is you get personal service.'

The wedding was only three weeks away and Faith's mind was already running ahead, wondering how she could pull together the staff to help her. Erica was off to South Africa straight after Christmas, and they'd be flat out for the ten days before she went.

'Good.' The bride sighed. 'Now, what's the best thing? Shall we meet to discuss the menu?'

'E-mail me what you've agreed with the other firm and I'll let you know if there's a problem,' Faith suggested. 'I can supply references–'

'No need for that. You were recommended by a friend whose judgement I'm happy to rely on.'

'That's nice to hear.' Word of mouth, thought Faith with satisfaction. What had she always said?

'Maybe we should meet at St Saviour's anyway,' the bride said, with the no-nonsense tone of a woman used to people doing what she wanted, 'so you can get a sense of the layout. I did tell you it's two hundred people?'

'You did.' God help me, Faith thought. 'Next Monday any good to you?'

Things had felt a bit weird with James since the birthday evening that went so horribly wrong. He was as sweet and loving as ever when they were together, but despite her business being quieter, it had been harder and harder to find time to see him. Or perhaps now Faith had more time on her hands, she'd realised how busy he was, and how hard to pin down? Either way, she hadn't seen him for two weeks now, and the phone was no good. James had always been funny on the phone.

The thought of this wedding, another happy bride agonising over her big day, made Faith feel doubtful and hopeful all at the same time. She hadn't forgotten how she'd let herself fantasise about marriage the very first time she and James went out. Faith the lifelong independent woman, dreaming of a white wedding to a handsome doctor: what would her old mates say? And what would they say now, she asked herself ruefully, as she pinned her hopes on a bloke who didn't even answer her calls?

But as luck would have it, James left a message the very

day she got the phone call about the wedding. His private clinic was cancelled, he said. Was she busy later? Faith was chuffed about the timing. It was always at the back of her mind that she wasn't quite good enough for James. For a consultant gynaecologist. She wanted to make a go of her business partly so she could show him she was a woman who could stand on her own two feet. There she'd be this evening, cool, calm and collected, with a big function to plan for.

By the time James arrived, though, Faith was panicking. The menu the bride had agreed with the original caterers had come through on the e-mail and she was definitely going to need an Erica to help with the cooking, even if she could hire a few extra girls to serve on the day. When James rang the doorbell she was still sitting in front of the computer, staring at columns of words and figures.

'God, I'm sorry,' she wailed. 'Look at me, not even changed!'

'You look gorgeous as you are,' James said. 'What have you been so absorbed by?'

'A new booking. Big wedding, in three weeks' time, at St Saviour's College.'

'That sounds like a reason to celebrate.' James produced a bottle of champagne from behind his back.

'Well.' Faith beamed. 'Aren't you a love?'

'I like to think so.' He grinned, and kissed her ostentatiously.

Faith wriggled out of his arms with a consolatory squeeze and went to fetch a couple of glasses.

'What was it really for?' she asked.

'What?'

'The champagne, you prune.'

'Do I need an excuse to drink champagne with the sexiest woman in Oxford?'

Faith settled herself on the tiny sofa and patted the cushion beside her. 'Well, I think we'll have to look into that, Dr Young.'

James had explained the whole thing about gynaecologists being surgeons, but although she got that it was more exclusive to be a 'Mr', Faith still liked thinking of James as Dr Young. It gave her a thrill, addressing him like that, and because it wasn't his proper title any more she thought of it as their private game. She glanced over his shoulder at the clock on the mantelpiece and was pleased to see that it was only six thirty. Plenty of time for some private games before dinner, she thought. Probably that was why he'd brought the champagne.

'Here's to the big wedding,' James said. 'Why such short notice? Is it a rush job?'

'The catering yes, the wedding no. The bride found out the caterers were double booked and she wasn't getting the head honcho, so she pulled out.'

'High risk strategy.'

'Not if you land with your bum in the butter and Faith's Functions doing the business for you.'

James frowned. 'There was something interesting in that sentence, Miss Sargent: could you run it past me again? Something about bums and butter I didn't quite catch...'


'I'll help out,' said James, as he scooped up the last spoonful of pannacotta. 'I'm not on call that Saturday. I'll be your gopher.'

Faith stared. Every time she reckoned she'd got James

figured out, she thought, he'd pull something unexpected like this.

'Why would you want to do that?'

'Why not? Bit of fun for me, see what you get up to when I'm not around. I did some waitering when I was a medical student. I wasn't bad.'

'I don't pay much.' Faith grinned.

'You can pay me in kind. I'll prepare an invoice.'

She laughed, and took his hand across the table. 'You're full of surprises,' she said. 'What d'you usually do at the weekends, then?'

'Ah, that's for me to know and you to find out.'

'Twenty questions?'

'All right.'

Faith sat back, and stuck her tongue into her cheek. What she wouldn't give to know the real answer to that question. Now she thought about it, it was obvious James didn't work all weekend, every weekend, even with his private patients, but apart from that one time he'd taken her to Aldeburgh he never seemed to be free. The Aldeburgh weekend and this one: that was only two in almost four months. When they were together it didn't seem to matter, any of that. What counted was the moment, how he spoke to her and looked at her and touched her. But now she'd asked, she wanted a straight answer. And she knew, part of her knew for sure, that she wasn't going to get one.

'Golf?' she asked.

'Hate golf. Play occasionally, mainly with my father, who still beats me hollow.'

'Gardening?'

'Ought to, but no. Mow the lawn once in a blue moon and leave the rest to its own devices.'

'Conferences?'

James pulled a face.

'Too many conferences. Damn patients, expecting me to keep up with the latest developments, as if last year's knowledge wasn't good enough.'

Faith considered. What else could she ask that he wouldn't mind answering? Friends he didn't want her to meet? His ex-wife? Other women, old or new?

'Must be call-girls, then,' she said.

James mimed horror. 'My secret's out! Will you ever speak to me again?' Then he lifted his hand to stroke her cheek. 'The truth is I'm a very boring person. I work, I sleep, I watch the telly, I dream about my beautiful girlfriend, and when she can fit me into her busy life I ply her with champagne in the hope that she'll decide I'm too fascinating and lovable to resist.'

Faith's lip quivered, despite herself. 'You don't need the champagne,' she said. 'You're fascinating and lovable all on your own.'

James smiled. 'And so are you.'

# Chapter Thirty-Eight

The Christmas decorations were up at the day centre, a modest tree in one corner and streamers made of garish metallic ribbon strung across the ceiling. Olivia arrived early, in time to help Shirley load mince pies onto trays to warm up while they sang.

'Carols today?' asked Shirley, although she knew the answer. 'I thought of getting the playgroup children in to sing to them, but they don't learn carols any more. Not the kind our lot would recognise.'

'Frosty the Snowman,' said Olivia.

Shirley pulled a face. 'Jingle Bells, maybe. But it didn't seem worth it. How many of these d'you think we'll need? I reckon I've bought too many again.'

Olivia was grateful for the diversion of fussing over foil trays and tubs of brandy butter. There was more in store this morning than carols and mince pies: Clive Shotter had phoned the night before to confirm that he was coming to Oxford today. They'd agreed that the Wednesday Club would be the best place for him to meet Georgie. It kept things simple, meant no one else had to be involved except Shirley. But now the time was approaching Olivia felt queasy with anxiety. The thought of Clive having a wasted journey was the least of it: what might the shock do to Georgie?

She'd mentioned the visit to Shirley as casually as she could manage, and if Shirley was unduly surprised she hadn't shown it.

'Clever old you!' she'd said. 'How did you track him down, then? Oh, that'll be a nice surprise for Georgie.'

Olivia had shrugged her shoulders and swallowed her misgivings.

'It's gone half past,' Shirley said now. 'You ready, Olivia?'

Olivia handed round printed word sheets, smiling; regretting Kenneth's absence again. 'Three Kings from Persian lands afar', she thought. That would have been a treat.

Georgie was in her usual chair, wearing her usual white blouse and a crisp navy skirt that seemed to have resisted the degrading effects of the communal wash. Olivia's stomach turned over again at the audacity of her interference.

'How are you today, Georgie?' she asked, and Georgie smiled – a plain, thin-lipped smile, but a smile nonetheless.

'Very well, thank you.'

'I hope you like carols,' Olivia said, passing on along the line.

She spotted Clive halfway through 'Once in Royal'. Shirley must have let him in, and the two of them were standing together by the door to the kitchen. Olivia saw Shirley pointing across the room towards Georgie, and then Clive caught her eye and grinned. His sparse grey hair was slicked down today over his smooth scalp, and he was wearing a tweed suit. He looked like a different species from the Wednesday Clubbers, even the ones who were only a few years older than him. He belonged to the outside world, Olivia thought. He'd come from his den, with its watercolours and its espresso machine. She played another couple of carols, as much to delay the moment as anything else, and out of the corner of her eye she watched Clive Shotter surveying the room.

Eventually she saw Shirley duck back into the kitchen, the sign for her to draw the music to a close.

'We wish you a Merry Christmas,' Olivia called over the lid of the piano, and she struck up the introduction. The singing had been more vigorous than usual today. Nothing like Christmas to get people going, she thought. Nothing like a babe lying in a manger, a star in the sky, a few shiny streamers strung across the ceiling. They serenaded the figgy pudding with gusto, their papery faces lit with enthusiasm, Elsie and Betty, Marjorie and William and the rest.

'Mince pies, everyone!' Shirley announced, appearing from the kitchen with a tray.

Amid murmurs of approval and pleasure Olivia moved quietly towards Clive.

'Moment of truth?' he asked.

'I hope this isn't a terrible mistake.'

Clive laughed shortly. 'Nothing ventured.' He clapped a hand on Olivia's shoulder and she led him across the room to where Georgie sat, a mince pie balanced now on a plate on the arm of her chair.

Olivia knelt down beside her.

'Georgie,' she said, 'there's someone here to see you.'

Georgie looked up, her eyes shaded by heavy lids.

'Hello,' said Clive. 'I'm afraid you don't know me from Adam.'

For a moment Georgie said nothing. For a moment Olivia thought her alertness earlier had been misleading; that she was too hazy, today, to register Clive's presence. Then her face twisted into an expression Olivia couldn't read.

'Oh, I know you,' she said. 'The spit of Henry.'

'Blow me,' said Clive. 'No flies on you, eh?'

Georgie regarded him gravely. Her bearing remained stiff, the emotion in her face still too finely balanced to call.

'They've sent you, have they?' she asked.

'There's only me left,' Clive said cheerfully. 'Me and you. Last remnants, eh, Aunt Georgie? I'm your nephew, Clive. Eliza's son.'

'Eliza's dead,' said Georgie with a hint of satisfaction.

''Fraid so. Long time ago, now. Henry too, and Edwin. Remember Edwin? Eliza's husband?'

Georgie gave a tiny nod of acknowledgement.

'Glad to have found you,' said Clive. 'Flesh and blood.'

Georgie flinched slightly, and Olivia felt her eyes fill with tears.

'You'd better sit down,' Georgie said, and Clive settled himself in the chair beside her. He hadn't brought the pug after all, Olivia noticed. He'd decided to rely on his wits instead.

The sight of the two of them left Olivia with an empty feeling; an unexpected sorrow. She realised that she'd imagined a kind of magic when she thought about this scene. She'd pictured Georgie transformed into a young woman again, Clive as a little boy leading her off to recover the lost years of her life. But here they were, simply two old people, the last survivors of their family. There was no going back, after all, and precious little time left to them. Precious little time for a happy ending, even if by some miracle Georgie wanted to see him again after this awkward first encounter among the plastic chairs and murmured conversations of the Wednesday Club's Christmas party.

Shirley approached, handing round a second mince pie to the few whose appetites matched their enthusiasm.

'OK?' she asked.

Olivia nodded. She stood up as gracefully as she could and followed Shirley back towards the kitchen.

'What a nice man,' said Shirley. 'I wouldn't mind him for my nephew. Was she pleased to see him?'

'Hard to say,' said Olivia. 'She was polite, anyway. She recognised the family likeness.'

Shirley shook her head in wonderment. 'Amazing,' she said. 'Seventy years since she saw any of them. Ooh, I feel quite excited, Olivia. It's a red letter day, this, isn't it?'

They both looked across to where Clive sat squeezed tight into an upright chair, leaning slightly towards his aunt.

'I wouldn't have known what to say, in his position,' Olivia said.

'Gift of the gab.' Shirley winked. 'I bet he's talked himself out of trickier situations than this in his time. And into them, too. Proper charmer, don't you reckon?'

It was what people said about a certain kind of man, Olivia thought. What people said about her Alastair, sometimes. Out of the blue she remembered their voices breaking, her older boys; how she'd heard men upstairs one day and wondered who they were. New people living in her house, with their unfamiliar mannerisms and their long legs, patting her on the shoulder rather than pulling at her skirts. She felt tears gathering in her eyes again, not for Georgie and Clive but for herself.

On the other side of the room Georgie was staring straight ahead, something approaching a frown on her face. But she was listening, Olivia surmised, to whatever Clive was saying. She hadn't thrown him out, however vehement her objection had been when Olivia had raised the possibility of tracing her family.

She felt exhausted suddenly. Perhaps Clive might expect her to wait for him, but she'd done her part. She ate a mince pie to please Shirley, exchanged a few words of banter with Rex the driver, then slipped away.

It was a relief to get out into the fresh air. The layers of papier mâché leaves on the pavement were overlaid with a sparkling of frost, and the sky was the pure powder blue of midwinter. Olivia looked up at the houses with their neat front gardens and red brick façades, the decorated trees in their windows marking their occupants' cheerful progress towards Christmas. She had a familiar sense of yearning, recognising the tug of a communal spirit that she never entirely felt part of. Did other people have the same doubts, she wondered, or were they happy to take their own lives at face value?

She was on foot today; she didn't trust her bike on icy roads. She joined the canal path at Aristotle Lane, passing fishermen with their camping stools and tubs of bait, the occasional narrowboat dweller taking in the midday sunshine. Under one of the bridges was a curiosity: two mangled bicycles that had been pulled out of the canal, entwined like lovers drowned together and encrusted, improbably, with clusters of mussels. Olivia stopped for a moment to marvel at them. She wouldn't have believed mussels could grow in the canal, especially not in such profusion. They had erupted through the saddles, strung themselves along crossbars and spokes, curved around the distorted rims of the wheels: a surreal sculpture of city trash colonised by sea creatures. Such strange sights life offered, she thought. Such extraordinary things could be buried beneath its calm surface.

When she got home Alastair was sitting in the kitchen.

'Boiler's broken in the Year Eleven block,' he said cheerfully. 'They sent us home. Where've you been?'

'Playing carols at the day centre.'

'Ah – community service among the crumblies.'

'Shush.' Olivia batted at him with the glove she'd just pulled off, but she felt a rush of pleasure at the prospect of his company. 'Shall we have some lunch?'

'A strange thing happened this morning,' she said, as she heated up soup. 'You know Georgie, the old lady at the day centre?'

'The one whose family you've been looking up?'

Olivia nodded. 'Her nephew came to see her today. She'd never met him before. Didn't even know he existed.'

'Huh.' Alastair tipped his chair back, balancing for a moment on the rear legs. 'It must be weird to have no family.'

'Georgie might have been better off without a family, considering what they did to her. But I hope the nephew might be a good thing.'

Faced with her flesh and blood, she thought, Georgie had opted for tolerance, and perhaps acceptance. Olivia hadn't dared hope for joy. Was Georgie capable of joy? Had her baby been conceived in a state of joy? Olivia hoped so, because there'd been precious little of it since for Georgie.

She glanced over at Alastair, imagining him, for a moment, at Clive Shotter's age. And then, turning off the hob, she carried the soup over to the table.

*FOR A LONG* time the monotony was a torture, but now you crave it: an emptiness to lose yourself in. Time slips through the blank days; months slide over each other into years. Their passing is marked by the slackening of your skin, the stiffening of your joints. The people change, the names and the faces, but you don't care any more. They move you, but you hardly notice. They speak more softly, but you don't hear. So much of you is gone: they cannot reach the rest of you, the remnant locked up with the seed of your baby, deep in the core of your shrivelled womb. You can speak to them, you can answer their questions, but you can't let them in.

It comes down to this: has the endurance of your body claimed victory for you? You shut your eyes and imagine the whiteness of the walls. The sting of the nettles at your ankles is a distant memory, but death eludes you still. And if, in the corner of the mirror that lines up the days, one behind another, there is the reflection of a face you have known, a face distorted and transformed but recognisable, still: if there is something to stir the memory of that little girl, that young woman, will it reach you?

# Chapter Thirty-Nine

Sarah's cast was removed on schedule on the twenty-third of December. The occasion had a festive air: the trauma unit was almost deserted (waiting, the plaster technician said drily, for the Christmas rush) and a little clutch of staff gathered to chat to Sarah and Guy while the plaster was cut off.

'Have a chocolate,' said the charge nurse, proffering a tin of Quality Street. 'We've got far too many here.'

'I was on an orthopaedic ward one Christmas,' Guy said. 'I thought I'd never eat chocolate again after that.'

'Road accident, was it?' asked another nurse, peeling the wrapper off a toffee.

'Mountaineering.'

And so Guy embarked on an account of his fall and the treatment that had followed. Then, encouraged by his reception, he recounted a tale of disaster narrowly averted on the higher slopes of K2 a few years before.

'We were lucky,' he finished, to appreciative murmurs from his audience. 'A week later, the weather was much worse. Things could have turned out differently.'

'You've never told me that one,' said Sarah. 'How many stories are there that I haven't heard yet?'

'An almost infinite number.' Guy raised one eyebrow. 'You're doomed, I'm afraid, to a lifetime of climbing anecdotes.'

The nurses chuckled, and Sarah felt a frisson of pleasure, registering their admiration for her fiancé's modest celebrity. It was rare for her to see him in public like this; easier to feel sure of his attractions when there were other people to share them with. He looked dapper, tanned, wiry: by contrast, the crew of the trauma unit looked pale and tired, as though it was a long time since they'd seen the outside world.

'When's the wedding?' asked the charge nurse.

'Two weeks tomorrow.' Sarah wriggled her toes as the plaster was finally lifted away. 'And I'm determined to walk up the aisle unaided. Except by my father, of course.'

'Speaking of your father,' said Guy, 'we should get going. The roads will be busy today.'

'It feels wonderful to be free again.' Sarah lowered herself gingerly to the floor. Guy took her arm, and one of the nurses handed over her crutches.

'Hang on to them for now, eh?' she said. 'Don't run before you can walk. You've got a follow up appointment?'

'Physio, heal thyself.' Sarah grinned. 'I'll see you in clinic next week. Thank you so much, all of you. Happy Christmas.'

Sarah and Guy made their way back through the winding corridors to the car park. They were going to Hampshire for Christmas. Her last Christmas as a single girl, Sarah's father had said, but she'd needed no persuading: much more satisfactory, she thought again now, to decamp for the duration than to shuttle between her flat and Guy's house. Both properties were on the market, and each had acquired a dejected air as they'd been prepared for viewing by prospective purchasers. Anyway, Sarah's brother and his family were flying over from Canada, coming for an extended stay that would include the wedding. After the quiet Christmases of the last few years the house would be filled with people again. Sarah was looking forward to it with a childlike mixture of excitement and dread.

Guy's car was already loaded, ready to drive straight on from the hospital. He stood by while Sarah settled herself in the passenger seat, tucking her crutches on top of the boxes of food and presents on the back seat.

'OK?'

Sarah nodded.

As they headed out of the hospital grounds, she recalled her conversation with Olivia a couple of weeks ago a little bashfully. It had never been her way to wallow in uncertainty. Olivia was right: she was good at making the best of things, and marriage was a worthwhile focus for her energies. She felt a sense of relief at coming to her senses, returning to the rational sphere in which she usually lived.

'Do you want to ring your father?' asked Guy. 'Let him know when we'll be there?' He pulled his mobile out of his top pocket and offered it to her.

Sarah shrugged. She wouldn't usually ring ahead; but then, she couldn't usually, because she'd be driving herself. She dialled the number, heard the ring tone, waited. Her father didn't have an answerphone.

'No reply,' she said. 'He's probably gone for a walk. I said mid-afternoon, but he won't fuss if we're late.'

The traffic was fairly clear for the first stage of the journey, but it thickened abruptly when they reached the M25.

'I wonder whether we'd have been better going cross-country,' said Guy. 'Heading down the A34 then cutting across. We could try that next time.'

Sarah grinned. 'You sound just like Dad.'

'I assume that's a compliment.'

There was silence for a minute or two while Guy shifted lanes, overtaking a couple of lorries that appeared to be tracking each other, side by side. Then he glanced across at Sarah as though weighing something up.

'We might not have much time to talk once we're there,' he said. 'I thought perhaps we should have a chat before we're swept up by Christmas and your family.'

'What about?' Sarah's laugh sounded ill-at-ease. 'Should I be worried?'

'No.' Guy frowned, putting his foot on the brake as the cars in front slowed again. 'No, I don't have any doubts. But I've been wondering whether you do.'

'Doubts?' Sarah was stalling for time; she knew exactly what he meant. *A la maison*, she thought. This was the last thing she'd expected, but perhaps it shouldn't have been. There wasn't much Guy was afraid of, and what he was, he faced head on. Unlike her, clearly.

'You've seemed a little distracted lately,' Guy said. 'Not quite yourself. I've wondered whether you're sure about all this.'

'Oh dear.' Sarah didn't look at him. 'I mean, oh dear that you've been worried.'

Guy shook his head briefly. 'Not worried, concerned.'

331

'You don't need to be,' Sarah said. 'I really don't think you need to be. I'm not one of those complicated women. What you see is what you get.'

Which is why her distraction troubled him, she thought. Had she expected him to notice nothing?

'I wouldn't want you to feel trapped before we begin,' Guy said.

Sarah stared out through the windscreen. The line of traffic stretched as far as she could see, cars and lorries nose to tail like migrating birds beneath the dense, milky sky. She felt a sudden sense of disorientation, and with it a surge of nausea. She'd been terribly travel sick as a child and she still hated being a passenger, still easily felt claustrophobic in a car. She took a deep breath, mustered her self-control.

'It's a big step,' she said. 'Of course it is, for both of us. But it's a normal thing to do, not some madcap plan...'

Her voice trailed off. Guy wanted a declaration, she thought, not an assurance of her good sense. But she was wrong.

'I should have told you this before,' Guy said. 'I feel bad about that. I can tell that you're not sure about marrying me because I've been in the same position myself. A long time ago, I was engaged to someone else. From the beginning I had doubts, but I pushed them away, put them down to nerves. I expected to feel better as the wedding approached, but I didn't. Finally, the day before, I confessed. I told her I'd made a mistake, that I couldn't marry her. It was an agonising moment, but it was the right thing to do. I've never regretted it.'

'Goodness.' Sarah's heart was beating hard. He must be very sure, she thought, to risk himself again. And to trust her with his secret.

'I should have told you before,' Guy said again. His voice was quiet, controlled, but even so Sarah could hear in it the possibility of an emotional range she hadn't detected before. 'But you can see it was a difficult thing to admit to a fiancée. Now you know I'm fallible. You know I let someone down badly. But I couldn't bear you to be in the situation I was in, and I know my limitations. I'm not an exciting person. I've had an exciting life, but I don't confuse that with being original or entertaining in myself.'

'That's not it,' Sarah said. She felt a rush of wind in her head, a sudden chill in her chest. 'It's nothing to do with you. There's something I should have told you, too. About my mother.' Her voice sounded shrill and distorted, rising above the thrum of the car engine. She swallowed hard, struggling to get the muscles of her throat under control. 'My mother didn't just die: she committed suicide. I was a disappointment to her, and when I was thirty she gave up on me. I think that's why – maybe it's why I've found this – hard.'

There was complete silence; only for a short time, but it felt to Sarah like a moment of levelling, of absolute zero.

'Surely,' Guy said, 'surely that can't have been the reason. Surely no mother–'

Sarah shook her head. The words came in a rush now. 'I let her down. She'd always wanted to be a doctor, and she couldn't, so she hoped I would be instead. When I didn't manage that, she at least wanted me to be beautiful and successful and marry well. She had high hopes of one boyfriend, someone I brought home a few times. She killed herself the day after he left me.'

'My dear Sarah.' Guy's face looked deeply riven, years of crags and crevasses scored into his forehead and the folds around his eyes. 'I'm so terribly sorry for you, but

333

I simply can't believe you were responsible. There must have been something else, some other explanation.'

'She'd been depressed,' Sarah said. 'She'd had bouts of depression, but she'd been much better for the last couple of years. Happy.'

'And the rest of your family – did they think–'

'We've never spoken about it. My brother was abroad when she died. My father and I don't talk about my mother. I've wanted to apologise to him, but I've never managed it.'

She ought to be crying, Sarah thought, but she felt icy calm.

'And so you've never married because you blamed yourself?' Guy asked. 'Because you felt you shouldn't have that happiness without your mother?'

'I haven't exactly been fending off suitors all these years.' Sarah laughed, another squeaky, incongruous trill. 'But – maybe. For a long time I thought I'd never get married.'

'Then why me?'

Sarah turned to look at him. 'Because you were so certain,' she said. Perhaps she'd only just realised this, but it seemed perfectly clear, now, that it was what had swayed her. She'd needed not someone who would settle for her, but someone who'd fall for her, who'd be determined to have her. Every year she'd have needed more convincing, and every year the likelihood of finding someone to do it diminished. Her eyes filled with tears now. Just for a moment she considered saying more, making another confession, but she thought better of it. What had there been to that, after all, but the mysterious workings of self-doubt?

'And because you were right,' she said, and Guy

reached a hand across to take hers, clasped tight in her lap.

It was dark by the time they turned off the motorway. As Sarah watched the familiar landmarks loom and pass, the houses of her parents' friends and the sign pointing to her old school, she thought that more than one plaster cast had been removed today; more than one thing inside her had mended. Or at least, the mending had begun, the slow knitting together of jagged edges. But as they approached the village her apprehension grew. Now that she'd told Guy about her mother's death, admitted what it had meant to her, she could see that it wouldn't be possible for things to go on in the same way any longer with her father. And then she remembered how they had veered close to the subject last time she'd been home, and it struck her that despite all the pretending and avoiding, the not-talking, her father had made sure she knew how pleased he was that she was getting married. He had done his best, all these years, to look after her.

'I ought to talk to Dad,' she said, 'before the wedding.'

Guy looked at her. 'I'm sure he doesn't blame you. Depression is unpredictable. It can overwhelm people suddenly, for no obvious reason.'

'But there was an obvious reason,' Sarah said. 'I know she was upset, because I was there. I came down for the weekend, after Mike – I came to tell them.'

Guy didn't answer, but he squeezed her hand hard. Whatever the truth was, Sarah thought, it was good to have him beside her. She thought of the years ahead, his lean body in her bed every night. She thought of arriving at her father's with Guy, not having to face the house on her own. She shut her eyes for a moment as they reached the final crossroads beside the Hare and Hounds, letting gratitude sink in. It wasn't enough to quiet her nerves, the plunging sense of stepping off a cliff, but it was a consolation, a promise for the future.

Despite the lack of streetlamps, the village was brightly lit. Strings of fairy lights twined around branches and along the fronts of houses; the solid tower of the church was illuminated by floodlights. Sarah felt a twinge of sadness and pleasure at the familiarity of it all. But as they turned in through her father's gate posts, apprehension was replaced by surprise. The house was in darkness, the curtains open but no lights visible.

'That's odd,' Sarah said. 'He was definitely expecting us. I rang him last night.'

'Visiting a neighbour?' Guy suggested. 'A drinks party or something?'

'He didn't mention anything. More likely he's having a nap, building up his strength for the onslaught. I've got a key, anyway.'

The house was warmer than she'd expected; her father must have turned the central heating up in preparation for their arrival.

'Dad?' she called, as they walked into the hall. She turned to Guy, uncertain.

'Shall we look upstairs, in case he's asleep?' Guy asked. 'Or would you prefer not to disturb him?'

'I'd prefer to find him.'

Could her father have wandered off, become confused? There had been no suggestion of that, ever. Sarah started towards the stairs, awkward on her crutches in the confined space of the hall. She remembered the last time she'd been here, watching her father with his stick as she hauled her cases upstairs.

Guy followed her up to the first floor, along the landing to the bedroom at the front. Sarah knew her way around the house in the dark, but Guy lit a trail of lights behind her. As they crossed the threshold of her father's bedroom he flicked the switch inside the door. The bed was empty, tidily made.

'Might he have gone out shopping?' Guy suggested. 'Some last-minute Christmas presents?'

'I suppose he could have taken a taxi into Petersfield. But look.' On top of the chest of drawers was a stack of wrapped presents.

'Well,' said Guy. 'Wine, or something. A sudden panic about playing host to all these people.'

'But I'm doing the catering.'

There was a petulant edge to Sarah's voice. Guy put his hand on her shoulder; the first time he'd touched her since they'd got out of the car.

Sarah felt suddenly that they'd dawdled, failed to register the seriousness of the situation. Moving as fast as she could on the crutches, she swung herself back along the landing, leaving Guy to peer into the other rooms on that floor as he passed.

'Careful,' Guy called as she started down the stairs. 'Don't fall.'

Before she reached the bottom he was beside her again, turning on more lights, opening the door to the sitting room.

And there was her father, exactly as Sarah had last seen him, sitting in the high-backed armchair by the fireplace. Except not as she'd last seen him, because Sarah knew in that first instant that he was dead.

# Chapter Forty

C hristmas crept up on Olivia almost without her noticing, in the end. Her own preparations weren't as demanding as they used to be, now the boys' presents consisted entirely of hard cash or pre-ordered electronic gadgets – and since their taste in food was equally unadventurous, she had long since given up any culinary creativity in honour of the season. If there were Christmas concerts at their schools, her sons didn't feature in them. Instead of the melée of nativity plays and letters to the North Pole that had characterised Christmases past, there was a week or two of vague anticipation, then a furious rush to fill the fridge and post presents to godchildren and cousins, and suddenly it was December the twenty-third.

She and Robert had been invited to a few parties of a sedate but pleasant kind, but the boys' social calendars – even Benjy's – were much fuller. Olivia had made an attempt to keep track of their plans, noting the events she got to hear about on the communal planner in the kitchen, but after school term finished she gave up. Tom's whereabouts had been beyond her sphere of influence for some time, and now it seemed affable Alastair was moving out of range too. The younger two occasionally needed ferrying to some engagement or other, but more often they went by bike, shouting farewells from the hallway then slamming the front door cheerfully behind them.

'Should I be keeping closer tabs on them?' she asked Robert, when he came home from work on the evening of the twenty-third to find her alone in the house. 'We always said one of the nice things about living in Oxford was that the boys could be independent, but Benjy and Angus aren't very old.'

'Don't you know where they are?' Robert took a bottle of wine out of the fridge and held it up enquiringly.

'Yes, please. I do in theory. Benjy's at Paul's house and Angus said he was going to the cinema, but they just head off. I feel a bit ineffectual.'

'Don't. Feel liberated instead. Cheers.'

Robert led the way through to the sitting room, in which an asymmetric Christmas tree had been installed at the weekend. The garden centre had almost run out of large trees by the time they got there, and they'd settled for one that had clearly been rejected by earlier purchasers. Decorations charting the years of family life hung from its branches, including a sequence of salt-dough stars made at playgroup, and a set of nativity figures from the expensive crackers Olivia had bought one year.

Robert settled into the sofa with a sigh.

'Good tree,' he said. 'I like the wonkiness.'

'When's your mother arriving?' Olivia asked, although she was fairly sure she had spoken to her last.

339

'After lunch tomorrow. She's getting some horrifically early train.'

Robert's mother always came to them for Christmas. Her other sons lived much closer, so she had less need to catch up with their families. Olivia suspected there was also less justification for her to stay any length of time with them, and she liked to bed into the household for at least a week, to get what she called her penn'orth. Olivia was happy to have her, anyway. She'd been a godsend at Christmas when the boys had been little, and now they were older she was remarkably tolerant of their noise and arguing. Olivia's own mother was staying in Italy for Christmas. She had an invitation, apparently, from a colleague who lived in Fiesole.

'We should have a family get-together next year, while we can still make the boys come,' Olivia said. 'They haven't seen their cousins for a while.'

'Mmm. Speaking of which, have you heard any more from your friend Mr Shotter?'

'No.' Olivia paused, considered. Things had been different between her and Robert since the Southwold trip, easier and warmer and more impulsive, but they hadn't mentioned 1983 or its ramifications again since they got home. She was conscious of the need not to ruffle the surface too much, just at the moment: she thought of something setting, or healing, or regrowing. She said lightly, 'But I wrote to Eve today.'

'Ah!'

'I did what you suggested. I told her neither of us was more to blame than the other, and that we'd done our penance.'

'Good.' Robert raised his wine glass. 'Good for you.'

'She can take it however she likes,' Olivia said. 'You

never know, with Eve. I don't expect to hear anything from her, but who knows?'

'Who knows indeed.' He grinned, pleased with her. 'How long are the boys out? Do we have time to slip out for supper somewhere?'

'I don't know. I don't suppose we'd get a table, anyway.'

'We could try.' Robert drained his glass. 'They've got keys, haven't they? It has to work both ways, this independence thing.'

'It doesn't, though.' Olivia hesitated. 'I suppose I could check in with Paul's mother. We could take our mobiles.'

In the end they cycled to a pub near the river that had changed hands recently. Its reputation was growing fast, but apparently not fast enough to fill it two days before Christmas. The food was unexceptional, but the occasion wasn't: it was a long time, Olivia thought, contemplating her husband in the candlelight, since she'd felt like the slip-of-a-girl he'd taken home to meet his mother in 1985. Lucky none of the children were there to see them sharing a chocolate soufflé, twining fingers under the table. Lucky them, to have this moment before Christmas descended in its full glory.

At ten o'clock Olivia phoned home and got Angus, returned safely from the cinema and indignant to find his parents absent.

'Where are the others?' he demanded.

'Paul's Mum's dropping Benjy back in a little while,' Olivia said. 'We'll be home soon.'

Angus hung up, and Olivia frowned. 'We should get back,' she said.

'He's almost fourteen. Old enough to fend for himself for an hour or two.'

'Even so. If any of them are going to cause us trouble, it'll be Angus.'

'Darling, he'll be plugged into the Xbox by now. How much trouble can a boy come to in virtual reality?'

Olivia accepted another glass of wine, but when the waitress passed again they ordered coffee and the bill.


When Olivia looked back on that evening later, she was conscious of a number of ironies, the first of which was that – having cycled to the pub because they'd already had a glass of wine each, exploited that fact by consuming another bottle over dinner, then arrived home merry enough to take down the bottle of Laphroaig – both she and Robert were more drunk than they'd been for a while when the phone rang at eleven thirty.

'It'll be one of the boys,' she said, as Robert got up to answer it. 'Tell them to call a taxi. The number's on the board.'

It was clear from Robert's tone that it wasn't one of his sons he was speaking to, but not immediately obvious that anything was wrong. Half-listening to his end of the conversation, Olivia admired the fact that at this hour of night, and after so much to drink, he could sound so measured and reasonable in what she took – absurdly – to be a business negotiation.

'When was this?' Robert said, and 'Who else is involved?' and 'Will there be any charges?' and Olivia dreamily remembered him as the whizz-kid of the

Leytonstone flat, speaking to investors in America late at night while she lay curled up in bed.

Then he said, 'We'll be there as soon as we can,' and she jerked upright as he put the phone down.

'What's happened?'

'Alastair.' Robert came back to the table and put his hands on her shoulders. 'He's all right, unharmed, but he's in a police cell. Caught in a raid on a pub in Jericho.'

Olivia relaxed slightly. 'Drinking,' she said. 'Silly boy.'

'Marijuana,' said Robert. 'Not much, but he might be charged with possession. I'll order a taxi.'

Olivia hadn't been inside the police station in St Aldate's since she'd accompanied a trip there six years before as part of the new citizenship curriculum, with – another irony – Alastair's primary school class. After that visit, she reminded Robert on the way down, Alastair had expressed a firm intention to join the police force.

'He still could,' Robert said. She couldn't judge his mood: he'd hardly spoken since the cab arrived.

'I would never have guessed it would be him,' she said.

She knew from the brief squeeze of her hand that Robert understood what she meant; that he knew she blamed herself, and that there was no point telling her this was a common enough predicament. Like a teenage version of headlice, she'd heard someone say, horrifying until you realise everyone's in the same boat. But not everyone in the class was arrested at sixteen. She shut her eyes, conscious of a headache throbbing in her temples, a long night ahead of them. Conscious of the fact that it was unreasonable to be more disappointed by

Alastair than she would have been by one of his brothers.

In fact the whole process, though bureaucratic and undignified, was blessedly quick. Olivia let Robert do the talking, sign the forms, be polite to the officer at the front desk and a succession of others whose role and rank she didn't grasp.

'We might've kept him overnight if it wasn't Christmas,' one of them said, and Olivia felt as though they'd slipped into an episode of a TV cop drama: the middle-class boy arrested the night before Christmas Eve; the parents worse for wear after dinner at a gastro pub. The uniformed officers who'd seen it all before.

It wasn't until Alastair was brought through to them that the twist in the episode became apparent. Olivia had been dimly aware that another couple had arrived just after them, but she hadn't made the connection with Alastair. But when he appeared there was another boy beside him: a boy of eighteen or nineteen with ginger hair, visible to Olivia for a few seconds before he was escorted to his parents. A narrow face, a sharp chin, incongruously large eyes. A few seconds, and a different context, but Olivia recognised him immediately, was certain beyond reasonable doubt that he was the boy who had attacked her that day on the canal bridge.

# Chapter Forty-One

The thing that struck Sarah most forcibly was the silence. After the flurry of their entry, the clatter of crutches on flagstones, the exclamations of grief and shock, there was nothing to disturb the stillness of the scene now. Deathly stillness, Sarah thought, kneeling beside her father and finding his limbs already stiff, his skin clammy despite the warmth of the room. A deathly hush. As she laid her head on his knee and waited for tears, even the usual small sounds of the house seemed quieted.

Guy put his hand on her shoulder, but he said nothing. Astonishing, how long he said nothing for, resisting the temptation to offer consolation, tea, phone calls. Sarah's mind wasn't working in its usual way, one thing following another, but spiralling downwards, backwards, inwards. She wasn't capable at first of registering Guy's restraint, or being grateful for it, but when the necessary observances were completed – when, slowly, slowly, there was a feeling like blood flowing back into a blanched limb – she was glad that he knew the silence mattered. She was glad, too, for the weight of his hand; that was also necessary, just then.

'What should we do?' she asked. 'Are we supposed to call an ambulance?'

The memory of that other occasion was unavoidable, the terrible flurry of ambulance crews and police officers, the drama they had watched helplessly, hoping it might have a different ending.

'I don't think so. No need for paramedics.'

'No one, then?'

'Perhaps his GP. The duty doctor.'

'His GP lives in the village,' Sarah said. Her father had been scrupulous about not exploiting this fact, but surely... 'By the phone, there, in the red book. Ashworth.'

'Shall I ring, or you?'

'You.'

Her tears were flowing now; now that the moment of vigil was past, and the long stretch of death was beginning. Sarah reached for Guy's hand as he moved away: a primitive instinct, to hold on to the living. He stopped, turned back to her.

'Did you find your mother?' he asked.

'Yes,' she said. 'Not in here, in her bedroom.'

Guy waited a moment longer, then he squeezed her hand again and released it.

'Dr Ashworth?' she heard him say. 'I'm so sorry to disturb you. I'm Sarah Brewster's fiancé.'


After that there wasn't silence but noise and people, an impromptu wake, as the villagers came up the road in their Christmas coats to offer their respects and condolences and assistance. It was, Sarah thought afterwards, as though they had slipped into an earlier century when death was played out in cottage sitting rooms, flanked by hearth rugs and wing chairs, not in overlit wards where there was no escape from clinical certainty. She imagined her father's spirit lifted and given flight by the voices and bodies he had lived among. Old men close to his age pressed her hand and praised him; well-meaning women advised about the likelihood of a funeral before the New Year. It was a fiction, a drama, a rite of passage. Impossible not to see, already, how a natural death was part of the natural order. People knew what to do. Thank God, people knew what to do. Sarah couldn't stop weeping, but not all the tears were for her father.

Guy found the Christmas cake among the boxes in the back of the car and passed it round on a tray. He made tea, produced bottles of sherry, with the same aplomb he might have shown at a village gathering in the Himalayan foothills.

'I saw him last week,' Gillian Ashworth told Sarah, before the house had filled with their neighbours. 'He'd had a bit of angina; his blood pressure was rather high. I started him on beta-blockers and arranged some tests for the week after Christmas.'

Sarah nodded. The words didn't mean anything yet – they had the same deceptive feel as a logical explanation in a dream – but she saved them up in her mind. She would have to tell her brother.

Dr Ashworth put a hand on her arm. 'At least there won't have to be a post mortem,' she said. 'I can sign the death certificate.'

Sheila Morrison, who had supplied Graziana the au pair, handed Sarah a glass of sherry. 'You may not think so, but you need it,' she said. She made a noise between a laugh and a sigh. 'Graziana's gone home to Zagreb for Christmas, or she'd be weeping too. She adored him, you know. Spent hours here, much longer than he paid her for.'

The new vicar came, even though Jock Brewster had not been sympathetic to his evangelical leanings. He accepted a piece of cake and held it carefully in the palm of one hand.

'You're about to get married, I understand,' he said.

Behind him on the grand piano the family portraits reflected back the bustle and strangeness, their frames polished for Christmas.

'We haven't had a chance to discuss–' Guy began, but Sarah interrupted him.

'Yes,' she said, 'we're getting married in a fortnight.'

# Chapter Forty-Two

'Well,' said Robert. 'It's Christmas Eve.'

They were walking up St Aldate's, passing Christ Church, the looming grace of Tom Tower rising above them. The city was quiet, but not deserted: knots of people passed them, most high-spirited, some rowdy, heading up towards Carfax or down towards the Abingdon Road. Lights in the shape of stars and crescent moons were strung across the street, their reflections glittering off the damp paving.

It was odd, Olivia thought, that amid the unfamiliar emotions, the awkward business of pitching a reaction that was responsible but not absurdly reactionary, there could be a sense of occasion. Was that what Robert was acknowledging, the strange festivity of this night-time walk, the two of them and their son alone in the streets of Oxford, or was his intention entirely ironic?

She was grateful for the frosty air, which helped to clear the fug of whisky from her head. She was grateful, too, for the unspoken consensus with which they'd set off on foot through the centre of the city. It felt important, somehow, to walk out of the police station, not to linger in the building waiting for a taxi. Apart from anything else, she wanted to get away from that other family as fast as possible. As they approached Cornmarket she was conscious of the silence that only Robert's brief remark had broken, and of the invisible thought bubbles hovering over their heads, waiting to burst into speech.

'Are you OK?' she asked Alastair eventually.

'I'm fine.' He turned a little towards her. His face was hollowed by the streetlights: he looked, Olivia thought with a shock, as though he'd aged ten years. She hadn't expected such a cliché; or if she had, she'd expected it for herself. 'Mum, honestly, I'm sorry. I'm an idiot.'

'For getting caught,' Olivia asked, 'or getting involved?'

'Both. Getting in over my head.'

'Has it been going on a long time? A regular thing, I mean?' She cast her mind back for signs, tried to assess how much he'd been out in the last few months. All she could remember was his pleasantness that recent lunchtime, and her gratitude; the memory of that sharpened her wits.

'Not exactly.'

'That other boy,' Olivia said. 'The one who was in there with you. Do you know him?'

Alastair looked down at the pavement. He was easy to read, Olivia thought. He'd always been easy to read.

'Is he the supplier?' she asked. Alastair shrugged. 'I've seen him before,' Olivia said. 'He ran into me one day, on the canal bridge. Hit me.'

'Oh, God.'

Robert had stopped. 'What?' he demanded.

'How did he know who I was?' Olivia asked.

'Probably saw you coming out of the house.' Alastair's voice sounded unfamiliar. 'When he was waiting for me.'

'Hold on,' said Robert. 'I've got my head around a one-off slip, but what are we talking about here? How on earth can this have involved your mother?'

'I'm sorry,' Alastair said again. 'I really am. I promise you, it's not as bad as it looks.'

'Explain,' said Robert. 'Explain everything.'

'That boy you saw – he gave me some weed at a party, a few months back. A few parties.' Alastair sighed. 'I was just trying it. I thought – I was kind of bored of being a nerd, you know? There's lots of it around. I didn't expect it to go anywhere.'

'But?'

'One night – I don't know why, I guess I was just there, and I looked innocent, or something – one night he gave me his stash to look after, but then people said the police were coming and I panicked and chucked it. He waited for me outside school the next day, said I owed him for it. More money than I expected. I was a bit freaked out. I brazened it out, but he said I'd be sorry. I didn't know–' He put a hand on Olivia's arm and she flinched; exactly the spot where she'd been punched, she thought. He couldn't have known that. 'He said something, next time he saw me, but I thought he must have got the wrong person. I didn't... After that I paid him for the weed and kept away from him.'

'Found another supplier?' Olivia could tell that Robert was angrier than he sounded. Perhaps Alastair could too.

'It's really not like that, Dad. I'm not that into it.'

'All very well for you to be so blasé, when it's your mother who's been assaulted by a drug dealer.'

'He's a bit crazy, but he's not–' Alastair stopped.

'So how did you end up with him tonight?' Olivia asked.

'Bad luck,' Alastair said. 'Bad judgement.' He looked at her beseechingly. 'I'm so sorry.'

They were at the top of Cornmarket now, emerging onto Magdalen Street.

'Look, there's a taxi.' Olivia raised her arm and the cab swerved over to the kerb. Good timing, she thought; she'd walked far enough now. It must be well past one.

None of them said anything more as they swept up the length of St Giles. They sat in a row, Olivia between her husband and her son, the swoon of a late-night radio station filling the silence. God only knew, Olivia thought, how much of the truth Alastair was telling. How much they really wanted to know, or ought to interfere. She felt old and out of touch; adrift in a place where anything she said or asked would reveal her ignorance. Not even the fact that she'd hardly been an innocent herself, in her time, could make Alastair's world, Tom's world, even Angus's and Benjy's world, less mysterious and inaccessible.

'OK,' Robert said, as they turned into their road. Olivia thought at first he was addressing Alastair, but he leaned towards the cab driver. 'Just here is fine. Thanks.'

'Happy Christmas.' Olivia smiled at the driver as they climbed out of the cab. The mother's part, observing the niceties of social engagement.

She was surprised to see that the house was in darkness. Usually the boys left lights blazing everywhere; she imagined them creeping around tonight, awed by the situation, being responsible.

Robert halted in front of the door, as though he wanted the subject closed before they went inside.

'You've got off damn lightly, Alastair. I hope you know that. You've put your mother in jeopardy; you've let us both down.'

'It won't happen again,' Alastair said.

And maybe it wouldn't, Olivia thought, as she came into the hall, inhaling the evocative scent of pine needles, but maybe it would. Who knew? Sweet Alastair; she couldn't really manage to think differently of him. Part of her, bizarrely, was grateful. It was better to have an explanation for that thump than to be the victim of a chance act of violence. Much better than being targeted for some fault of her own. Her desire for punishment was subtle and specific, and the events of this evening had diminished it, in some odd way. It wasn't her failing that had led Alastair into a police cell or incited her assailant: she was responsible for her sons' begetting but helpless, in the end, to shape their lives. She had never done less than a good mother would, not even on that horrible day in Suffolk, and there had always been things beyond her control – well-meaning decisions that would turn out to be flawed, failures of judgement to be learned from – just as there would be for her sons.

She went down the passage towards the kitchen, but the door of the music room was standing open as she passed, and on a whim she went in and sat down on the stool. A book of Chopin nocturnes she'd got out for a pupil stood open on the stand: the same book she'd played from when the boys were babies. She couldn't make out the notes on the stave in the dimness, but she didn't need the music to play these pieces. She laid her fingers on the keyboard and the first few bars of the B flat minor

353

nocturne floated up around her, like something conjured from nowhere, from her subconscious. Like an emotion she didn't have to find words for.

After a few moments she heard the click and slide as Robert locked the front door. Without breaking off from the music, she shut her eyes and waited for him to come and join her.

# Chapter Forty-Three

The week between Christmas and New Year was a busy one. Sarah had rung on Christmas Eve to break the news of her father's death and to ask Olivia and Robert to come to his funeral on the twenty-eighth. Later that morning, Clive Shotter had called to say he'd be in Oxford on Boxing Day to take Aunt Georgie out, and hoped Olivia would join them for tea at the Randolph. And Olivia made a phone call of her own, the same afternoon, to confirm an arrangement she'd made for the thirtieth. Pieces of life, she thought, to stitch together like a patchwork quilt: deaths and births, coincidence and reconciliation. Appropriate for the turning of the year, this collage of endings and new beginnings.

Alastair offered to come with her to the Randolph. His scrupulousness over Christmas had surprised Olivia. She'd expected the ties between them to be strained by the drugs incident, but instead there had been what she described to herself as a rebound. She could see him, all of a sudden, as a grown up: a man like Clive Shotter, holding his mother in affection even as he teased her. Her reaction to this insight was more than she could have anticipated, too; the absurd pride of having raised her sons to adulthood, flawed but whole.

Nonetheless, she went alone to the tea party. This wasn't an occasion for Alastair to exercise his charm or his tact or anything else. There was already quite enough in play.

Clive and Georgie were well ensconced when she arrived, settled in matching chairs either side of a linen-clad table. Clive rose to greet her, indicating the third chair with a waft of the menu. He looked entirely at home; the Randolph was very much his milieu, Olivia thought. The walls of the tea room were adorned with Osbert Lancaster's famous illustrations of *Zuleika Dobson*, and it seemed to Olivia that Clive Shotter would have fitted admirably into these scenes of undergraduate frolics a century before, with Zuleika creating merry mayhem among the bright young things.

'We've ordered the whole caboodle,' he said. 'That do? Cake, sandwiches...?'

'Perfect.' Olivia smiled, concealing her nerves, or perhaps failing to.

'We're hungry,' Clive declared. 'Aren't we, Aunt Georgie? Energetic day.'

Georgie had her eyes fixed on Clive. Did she look different, Olivia wondered, or was it the effect of her plush surroundings? Her clothes were the same, although she had selected, perhaps by accident, a variant of her navy and white range that was less institutional than the rest; she looked almost like any other aunt being taken out for tea.

'What have you been doing?' Olivia asked.

'Aunt Georgie has pronounced my person

acceptable, but not my education,' said Clive with satisfaction. 'She's pledged herself to improve me. Today we've visited the Pitt Rivers Museum, and her old college.'

Georgie's eyes swivelled towards Olivia. 'I was a student of English Literature,' she said, 'at Somerville.'

'Great reader.' Clive beamed. 'Puts me to shame. But I can do paintings. Tit for tat, eh?'

The tea, when it came, was sumptuous, set out on a three-tiered cake stand. Olivia had thought she wouldn't be able to eat much, but she surprised herself. It was a long time since anyone had offered her a plate of cucumber sandwiches, and Clive's enthusiasm for the occasion made it hard to resist. Perhaps Georgie felt the same: she certainly ate with gusto, although she said little and revealed even less, after that brief allusion to her Oxford past. Clive filled the gaps in conversation with accounts of their day which implied a rich seam of roguish banter. Olivia wondered whether her arrival had silenced Georgie, or whether Clive was cheerfully reconstructing the outing in terms that suited his purposes. In any case, they both seemed content with the arrangement.

'All right, Aunt Georgie?' he asked, as she refilled her plate. 'Sandwiches acceptable?'

'Very nice, thank you.'

'National Gallery next, then? Chauffeur-driven excursion, all expenses paid?' Clive winked at Olivia. 'I know my place, you see. Education comes at a price. Speaking of which, don't think I've forgotten your place in my grand scheme. The board's keen to have you. Grand name for a collection of old buffers, but the work's serious. Counting on you to talk sense to us.'

'I don't talk much sense,' said Olivia, 'but I'm happy to help if I can.'

'I've heard you play, don't forget.' Clive looked at Georgie again. 'First rate pianist, isn't she? First rate people, both of you. Lucky fellow.'

Olivia, dipping her head modestly, almost missed Georgie's smile.

The weather stayed very cold all week, and there was a heavy frost on the morning of Jock Brewster's funeral. The roads were empty that morning, the country enjoying its extended Christmas break. Nonetheless, Olivia was glad of Robert's company, even if they didn't talk as much as she'd expected, or about the things she'd expected, on the way down to Hampshire.

Perhaps, she thought, as the miles sped by, there wasn't any more to say about Alastair, or about Tom, who had used his brother's notoriety as an excuse to slip even further into the background in the last few days. Robert's mother was on Olivia's mind too: she was noticeably frailer than she'd been when they last saw her back in June. That was the next chapter, Olivia thought, another unfamiliar stretch of life to negotiate. Both their fathers had died young; they had two widowed mothers to think about in the years ahead.

That thought brought her back to the purpose of their journey.

'Poor Sarah,' she said. 'I do feel sorry for her. She must be wishing she'd picked December for the wedding, not January.'

'Better than it happening the day before,' Robert said. 'Better than the middle of the reception.'

Robert's outside elbow was propped on the arm rest, his habitually casual driving position. Olivia prodded him. 'Unfeeling brute.'

'What kind of funeral do you think it'll be?' he asked.

'What kind?'

'Haven't they diversified, like weddings? Rock music, video testimonies?'

'I hardly think we'll have either of those today.'

'Modern vicar, maybe.'

Olivia laughed. 'Sarah's a match for anyone,' she said.

Though as it turned out, the surprising thing about the funeral was that it bore Sarah's imprint rather lightly. The church, decked with holly and ivy, was full, and the proceedings followed the Prayer Book almost to the letter. The village choir made its way valiantly through Purcell's funeral sentences, and Sarah and her brother each read a passage from the Bible. The whole service, Olivia thought, was unexpectedly moving: the power of ritual, unadorned.

Afterwards, in the churchyard, Sarah hugged Olivia. She looked dramatically thinner, even though it was barely more than a week since Olivia had last seen her.

'You remember my brother, Andrew? He was a baby last time you saw him. Fifteen or sixteen, maybe.'

Olivia did remember. He'd been a very beautiful teenager, rather shy. The romantic poet look, Sarah had called it. Somehow he'd turned into a solid, smiling man who bore a much closer resemblance to his sister, these days.

'How nice of you to come,' he said, shaking Olivia's hand and then Robert's, the trace of a transatlantic accent attractive. 'I hear you've been a terrific help with the wedding preparations.'

Nearby, his children circled their mother like a maypole, a trio of strawberry-blonde girls somewhere between five and ten. Olivia felt a rush of warmth: not just for the children, she thought, though that was part of it, the sweetening that children brought to funerals, but for the occasion, the village, the family.

She and Robert were turning away when Olivia felt Sarah's hand on her sleeve.

'Olivia,' she said, 'I need to talk to you.'

It was surprisingly easy to manage a private conversation at the edge of the knot of mourners and well-wishers. Sarah drew them a few yards away, into the shadow of the yew trees that guarded the east end of the church.

'I'm not good at confiding,' she said. 'We're such a terribly secretive family.' She stopped, sighed, tugging at the wool scarf that provided a leavening of colour against her black coat.

Olivia thought of the things Sarah had confessed to her and wondered whether this entrée was a prelude to asking for discretion. 'I haven't repeated anything you've told me,' she said.

'No, no.' Sarah shook her head. 'This is something I haven't told you. I've never talked to anyone about it. About my mother. She committed suicide, you see.'

Olivia said nothing, but she grasped Sarah's hand more tightly.

'I always blamed myself. Maybe it sounds strange, but I thought... But the thing is, I found some letters in my father's desk, the day before yesterday. Love letters to my mother from someone else.'

'Oh God!' Olivia bit her lip. 'Oh Sarah, how dreadful. I'm so sorry.'

Sarah brushed tears away from her eyes. 'I read them,' she said. 'All of them. I couldn't stop myself. It was the strangest feeling, like seeing my mother again. Like one of those dreams where people come back quite different.'

'Do you know who he was?' Olivia asked.

Sarah shook her head. 'Hugo,' she said. 'I think – I got the feeling they'd known each other a long time. But most of the letters were from the final two years. The time–' she rubbed fiercely at her eyes '–the time when she was happier. But the last few – it's not clear, but either he was going abroad somewhere or pulling away from her. I guess that's what – that's why...' She shook her head again, more slowly. 'I feel so dreadful for my father. I feel so dreadful that he never told me.'

'Poor man,' Olivia said.

'But the worst thing – the worst thing is that it's also the most extraordinary relief. I know it's terrible to be glad that it was someone else who made my mother so unhappy, but it's the truth. I only wish...'

For a moment she couldn't go on. Olivia waited.

'The awful thing is, I was going to talk to my father about her this Christmas. Guy and I discussed it on the way down in the car. I can't bear the idea that he felt guilty too, all these years. That he might have thought I blamed him.'

'If he thought that, wouldn't he have told you about the affair?'

Sarah pulled a handkerchief out of her pocket – one of her father's, Olivia guessed – and blew her nose. 'I don't know. We were no good at talking. Maybe he thought he was protecting me.'

An elderly couple were hovering a little way off,

waiting for Sarah's attention. She glanced at them, then turned back to Olivia with a tiny smile.

'At least it doesn't look strange to cry at a funeral,' she said. 'It doesn't even look that strange to be crying for one parent rather than another. I hardly know why I'm crying, in fact. Partly because I've realised how lucky I am, having Guy. And you, Olivia. I wanted you to know how much it's meant to me, having you to talk to these last few months. Even if I haven't told you the most important things.'

Olivia remembered her fickleness, in Eve's presence, and her lingering guilt about their schoolgirl mockery. She cast about for words that would make Sarah feel better rather than worse, but before she found them Sarah had squeezed her hand one last time and turned to the couple behind her.

'Cyril, Beverley,' Olivia heard her say. 'How lovely of you to come.'

Olivia was on the edge of tears herself when Robert approached. She stood very still while he put an arm around her shoulder.

'Come on,' he said. 'I expect there's a cup of tea somewhere.'

By the thirtieth Robert was back at work. The weather forecast mentioned freezing fog, and Olivia's resolve wavered.

'Go on with you,' her mother-in-law said, over breakfast. 'We'll be fine here.'

And because it was impossible to explain her qualms, Olivia went.

It was a strange experience, travelling all that way

alone. She sat in the corner of an empty carriage, staring out of the window as the final train rattled through the outskirts of London and on into the broad stretch of East Anglia. As they passed through Chelmsford she remembered a friend from university who'd got a job as organist in the Cathedral there, and at Colchester she thought, inevitably, of Georgie, born in its outskirts more than nine decades ago.

The train pulled into Ipswich two minutes behind schedule, and Olivia stepped down onto the platform with a queasy feeling that reminded her of going back to boarding school.

'To the hospital, please,' she said to the taxi driver.

# Chapter Forty-Four

St Luke's Hospital had changed considerably in twenty-five years, but it still sprawled; it still looked less like one institution than several stuck incongruously together. Olivia stood for a moment where the taxi had dropped her, looking at the signs, the arrows directing her to each corner of the site.

She hadn't been sure how to begin, when she'd first thought of contacting the hospital for information. She was sure the records in the Accident and Emergency department wouldn't go back twenty-five years. The Special Care Baby Unit was more likely to keep information about babies who'd died, she'd thought, but she didn't even know if the SCBU had existed in 1983, and if it had, the phone box baby had never been near it. In the end she'd dialled the main hospital number and braced herself to explain her mission.

After a long wait for the switchboard, she'd been referred first to the Patient Advice and Liaison Service, then to a glum woman whose job seemed to be connected with the disposal of patients' effects and the processing of death certificates, and finally to the Medical Records Department, where a data clerk was dumbfounded by the notion of searching for a former patient without a name. Eventually, when she asked, with what might by then have been a desperate edge to her voice, if there was anyone at all she could speak to about a baby who'd died at the hospital years before, she was passed to the hospital chaplain.

And then at last she'd struck lucky. Father Timothy had been connected with the hospital for thirty years. He thought he remembered – he couldn't be sure, but he had records, he could look back – but in any case he would be happy to see Olivia, to talk to her about the baby. And so here she was, walking through the main entrance, following the trail of her nineteen-year-old self with that little woollen bundle in her arms.

Father Timothy was enormous. That was Olivia's first impression: a man like an Old Testament prophet, above average height and immensely wide, with a beard that bloomed from his face in every direction. He was crammed into an office so small Olivia wasn't sure she could fit into it too.

'Come in, come in, close the door, give all that a good shove, that's the way. There's a chair under there that's comfy enough. I've some filing to do, as you see.'

He didn't smile – or if he did it wasn't easy to see, through the beard – but his voice was as bountiful as his body, a rich bass that made every phrase sound like a piece of recitative.

'Olivia,' he said. 'You are Olivia? In search of a baby.'

'A particular one, yes.'

'Twenty-sixth of August, 1983. Date of birth,

presumed.' Father Timothy raised his eyes and looked straight at Olivia. 'Date of death.'

Olivia nodded.

'I do remember. My notes are very descriptive. It was an unusual situation, a sad mystery that was never solved.'

'I don't have the solution,' Olivia said, her heartbeat swooping. 'I'm afraid I'm seeking information, not offering it.'

Father Timothy nodded slowly. 'I understand that. Seeking information.' He cocked his head to one side, considering this idea, then lifted two pairs of fingers in quotation marks. 'Seeking closure.'

'I suppose so.'

There was silence for a moment, then Father Timothy moved abruptly into action, excavating under the heap of books and documents on his desk, risking a small avalanche, and emerging with a bound leather volume and a battered hardback notebook.

'You can read these,' he said. 'I can copy them for you, if you like. I don't know whether they will give you what you want, but they confirm what happened.' He fixed his eyes on Olivia again. 'They attest to the baby's existence.'

'Thank you.'

'The Book of Remembrance–' he waved the leather volume '–is kept in the Hospital Chapel, which is shared these days with our brothers and sisters of other faiths, or of none, but it has no formal status except in the eyes of God. There is also, of course, the Coroner's ledger, to which you could request access, and which contains the official record of her life and death. Her hospital notes I regret I have been unable to locate, but I took the trouble to copy the entries into my own notebook at the time.' The other book was lifted in the air. 'Apart from the events you yourself were party to, my notes record the efforts made to locate the child's mother, and the rites I undertook on behalf of her soul.'

'Thank you,' said Olivia again.

'I baptised her,' Father Timothy said. 'I gave her a Christian funeral, before her body was cremated. It is what I felt called to do. I am answerable to God: I have found that is the only way to look at things, sometimes.'

He leaned back in his chair, then abruptly forwards again as though he had collided with something behind him.

'You are not the child's mother?' he asked. 'That isn't what you've come here to tell me?'

'No.' Despite the bizarre nature of the meeting, the distinct strain of comedy, Olivia felt close to tears. 'I became very attached to her that day, but I wasn't her mother. The story is exactly as we told the staff on duty that night.'

Except for one detail.

Father Timothy nodded again. If he scented the missing detail, he didn't pursue it. He was the kind of man, Olivia thought, the kind of priest, who believed guilt was between you and God. This thought brought both relief and something a little like disappointment. Father Timothy didn't speak again, and in the cramped silence Olivia was aware of the fact that almost everything known about the phone box baby was here between them, in this tiny room. She felt more and more certain that the chaplain knew, had known for twenty-five years, that something was missing from the account in his notebook. He wouldn't insist on hearing the truth, but if she told him, if she asked him, perhaps he could absolve her. He could at least hear her confession on God's behalf: was that what she wanted?

'I dropped her,' she said, before she had time to think again. 'We stopped to buy petrol, we were flustered and arguing, and I dropped her. I think that's what killed her.'

Father Timothy said nothing.

'We should have told the nurses, I know that. We should have faced the consequences. God knows it's been on my conscience all these years, the death of a baby.'

Her voice quavered into silence, and Father Timothy leaned forwards across his chaotic desk and laid one huge hand on hers. With the other hand he flipped open the notebook and laid it in front of her. Olivia read the lines he indicated.

*Marked hypothermia, hypovolaemia, hypoglycaemia*
*(glucostix <2)*
*Head injury probable cause of death – ?timing*
*Olivia upset ++*
*Discussed with Dr Maitland – has spoken to both girls –*
*no further action*
*Chaplain informed*
*Signed: FS (Sister F. Sawyer) 6:40pm, 26/8/83*

Father Timothy started to speak again while Olivia stared at the page. 'It would be different now,' he said. 'Structured questionnaires, batteries of tests, no stone left unturned. Better or worse, I don't know.'

Olivia looked up at him, dry-eyed, astonished.

'I prayed for you,' Father Timothy said. 'I asked for God's blessing on you. It was a liberty, another liberty, but I inferred repentance for any sins of omission or commission.'

'My friend was pregnant,' Olivia said. 'I didn't know. She couldn't stand the smell of the petrol because she was pregnant, but I wouldn't give her the baby and fill the car myself.'

'I prayed for you both,' Father Timothy said. 'I baptised the child for you both.'

Now he laid the other book in front of her, the leather-bound Book of Remembrance, and indicated more words in the same curving hand, the same thick black ink.

*Baby Olivia Eve, 26ᵗʰ August 1983*

# Chapter Forty-Five

There was frost on the ground for Sarah's epiphany wedding. The gardens of St Saviour's looked magical, laced with icy spiders' webs and the silvered skeletons of specimen trees. For those who ventured as far as the river, carrying a stray bottle of wine or escaping the hubbub of the reception hall, there were skeins of ice in the backwaters and disconsolate ducks perched on floes in the shadow of overhanging branches. The rose gardens, crisp and flawless underfoot, were populated by arches and arbours hung with frosted tinsel and thorns edged in platinum.

Inside, the bride's meticulous attention to detail had yielded an equally spectacular setting. White lilies and trailing ivy were offset by starched linen and the College's mellowed silver cutlery; small children frolicked decorously, as though aware of their part in the *mise en scène*, and a string of bridesmaids of different ages and sizes were flattered by ice blue. The domestic bursar, despite his moustache and his air of disapproval, proved entirely competent, and the bridegroom's choice of champagne proved entirely satisfactory to him.

'Moet,' he murmured, to anyone who cared to listen, 'always pours like a dream.'

The bride looked perfect too, her homespun wedding dress a triumph. Fifty pearl buttons flowed down the length of her spine, and the lace of her veil, thrown back over her head as she emerged from the chapel, crowned her in a cloud of gossamer.

It wasn't until the gong had been rung, the canapés had been gathered in, the guests had been seated and Faith's Functions had begun serving the main course that anything untoward occurred.

'Salmon en croute or beef Wellington, madam?' enquired the dark-haired waiter, leaning down to catch the reply over the ambient noise of wedding-guest chatter.

'Salmon, plea– my God, it can't be James?' The lady guest, tilting her head back far enough to get a good view of his face beneath the ample brim of her hat, gawped at him. 'It *is* James, isn't it? James Young? You don't recognise me.' She laughed, equal parts incredulity and delight and mockery. 'Eve de Perreville. I haven't seen you for – oh, I hate to think. What the hell are you doing as a waiter?'

'Helping out.' James smiled. There was nothing to do but smile: it was, after all, a stock in trade of his usual profession as well as the one he was impersonating. 'I'm a friend of the caterer.'

'Well, good Lord. I wouldn't have been surprised if you'd chucked in medicine for cookery, actually; you always did like faffing around in the kitchen. Samphire: do you remember the samphire at Aldeburgh?'

'Samphire, yes.' James smiled again. 'It's good to see

371

you, Eve.' This was a risk, but he had the perfect excuse to move on; he had twenty-five portions of salmon en croute to serve before it got cold.

'You're not to run away.' Eve grabbed at his cuff, discreet but insistent. 'I don't mean now: you're not to run away later without coming back to speak to me, OK? I can find you, anyway. I can find you through the caterer, can't I? I really can't believe it's you!'

'Nor can I,' said James. 'I shall look forward to the pleasure of speaking to you later.' He gave a little bow, the essence of the well-trained waiter, and moved gracefully to Eve's left.

'Gracious heavens,' he heard Eve say to her neighbour. 'I'd forgotten what a small country this is.'

James's progress around the room wasn't destined to be a smooth one, however. Having rounded the end of the long table below the dais which held the bride and groom and their party, he was accosted by another lady guest a little way down the opposite side.

'James! How extraordinary! Are you bride or groom?'

'Neither.' James's smile was tighter, this time. 'Serving staff, in fact. You could call it moonlighting.' He laughed, not entirely successfully.

'Well, well.' This guest, clad in an unflattering shade of primrose, was too well-mannered to grab at cuffs or insist on an explanation, but her expression eloquently revealed her perplexity. 'How's Amelia?' she asked brightly. 'And the girls?'

'Skiing with her parents,' he said. 'Would you like salmon or beef, Barbara?'

'Oh: beef, I think. One shouldn't, I know. Is it good?'

'It's excellent.' James slid gratefully away. 'My colleague is following with the beef.'

He was about halfway down the table when he heard her voice again, its timbre carrying effortlessly over the thrum of conversation.

'How funny that you should know James,' she said, as Faith reached her. 'I'm a great friend of his wife's.'

Faith said nothing at first when she came back into the servery. She laid down her empty platter on the side and slid another out from the warming trolley. Then she looked up at James.

'The salmon's under there,' she said. 'Chop chop.'

'Faith,' said James.

'Not now. We have a function to service. This is my livelihood, remember. Ruin this wedding and you'll regret it for the rest of your bloody life.'

'I'm going to regret it anyway, Faith.' James moved towards her.

'Fuck off,' she said. 'Take the fucking salmon and serve it to the fucking guests, and don't speak to anyone, do you hear?'

She banged out of the door and nearly collided with a woman hovering in the passage outside.

'I'm sorry, madam.'

'My fault, I'm in the wrong place. Do you know where the loo is?'

'Down there and first left.' Faith swivelled to apply her shoulder to the swing doors into the hall.

'The food's terrific, by the way,' the woman called after her. She hesitated for a moment, and so she was still standing in the corridor when James emerged, a full plate of salmon en croute balanced on his left arm.

'Heavens,' she said. 'James.'

His expression was so horrified that she laughed.

'Is it that bad? We've met before, that's all. I'm Olivia.

Olivia Conafray. I stayed at Shearwater House, years ago. I thought – actually, we ran into each other a few months ago. I thought you'd recognised me then.'

'Yes,' James said. 'I couldn't place you.'

'On the bridge?' Olivia asked. 'After that boy hit me?'

James glanced towards the hall.

'I'm so sorry; you've got a job to do. We must catch up later. Eve's here, you know. We were at school with the bride.'

'Of course.' James raised his eyebrows. 'Small world.'


'The most extraordinary thing,' Olivia said, as she slid back into her seat at the end of the bride's table.

'What is?'

Robert slipped a hand onto his wife's thigh. He was enjoying himself: he'd already had a couple of glasses of champagne, and it continued to flow very freely, at least on the bride's table.

'That waiter over there: that's James Young. As in Aldeburgh.'

'I thought he was a doctor?'

'So did I. To tell the truth, I don't think he's usually a waiter. He's making rather heavy weather of the silver service. But it was definitely him I saw on the bridge that day.'

'Well, that's one mystery solved. Have you spoken to Eve?'

'Briefly.'

'Did she say anything?'

'Hello.'

'Thank you for your letter?'

'Not in so many words. But I think *hello* conveyed that general sense.'

'Uh-huh.'

'I'm glad I caught her early on,' Olivia said. 'James's presence complicates things rather.'

'Yes,' said Robert. 'Yes, I can see that it might.'

The next time Faith returned to the servery she set down her tray of dirty plates on the trolley, then moved across to the corner where she and James had hung their coats. James's mobile phone was tucked into the top pocket of his overcoat. Flicking the screen open to check that it was on silent, Faith slipped it into the invisible pouch in her belt. Then she opened up the refrigerated cabinet and took out two trays of desserts. By the time James returned with the last of the cleared plates, she was already moving down the first table, beaming with enthusiasm for her strawberry pavlova, her chocolate cheesecake, her lime pie.

The speeches hit, as was to be expected, a bittersweet note. The loss of Sarah's beloved father -- and of course her mother, a few years earlier -- featured in the opening sentence of Guy's address, before he moved on to praise Sarah's devotion, fortitude and grace under pressure, and then to attest to his own good fortune and the privilege of joining her family at a time of such emotional consequence. He ended with a nicely-judged remark, straddling the awkward ground between humour and pathos, about the fact that his own position in his wife's affection might at least now be unassailable. Few in the audience understood the full import of this observation, but one who did squeezed his hand with unreserved feeling.

Sarah's brother Andrew, who had given the bride away in his father's place, and whose children constituted the majority of the bridesmaids, spoke more briefly and more simply, but none who heard him could doubt his affection for his sister nor his esteem for his brother-in-law. Wiping a tear from his eye, he confirmed that his only regret was that his father – and, of course, his mother – couldn't be there to see Sarah looking so beautiful and, despite the circumstances, so happy.

The best man, a model of discretion rarely seen in that role, gave a modest summary of the bridegroom's achievements in scaling the higher points of the planet, declared that no one less charming nor deserving than Sarah could have tempted him to forsake them for matrimony and an accountant's office, and sat down again without a whisper of a double entendre about early conquests or soaring peaks.

Sarah herself, blushing in the best tradition of bridal bliss, stood up to thank all her many friends and relatives for their support and sympathy, making special mention of Olivia Conafray (which elicited another blush a few seats away from her) and her sister-in-law Karin, who had been a tower of strength in the last fortnight. She also wanted, she said, to express her gratitude to Faith Sargent of Faith's Functions, who had stepped into the breach so magnificently at very short notice. Her eyes scanned the room enquiringly, and the assembled company turned in its seats to salute Faith. And so, in the moment of silence when it became clear that Faith was no longer in the hall, two hundred guests were collectively privy to the unmistakable and startlingly extravagant sound of smashing crockery.

Olivia was on her feet in a moment. James, she thought. There is something very odd about James being here, after all. She glanced at Sarah, indicated that she was going to see what was happening, smiled reassurance. The initial shocked silence in the hall had given way to nervous laughter and curious chatter. When the bride and groom sat down again, the noise rose gradually to its former volume and the backstage drama was dismissed.

Eve saw Olivia making her way down the hall and pushed her chair back before she had time to think. She wouldn't be surprised if there was more to James's presence today than met the eye, and if there was anything to uncover she wanted to be there. If there was a denouement to be played out, she was damn well going to be part of it.

Robert hesitated for a moment, then followed Olivia. He had no idea what was going on, but he hadn't relinquished the notion that there was something suspicious about this James person, and about Olivia's fascination with his damn house. In any case, Olivia was fragile at the moment; he wanted to be there to offer a comforting arm, in case things got out of hand.

It was perhaps fortunate that the domestic bursar had gone home before the speeches, leaving his deputy to oversee the end of the function, and was therefore not present to witness the College crest skittering in every direction across the floor of the servery, among scraps of pastry and root vegetable. A final volley of crashes echoed from the polished tiles as Olivia pushed open the swing doors, Eve and Robert close behind her. James had positioned himself behind a stainless-steel trolley stacked high with dirty plates, but the distribution of china around the room suggested that Faith's aim tended more towards drama than accuracy.

'Bastard,' she was hissing. 'Lying cheat. How dare you? How did you think you could get away with it?'

There was a moment, just a moment, of silence while the new arrivals took in the scene, then Eve started laughing.

'Good on you,' she said. 'Once a bastard always a bastard, eh, James?'

'For God's sake.' James held up his hands in a desperate attempt at a truce. 'What is this: an inquisition?'

'The ghosts of the past.' Eve's eyes were glittering. 'You here to defend him, Olivia?'

'No,' said Olivia. 'To clear up a few things.'

'Me too,' said Faith. 'Though James is going to clear up this mess.' She dropped another plate on the floor just in front of her. 'You know what I can't believe? That you offered to come here, bold as brass, never thinking there might be people you knew. Was it just a game, taking that risk? A bit of a thrill? Did you reckon you'd get away with it, or are really past caring about anyone except yourself?' She threw another plate over his shoulder and it shattered against the wall behind him.

In the brief silence, Olivia seized the initiative. There

was no need for logic, she thought. Faith's approach was just fine: chuck things at random and watch him duck and dodge. This was showdown time.

'Who's Amelia, James?' she demanded.

'Amelia's his wife.' Faith brandished a mobile phone in the air. 'I've just been on the phone to her, in fact. You know what: she's been trying to get hold of him this evening because one of his daughters has broken her leg in a skiing accident. His daughter who's almost the same age as me.'

'So you married someone with the same name as your cousin?' If Olivia was aware that this avenue of enquiry was of less interest to the rest of the company, that wasn't going to stop her pursuing it. They'd all get their chance.

'What?' James looked perplexed. 'Which cousin?'

'The one with Down's syndrome.' Olivia stared at him, realisation dawning. 'She doesn't exist, does she? Poor little Amelia, such a consolation to her parents. Was she a figment of your imagination all along? What about the little boy cousins who drowned?'

'Or the wife who drowned?' demanded Faith. 'Did you make her up too, you sick bastard?'

James shrugged his shoulders. 'You win,' he said.

'We *win*?' Eve laughed. 'We *win*? God Almighty. A pretty hollow fucking victory, at this point. What's the prize? A trophy for the victor ludorum?' Her eyes scanned the shelves: if there had been a silver cup anywhere about, a claret jug or a gravy boat, she might have thrown it at James.

Olivia's mind was moving slowly. But surely it was too much of a coincidence, she was thinking, for that name to have come into James's mind back in 1983, unless...

'How long have you been married?' she asked. 'How old is your daughter?'

'Twenty-four,' said Faith. 'Unbelievable. Born when he was ten, eh, James?'

Olivia looked at Eve: the maths didn't need to be spelled out. The real maths. The birth in 1984.

'I'm amazed she's stuck with you,' Eve said. She looked almost jaunty, but Olivia knew her too well to be deceived. 'Amelia. Rather her than me, that's all I can say. That's the only consolation: my disappointment came all in one go. Were you married then, or just engaged? Was she pregnant too, that summer?'

'What do you want?' James asked now, his voice veering between petulance and aggression and settling somewhere dangerously close to amusement. 'What exactly do you want from me? Such old scores.'

'Brand new scores in my case,' said Faith. 'Though I can tell you flat I don't want anything from you after you've cleared up in here and paid for the damage. Not a single thing, ever again.'

'I should have blown your cover years ago,' said Eve. 'Suave, charming James, left to go about his nefarious business all this time. Spinning his bloody web.'

'I should have known, sod it,' Faith said. 'I can't believe I swallowed it all. Being fitted in when your wife was away, all these months. Not asking questions. Even that story about the dead baby, after you missed your birthday dinner.'

'Dead baby?' Eve looked venomous.

'Some story about being up all night looking after a girl who'd left her baby to die in a phone box. That wasn't true, was it?'

'It was true,' Olivia said, swaying slightly as the world

shifted around her like a stage-set moving into position for the next scene, 'but it happened a long time ago. It happened to us.'

She was standing close enough to touch Eve, but she didn't. She'd lost track of where they were now on the spectrum between tragedy and farce. And it seemed that no one else knew the next lines either; that the run of ad lib dialogue had dried up.

'Come on,' said Robert, when the clock on the wall had ticked its way round a full circuit of silence. It was the first time he'd spoken, the first time any of them had noticed him standing there. 'I think we've heard enough to satisfy everyone's curiosity. Shall we go back into the hall? Olivia? Eve? Faith, the bride was looking for you to say thank you.'


As they moved back into the corridor, Olivia's arm brushed against Eve's. It was too late now, she thought, to set the record straight about her and James. She imagined herself explaining clumsily that nothing had happened between them, and Eve's sneering response: *Aren't you the lucky one?*

# Chapter Forty-Six

Olivia and Robert left the reception well after midnight, cycling away through streets bright with sodium light and dotted with merrymakers returning from late night revelry. The midwinter cold had mellowed as the night wore on, so that there was, despite the sparkle of frost, an almost spring-like freshness in the air as they made their way towards home.

During the last hour of the wedding, when the final bottles of champagne had been drunk and the scene in the servery had begun to pass into folklore, Olivia had felt strangely solemn. She had been moved by the sight of Sarah dancing with her husband, brimming with happiness, and of Eve slipping away alone. She had marvelled at the thought that it was twenty years since she and Robert had got married, and that their children were fast approaching the age they'd been then. The circularity of life was inescapable: the chain-link of weddings and funerals, deaths and births, and the glorious, laborious business of striving towards one landmark or another.

But now, liberated by the mystique of moonlight, she felt skittish. This was life too, freewheeling in the dark, balanced on two narrow tyres. The past she'd revisited over the last few months was confined at last to history; the world lay open, expectant, before her. She steered a fanciful sine wave along the deserted roads, watching the feeble beam from her headlight swooshing to and fro over the tarmac and Robert's back proceeding steadily ahead of her, faintly comical, as large men always are on bicycles. She would recognise Robert instantly from this view, she thought. She would recognise him from any view: his gait, his voice, his silhouette. She knew his laugh in another room and his shape in the dark. This was one certain thing she had to show for her life: an understanding of intimacy.

As they turned into their road she felt a shiver of pleasure at the thought of arriving home together, late and tired and slightly drunk, amorous from the romance of a wedding. She felt the potency of having stayed the course; the way twenty years had made the bonds between them more vibrant and vital, not less. It was no longer a question of whether she had made the right choice or the wrong one: this was the choice she'd made, the only one it was possible to imagine now. She wouldn't swap places with Sarah, she thought, for all the allure of bridal lace, all the suggestive possibilities of that tracery of threads and empty space.

She dismounted in front of the house, and while she unlocked the front door Robert bolted the bikes together under the bare winter branches of the silver birch tree.

'Hey,' he said, catching her on the doorstep, and she turned to kiss him, still skittish, smiling in the way she remembered doing when they were students, still exotic to each other.

'Come on,' she said. 'Let's...'

They saw the light in the kitchen as soon as she pushed open the door. For a second they stood together just inside the hall, Robert's hand still on her waist, and looked at each other.

Tom was slumped at the kitchen table with a glass of beer untouched beside him. A glass, Olivia thought, not a can: what were they to read into that? An adult distress, perhaps. A lack of conviction in the necessity of the beer except as a prop.

'Hi,' she said. 'Everything all right?'

Tom lifted his head slightly. 'Yeah.'

'Sure?'

There was a grunt and a sigh. 'I've been dumped.' The word came out hollow-sounding, full of self-deprecation.

'Oh dear.'

And there it was, Olivia thought: the adult world spread before him. Pain, great and small, from which she couldn't protect him.

'Should've seen it coming,' said Tom.

'Easy to say with the benefit of hindsight,' said Robert. 'How about something stronger? Fancy a whisky?'

'Yeah, all right.'

Olivia sat down opposite Tom. 'Was it someone we've met?' she asked lightly.

Tom shook his head. 'Don't think so. Bit older than me. Should've known it wouldn't last.'

Robert slid a glass of whisky along the table. He raised his eyebrows at Olivia, who shook her head, then relented.

'Just a small one, though. Too much champagne already.'

'How was the wedding, anyway?' asked Tom.

Olivia grinned. 'Eventful.'

'Your mother,' said Robert, 'was like one of those TV detectives this evening, uncovering a ring of vice.'

'Hardly a ring,' Olivia protested, laughing. 'And hardly vice, either.'

'At a wedding?' said Tom. 'Sounds more interesting than I expected.'

He took a long swig of whisky, pulled a face, set the glass down in front of him.

'I'm sorry about your girlfriend,' said Olivia. 'D'you want to talk about it?'

Tom shook his head. 'Nah. Probably better off, to be honest.'

'Mocks next week, isn't it?' asked Olivia.

Tom grinned. 'More fish in the sea, Mum.'


'You're a force for good, you are,' Robert said, as they curled up against each other half an hour later.

'I'm not,' Olivia murmured into his back. She felt too tired, now, for anything except sleep. 'When have I done anyone any good?'

'All the time. That poor girl this evening.'

'Faith's Functions?' Olivia made a little laughing noise, but she felt a shaft of pity for Faith. For the imaginary drowned wife and the string of deceived women stretching back twenty years. For Eve. It was almost funny, except that it wasn't.

'She's been spared some misery, perhaps,' said Robert.

'That wasn't me, it was chance. The pure chance of us

385

all being there together. The weirdest thing, don't you think?'

'Life is weird.'

'Sometimes.'

Robert rolled onto his stomach and lifted his face towards her.

'What about Tom's girlfriend?' he asked. 'Might she be your ghost, do you think?'

'Who knows.'

Part of Olivia didn't want to think so. She knew Lucy wouldn't be back, either way; and either way, she was sorry to lose her. Lucy had played a part in the last few months, she thought, at least in her imagination.

Robert yawned, smiled. 'I love you,' he said. He kissed her clumsily, then rolled onto his back again with a sigh.

Olivia laid her head on his shoulder. She'd let the wave of sleep pass her by, she realised, while they talked. She'd let things into her mind that wouldn't melt away at once. But she could feel Robert's warmth, the rise and fall of his chest. Her skin was pressed so close to his that she wasn't sure where she stopped and he began. It was incredible, she thought, what their bodies could do. Conjuring life out of nowhere: out of sheer lust. One moment of reckless pleasure could make a whole new being – a trail of dates in the ledgers of the registry office; a thread of humanity reaching down through the generations. A force for good or bad. She would never get over it, the miracle of procreation.

'You know something,' she whispered into the darkness, 'I love the boys dearly, but I've always wanted a baby girl. Do you think it's too late? Would it be a mad thing to do?' She ran her finger down the length of Robert's back, and he sighed deeper into sleep.

'Someone like me,' Olivia said, into the hollow behind his ear. It had always seemed to her that there was something magical about mothers and daughters, something she'd missed out on. Something magical about babies altogether, come to that. She could feel now the soft heat of an infant's newborn scalp, the magnificent sense of being necessary, important, omnipotent. It was the best thing in the world, she thought. The thing she was best at. She felt her mind drifting towards a dream, her limbs floating away from the bed. She let her eyes shut, then forced them open again. 'I am the end of the line,' she murmured. 'None of my children will be mothers, and it's all I've done. All I will do now.'

Her words faded into silence and her eyes closed again. But then she felt a movement beside her. She couldn't see Robert's face in the dark, but when he spoke she could tell he was smiling.

'It might be another boy,' he said. 'Have you considered that?'

Olivia didn't answer.

'It's not too late for you to do something else, you know. To find a new way to be yourself.'

'We could adopt,' said Olivia. 'Then we'd know it was a girl.'

'What about your friend Clive? His charity?'

'He doesn't really need me.'

'Why not? You'd be excellent.'

'Maybe.'

He reached his arms to enclose her.

'My love,' he said, 'it's your life. You must do what you want with it. Whatever you want.'

# Epilogue

The British Airways 747 is approaching Heathrow through the straggly grey clouds of a February afternoon. Eleven hours out of Beijing, having lapped nearly a quarter of the earth's circumference, it's just a few minutes behind schedule. It is a creature of the technological age, its path mapped by computer, its movements precisely controlled by slats and spoilers, flaps and ailerons. Twice it banks and circles wide again, like a predator prowling around a water hole, waiting for a gap to open in front of it. Twice the passengers feel the lurch and tug of its shifting momentum and see the flat world beneath them drop away. Then it sets its nose downwards and makes for the ground, descending towards the runway with the heavy, deliberate grace of an oversized bird on the road to extinction.

As the engines' pitch sinks through a slow glissando, the tiny doors are already opening, mobile stairs and landing staff and luggage carts are already congregating. Within minutes the first passengers are discharged onto the tarmac outside Terminal 5, swept along towards the glass palace of the arrivals hall.

Among them are three women holding babies who were not with them on the outward flight. Li Jing-Wei gave birth in her home city of Shenyang, her baby delivered by her uncle, the professor of obstetrics, and cared for by her mother for six weeks before her return to London to join her husband in the postgraduate students' accommodation at University College. By the time they return to Beijing in two years' time, their son will have a smattering of English words which will prove a curiosity to the extended family waiting for him on the other side of the world.

The other two women have only known each other for a few weeks, but they have established a strong bond in that time. They carry older babies, little girls who have spent their first few months in the Children's Welfare Institute in Tianjin City. The shorter of the two new mothers, her dark hair held back in a tortoiseshell clasp, keeps close to her husband, their bearing betraying both exhaustion and elation as they shape themselves, already, into a family unit. The other woman, taller and blonde, walks close enough to show that they have travelled together, these three. The dark-haired woman's husband pulls two sets of luggage off the carousel while the women stand together behind the press of passengers, hugging their babies close.

When they have come through Customs, the two women hug farewell, wipe tears from tired eyes, take a last look at each other's new daughters. They are travelling in different directions now, but they promise to see each other soon, to keep in touch. It's a shame, they have said over and over, that they don't live closer, that their girls can't grow up together. Then the little family makes its way towards the bus for the long-term car park, the minds of the new parents turning to the long drive back to Cornwall, the bedroom prepared there for the baby, the grandparents waiting to welcome them home.

As crowds swell and part around her, greetings and reunions bursting like firecrackers to left and right, the other woman stands, uncertain, the child wriggling and worrying in her arms as though she senses the enormity of what is happening to her. A beautiful child, with sleek dark hair and smooth skin and perfect, delicate features, her name symbolic of a happiness she hasn't yet known. Shushing and soothing, swaying from foot to foot, the woman surveys the collage of faces filling the hall.

Watching her, you couldn't be sure whether she was expecting to be met, or searching the crowd on the off-chance of seeing a familiar face. You could only guess whether the message she left ten days ago had been picked up, or how it had been received. Or whether, in the end, she had clicked 'cancel' instead of 'send'; had replaced the receiver without speaking.

So if the mass of people, anxious and impatient, joyful and fearful, coalesce into a single person, and above the hubbub a name is called, will it be hers? Will she hear the single syllable – 'Eve!' – and in its inflection recognise three decades of feeling? Across the airport arrivals hall, will she see in the face that greets her a sign of the smooth, hard core of friendship?

THE END

# A note from the publisher

**Thank you for reading this book**. If you enjoyed it please do consider leaving a review on Amazon to help others find it too.

**We hate typos.** All of our books have been rigorously edited and proofread, but sometimes mistakes do slip through. If you have spotted a typo, please do let us know and we can get it amended within hours.

**info@bloodhoundbooks.com**